All I Want is Link

Bad Boys Book Nine

Christine Young

Published by Rogue Phoenix Press, LLP

ISBN: 978-1-62420-652-8

Editor: Sherry Derr-Wille
Cover Art: Designs by Ms G

Chapter One

Virginia 1826

"Blessed hell," Link Stewart murmured. "Don't believe I've ever been this cold.

Link knew he had never been so bloody cold in all his life. The scent on the air was wind, coldness permeating the soul coupled with snow. Wind whipped through his heavy coat as if he wore nothing at all. Flakes of the white stuff poured from the sky, the white flecks piling high on his shoulders. He crossed his arms in front of him, his head down as he plowed forward through the blinding snow, heading for the alehouse just down the block from where his ship was birthed. He grimaced as a gust hit him square in the face with gale-force power sending him back a step. Looking up had been a mistake.

Stepping into the pub he let his eyes adjust to the darkness of the room. In the pub the scent of male sweat and ale filled his nostrils. Cigar smoke curled in blue spirals through the meager light. He found an empty table and sat down, absorbing the warmth it presented. A few minutes passed before he was willing to rid himself of his outerwear and enjoy the atmosphere the small tavern offered. A blazing fire crackled in a fireplace situated on one wall at the side of the room. He was tempted to take up a position in front of it and warm his hands.

The serving maid who stood beside his table now slowly eyed him. Ogled might be the better word. She was a pretty young thing but her profession would make her old before her time. He grinned at her not wishing to encourage her attention, but the smile was natural for him when he saw an appealing girl. "What can I get you?" She looked to the upstairs then back to him, her meaning clear. She wouldn't be averse to a dalliance.

He wanted to laugh at her audacity, knew it was the way she made extra money. Ah, but he supposed things didn't change much from one country to the next. His mind was fixed however not on new dalliances with the local maids but on the rumors swirling around one Sophia Carter-Brown.

The lady was an enigma to him. She was part of why he was here. He meant to find out everything he could about the lady who did not act the role of a lady.

Link flashed the serving maid his signature grin, his smile wide, understanding the affect he had on women. "A hot toddy would be nice. Might take the bite of cold away," he told the young woman, casting his gaze away from the girl and to the groups of men enjoying a drink this wintery afternoon.

Nothing he read about the area prepared him for this blast of frigid weather he encountered. He loathed the idea of going outside but knew in about an hour Grayson, his plantation manager, would be at the docks to pick him up. Best he learn as much local gossip now that he had the chance.

Sophia was said to have three lovers so far. It was the so far that stopped him cold. If any of this were true, she was a harlot, willing to sell herself, but for what purpose? Why would a young lady of good breeding suddenly assume a life of prostitution? What was the price she put on her body? He heard it was quite high. Listening to the conversation in the pub, she seemed to be the main topic along with who might be her next conquest. He decided he might put himself in line for that seemingly coveted role. She would know from the start, however, that he didn't share. No, if she were to become his lover, she would have to get rid of the others.

Every last one of them.

He would tolerate nothing more.

The idea became more and more intriguing as he thought on

taking her for his paramour.

His grin widened thinking about bedding the experienced young lady. He also heard she was beautiful. Link enjoyed the experienced ones. They were usually not looking for a husband, so all he needed to do was appreciate as well as adore and pamper the ladies to his heart's content. He would look forward to seeing this woman for the first time. Wondered how she would react to him. The drink curled warmly in his belly. He would have to remember this particular concoction when he returned to Scotland. The drink was suitable for a cold winter night.

He sat back, his legs stretched out in front of him, his ankles crossed, feeling the first moment of relaxation since he stepped off his ship an hour ago and into this frigid arctic weather. Yes, now that he knew what he intended, he would proceed with his plan accordingly. He wasn't at all sure if Sophia had anything to do with the dark magic being perpetrated in the area, but she would know more than he did. Perhaps she could shed some light on the happenings, as well as why.

Strangely, he was no longer bored.

By listening to the table nearby, he heard one of Sophia's lovers sold his plantation to Sophia's uncle then headed back to Scotland. He wondered to himself, thought of different scenarios that might have been the cause. Perhaps she also understood the reasons for one of her lovers suddenly moving back to Glasgow. So, now there might only be two for her to get rid of when he told her his plans.

The hot toddy had the affect he wanted. His insides were suddenly feeling normal again. Normal until he left the warmth of the tavern to wander outside. Pulling out his pocket watch he noticed he still had about thirty minutes before he needed to head for the port.

The bar maid stood by his side again, moistening her lips while thrusting out one hip. She was plump and pretty, her breasts large enough to fill his hands. Her lips were soft pink as she moistened them. He wasn't interested though. There were too many things occupying his mind. A sexual distraction was not something he wanted or needed at the moment.

He smiled, held her hand in his before he briefly kissed the back. "Maybe another time, sweetheart," he murmured softly.

"You don't know what you're missing," she told him her voice assuming a seductive quality as she sashayed to another table.

Ah, but Link was sure he did know what he was missing. No, he hadn't even seen Miss Sophia Carter-Brown. Still he wanted her. No one else would do for him at least not until he learned the secrets she was hiding. She would learn quickly enough he was not a man to be played with.

If he understood women at all, he knew there were riddles to uncover then solve. He was just the man to accomplish such a feat. He looked forward to doing just that with a resolve he didn't quite understand.

Bits and pieces of information filtered through the smoke-filled air. Sophia was still the main topic. Her latest conquest was a young man, Devon Masters. His father owned a nearby plantation, but Devon had a penchant for gambling as well as whoring. He spent his father's money as if there was a never-ending supply. Perhaps there was. This plantation while still thriving could be brought down, he assumed, if the man did not concede to his father's wishes. Link decided he would have to look into the finances of each of her lovers a bit more closely.

The third lover was an older man. The scenario did not ring true in this case. Once again Link decided he would have to learn more about the man. It would be gratifying to discover a common thread. The rumors spoke of his longing for Scotland though. Perhaps it was innocent. Possibly Sophia was just a woman with questionable scruples, a woman who enjoyed what a man could give her. After all he would never condemn a woman for enjoying sex. He enjoyed sex. No responsibilities attached. She was allowed to be free just as any man. It was just...

Well hell, just what?

He knew what he was thinking, didn't like the gist of those thoughts either. Just then a cold rush of air filled the alehouse. The open door brought a smattering of snow, a blast of cold air as well as a man swaddled in a thick coat. A wry grin touched on Link's face as he stood to greet Grayson, the manager of the Stewart plantation. The description he'd been given fit him to a tee, salt and pepper hair included.

"A drink before we brave the weather?" Link asked, extending his hand in greeting.

Grayson shook snow off his coat before shaking his hand, "No, we need to get going. There is a break in the clouds as well as the snow. Should make use of the time the weather is giving us. I thought perhaps you weren't coming until I spoke to the captain who said you were the most enjoyable passenger he ever had. We should get going."

"Very well, I'm sure you know what you're about. Don't need to get any colder."

Link left money on the table to cover his drink. He looked at his coat, wishing he were in the south of France right now instead of Virginia then slipped his arms into the sleeves, buttoning it up to his neck. Sprawled on a chair watching the waves lap at a beach was his idea of heaven. Mayhap in time he would get used to the ice and snow. Perhaps in time the weather would change and the sun would come out.

Fact of the matter was the ship's captain liked him simply because he did not sleep with his new wife, a young lady making her first voyage with her much older husband. She tried to seduce him in the companionway during a storm. What the woman didn't know was that he would never cuckold a man. Evidently, the captain discovered what she was about. A solid rule of his was to never get into bed with a married woman; too many complications, way too many to make it a prudent venture. No, widows and adventurous women were the only ones for him.

They stepped outside. Grayson was right. The snow had stopped and the sun was shining down on them. Dark clouds lined up to the south threatening more of the same in an hour or so. He hoped an hour was enough time to reach Leslie Hall. He lifted his face to the sun with every intention of soaking up as much warmth as possible now that the sun was shining. Ah, but the manor was named after his brother the duke. Leslie Stewart. Until he was born it had just been a nameless place in Virginia. Their father believed naming the plantation after his first born to be a nice touch. Either that or they could have called it Southcliff the Second.

The wagon taking them sat in front of the tavern, piled high with supplies. "Well, I can't tell you enough that I'm thanking God over and over again that you are here. We've had trouble but then I'm sure you read the letter I sent to the duke. I don't know what to do about the black magic along with all the bizarre happenings. I'm afraid these nightly visits are escalating. Don't mind telling you they scare the very daylights out of me as well as all our slaves and free people. As to the cold, the weather will improve. By May you'll be praying for some snow before you succumb to the heat. It will also be so humid when you take a bath and try to dry off, you'll still feel damp. Horrible weather."

Link wasn't sure he would still be here in May. At least he hoped he'd solve this little problem, take stock of Sophia Carter-Brown then be on his way home by May. Two months should be more than enough time to figure out all this duplicity. After all, he was a very astute man.

"You will see to the—"

Mr. Grayson's voice broke off abruptly. He sucked in his breath. Link followed the line of sight and in turn saw a vision of his own. It was a woman...truly just a normal woman. He saw nothing special about her. Even from this distance, he realized who she was. Yes, he was certain this was the woman who dangled three men so skillfully. When she bade them dance, they most assuredly played right into her small adept hands. A woman should never be able to wield so much power over the male species.

Link grinned. He wondered what other delightful things she proposed they do. What would she propose with him? He sighed, too tired and cold from the weeks on board the ship to wonder about something he would discover soon enough. The intense cold was sapping his strength. He'd never experienced anything like it before in his life. He hoped Grayson's prediction was correct and either he'd adjust or the weather would improve or he'd just sit next to the fireplace and drink hot toddies, while doing so gaze at the flames.

His attention went back to Grayson. The man was still staring at the woman, salivating at her, drooling by God, knowing she'd never be his because more powerful men coveted her. That was the kind of man it seemed she preferred. Men who owned plantations...that was an interesting thought. Perhaps, just possibly she was part of a plan to buy out other plantation owners. A monopoly of the tobacco plantations in the area would generate a fine profit. Would not be the first time a woman used her body for personal gain and greed. Even while thinking this, he understood a man was most assuredly behind the plan.

"Mr. Grayson, I'd like to go to Leslie Hall now. You can tell me all about the troubles you're having on the way. Also, I'd like to hear everything you know about that lady you can't tear your gaze from." He nodded in the direction every male on the street was looking.

"Yes, yes Master Stewart, but that's Sophia Carter-Brown, you know." He pulled the hood of his coat over his head, hunkering down as if the snow was falling still. "Know enough about her. Known the young lady since she and her sister arrived penniless and without parents."

"Ah," said Link, his voice a blend of irony and curiosity. "Onward, Grayson. Pull your tongue back inside your mouth, if you please. We need to get myself and these supplies to warmth before the next storm hits and buries me in the white stuff."

Bloody eyes but the day he arrived in Glasgow it was snowing like this, damn near lost his way when he tried to ride to Southcliff.

Samuel Grayson stuttered a few times, tried valiantly to remove his ardent focus without success. The woman in question was being helped down from her horse by a man and had just shown a glimpse of silk-covered ankle. To render men slavering idiots with an ankle caused Link to shake his head in wonder. Her ankles were no different than any other lady's ankles. Over the course of his adult male life, he'd seen many ankles, legs, thighs and everything else feminine that at this exact freezing time he far preferred a roaring fire than seeing anything the woman had to offer. At least at this moment that's what he preferred. Once he warmed up, he'd see things differently. Discovering her more feminine assets could wait.

"Back to the task at hand," Link said growing impatient.

Grayson nodded his focus still on the so-called vision. "I don't understand," he said more to himself than to Link as he urged the two horses pulling the cart forward. "Look at her. Well, I know you did but you're obviously not affected by her beauty. She is exquisite. One can understand why the men want her. What I can't quite conceive is why she wants them."

"She is a woman, Grayson, nothing more, nothing less. Just as a man she has needs. Seems she hasn't found the right man yet. Can we go now?"

"It's nearly an hour to the plantation. The road curves along the river. It is really quite beautiful. You will appreciate the scenery. Many of the largest farms have their own docks. The water is deep enough to handle most ships. You should enjoy the ride. The main house looks over the river. There is a small summer cottage close by. You might enjoy its solitary aspects. It also looks at the river and is very pleasant during the summer months when cool air can flow from the front door to the back.

Again, Link thought he wasn't planning on being here in the summer. He would check out this cottage though. It might be a nice place to get to know Miss Sophia Carter-Brown better. If the cottage was secluded, he liked the idea even better. He began to formulate a few plans.

While they rode Grayson talked endlessly. He spoke of the weather then switched to the strange happenings, how even the slaves as well as the free-workers were terrified. The blue and yellow smoke unnerved him and everyone else. The foul odor reminded him of what hell must smell like. It wasn't right. It had to be something supernatural to cause all this horror. The rattling sounding like bones was even more terrifying as were the moans and groans as if someone was dying.

He didn't understand. No, he didn't understand at all. No one wanted to go outside and investigate. Leastwise, no one but his son, Edward, who didn't seem to be afraid of anything. Just last week there had been a fire set in a storage shed near the main house. Edward put it out, believed it was the work of men who were trying to scare him away. Things like that was one of the reasons why he sent for help. Two nights ago a tree nearly fell on the veranda roof. The tree had been very large and sturdy. There was no wind or anything that could have brought it down. Strange happenings just like this had been going on nearly a year now.

Link wondered when the lady took her first lover. Interested in the description of happenings that he was sure could be explained in earthly terms he continued to search for answers. "Did Edward find any saw marks on the tree?"

"No," Mr. Grayson said, firmly shaking his head at the same time. "No, there was nothing to indicate any man had a hand in this. It's the work of the supernatural. I tell you true. There is no reason for those things to happen. Even Edward had to acknowledge what I said. He didn't want to but he couldn't figure out how the tree fell."

Grayson tugged in a deep breath, looking over his shoulder as if something was about to attack him. "One of the slaves said he saw smoke swirling around the tree, white smoke then it turned green and red. Soon as the smoke was gone, well, the tree fell."

"Ah, so this also makes you believe this is the work of the supernatural. Personally, I don't take much stock in witchcraft and the like. There will always be a scientific reason behind what takes place around man. All kinds of chemicals when mixed together can make colored smoke. It is a flesh and blood man who is causing this, nothing supernatural, no ghosts, no black magic or voodoo. All you need worry about is catching the men who are perpetrating the crime then figure out the motive behind it."

"Don't believe anyone around here has that kind of knowledge," Grayson muttered. "Chemicals? Not a chance. Who here would know how to mix chemicals? Never heard of such a thing."

Link wanted to laugh but carefully kept it behind his teeth. He didn't want to antagonize this man or belittle him. No, he needed his help as well as Edward's to ferret out what was going on here. He was a man well pleased. His boredom would not return anytime soon. He looked forward to the following weeks. There would be so much to keep him entertained. When he wasn't fighting what appeared to be black magic, he would be deciphering Sophia Carter-Brown.

"Speaking of your son, tell me more about him. There was nothing in the letter speaking of his abilities or thoughts."

Grayson puffed up, a grin flashing across his face. The man was clearly pleased with his son. A moment later he was fidgeting with his heavy gloves. "He is a good boy, Sir. He does a lot for me—for the Stewarts—now that I'm getting on in years. He didn't want to leave the hall unprotected so he is waiting for us there."

They passed dozens of small homes. Link wondered if these were the slave quarters or the quarters of those who'd earned their freedom. He yearned to set all of them free, but knew he couldn't go that far. He didn't understand why they were slaves in the first place even though he understood most cultures had slaves. Had been that way since the beginning of time. Didn't know why the Stewarts bought them in the first place. He decided to write Leslie for more information and a suggestion of his own as well.

Well, hell, the fact didn't make it right.

The countryside wasn't all that different from the Scottish landscape where Southcliff Manor was situated. Virginia was different though. It was completely foreign to the Bordeaux region of France where he spent most of his life. Here, instead of miles of vineyards, one saw miles of tobacco plants. He wondered if he'd see wild animals; wolves perhaps, deer maybe a bear. Perhaps not, he had enough to contend with as it was without dealing with wild animals. He might see one of the Native Americans who owned this land first.

"We are nearing Mayfair Hall," Grayson said suddenly, his voice falling to nearly a whisper.

Link raised a speculative eyebrow wondering about the significance even though he had a guess.

"It's her home, Sir. Sophia Carter-Brown's home. She lives there with her uncle and her younger sister. There is one plantation between Leslie Hall and Mayfair Hall. As I understand, her uncle is about to buy that place substantially adding to his holdings.

Link thought that fact to be very interesting. He wondered why the man was selling and if he was one of Sophia's three lovers.

"Charles Ewing. Some say he wishes to move to New York. It's north of here as I'm sure you know. Doesn't make a lick of sense though. He always told me he loathes the city and would never want to live there. He has four older children who don't work, just idle away their time. His wife is said to be a trying witch by some. It's a sad story, a real sad story."

Link was certain he heard the man's name in the alehouse earlier this afternoon. He was wracking his brain to recall what was said about the man. He'd heard so much it was difficult to sift through all the information. What he was searching for would come to him.

Then he remembered. He spoke very slowly, "I understand this Sophia Carter-Brown has three men currently in her bed. I seem to recall that this Charles Ewing was one of them. Am I right?"

Grayson flushed to the roots of his graying hair. "You've only been here a short time. How would you know?"

"It's what all the men were talking about at the alehouse when I first arrived. The topic was Sophia. As you know, I went in there for something to warm my insides as well as my outsides. If this older man was one of her lovers, why? Why would such a beautiful young woman want an old man in her bed?"

"No, no, none of what you heard said is true. She is beautiful inside as well as out. She has not taken lovers. I'm positive she is still a virgin, innocent in fact of the wicked ways of men. Rumors, idle rumors that's all you heard. Never take any stock in rumors. There are many men who are not gentlemen. They don't speak the truth about the young lady. She is exquisite. They want people to think she took them into her bed when she hasn't. They want to preen, strut about and talk of their prowess while making Sophia their victim."

"It is the rumors, is it not?"

"What you heard is a viscous lie. Don't believe what you hear about Sophia. As I just said, she is sweet and innocent. She has no lovers. Don't mistake me. Customs on plantations are different. Many of the white owners have black mistresses. That doesn't have anything to do with Sophia. She is a lady."

Grayson was sputtering now. He was in distress over the conversation and obviously believed the young harlot was guiltless.

"Do you bow down to the local customs, Grayson?"

"Not in the beginning. Not when my wife lived. I was loyal to her. After she died, I was lonely. Yes, I took a mistress. Life here is different from Scotland in many ways. In other ways, you'll find it very much the same. You'll get used to the idea of white men bedding their slaves."

Link didn't think there were some local customs he would ever grow accustomed to. He knew he wouldn't be here long enough to do so. Nor would he be here long enough to make a difference. He couldn't free all the slaves but he could try to find a way to free the ones at Leslie Hall.

Link subsided, letting his body relax and absorb the rolling, bouncing sway of the wagon. He closed his eyes a moment, breathing in the cold stinging air coupled with the smell of the nearby river. "Why is Ewing selling out then, in your opinion?"

"I really couldn't say. Never truly thought it was any of my business. So, I never asked. Once again there are rumors. It was a sudden decision I was told. He and his family are leaving next week. I have heard he lost a lot of money to Devon Masters, a wastrel but lucky with the cards. You should not gamble with him. Some say he cheats, too, but it has never been proven."

"Another rumor."

"Yes."

Link turned to face the man, his manager, a man he needed to trust. He needed information not gossip, "There is every bit as much talk here as there is in Scotland as well as Bordeaux. I don't believe I'll be the least bit uninterested. Perhaps we'll have some mysterious manifestations tonight to welcome me. Yes, I would relish a ghoulish spectacle of any type. Perhaps we can catch whoever is scaring people witless. Isn't this young Devon reputed to be one of her lovers?"

Link wondered if Grayson would denounce this rumor too. He opened his mouth then managed to keep his words behind his teeth. After a few moments of reflection Grayson said in a very calm manner. "I repeat, Link, all of this is utter nonsense. Her uncle, William Brinkmeyer, is a good man; solid, dependable. He is amiable, his business dealings above reproach. I imagine the vicious rumors about Sophia Carter-Brown hurt him very much. He never speaks of it because he is a gentleman of the finest type. His overseer, however, is a different story. Felix Campbell is a rotten fellow, cruel to the slaves."

"If Uncle Brinkmeyer is such a fine fellow, why does he employ someone the opposite? Someone who is cruel to the less fortunate, a savage from what you say."

"I don't know. There are rumors about that too. Some believe the slaves need a stern hand or they won't work. Brinkmeyer doesn't have a cruel bone in his body, so the slaves would just idle away the hours if he didn't have someone with an iron fist to run his plantation for him."

"Yes, perhaps Brinkmeyer just feels pity for Ewing and is simply taking the plantation off his hands so the man can move on with his life. Brinkmeyer is the younger brother of Miss Sophia and Clare's mother. Do I have that right?"

Link wasn't sure what was going on here. There were too many holes in the facts, too much idle gossip. It seemed Grayson took a lot for granted. "What are the girls doing here?"

"Their parents were drowned when their ship went down about five years ago. The children were made wards of their uncle. They've been here ever since."

"Are they English?"

"Scottish. They lived near Edinburgh, a small estate that will belong to the children when they come of age. Miss Sophia is close to that age now. When she has children, a boy, he will inherit."

Link was silent going over everything that had been said as well as what had not been said. So, the girl had been raised in Scotland. Now she was here and she was a tart. His thinking turned back to the problem that brought him here to Virginia. Link strongly doubted the supernatural had anything to do with the problems occurring at Leslie Hall. Oh no, greed was the same all over the world. He said, "Did Mr. Ewing have any supernatural problems before he agreed to sell to this Brinkmeyer.

"Not that I know of. Oh, I see the direction of your thoughts, Link, but I don't credit them. As I said, Mr. Brinkmeyer is an outstanding individual. He gives to charities and those less fortunate. He is always looking after others. No, if Ewing were having financial problems or if he were being besieged as we are at Leslie Hall, Brinkmeyer certainly would not be behind it."

Link wondered if Grayson spoke as passionately about the Stewarts as he did Uncle Brinkmeyer. He'd never met a man who deserved such accolades. Well, he would soon discover the truth for himself.

Grayson turned the wagon inland away from the river. The cart lumbered up a long winding driveway before it stopped in front of Leslie Hall. It appeared much as Southcliff did. Link supposed their father had it built in the same style for good reason. He would feel at home here.

"My home is beyond the main house about a quarter mile and the cottage I spoke of is just at the top of that hill. The trees surround it except for the front and back. In the summer they provide a host of shade, cooling the building down to an enjoyable level as breezes from the river flow freely through open doors," Grayson said.

Ah, but Link didn't intend to still be in Virginia in the summer. However, he did intend to discover its uses while he was here.

~ * ~

It was nearly midnight. Link thoroughly enjoyed himself in the small cottage. The fireplace blazed with logs crackling. A cozy warm glow filled the room. He stretched out on a white fur rug in front of the hearth, a glass of Bordeaux in his hand. The storm threatening to the south still had not reached them. The crisp air outside had taken on a decided chill. When he strolled outside for more logs to place on the fireplace, the snow popped and crunched beneath his feet. The scent filling his nostrils was one of impending winter and ice.

There was a half-moon shining above. He felt relaxed, ready to take on whatever real or supernatural powers that threatened the lives of these people. The night was so beautiful, the black vault of the sky overhead with the spattering of stars, so calm so silent that he felt peace flow through him. This was just how God planned life.

He wasn't a peaceful man. This newfound sensation of his was an odd feeling. He found that he didn't dislike the peculiarity, meant to soak up the moments because he didn't believe the serenity would last. Nothing peaceful ever did last. He stretched out naked on the fur wishing one of his widows from Bordeaux might have made the trip with him. Ah, Suzette, how he missed her. He did need to find a willing lady to see to his baser needs. He stretched again, relaxing even more, relishing the fur against his nakedness. Closing his eyes, he listened to the sounds he hadn't heard before. The sound of an owl came to him then the soft sound of a breeze curling around the eaves of the cottage. He thought he heard the croak of a frog but dismissed the idea. Somewhere a dog barked. He sighed when each sound became more distinct.

It was just so damn tranquil here, perhaps because he had only one purpose. He didn't have to please anyone, just ferret out the truth then go home. He was on the point of falling asleep when he heard something unusual.

The noise was too different to put a name on the sound, something he'd never before heard. Still lying on the fur, he held himself motionless while he waited. He listened hard. There it was again, that strange sort of low moaning sound that didn't sound remotely human. Although he knew it was. This was why he'd been sent here. Well, he didn't have to wait a day for the first confrontation.

He slipped on his pants and shirt then his boots, intending to discover the source of the sound. He forgot the air was frigidly cold. Forgot everything except his quest to discover the truth. The sound became louder the closer he got to the main house. He ran lightly up the snow-covered slope toward the back of the house. He eased around the side. The sound came again. A strange light welled up from the ground. It was a narrow, thready, light blue beam, and it smelled of sulfur as if it was coming directly from hell and the moans were of the souls entrapped there. Gooseflesh rose on his body. The hair on the back of his neck stood on end. This was beyond strange, bordering on ridiculous. There was an explanation. This was just a mixture of chemicals concocted by a mere mortal.

He heard a hiss. As he whirled to see who it was, he picked up snow, molding it into a hard ball, pounding more snow onto it until it was large and very hard.

It was Edward Grayson. He met the man upon his arrival at Leslie Hall. He was the estate manager's son.

Link grinned. He liked Edward. The young man had a good head on his shoulders, smart as well as possessing a great deal of common sense. Like Link he wasn't the least bit superstitious although he didn't once disagree with his father during dinner or their discussion later.

"What do you think it is?" Link asked in a deep whisper, shielding his mouth with his hand.

"Don't know but I intend to find out now you're here to help me. I've tried to get some of the male slaves, free men as well, but they roll their eyes and look at me as if I'm crazy. They mutter some nonsense in a different language. They won't dare go outside in the middle of the night to investigate the smoke."

"Very well," Link said resigned to the fact he and Edward were in this together with no other help forthcoming. "Go around to the other side of the light and I'll ease closer from this side."

Edward disappeared into the shadows to work his way to the opposite side of the smoky blue light. *A trap,* Link thought, pleased. Blood pumped wildly through him, thrilled by the new excitement. He thought about the two women he bedded on the long trip here. They were both charming delightful ladies but much the same. He was tired of the same. He didn't want to be bored here. This, now this was intriguing, exciting.

When Edward was in position, Link straightened, clenched one fist tight at his side, held the snowball in the other hand and walked directly toward the light. An unearthly shriek reverberated through the stillness then the moans followed. Gooseflesh rose again despite the fact he knew a man created the mournful rendition of a ghost. The noise was strangely eerie.

The blue light continued to rise higher into the black sky, the odor foul. Once more he reminded himself it was simply the igniting of sulfur, nothing more. Who was moaning? They were doing a blessed fine job.

Edward shouted while waving his hands in the air. He began to run following a flowing white robed figure. Ah, here we are. This is why

I came to Virginia. The identity would be discovered this night. He realized he didn't want to go home so soon. No, it wasn't even May yet. Nor had he discovered Sophia Carter-Brown's talents. No, not even if he solved this puzzle, he must remain to solve the second one.

The stealthy white figured turned then and fired at him. Link felt the bullet whiz by his temple. He touched his head. There was blood on his fingers.

"Bloody hell!" he yelled before racing straight toward the figure.

He meant to throttle this interloper. The man was tall and large, but Link could run fast and was gaining on him. Any moment he would have him. He slipped on a patch of ice, cursed, started forward again.

Without warning a shaft of pain seared his thigh. He stopped, staring down at the feathered arrow that was sticking out the side of his leg.

Damnation, the man was getting away. Edward, shouting at him was at his side in another moment. "Where the hell did that bloody arrow come from? The man had an accomplice, damn him!"

"It's nothing, Edward. Go after him. We've got to find out who the devil is creating all this havoc where there is supposed to be only peace and quiet."

"No," Edward said calmly. "The men will come back. It seems they can't stay away. Your leg needs to be tended to even though it is not much more than a flesh wound, no serious damage. I doubt if it's going to stop you for long."

With no more words Edward ripped a strip of his shirt then turning to Link he pulled the arrow from his leg and bound the wound. "We need to get you back to the main house. It needs to be cleaned and bandaged. You'll walk with a slight limp for a while."

~ * ~

He was careful not to hit her where the bruises could be seen. The first blow hit her ribs below her breasts. Her gasp made him pause then grin. The damage he inflicted would never be seen by anyone but him. He felt good when he hit her, when she crumpled to his bidding. She knew this was just the beginning. He relished hurting her. Sophia understood he wouldn't stop until she lost consciousness from the pain. She closed her eyes as another blow hit her in the stomach. No bruises there.

He hit her ribs again in very nearly the same spot as the first blow. Her body jerked, the agony searing inside her as she tried not to give him more pleasure by crying out. If she could, she would hit him back. He hit her temple then jabbed her twice more in the ribs. She knew her hair would cover the bruising as long as it didn't seep out to far onto her face. She cringed then sucked air, her hands trying to block each blow even though she understood the feeble gesture wouldn't stop him. He wouldn't end the relentless torment until he either grew tired or she blacked out.

Once again, he turned his attention to her ribcage, battering her until she was forced against the wall. She looked at him, pain excruciating, flaming though her body before she slowly slid to the floor. He wouldn't stop though. He would find a way to prop her up so he had easy access. Confused, she wasn't sure why she earned this beating, didn't know what she did wrong or didn't do. She wracked her brain for the cause. Couldn't think of anything. True, she'd been in town yesterday. But...

He was so unpredictable.

He usually only attacked when he was displeased with something. When she did something he disliked. Searching her mind again for the reason, she couldn't come up with any plausible motivation. He kicked her then, one more shot at her ribs. It wasn't hard enough to crack a rib.

He was truly very careful. Nothing he did would show.

"Little slut, think you can get away with acting as if you're not a slut? You aren't a lady. Stop pretending to be one." He stood over her, his feet braced on either side. Slowly he bent down, pulling her to a standing position. She blinked a few times in an attempt to clear her vision. One eye was swollen. She would have to use her makeup there. Still, she didn't understand what he was talking about.

Desperately, she tried to keep the bile in her stomach. She didn't want to lose it simply because she would have to clean it all up. Even if she spilled her lunch on his shoes, it would be fitting. He would only be angrier. Would hit her again.

"Why?"

Shaky as it was the sound of her voice surprised her. It was weak and pathetic, just the way he made her feel. She had no recourse except to obey him even though she longed to fight him. He threatened her daily with her sister's life. Allowing her little sister to become what she was, well it was something she wasn't going to allow.

"You didn't tell me. Why the hell didn't you tell me?" he was screaming at her now, shaking her until her head lolled back, until her ribs cried out more painfully than before.

She heard the soft moan come from her throat. Felt the bile start to rise in her throat. His scent of male sweat and whiskey was putrid to her. She turned her head in hopes of avoiding it.

She was standing now but only because he was holding her. She didn't know if he was going to hit her again. What happened to her next probably depended on her reply, but she didn't have any notion what he was talking about. She didn't care either. As long as he didn't take his anger out on Clare, she would do anything he wanted, say anything.

"Tell you what?" she managed to say just before he jerked her close. His foul breath wafted against her cheek. Revulsion nearly sent her to the ground again. This time truly she almost lost the contents of her stomach. His hand wound into her hair tugging her head back ripping at her scalp. She couldn't even turn away from him.

"Don't lie to me, girl. I don't like it. You know exactly what I'm talking about. You were in town yesterday. You saw him."

Spittle was flying from his mouth, landing on her cheeks and lips. Once more she closed her eyes for a moment then another one, trying to soak in strength. No matter how she wanted to ignore him she couldn't.

He would go away only when it pleased him.

She swallowed hard wishing she had the answer he craved. Her voice trembling, she finally asked, "Who?"

"Link Stewart. You must have passed him just outside the alehouse. I know you saw Devon yesterday. Grayson saw you. Link was in the wagon with him. I gave you permission. Devon took you to lunch then brought you home. I watched from the balcony. Didn't he tell you Link was there? He would have noted a new arrival. Would have spoken of him." He was pale now, his eyes narrowed with fury. "I should have been told."

"I don't even know who that is. Link Stewart?"

She was cringing again, hating her cowardice yet feeling rage boiling up inside her. It was stupid of her, this temper of hers, this habit of saying what she was thinking instead of using prudence. She was going to make matters worse, but she just couldn't help herself. "I wanted him to be here, to catch you at your evil games. I prayed he would come, the voice of reason, a man who would see through the ridiculous. He wouldn't believe any of that supernatural stuff. I knew if anyone could do it, he could stop you. I didn't say anything because I wanted to see you suffer."

She waited for the next shot to her face or ribs. It never came. Instead, she heard his laughter, saw his grin, his yellowed teeth behind his lips. For a moment she saw what others in this small community saw, a man with humor and wit, a gentle man, a man of breeding. In the next moment it was gone. He was back as she knew him to be. The once pleasant grin was evil now. "If Felix hadn't shot him with the arrow, he might have discovered us. I didn't expect any of what happened last night. Here was this fellow, running at me, yelling like a banshee, a snowball in his hand. Felix shot him.

"He was going to throw the damn snowball at me. He was packing it harder as he ran. I might have died. You would have liked that wouldn't you?"

Sophia felt the blood drain from her face. She couldn't fathom what he just told her. This wasn't possible. No, he couldn't be saying what she thought he was saying. "You killed him? You killed the owner of Leslie Hall?"

"Oh, no more's the pity. The arrow nicked his thigh. Didn't do much damage. Felix is always careful. Strange, truly strange you know. Since the man was probably having a tryst in that little cottage on the hill. Which brings me to the next part of our plan. Stewart is going to be your next lover. I want you to be the woman having the tryst in that little cottage with him. No one else, you hear me? He's a man with strong appetites. He'll play right into your lovely harlot's hands. That's the only way I'll be able to control the man. He has to fall madly in love with your sweet charms. He must be so in love he will overlook the fact that you are the town whore. You have to give him anything and everything he wants. Don't deny the man anything."

She said nothing more. Air forgot to find its way into her lungs for a moment upon another moment. She should have told her uncle she'd seen Stewart in town and perhaps he would not have been shot. It was her fault. Yet, it never occurred to her the man, the owner of Leslie Hall could be in any danger or that he was a threat of any kind to her uncle. That this man's appearance in Virginia was the reason he was beating her. She'd been a fool and Mr. Stewart had been the one to pay for her mistake. She paid, too, but that was nothing new nor would it be the last time. She tried not to move knowing if she did the pain would increase. It hurt her to breathe, but she had to take in air. If only she didn't.

Uncle William moved away from her. Walked around his desk to bring a chair so he could sit right in front of her, stare at her. "You're not a fool. Stupidity doesn't suit you," he said finally after staring at her for what seemed an eternity. "How many times do I have to remind you of your sister's predicament if you don't do exactly as I say? Now, think, if I had been caught, what would happen to you as well as Clare? Hmmm... Doesn't take a hell of a lot of imagination to come up with the unpleasant scenario. You won't be the only whore in these parts, my dear. Since you, my sweet niece, are underage and I'm yours and Clare's guardian, there will be no one to see to your future. No, miss, you won't lie to me or try to do me in again or I swear to you…" he paused, rose and strode back to hover over her.

What would he swear to her? She had her guesses.

She shrank back against the wall terrified he'd start pounding her again. He sank down on his haunches, grabbing her chin, his fingers tightening as he jerked her head upward. She had no choice but to look at him, his eyes simmering with hatred for her. "I swear to you, Sophia, I will kill you if you try anything like this again. Do you understand me? Then what will happen to the little sister? Why, she'll be just like you. Not sure what I'll hold over her head though. I'll have to think about it for a time. Perhaps I won't kill you. Chain you somewhere."

She said nothing, knew he saw the hatred glaring at him in her eyes. She also knew he saw the fear. Then his expression changed to a slow evil smile spreading across his face. "No, I don't believe I'll kill you. I'll kill your sister instead even though she would garner me a lot of money in the future just as you are doing."

He let go of her chin, standing so he would tower over her. "Tell me you understand, Sophia."

Unable to help herself she nodded her head. "Yes," she finally said, "I understand everything. It's perfectly clear." She understood she had to find some way to save her sister, to get her back to Scotland.

"Good." He offered her his hand. She stared at it knowing the injustice he could met out so easily, remembering the feel of his fist as it hit her earlier. She felt helpless, but she wasn't going to give him satisfaction by accepting any kind of help from this man she detested.

"You're stubborn. That's not entirely bad in a woman in your position. Means you'll pursue this until I get what I want. You can hate me too. Doesn't matter to me. I find your hate amusing, even invigorating at times. If you were my mistress, I would enjoy whipping that insolent look out of your eyes. The welts on your back would please me sufficiently to keep you alive just to whip you again. I would break you, Sophia. Ah, but I don't want you broken, at least not yet. There will be time for that." He stroked his chin, staring out the window. "Yes. The Duke of Southcliff finally reacted to Grayson's messages. He sent his brother just as I intended. Now it is time to put my plan into action. I mean to have Leslie Hall by summer. You will help me."

Despite her revulsion she understood her choices. There were none.

"Ah, yes, sweet Sophia since you've seen a number of naked men you won't be disappointed with this one. He is extraordinarily built and pleasing to the eye. This man should not be too incredibly hard for you to seduce. After all, he is only a man. He will succumb just as easily as the others to your feminine wiles. This one is not a fool though. He won't be quite so easily seduced as Devon or Charles. I will tell you in the morning what is expected of you. I'm quite looking forward to the inevitable outcome."

At eight o'clock the following morning Sophia was trying to fasten the front buttons of her gown. Every movement hurt. She tried not to groan even though there was no one there to hear her. Tried not to let the moisture in the back of her throat move to her eyes. The flesh on her torso turned all sorts of blues, greens and yellows. He wouldn't see her pain, but he knew she hurt. Uncle William expertly inflicted the intended punishment. She was truly trapped here where he controlled her every action, her entire life. As she slipped another button into its hole, she felt the pain so deeply she doubled over, her breath catching in her throat. She froze for a few moments, closing her eyes to let the pain ease from her.

There was nothing to do, however. No, she had to protect Clare, do what he wanted. For her there was no end in sight. She knew if she did what he wished, he would keep his promise. At least she hoped he would. There were no guarantees. Clare poked her head around the corner, a large smile on her face. "Don't you want breakfast? It's growing cold and you know how Uncle William is. You won't get another bite until luncheon if you don't come down soon."

"Yes, I know," she said, but she wasn't sure she could eat anything.

A hot cup of tea would be nice though, maybe a little lemon and milk in it.

Clare sat down on the bed, her hands clasped in her lap watching. Her blue-gray eyes seemed to see into her mind. She didn't want Clare to know how much pain she was in or why.

She finally finished dressing. She glanced in the mirror intending to brush her hair, knew she couldn't. She looked pale and disheveled, about as seductive as a cow. Some harlot she was. If Link Stewart was a man of the world as he was reputed to be, there was nothing about her he would find attractive. There were dark circles under bloodshot eyes. Only the makeup Uncle William insisted she wear would hide the circles. Nothing would hide the redness of her eyes. She wasn't sure she could put on enough makeup to hide the agony.

She finished, every move sending more ripples of pain through her body. She pulled back her auburn hair and tied it at the nape of her neck with a black ribbon. It would have to do. "Let's go eat."

"You don't feel well do you, Sophia?"

It wasn't' a question. Sometimes Clare saw more than she should. Sophia wasn't at all sure how long she could keep the truth from her little sister. Clare was growing more intuitive every day. Soon enough she would know what was happening. "All I need is a bit of breakfast to make me feel better. Yesterday was busy. I didn't get a chance to eat. I didn't sleep well last night. I'll be fine once I get some food into my stomach." Sophia didn't believe that nonsense and it seemed neither did her sister.

Clare looked at her, shaking her head, clearly not trusting a word coming from her mouth. No, her little sister didn't appear reassured nor did she look as if she believed her. She took her hand in hers walking with her. "If there is something wrong, you'll be sure to tell me. Promise?" Clare's wide blue eyes stared trustingly into hers.

A wave of guilt coursed through her. It was a feeling she would have to ignore. "Promise." Sophia loved Clare more than life itself. She vowed she would never let anything bad happen to her. Clare was the only person in the world who loved her. She would have to do everything he asked of her, perhaps more. She was terrified though. Sophia didn't understand how she knew it, but she did know Link Stewart was not like the other men she seduced. Even her uncle saw the difference.

Uncle William was in the breakfast room. She hoped he'd be gone, a false hope she knew. He told her last night he would explain what he wanted from her in the morning. So, she knew he would be in the room sitting on his chair, waiting, needing to see first-hand the damage he inflicted. He waited here to torment her until they were alone again and he would tell her what he expected from her. She didn't want anything to do with Link Stewart, having the sinking feeling she would lose if she went up against that man.

Thirteen months since she'd become a whore, a harlot, a piece of muslin any man could use. Well, not just any man, only the ones her uncle wanted something from. Thirteen long months since the women in the community shunned her, whispering behind her back. The rejection hurt her deeply yet she learned to ignore them when she was in town, learned to hold her chin high and look the other way. They didn't shun her when they came to visit at Mayfair Hall. No, they admired her uncle too much to do that. So, they hid their dislike behind the fans they used to flirt with.

She looked fondly at her sister, hoping somehow she would fare better when she came of age. The sinking sensation Clare would not, had her ever more determined to find a way out of here for her sister. "Sit down and eat your breakfast."

"I think I'll just have a cup of tea."

William looked up from his newspaper, the imported London Times only two months old, for English ships were regular in their arrivals. One could think they were keeping up with the current news from abroad. He seemed to study her face even as she lowered her lashes not wishing to see him.

"You and I will meet after you've eaten. You must eat, Sophia. Don't want you to waste away to nothing. Your men friends won't like it if you are skin and bones. Men don't appreciate women who are too skinny. They want something to hold on to when they kiss when they think about marriage." He cleared his throat, still studying her before changing the subject slightly. "There are things we need to discuss. I know you always wish to accommodate yourself to my wishes. Ah, do not take too much time eating. Plans need to be made and put into action." He was rising, folding the paper to set it on the table before he moved to the other room, his office, where they would have the much-needed privacy.

Clare glanced between them, her eyes narrowing thoughtfully. She was smart. The little girl knew something was going on, had been for quite some time. Sophia wished Clare would stay young and carefree a bit longer. She also wished their parents hadn't died. She supposed none of her wishes would ever come true.

"Very well, Uncle," Sophia said in a purposefully soft voice. "In your study then. After breakfast. I'll be along shortly."

"Yes, my dear, that is exactly what I wish."

He turned his attention to Clare. "As for you, my fine young lady, you will accompany me into town today. It seems you've outgrown all your clothing. Don't want your ankles to show now, do we. We will get you an entire new wardrobe, one that will usher in the spring and the summer as well. Would you like that?"

The pleasure in Clare's eyes made her ribs hurt.

Chapter Two

Link spent the morning riding over the plantation in order to survey the land. While the snow fell from time to time, the sun also peeked from behind dark storm clouds. His leg throbbed, hurt like hell, but he tried to ignore the pain. He cursed silently every time he thought about how close he and Edward came to finding the man behind the white sheet and sulfurous smoke. When they found the man, all this supernatural garbage would be over.

A man in a white sheet. Nothing too creative about that.

Now he settled into the main house, making himself comfortable. He had thoughts of riding to the cottage to eat. He ignored them. His lunch was served to him in a room encased in glass, a bit chilly except for the fact sunshine filtered inside warming the area with natural heat. It didn't hurt that the fireplace in the room was blazing. He gazed on the river, thinking of the coming spring. Grayson joined him, sitting down to pour himself a cup of tea before handing him what appeared to be an invitation embossed with gold lettering.

Link arched an eyebrow wondering just what ploy this could be. "What is it, Grayson? Looks much too fancy. Don't like balls and things."

"Pretty much what it looks like, Link. It's an invitation from William Brinkmeyer of Mayfair Hall. There is to be a ball this Friday in your honor. He wants to know if you will be there."

"A ball."

Link tapped his finger on the tabletop before folding them thoughtfully in front of him. He didn't like those stilted affairs, nor did he want the gala to be in his honor assuming it was something he would enjoy. Yet he didn't think he would miss the event for the world. It might be the best time he could meet Sophia, the woman who could juggle sleeping with three men without showing her hand.

"No one will be able to plow their way through the snow if the threat of the storm on the horizon materializes. Surely this Brinkmeyer fellow isn't serious about an affair such as a ball in this weather." He was appalled at the thought of more cold weather on its way.

"There will be lots of food and drink. He will most assuredly invite all the people in the area you should know, all the well-connected money folks. I suppose some will get out their sleighs if necessary. You might enjoy it. Every room will have a fire burning. I'm sure once you get there you will be splendidly warm. You won't suffer from a chill if you decide to attend. The most important benefit for you is that you'll see Miss Sophia Carter-Brown at her best. You will undoubtedly come to realize she is sweet, nothing like the horrid rumors."

Link was silent still thinking of the woman who could be a key to all the things plaguing this tiny part of Virginia. He wanted to meet her. He didn't agree with Grayson's evaluation of her character. From everything he heard about the woman she was anything but sweet.

"There is a young man waiting for your response, Sir."

Link slanted him a languid smile. "We'll go, naturally."

Grayson nodded then left the room to write an acceptance. Link closed his eyes again thinking of warm sunshine in the south of France, a sweet bottle of Sauternes along with a willing woman. He might go there before he returned to Scotland. It would still be cold in Glasgow. He wanted to go back to the cottage and lie on the white fur rug in front of the fireplace soaking up the warmth. He also wanted a willing woman to lie there with him.

Link closed his eyes, drifting asleep.

When he woke the sky was becoming dark, the sun hovering between the storm clouds and sinking below the horizon. Colors blazed in the sky while shadows danced across the lawn. Edward was sitting beside him, his long legs stretched out in front of him.

"Your father doesn't think the cold weather is much of a hindrance to anything as well as the snow and the ice. It shouldn't stop people from going about their business. This is nasty stuff. I don't believe one word out of his mouth. He's besotted with Sophia."

Edward grunted. "Most the time that is what everyone does. The only weather that actually stops anyone are the hurricanes and a possible blizzard. Otherwise, we do go about our business. If we didn't, life as we know it would come to a halt."

"Is it ever too cold to make love, I wonder?"

He thought on that now as a stupid question. One could always build up the fire or snuggle beneath layers of blankets when one held a willing woman in his arms. He much preferred to see his women naked not covered with layers of fabric. If he was going to stay here very long, he would have to figure out this warmth thing.

Edward laughed. "Yes, if one lets the fire die down to embers. I hear we are to go to a ball at Mayfair Hall this Friday night. Sounds to me as a great way to meet Sophia."

"Yes, for some reason I can't fathom I'm to be honored. Meeting Sophia, well, that is also what your father said. I think, however, that I would rather try out a sleigh and go for a ride all bundled up with a beautiful woman sitting next to me. My hands...well... Ah, well, don't suppose that will be possible anytime soon. Of course, it might be preferable to chase a villain wearing a sheet. Like to catch that man."

"If he's smart, he won't show up anytime soon. In any case the ball should be amusing, Link. You will meet all the planters and merchants from this area as well as their wives. You will hear so much gossip your ears will ache. After that it is up to you to decide what is true and what is not. There is little else to do here this time of year, you see, except drink hot toddies, which most do to excess. As you noticed already, father is much taken by Sophia Carter-Brown. She is Brinkmeyer's niece and hostess. She will be there decked out in her best finery and flaunting her body for everyone to see. Her dress will be cut low, revealing more than a young lady should while daring anyone bold enough to touch. I don't doubt father would challenge me to a duel if I dared insult or say one derogatory word about Sophia. He thinks of her as a goddess."

"I also understand she is a good horizontal."

"True," Edward said, keeping his gaze focused outside, "that's what is understood. Do you plan on discovering the truth of those rumors?"

"You sound upset. You've known the girl for a long time?"

Link was interested in the answer more than he wanted to admit. After all she was just a woman with all the same parts as any other woman.

"Four years, as long as she's been living with her uncle. She wasn't always like she is now. There was a time when I thought her sweet and innocent, a fine person just as my father still does. A little over a year ago all that changed. She's lived here since she was fourteen. She is now seventeen nearly eighteen. Her exploits with the men and thus her tarnished reputation began thirteen months ago. You see through my feelings. Sophia displeases me and disappoints me even more. Before all this started, I quite liked her. She was a spirited girl, always ready for a prank or an adventure, without guile or vanity. Indeed, I once thought that we might—but that's no longer important." He looked away for a moment as if he tried to hide his emotions.

"You know all this as fact, not rumor."

"She meets her lovers at a small cottage near Mayfair Hall. It's not unlike the one on this property. I chanced to visit the cottage following a night she spent with Devon Masters. When I saw him, the man seemed pleased with himself, a smug grin on his face. He was drunk though. Still drinking what I thought to be a hot toddy. I was surprised since it was morning. The place reeked of sex. He spoke of her freely; her attributes, her skills at pleasing a man, her daring at flaunting convention. He told me she was an amazing lover, knew just what a man liked as well as what he didn't."

"You didn't see her there."

Link was going over in his mind what he liked as well as what he didn't. He didn't suppose all men were the same in their sexual preferences.

"No, I've been told she leaves her men to wake up by themselves. That's what Devon told me. However, there are female slaves there to tend to their needs when she is gone. None of the men seem to mind this idiosyncrasy. It seems they feel well satisfied even though she doesn't want to spend the early morning hours with them."

"You trust and believe Master's tale."

From what he'd been told about Devon Masters, he wouldn't trust the man's word father than he could spit.

Edward's voice was stilted as if it took a great deal of effort for him to speak. Still, he didn't look at Link. "As I told you, the cottage reeked of sex. Plus, he was too drunk to make something like this up. He spoke of her quite explicitly. The size of her breasts, her hips, her woman's parts as well. Disgusting. I've never liked the man. He's a pompous rich bastard who takes advantage of everyone. However, there was not a single reason for him to lie. He did not take anything from Sophia she was not willing to give."

"I see," Link said rubbing his chin, thinking over all Edward said. "So, the girl turns seventeen and decides to flaunt all her uncle holds dear, his reputation and so on. Sounds peculiar to me. Surely, in her situation no man would wed her. Her future would be bleak. Why do you think she changed so dramatically and started making herself available to men in the first place? There must have been a catalyst of some sort. Most importantly, no one does something like this without an exceptional motive. A well-born woman doesn't set out to be a whore."

"I've thought on it enough to realize there is no explanation, at least not one I can contemplate. She was always a strong-willed girl, spirited, as I told you, and very protective of her little sister. One of the planters called her a little hellion because she defended her sister from the advances of an older boy. That was about two years ago. She could have had her pick of the gentlemen in the area, for it's well known she is handsomely dowered. She is pleasant to look upon as well. I have always been given to understand that females don't wish to have sex as much as men do. Thus, why would she want it so badly to give up everything that women are raised, even expected to want?"

"That is such a good question. I believe I'll make it my mission to discover the reason or reasons as the case might be. Yes, where women are concerned it's nice to have a mission, a way to proceed." He stood and stretched before walking over to the fire, rubbing his hands together, seeking the meager warmth. "It will be blessedly nice when my hands are not always freezing."

Edward grinned broadly at him. "I heard father order cook to make you something hot for dinner, a bowl of venison stew might warm your innards along with some fresh baked biscuits. Cook does like to bake biscuits. They are truly very good. He doesn't want you to shrink away for lack of sustenance. In time you'll get used to the cold. By the time that happens the weather will be so muggy you'll drown in your sweat."

Link waited for what, he truly didn't have a clue but he stared out toward the river as if something was going to happen. He knew in his heart, he would discover the truth about Miss Carter-Brown. It was dark now and the half-moon was rising again, casting a shimmer of light over the yard. He sighed realizing the man wasn't going to come back any time soon for an encore performance. He would have frightened him.

"As I said before, there is always something that drives men and women to behave as they do. There are three different men involved, I understand, and there were probably more before that. Of course, she will have a motive or two, perhaps unique motives for each man. Whether or not any of us are able to understand what they are, is up in the air." He inhaled long and deep, enjoying his thoughts more with each passing moment. "I rather fancy that I will amuse myself and just find out what it is that makes this hellion part her legs for so many men. Perhaps she will do so for me."

"I don't see how..."

~ * ~

Friday night was here and Link actually felt a bit excited for the upcoming ball. He had to admit he did want to meet his neighbors as well as some people from the nearby town. Learning what motivated these people seemed to be important.

The cold wasn't all that bad. The day turned a bit warmer as the snow began to melt. Instead of taking a carriage, he chose to ride the large black stallion they called Thor. The horse was remarkable, strong, with a regal bearing. To his disappointment, after the incident his first night in Virginia, there had been no other strange occurrences. No, burning sulfur, no sheeted man, no moans or groans, no guns or bows and arrows.

He was disappointed.

Over the last few days, nothing out of the ordinary occurred. He met Grayson's housekeeper, a young black woman with laughing eyes, a slim lithe body and a ready smile. She lived in Grayson's room and worked in the house during the day. Her name was Alice. Edward on the other hand also had a housekeeper, a thin slip of a girl who answered to the name of Josephine. Her eyes were always downcast in Link's presence. She never uttered a word that Link heard. Alice couldn't have been more than fifteen. Edward paid her no attention whatsoever, except, Link assumed, at night, when he took her to bed. She worked for him during the day and slept with him at night. For some reason Link wasn't amused at all. In fact, he was quite put off with this custom. It felt wrong and dirty, just as the fact Sophia slept with so many different men felt wrong. The women were far too young for this flagrant use of their bodies.

The morning after he arrived Grayson offered him a woman, and Link, for the first time in his adult sexual life, refused. The practice seemed too heartless to him, too artificial, too expected. That was it. He didn't want to do the expected. He chuckled at his arrogance at the pretentiousness of his conduct. He realized he was saving himself for Miss Sophia Carter-Brown. Something else he'd never done before.

The three men rode to Mayfair Hall at nine o'clock on Friday night. It was dark and the moon was fuller than it had been when he first arrived nearly a week ago, the stars filling the sky overhead. Link could never get over the clarity of the night sky when the weather was cold and crisp. Even in Bordeaux after a solid rain sometimes the sky wouldn't be this brilliant. Perhaps it was the reflection off the snow.

He could see the lights of Mayfair Hall in the distance, even hear the music as the sounds rippled across the snow and ice. He might put a few of the pieces to his puzzle together tonight. The random notion caused him to grin. There were carriages despite the condition of the main road. The snow was not deep enough now that the weather was warming to warrant a sleigh ride. He would truly like to ride in a sleigh. Maybe it would snow again before he left. Perhaps he would treat Miss Carter-Brown to a sleigh ride with him.

The house glistened and shimmered.

Link saw her immediately, his breath catching in his throat. She was standing next to a young man at the entrance greeting all the newcomers, acting the perfect hostess for her uncle. She was gowned in white, pure virginal white, her shoulders bare, her auburn hair piled high on top of her head with two thick tresses falling over her shoulder to lie on that bare white flesh. Link looked at her and nodded, a smile on his face just as she looked up and saw him. She went very still, seemed to freeze for a moment. She didn't smile back. Belatedly, he realized there was something akin to disdain in his smile. He removed the expression. He relaxed. It didn't matter if she slept with every man in the state. It simply made no difference.

When she slept with him, he would be her only lover.

Her motives still interested him. She captivated, intrigued, enticed...and yes, she excited him. He meant to take his time with her. Somehow, he knew she would never be an easy conquest. Neither would he.

He strode up the steps, beside a worshipful Grayson, toward her. He noticed under more careful scrutiny she wasn't the goddess Grayson saw her as. She looked much older than almost eighteen. Her eyes were an arresting silver gray, her skin as white as her bare shoulders, too white. She was wearing more makeup than any lady should wear, especially a young woman of her age who needed no makeup at all to look her best. She appeared more like a London actress or an opera girl than a young lady at a ball in her home. Her mouth was thick dark red, kohl lined her eyes and darkened her brows. She applied rouge to her cheeks, a heavy layer of white powder to her entire face as well. Why did her uncle allow her to appear a harlot in his house? The damned white virginal gown she wore, the picture was entirely too much. It was as if she ridiculed her uncle, mocked all the people present, perhaps even scorned herself.

It seemed every time he learned something new about her there were more questions.

Link heard the introduction, accepting her hand in his, turning it over and lightly kissing her palm. She jerked. He released her hand, slowly, very slowly savoring the moment as well as the terrified look in her eyes. He wasn't wrong. She truly didn't like him. In addition, she feared him.

In due time he would change that.

William Brinkmeyer was of an entirely different ilk. A tall man, thin as a reed, with a hard face and narrow chin. He seemed exceedingly reserved. He also seemed oblivious to the almost eighteen-year-old who flaunted herself beside him. He shook Link's hand with little strength and said, "A pleasure to meet you, sir, a pleasure. Mr. Grayson has often spoken of you. He has amazing things to say about you as well as the rest of your family. You are always welcome here. You will make sure to dance, of course, with my sweet niece."

Was the bloody fellow an idiot? Was he blind as a bat?

The sweet niece looked like a painted hussy. Link turned politely, a smile on his mouth that didn't reach any farther than his lips, "Would you like this dance, Sophia?" Sarcasm rolled from his mouth. They were playing a minuet, a perfect slow dance for perhaps a bit of conversation. He wondered if she would speak to him at all. She looked as if she would rather skewer him through.

She nodded, saying nothing, a wary look in those silver gray eyes of hers that appeared as hard as steel. He could swear she wanted to tell him no. That the last thing she wanted was to dance with him. Ah, but she would dance to his tune soon. Lightly, she placed her hand on his forearm, following him onto the dance floor. The smile he sought failed to appear.

Another time perhaps.

As they walked onto the floor, he realized she said nothing at all to Edward. She ignored him. Obviously, they were no longer friends, more tangled and strange behavior. He became increasingly fascinated. She was composed of more twists and turns than a maze.

"I thought you and Edward have known each other since you were children," he told her, then released her to perform the steps in the minuet his gaze focused on her eyes.

When they came together again, she said, "Yes." Nothing more, no explanation or comment about how they didn't get along if they ever did.

"One would think," he began when she was near him again, "why one would ignore one's childhood friend when one reached adulthood. Yes, I believe that is a question to wonder about. Do you have an answer, pray tell?"

Several minutes passed by before she was back to him and her hand was in his. She said, "I suppose one can wonder about a lot of things and never get an answer. One can also ask a lot of questions without being satisfied."

Nothing more. Curse the chit. She meant to lead him around by the nose. He would have none of that. He would be satisfied.

In more ways than one.

The music stopped. He felt quite pleasantly warm. Even with the doors opened to the terrace the room was comfortable. Grayson hadn't lied. The ballroom brilliantly lit by myriad candelabras was nonetheless heated by the people as well as the well-positioned fireplaces.

Link strode back to Brinkmeyer, his hands behind his back. He said nothing more. He turned away, Grayson at his side to be introduced to other guests. He looked back to see Sophia standing very straight, her shoulders squared. Her uncle was speaking to her. His eyes narrowed. Was the uncle perhaps berating her for wearing so many cosmetics on her face or the whore's gown that revealed more than it concealed? He certainly hoped that was the case. For some reason he doubted it. Personally, if she was his niece, he would hold her face in a bucket of water then scrub it with lye soap until all traces of that horrid white powder, rouge, kohl and more were gone. He wanted to see what was beneath the powder and the goop. He wanted to know if she sported freckles. Ah, women detested them but he adored freckles, liked to taste each one with the very tip of his tongue.

Within an hour or so he was sure he danced with every daughter of every planter in Virginia. He was fawned over, complimented on everything from the shine on his boots to the lovely color of his eyes, simpered at until he wanted to yawn with the sheer boredom of it all. His feet hurt. He felt petulant and wanted to sit down and not move for a good hour. Finally, he was able to elude Grayson, three purposeful-looking planters, two more purposeful-looking wives with daughters in tow, and slip out onto the balcony. He never liked being places where mamas were hoping to wed him to their daughters. There were stone steps leading down into a quite lovely garden lightly dusted with snow. The scene was beautiful. He breathed in deeply the clean crisp scent of the air. There were stone benches. He sat down on one and leaned back against a sturdy oak tree. He closed his eyes, thrilled to finally be alone with his thoughts.

"I watched you come out here."

He nearly jumped out of his skin. She startled him so badly. He stood. It was Sophia Carter-Brown. She was standing very close to him, so close he could smell roses. He wondered if all of her smelled of roses. In time he would discover the truth.

She looked up at him, keeping the same expression, making no movement whatsoever now. Her hands were held together in front of her. Her lips thinned into a smile. She obviously didn't want to be there.

He felt compelled to speak. "I wanted to rest. I am not yet accustomed to the land. I don't like balls and all the people wanting me to dance with their daughters. My man's body is not a bargaining chip for marriage. I'm not on display."

"Yes, I understand. Dancing is what one does at balls," the soft almost shy voice surprised him anew.

When he listened to the deceptive undertones, she sounded haughty, very aloof, her expression giving nothing away of her feelings. By her tone she sounded as if she disliked him. Why did she follow him out here? Something else that made no sense. She didn't like him.

He didn't want to let her know what he was feeling or thinking.

He sat again stretching his legs out in front of him, crossing his ankles and crossing his arms over his chest. His posture was blatantly impudent. Never in his adult life had he been so rude to a woman. He was always most polite, a gentleman as well. He spoke in a voice that matched her coldness, "What is it you expect of me, Miss Sophia Carter-Brown? Could it be another dance since this is a ball as you sarcastically pointed out? One dances at balls. You followed me out here. Was that your purpose?" He wanted to unravel at least one strand connecting her secrets.

Her chin rose as she stiffened. Again, he wondered why the hell was she out here with him when it was obvious this was the last place on earth she wanted to be. Her spine stiff, she gazed out into the darkness. "You don't act like most men, Mr. Stewart," she finally said her voice still void of feeling. It was as if she spoke to herself. "I don't understand you."

"Ah, by that do you mean I don't drool at your feet? I don't gaze at your very red lips and long for a kiss or to suck into my mouth your undoubtedly enchanting breasts?" Once more his tone was insolent, rude to the extreme. He watched her for the reaction he was hoping to elicit.

"No!"

Well, he got more than he expected. "What is it that I don't do?" he spoke softly as he leaned into her.

She looked away. He watched her fingers pleating and playing with the soft folds of her silk gown, clearly nervous. It was a sign of some sort. She was very slender. Although her gown was cut high beneath her breasts in the new fashion mode, he could tell her waist was narrow. He wondered about her legs and hips. Were they long and slender and white? Were her hips gently curved?

He saw her breasts rise and fall then temptingly sway as she inhaled a large breath of air before turning to face him, this time a half smile on her garishly painted lips. "You are audacious, Sir. Gentlemen don't speak so bluntly, surely not even in Scotland."

"Not even to painted tarts?"

Everything about her was temptation.

Link heard the gasp as she sucked in her breath. He could have sworn she actually reeled back in shock. An emotion, it was what he was aiming for. He needed to disarm her so he could discover a weakness. Unconsciously, she raised a hand to her cheek and began to rub at the powder.

He wanted to offer her his handkerchief.

She stopped suddenly letting her hand fall to her side. She smiled now and the utter control baffled him. Still, he waited for the next round as he sifted through his thoughts. "No," she said calmly, too calmly, "not even to painted tarts. I had been told you had some wit, some manners as well. Told you were a gentleman. I was told wrong. I was mistaken to believe you might be well-mannered. You are rude and a bore."

He rose to stand over her, very close, so close he could once again smell the rose scent on her hair. She didn't move away. She stiffened. "Ah, you hit hard when it pleases you," he told her, "and you don't do it too badly. Not all that well either. I will have to explore this further. After all I'm only a man." He withdrew a handkerchief from his pocket and quickly wiped it over her red lips. She tried to jerk away, reached out a hand to stop him. He wasn't going to let her have her way. He grabbed her by the back of her neck and wiped her mouth yet again. He tossed the cloth to the ground. "Now," he said as he leaned down and kissed her hard on her mouth. He kissed her for a very long time.

~ * ~

After but a moment, he gentled. She understood his expertise was great, greater than she'd know before. His lips were stroking, caressing hers, his tongue seeking entrance, parting but not demanding, nibbling and enticing. He could wait. He was leaving this up to her, this mad coaxing of his, this subtle cajoling.

She knew it to be what it was. She allowed him the time, not moving, not responding. She couldn't give into this man or she would be lost. He was different, so sure of himself. She didn't understand how to deal with him. Her uncle would be angry with her. She couldn't help herself.

Suddenly his hands cupped her breasts. She jumped. She couldn't help it.

"Hush," he told her, his breath warm scented with wine. "Let me feel you. Is your skin as soft and warm as I believe it to be?"

Just as suddenly, as he spoke, his hands were down the front of her bodice, cupping her bare breasts, passing his thumbs across her nipples. He paused a moment. Lifting his head, staring down at her.

~ * ~

He knew in that instant he wanted to see her quite as naked as the day she was born. "Your heart was pounding, but not fast enough. I don't think. Your breasts are nice, Miss Carter-Brown. Is this the reason you came out here looking for me? You wished for me to fondle and caress you, stroke your nicely rounded breasts until you moaned with pleasure. Perhaps you wanted me to take you here in the garden. It would be too cold though. I'm not partial to snow and ice when I have sex. I like it in front of a blazing fireplace on a fur rug. You would look nice stretched out and naked on my white fur rug."

She stood quietly, didn't say one word while she allowed him to do what he wanted with her. He kissed her again, deepening the kiss this time, his open palm against her heart. The heartbeat quickened. He smiled into her mouth. She wasn't completely averse to him. He managed to elicit a reaction from her.

"Ah, but do you think to compare me to your multitude of men? You won't, you know." He wasn't about to play her game.

He knew his breath was warm, his tongue gentle and easy against hers. She wasn't kissing him back. She was passive. He didn't understand her. He wanted another response from her and by God he was going to get it. He pulled his hands from the bodice of her gown, grabbed the shoulders of the dress, jerked it to her waist. In the pale moonlight her breasts showed soft and white. They were not large breasts, but very nicely shaped, full and high, the nipples a pale pink. He leaned down and began kissing the warm flesh. She tasted of warm milk and peaches, of woman.

It was then she laughed, a teasing, wicked laugh. He stiffened from the pure surprise of the sound and looked down at her. Graceful as a dancer, she spun away from him. Yet she did nothing to cover herself. He was perplexed, infuriated as well.

"You are not lacking in the ways of men," she told him, her voice light and caressing, her breasts swaying softly as she moved, her shoulders back, thrusting them outward, taunting and teasing. "No, not bad at all. You are daring, egotistical, a man who doesn't wait for a lady to issue an invitation. You should show more restraint, Sir. Or perhaps it is an invitation you want, and you haven't the patience to wait for one to be issued. It is not well done of you."

"You might be correct," he told her, "perhaps. I don't share, Miss Carter-Brown. When I take a woman, I'm the only man whose rod comes inside her. There will be no comparisons, at least no immediate ones."

"I understand," she told him, that bloody stilted tone of hers, lilting and more seductive than any woman's voice he'd ever heard in his life. She was like a siren luring men to their death. "For this moment you may admire me, Sir," she said.

He stared at her breasts as she slowly with infinite fascination pulled the gown back to her shoulders, gently easing it into place. When her gown was straight and she looked as if she'd done nothing out of the ordinary, she said, "No, Mr. Stewart, you've not been a gentleman. You've moved far too quickly than you should have. You've displeased me with your excesses. You demand not ask. On the other hand, I do not dislike your arrogance. It is refreshing. You do not waste time in getting to the point. Tonight, when I'm abed I will think about you. Mr. Stewart. I have decided that I will ride with you in the morning. You will meet me here at ten o'clock sharp. Do not be late. I dislike waiting for men."

Link was tempted to take her riding habit, her horse, her bloody orders and tell her to go to hell, but he didn't. Nothing she did or said changed the fact she fascinated him nor did it diminish his curiosity. He was staring at her mouth, clean now of the bloody red paint. A beautiful mouth, truly. He wanted to taste her again.

She was still an enigma.

He grinned at her as he reached out and lightly stroked his fingertips along her jaw. "An order for you. Do not paint your face. I don't like it. You will excuse me now, Miss Carter-Brown."

~ * ~

Link grinned, feeling inordinately pleased with himself as he stared at the ormolu clock in the main salon in Leslie Hall. The time was now ten o'clock. She would be looking for him. Well, she wasn't going to find him, at least not until he was good and ready. Two could play at this game of cat and mouse, but there could only be one winner. He planned on being the winner. Ah, but she would expect to see him riding up to the front of Mayfair Hall, just as Her Highness had bade him.

He wasn't going to be there.

When it was ten-thirty, he rose, stretched and walked into the small breakfast room. Both Edward and his father were there, sipping on the rich black coffee cook always made in the morning. He looked for tea, gave up and poured himself the coffee he was just beginning to enjoy. Two servants were in the room, at least he hoped they weren't slaves. He didn't cotton to owning slaves. They were serving breakfast. One smiled at him, waving to him to be seated as if he were her guest.

Link accepted the eggs, bacon and fresh bread set in front of him. The scent was divine, his stomach grumbling. He downed the hot black coffee realizing he was beginning to prefer it over tea. Thinking about Sophia he was trying to picture the look on her face now that she must realize he wasn't doing her bidding, salivating over the minutest amount of time she was willing to give him. He grinned as he chewed on the bread waiting for the next confrontation.

"I heard someone mention last night you were planning on riding this morning with Miss Carter-Brown."

Link choked on a bite of food but he didn't look at Grayson. He was afraid that if he did, he would show his emotions and grin, for Grayson sounded jealous. He wondered how many men were besotted with Miss Carter-Brown, as well as why. He didn't find anything remarkable about her that caused all this devotion. How the devil did he know about the assignation with Sophia? Rather the supremely confident order she gave him.

"Whoever spread the gossip was wrong. As you can see, I'm here eating this delicious breakfast with the two of you. Please tell your cook how simply enjoyable it is."

"Her uncle told me the two of you were riding," Samuel said, looking at him. "He wanted to know if you could be trusted to be alone with a young lady. Brinkmeyer loves his niece very much and he is very anxious that no man take advantage of her. You don't plan on doing that, do you?"

Edward sputtered out a few drops of coffee then quickly wiped his mouth with his napkin, his brows pushed tightly together.

Link leaned over and smacked him on the back. "Are you alright?"

"You have no business acting like this, Edward," his father said harshly seeming to understand explicitly what his son thought. "You will not speak badly of her, do you understand? You will not act the leering young man."

Edward looked at his father, disgust clearly written on his face. "I said nothing. I merely choked. You can't keep living in a fool's world where Sophia is concerned."

"Damn you, son, I won't accept your damnable impertinence. She is a fine young woman." He waved his hand in the air. "Don't believe all the gossip. Use your eyes and look at her. You will see her sweetness."

"Grayson," Link said smoothly, interrupting his exchange with his son. "As to Miss Carter-Brown's reputation, no one seems to agree. Surely, you're aware of that. She is an enigma purposely trying to keep people wondering. For at least one moment last night I did see a trace of sweetness, but it vanished as quickly as it appeared."

"Makes no difference to me," Grayson said, his voice harsh. "I know the truth even when the rest of you do not. No one will change my mind about her."

"A change of subject might be nice here. There have been no more supernatural incidents. I'm quite disappointed. I was so looking forward to catching someone in the act then removing the white sheet. I do wonder why they ceased so abruptly with my arrival."

Yes, he had to consider his timely arrival did have something to do with termination of antics.

Edward spoke slowly. "It's a fact. Since you spent some time in town before my father brought you to Leslie Hall, everyone or practically everyone would have known within twenty-four hours that you arrived. The fact it happened the same days is telling. Someone didn't hear the fortuitous news."

"What does that mean?" Link continued thoughtfully as he stabbed at some egg with his fork, "That if they were meant to stop upon my appearance then the person responsible hadn't heard of my arrival before the first night. Is that what you're telling me?"

"True," Edward said. "All true."

"I am not certain there is a real person behind this," Grayson said. "None of this is natural. What you saw isn't normal. You said yourself, Link, there was no sign of the fire where you'd seen one, no scorching of the earth. Perhaps it wasn't a person in a white costume, perhaps it was another manifestation of evil."

"What Edward and I saw was a flesh and blood man running around with a sheet over him," Link said firmly. "Also, the arrow that went into my leg was shot by a real person. Thus, there were two villains at Leslie Hall that first night. A question, Samuel, do you know of any man nearby who is good at archery?"

"Good God," Edward said, appearing surprised. "I hadn't thought to ask. Yes, Father, let's think on that. Of course, there are the natives."

Both men thought for several seconds. It didn't take much longer. Link ate the fresh baked bread spread with strawberry preserves and butter, chewing thoughtfully. He thought of Sophia Carter-Brown, waiting.

Both the thought and the bread were delicious.

Grayson spoke up, "Yes, I do know of a man skilled in archery."

"Who?" Edward and Link asked at the same time.

Grayson waved his hand in the air as if to dismiss his thoughts. "It can't be. It's just not possible. I was thinking of Felix Campbell, William Brinkmeyer's overseer. He is noted for his exceptional abilities with the bow and arrow. Again, no, the fact makes no sense. Why would he come to Leslie Hall and shoot Link in the leg? Also, Charles Ewing is a devotee of the sport as is a Mr. Jennings, a merchant in town. Doubtless there are others in the vicinity. Most likely there are too many to draw conclusions as to the person who shot you. We would need more information to come to any valid conclusions."

Link grinned. Another part of the puzzle revealed. Another connection to that shameful little tart at Mayfair Hall who'd teased him and practically let him make love to her in the garden on the ice and snow. He toyed with a slice of bread. "Since the men who visited us that first night of my arrival didn't know I was here, why then, we can begin to narrow down the list of possibilities. I met many gentlemen that first afternoon in the alehouse."

Edward retrieved writing utensils. They began to make a list all the names Link could remember from the alehouse when he arrived. The list began to grow.

"Many aren't accounted for," Edward said quietly. "More, there are many more names. The number boggles the mind."

"Among the count are two of her lovers." Link said easily. "We can mark off Charles Ewing because I did encounter him. Obviously, he knew I arrived so he isn't the perpetrator of the crimes."

"Yes," Edward said.

His father set his coffee cup in its saucer before he angrily fled the room.

Link frowned after him. *Why could he possibly wish to overlook what the chit is about as well as what she has become? What truth did Grayson see that no one else did?* The very thought boggled Link's mind. Left him with more questions.

Edward looked across the breakfast room to an oil painting of a ship. Then with a shrug he focused on him. "Father wanted us to marry, but that was a long time ago. He won't give up on that idea no matter what

I've told him. He believes in her innocence. Why, I'm not certain. Her wickedness intrigues him, might even fascinate him. I'm sure you've noticed his housekeeper is a little flirt and he is fond of her. You mustn't take his anger personally. He means well but doesn't understand how drastically Sophia has changed. There is no longer anything sweet or innocent about her. I suppose even if he does realize, he would forgive her transgressions without batting an eye. He longs for her to be what she isn't."

Link made no more comments. Deep in thought he continued with his breakfast.

After a few more seconds Edward said, a grin on his face. "You were supposed to ride with her today, weren't you?"

Link smiled back at him, pure delight simmering through to his bones at the thought of Sophia waiting for him. "Yes, yes I was but I'll never allow a woman to dictate or order me to do something. I will be the one giving orders. She will know what I wish and when I wish it. I will do the asking not she the telling. So, here I am while she is waiting for me. Perhaps in a little while I'll wander over to Mayfair Hall and see what is in store for me. I'm sure she will retaliate in some manner. I'm anxious to see what that will be."

"This should prove interesting."

"Well, interesting is what I'm searching for. I didn't want to be uninterested while I was here. Didn't expect life here could prove this fascinating. Sophia is a perfect diversion," Link said and drank the rest of his rich black coffee. "Do you have the time, Edward?"

"Yes, It's nearly eleven-thirty."

"I believe I will go riding."

Edward slanted him a crooked grin. "Enjoy the hunt."

"I believe I will," Link said whistling a jaunty tune as he walked away.

Chapter Three

"What did you say to him? He's not here."

Sophia turned to face her uncle, her heart thundering. She looked at him, looked at his face and the way he sneered at her. She detested him. She feared him more. "I don't have the faintest idea what I could have said. I assumed I made myself clear. That he should be here at ten. He didn't say he wouldn't come. So, I assumed."

"You made him angry, damn you. You have no idea. This man is important to my plans. I need him."

He raised his fisted hand to hit her. Seemed to think better of it and let it drop to his side.

She realized he didn't punch her only because a housekeeper was walking toward the room. Her uncle never showed his true self to anyone but her. All the while she prayed Clare never discovered his wrath.

He lowered his arm then his voice. Even though his voice was soft his fury was obvious and vicious. "You put him off. You didn't succeed, Sophia. I'm displeased with your efforts. You will make this right or you'll be sorry. Must I do everything?" He held his hands up. "No, don't answer that. I will think about this and decide what you should do now. You've botched it and I wonder if you didn't do this on purpose. What do you say, Sophia? Did you plan this debacle? You don't like the man so you put him off."

He paced the veranda for several minutes. Sophia watched him with a disinterested eye and kept silent. She prayed Link Stewart would have the good sense to stay away from her, from the two of them. She didn't want to see him hurt. If he persisted it was inevitable. Her uncle always achieved what he set out to get. If she warned Link, she would suffer the consequences. Without a doubt her uncle would learn of it.

William paused, approaching her, sitting in a chair on the porch. "You took Devon Masters to the estate last night, did you not?"

It seemed he wished to change the subject. She was glad that he did. Speaking of Link Stewart was not something she could do with any ease.

Her hands clasped in front of her, she nodded, refusing to say anything more to him. She looked at the floor, the perfectly polished floor. Her heart was pounding so hard in her chest she thought she would truly die.

"Were there any problems?"

"Yes, he didn't like the fact I gave Link any attention, didn't like the fact I danced with him during the party or that we were to ride today. His is not a steady character. He is immature and self-absorbed; thinks he owns me. Once he has drunk enough, he is not difficult for me to handle, but last night his jealousy...well it doesn't matter now. It all turned out the way you wanted."

"You dealt with him."

"The way you taught me."

"Ewing will be leaving next week."

"That's what I've heard."

"You will detach yourself from Devon Masters now. There is no more use for him. I'm sure Mr. Stewart is not a man who shares his women."

"He will not go easily," Sophia said softly. "He's young and arrogant and considers himself to be my stud. He will not think kindly that I no longer want him. He will most likely vehemently protest the rejection. You are right about Mr. Stewart. He already told me he wouldn't share."

"You must find the proper words to let the young pup go. You realize of course, Devon's feelings make little difference in this scenario."

No, no one's feelings made any difference to her uncle.

When she saw Link Stewart ride up not ten minutes later, she wished she could find somewhere to hide. Sophia didn't know if she had the energy to deal with the detestable man nor did she want to do so. She wanted him to leave but understood he would not. Curse his male stubbornness. She understood the way men thought. No, she didn't like this, didn't like it at all. This was a lesson for her a punishment of sorts. He was making sure she understood she could not order him around, that he would do what he pleased when he pleased. He was meting out discipline, putting her in her place so to speak. She would have none of that.

Well, let him try.

If only he knew it was her wish to never see or speak to him again, he might vanish back to Scotland or Bordeaux. She heard he had a home there. Well, then, they would both be more than pleased. It was her wish he would book passage back to Scotland. Yesterday would not have been soon enough. She stiffened when she thought of the way he so arrogantly touched and stroked her last night. Was mortified knowing she had no recourse but to endure his haughty behavior simply because he believed her to be a harlot. If her uncle got wind of the fact she refused him, there would be more beatings. It terrified her when she realized she didn't want him to stop touching her. Was horrified when she realized she wanted to know what it would be like to have him make love to her.

Holding her breath, she didn't move, merely watched him as he rode toward the porch, dismounted and tied his stallion to the post some ten feet away from her.

He sauntered over to her, leaned negligently against the porch railing, and said easily, "Good morning. Nice to see you."

"It's closer to the afternoon," she shot back immediately regretting the words as well as the tone when she noticed the expression on her uncle's face. She didn't want to be polite to Link Stewart. With her uncle staring she had no choice.

"Ah, but indeed it is. I was busy this morning."

He frowned at her then lifted his broad masculine shoulders as if it didn't matter in the least that he was very late, not even fashionably late.

He was staring at her face and she knew he was displeased with the fact she wore the makeup he told her not to put on. She knew in the morning sunlight it would look brassy and tasteless. It was the way her uncle wanted her to appear even when she told him Mr. Stewart didn't like the cosmetics. Had explicitly told her not to wear them.

His voice gruff, "I told you to wash your face. You look ridiculous. You may be the harlot but there is no reason to advertise the fact, especially when you are with me. I won't have it."

He spoke slowly and clearly as if she didn't understand the words he was saying.

Slowly, Sophia stood up, her anger rising with each passing second, her fists clenched behind the folds of her skirt. She watched him for a very long time saying nothing, wishing she could fade away into the woodwork, knowing she could not. She would have to fight him every way she knew how. Then in what was meant to be an unconcerned light teasing voice, she said, "Are you here to take me riding or to decree conditions of surrender?"

"Surrender," he repeated seeming fascinated, his smile broadening. "That sounds quite fascinating to me, particularly with regards to you, madam. First, go wash your face. Then I will take you riding and we can talk about the terms of surrender. Your surrender, not mine."

"I didn't say I would ride with you. After all you are nearly two hours late. I've other things planned for this day, important things. You wasted my time. I'm not at all pleased by that."

"Am I? Do you? Dear me, how remiss of me and ungentlemanly. On the other hand, two hours ago, I wasn't in the mood to go riding. Now I am. Go wash your face. I will give you ten minutes, not that you need that long."

"I don't want to go anywhere with you. Go back to Scotland where you can be a bore with someone else."

Despite the fact there would be repercussions from her uncle, she blurted the words that would damn her for another beating. She could not keep her distasteful words behind her teeth.

"Mr. Stewart, how delightful to see you," William Brinkmeyer stood on the porch, his hands behind his back, rocking on his heels as he surveyed the scene. "My niece mentioned that the two of you would be riding today. It's so nice that you came. Sophia, you must accompany him. Where are you going? You must be charming to our neighbor. I'm sure he would appreciate your company. You can show him around, give him a grand tour."

Link was amused to see her so neatly trapped. Before her uncle appeared, he was sure she meant to disappear into the house and not return. "Yes, Miss Carter-Brown. Where are you going?"

She shot him a furious glare before speaking over her shoulder. "To freshen up."

"Excellent, well do hurry. While Mr. Stewart and I would love to chat I'm sure he would like your company much better than my own." He turned to Link, "Such a sweet girl, my niece. Charming, isn't she? Sit down, Mr. Stewart. Should you like a brandy?"

"At this hour? No, thank you, Mr. Brinkmeyer."

"Ah, do call me William."

"Then you shall call me, Link."

"I understand your brother is the Duke of Southcliff."

"Yes, he would have traveled here himself but he is newly wed. He wanted to spend time with his wife. So, I volunteered."

His wife, the beautiful Lacie with the bountiful breasts, his brother was indeed protective of her endowments. The thought gave him good reason to chuckle. Sophia didn't have breasts like Lacie's. Few women had such bountiful endowments. He liked Sophia's breasts. They were well shaped and soft. Just the right size.

"How long are you planning to stay?"

"Only until the ghostly apparitions are dealt with to my satisfaction. I won't have them plaguing Leslie Hall or the surrounding neighbors any longer."

"I also would not like to see them continue. They are such an annoyance. The slaves are terrified and refuse to work the day after," Brinkmeyer said as he looked toward Leslie Hall.

"Mr. Grayson has spoken to me of these superstitions. That's all they are, just superstitions. Everything can be accounted for scientifically and fabricated by man. Mankind, of course, is capable of anything. We are talented at pursuing the dark arts to our personal benefits."

"To my knowledge, nothing has happened for a few days. Do you suppose they have stopped?"

"If they have in deed ceased, I'm relieved. I was quite frightened on my first encounter."

"So, why do you suppose they have," William paused, "stopped?"

Link wanted to ask him a host of questions such as who he might know with archery skills, other questions about his overseer but he figured it was too soon for anything so probing. He needed to know things no one else did while not giving his thoughts away to a person he wasn't sure if he could trust. He relaxed back in his chair, slanting William a guileless smile, thoughts of Sophia at the forefront of his mind. He wondered what was taking her so long.

A house slave brought hot coffee at Mr. Brinkmeyer's request. It was delicious even without the cream and sugar he added to his coffee at breakfast. He quite liked it unadorned. Link noted that Miss Carter-Brown far exceeded her ten minutes. He finished the cup of coffee and gently set the cup in its saucer. He rose and extended a hand to William.

"It's grown late, William. It's also apparent your niece has no wish to ride with me today or perhaps has become occupied with the more important matters she spoke of. Good bye."

He strode away whistling nonchalantly.

William Brinkmeyer stared at his back. He could feel the hair on the back of his neck prickle. Then the man yelled, "Sophia!"

Link didn't stop. No, he wouldn't wait a moment longer for the little tart. He strolled toward his horse, still whistling as if he didn't have a thought in the world. He heard a noise from above, and curious, he looked up.

She was standing on a balcony some twelve feet up. In her hands she held a basin. He sidestepped but he wasn't fast enough. A good amount of water whooshed down on his head. He swore softly then composed himself along with his anger.

The laughter from above was faint before it stopped abruptly as if she realized she would give away her motive if he heard. He did hear. He also heard. "Oh dear, what have I done? Oh, Mr. Stewart, I'm so sorry. I wasn't paying a wit of attention. I was in such a hurry, you see. Your ten minutes was just not enough time. Do come inside and I will give you a towel. Wouldn't want you to catch cold."

The game was becoming more and more stimulating. He had to give her this point. She got him quite nicely. One battle in Miss Sophia Carter-Brown's favor. He would have to even the score.

He called back, "Thank you, Miss Carter-Brown. Actually, the sun is getting quite hot today. The water felt good."

"In any case you will want to dry off, I will be right down with a towel." She added with a voice of gentle sweetness so false he was forced to grin. "Do call me, Sophia."

When Link turned back to the porch, he saw something very unexpected, something he meant to log away in his brain for future reference. It was William Brinkmeyer's face and it was ugly and mean and something very frightening moved in his pale brown eyes., Abruptly whatever Link thought he saw vanished. Brinkmeyer was distraught and concerned and waving his hands as he moved quickly toward him, even wringing his hands exclaiming, "Come here, Mr. Stewart, do come here and sit down. Ah, my niece was careless, but surely she will make it up to you."

"I have no doubt she will do her best," Link said.

He would make sure he gave back to her what she so richly deserved. She would not have the last say. The ensuing punishment would fit the crime.

The brazen jade.

When Sophia appeared, she had washed only the most vulgar of the makeup off her face. On the other hand, his face was shiny and dripping with water. She smiled at him, her eyes glittering her triumph even though the words that spouted from her mouth seemed angelic. She prattled nonsense like a brainless twit. She hung about him, offering to pour him more coffee, offering him more towels, brushing imaginary water droplets off his shoulders.

It was all quite amusing. He was relishing this immensely, could hardly wait for the next round between them.

When she actually offered to dry his hair for him then comb it, he said. "No, thank you, Sophia. I'm truly quite dry now. No more of your tender concerns for my person. I do hope that bucket you accidentally spilled on me contained only fresh water."

She blinked furiously, her face paling believably then flushing, before finally settling into a patently false mask of chagrin. "Oh my, I do believe so, but you know...oh certainly my maid changed the water and cleaned the bucket, but then again, sometimes she is so lazy so perhaps not."

She was an incredible actress. At least he hoped she was acting. The water did taste and smell clean so he meant to dismiss the idea it was something other than pure fresh water.

"Wait, Sir, and I will ask." She struck a pose. "You know, if my maid didn't clean it out, she will never admit such a thing. So, I suppose we will never know for sure, now, will we? She jumped to her feet and as she passed him, she sniffed rather loudly and wrinkled her nose.

She was better than he originally thought.

He strode to stand beside her. "Sniff again, Sophia. Yes, is there anything untoward? No? Excellent, I see that your face must weigh a tiny bit less that it did before. There are still cosmetics, but not enough to make me send you back to your room to start over. Further, you have no more water to wash your face with, do you? Perhaps, I now have some of your powder and rouge on my head. Come, let's go riding before the sun vanishes and we have snow once again. I don't like the cold."

A boy appeared leading a beautiful bay mare with two white stockings. The horse nipped Sophia's shoulder. She laughed then patted her nose. It was a sound pure and sweet, something he'd like to hear again. He looked hard at her.

"You naughty girl. You are ready for a ride, now, aren't you?" she asked.

More matters to think about. Link frowned realizing the voice he heard was completely different as was the low quite charming laugh. It was perhaps the reason Grayson would forgive her anything. When she laughed like that, one might come to the conclusion she was sweet and innocent as well.

He didn't help her up. It wouldn't do him any good to all of a sudden become a gentleman. She did expect it, he saw that, but he merely mounted his stallion and waited, not even looking at her.

The boy gave her a foot up. She stared hard at Link. Her expression was as bland as his sister Merry's when she'd managed to beat him at a game of chess. Sophia might have a few things she could teach Merry. It was a good thing she would never get the chance.

"Do you have someplace you would like to go, Mr. Stewart?" she asked.

"Since I am to call you Sophia, why don't you call me Link?"

"Very well, where would you like to go, Link?"

He sifted through his mind for a destination. "Along the river, perhaps to that little cottage I've heard so much about."

She didn't hesitate for a moment but he would swear he saw her eyes widen in shock for just a second. She said with no emotion in her voice, "I think not."

She slanted him a tempting smile and a toss of her head. Her riding habit was of a pale blue, her hat a darker shade with a charming feather that curved around her face. It was very effective, that feminine head toss. He wasn't most men though. He knew exactly what she was about. "Besides, the cottage is most likely occupied. My uncle lends it out on a regular basis. One never knows who might be there. We wouldn't want to interrupt anything now, would we?"

Sophia kicked her mare Diamond into a canter. Off they went down the long, wide drive of Mayfair Hall as he watched.

She was audacious. There wasn't an ounce of humility in her. Those characteristics in a man would be credible. In a woman...

He'd have to think on that.

He followed her, content to watch her backside and the way she moved so gracefully on the horse. They rode onto the main road, following it only for a half-mile or so then she turned off toward the river. When they broke through the line of evergreen trees, Link sucked in his breath. The river was beautiful.

He held in his breath staring at the river and the beginnings of spring. Through patches of snow, daffodils poked their heads up. A few were in full bloom. Cherry trees melded with the pine, the pink-white blossoms showing a brilliant display of color. He wondered if the river was as cold as it looked.

Probably colder.

There was a stretch of beach that seemed to go on and on. It was beautiful. In many ways the same as Scotland but nothing like the Bordeaux area of France.

"It's amazing," he told her before he thought to censor his words and give her only what he wanted her to hear. "I'm sure you love this as much as I do the warmer climate of my homeland."

"This is my favorite part of the river." Her voice was soft well-modulated and sincere. "I like to swim here in the summer. It is far too cold this time of year."

He reclaimed control of his unruly body then raised a brow looking at her. "Would you like to swim now?"

"I normally swim..." She looked away. "It is too cold."

He guessed she wore nothing at all when she swam or just her chemise. "I would have never guessed you to be a coward. I've already seen and fondled your breasts. They are quite adequate you know. Not at all that large but finely shaped. No man I know of would complain about them. They are incredibly soft. Well," he paused, "I cannot say much about the rest of you which I've yet to see. Your hips, your belly, your legs, and your woman's endowments, I wonder, are they just as adequate? A man should be able to see what he is getting himself into before he makes a commitment, don't you think?"

For a moment she turned her head away to stare at the cold water. "Ah, well, Sir, do you think a woman should have the same consideration, Mr. Stewart? See a man's endowments before making a commitment?"

He let out a long indifferent breath of air. "You really should remember to call me Link since we, in a very short time are going to be very close, much closer than we are now. Of course, a woman should be given the same considerations. A commitment is just as important to females." He grinned then, showing her his perfect white teeth behind his lips. "Would you like to see me naked, Sophia? Now?"

He thought he had her, really did, but not a second later knew he underestimated her. She slanted him the hottest smile he'd seen in his adult life. Expertly, she ran her tongue across her lower lip before leaning her upper body toward him. How the devil could an eighteen-year-old know so much about seducement? "Why, I think that would be ever so nice, Link. Maybe you could strike a pose for me. I believe I would like that too. I could sit over there on that grassy spot beneath the cherry tree and direct you as to how to turn so I would get a better view. A man's buttocks, flexed, you know, are sometimes quite delightful. Yes, I believe that would be very nice."

Bloody eyes, he thought, picturing what those words conjured up in his mind. It was totally unbelievable. No, he would never have believed she said it if he hadn't heard it himself.

He realized he flushed. He truly turned red to the roots of his hair at her outrageous suggestions.

Sophia saw that flush and her satisfaction wasn't all that subtle. She couldn't hide her reaction. She shook her finger at him. "Truly, Mr. Stewart, it's never wise to make suggestions such as you did when you don't have the slightest idea what you're going to get in return." It was a hard-won fight but she managed it. She just didn't know how long she could wage battles against this man. He would win the war. This time she'd been so outrageous she'd made him flush. She was sure she must be the first woman to accomplish such a feat, for he was polished, suave. This man with his clear blue eyes, sophisticated and cynical and very sure of himself would never let a woman get the upper hand. Which was what she just did. Inwardly, she smiled.

By chance, she'd known exactly what she was saying. The first time she'd taken Devon Masters to the cottage, he'd already been three-quarters drunk. He'd stripped off his clothes, eager to show her that his body was firm and muscled, much nicer than that old man, Charles Ewing's, and how once she saw him, she'd dismiss all the other men. He'd posed for her, even turning his back to her and flexing his buttocks, and thus it was he she was seeing when she'd said those words to Link Stewart.

She watched him, refusing to say anything more for the time being.

~ * ~

Link was furious at the turn of events. His face rarely showed his feelings. He wouldn't allow her to keep the upper hand. No, this wasn't fathomable. He wanted to toss his head back and howl with the fury he felt. Instead, he inhaled a calming breath of air before smiling. He had to get the advantage back. Well hell, it was intolerable that a woman, a damned hussy, could do him in.

She had done just that twice.

"I do enjoy taking chances, Sophia," he said finally, in charge of himself and his damn voice again. "I haven't yet caught a Tiger or a Lion. Perhaps I've snared a rabbit or two and the good lord knows they are enjoyable to eat."

He slanted her an intimate smile but Miss Carter-Brown merely looked at him, one eyebrow arched, and Link would swear she had no clue as to what he was talking about. No, impossible, she was just toying with him again, pretending to innocence this time.

She said on a laugh, "Perhaps I should introduce you to a porcupine. They're quite slow on their feet, not intimidating at all but somewhat dangerous if provoked. They can sting you with their quills when you least expect it. Then there is the skunk who is quite deceptive if you know nothing about the critter. They can be mistaken for a house cat. Do they have skunks in Scotland or France? All in all, a very stinky fellow, one would say."

"I'm at a distinct disadvantage. I'm not at all sure where all this is going. It seems you could go on indefinitely about animals and their unnatural qualities."

"Perhaps you should not start something you don't know how to finish."

"Perhaps I shouldn't but then who knows. I might run into an animal that is tender and spicy. I wouldn't want to hurt one such as that. Ah, but some animals are shy and some too bold for their own good, finding themselves in trouble when they least expect. As for their bodies, who can say? I wonder about their taste. Bitter, do you think? Perhaps even deadly? Surely not sweet and juicy."

"Your comparisons are getting stranger and stranger by the second. Let's canter up the beach. There are some rather interesting spots farther ahead. In the summer there is a field of wildflowers. Now, there will most likely just be patches of snow, perhaps some crocuses and daffodils."

He followed her, appreciating the warmth of the sun, which was still choosing to shine down upon them. At the moment, he was furious with himself, not with her. She was what she was. The only problem with that conclusion is that he didn't know what exactly she was any more. All his previously formed conclusions were being whisked away with each new outlandish statement from her lips. Lips he would enjoy kissing again, depending on their taste then maybe more times.

Reigning in she dismounted, shaking her skirts then led him along a narrow foot path toward a field a good quarter mile from the river. One could see a line of trees in the distance. She headed that way. He followed, wondering if she was aware of anything. It seemed she tried to rid herself of him. Thought she could do just that by walking away from him.

She would have a difficult time with that. He would leave when he wanted to leave.

They passed through the line of trees, turning. The landscape changed dramatically as they wound their way farther inland. A cliff rose in front of them. There was a narrow opening that led into the side of the hill in front of them. Link stepped into the black stillness then out again. He didn't like caves, never had. "So, there truly are caves here. I heard talk when I was at the alehouse the day I arrived. Were these used for smuggling? Perhaps they are still used in that manner. I heard guns and ammunition were stored here during the revolutionary war. Is that true?"

"It is deep. As far as I know it has no other openings. At least none that I could find."

"Have you supplies in there?" He wondered if she used the place for some of her trysts.

"I don't understand."

"Oh, things like blankets, a sheet, a bottle of wine, things to ply your trade?"

She was shaking her head then nodding seemingly confused. A blank expression came upon her. "Ah, I see. Do I bring men here on occasion to seduce them? Is that what you are wondering? That I mean to seduce you here today?" Momentarily she appeared thoughtful, nothing more. The bland expression once more covered her face. "No, not to date. I don't suppose it's a bad idea though. Yes, perhaps your implication has some merit. This is relatively isolated although there is not a lot of privacy."

"What I believe is that a man would have to be absolutely crazy to be naked in this place despite the amazing, touted skills of his escort."

She smiled at him before turning away, a sly grin on her face as she went on to say. "Oh, I do think the opposite. In my experience men, gentlemen, are much the same. They tend to forget themselves entirely when promised sex with a woman. They think only with their manly parts not their brains. She doesn't even have to be particularly beautiful. They could be on the moon and dismiss it as unimportant when they are otherwise occupied."

A shudder swept through Link. He remembered telling his brother that he would forget his name once he was inside a woman, forget everything when the pleasure was so intense and startling, he couldn't think. In the presence of this tart, he flushed a second time. This time he hoped he controlled the emotion enough so she wouldn't notice. If she did, she didn't say a thing.

Damn her.

"The fact you can keep so many men happy and well satisfied when each knows about the other tends to support your hypothesis."

"Crying uncle, Mr. Stewart? Hypothesis?" One perfectly sculpted eyebrow shot upward. "It is not a theory to be proved."

"No, I take that back. What you say happens to be fact, not theory or hypothesis. A man has to be stupid not to face up to the truth when it's staring him in the face. Remember, my name is Link. I would be severely disenchanted if you screamed Mr. Stewart when you have your very first orgasm with my hands pleasuring you. I would feel very strange if you did something like that. No, it's just not right."

She should be blushing to the roots of her hair but she didn't look the least bit embarrassed. Curse her. What she looked was disgusted and totally contemptuous. He smiled at her, soaking in the moment while trying to gauge her true feelings. "Would you like to walk back to the horses? Incidentally, do horses get frostbite?"

She gave a lilting laugh.

~ * ~

The sun was about to go down, darkness would fall any minute. Only one candle burned in Sophia's bedroom. Blankly, she stared at the window, seeing the moon and the few stars surrounding it. She was wearing a robe, had pulled it tight around her as if that would give her the comfort she wanted no, needed. This scenario with Link Stewart was all becoming such a travesty. She could no more handle the man than she could the stallion her uncle bought about a month ago. They were both wild and untamed, unwilling to let a female handle them. She was totally silent. She felt utterly defeated.

Link Stewart wasn't like any man she'd ever come across, any man she'd manipulated and seduced. It was true she did him in, confused him, even brought a flush to his face. She was able to do it simply because he'd never met a woman who spoke so boldly before. He was already accustoming himself to her. If he continued to see her, he would turn her world inside out. She had the feeling she would never get the upper hand again.

What to do?

The hair on the back of her neck stood on end. She knew her uncle was in her bedchamber even though she didn't hear him enter. At times he was way too quiet. She didn't understand how such a big man could move without making a sound. For her actions today, there would be repercussions. She inhaled a ragged breath meant to keep it inside her lungs for as long as possible.

"How did your day go with Mr. Stewart?" The tenor of his voice was bland. She knew if she said the wrong words, he would beat her again. She had to step cautiously.

She continued to stare out the window, unwilling to look at him. She said in a flat voice. "We rode. I showed him the field of wildflowers and the little cave beyond the line of trees just west of here. He is a man, Uncle, but a man like no other. He didn't try to kiss me although there were opportunities. He didn't try at all. He spoke frankly of sexual things. He was relentless in his intimidation." At the thought of facing Link again, her stomach rolled.

"You will seduce him. Plan on taking him to the cottage tomorrow night. I'll make the rest of the arrangements."

She turned to face him. He was sitting on her bed, his back resting against the headboard. When she saw his face for an instant, just the tiniest instant, he looked good and kind and gentle, the man with the mask he presented to the world now one and the same.

Beside herself she let out a long slow breath of air. "You can't possibly comprehend. He does what it is he wishes to do. He will tell me when he wants to have sex with me, not the other way around. I could probably saunter around him with nothing on and if he felt he didn't have absolute control over me, over the situation, why, he would grin, say something shocking, and stroll away. He would not even bother to look back to see my reaction. If I tell him to meet me at the cottage tomorrow night, he won't show up."

William Brinkmeyer scowled. “You’re right, although I hate to admit it. I spoke with Link Stewart long enough this morning to see your point. It’s valid. We’ll have to find a way around it. We will simply have to get the man to the cottage another way.”

“Good luck with that.” Her sarcasm she understood was very evident

There was nothing more she could say even if she wanted to speak, which she didn’t. She felt very cold suddenly, very cold, very tired. Old to the marrow of her bones. The only thing she knew was that she didn’t want to see Link Stewart again.

“Did he mention his wounded leg?”

She shook her head. “Nothing.”

“He isn’t a stupid man. I imagined he inquired about who hereabouts could shoot a bow and arrow. He plays a game, but you and I, Sophia, we are the only ones who know the rules. Despite what he thinks, he can’t win.”

She despised the rules. He, not her, dictated the rules. When would her uncle understand that fact?

This evening she had to tell Devon Masters she wanted nothing more to do with him. She had no idea how to accomplish the feat, sure Devon would have an argument to anything she suggested. He was young and arrogant. She knew he wouldn’t be able to imagine anyone not wishing to see his wonderful self any longer.

William Brinkmeyer devised the way to accomplish the feat. For the first time Sophia laughed. It was sincere laughter, not contrived. For a single moment one heavy weight lifted from her shoulders.

~ * ~

It was very late when Sophia arrived at the cottage. The weather was taking a different turn. Clouds now dotted the sky. She was sure it would begin to rain before she accomplished her task. She would get soaked on her way home. Devon’s horse was tethered in front.

When she entered, he saluted her with a hot toddy. It didn’t seem as if he were inebriated yet. That should make it easier to break the sordid news to him. He sat on a chair, his legs stretched out in front of him, leering at her, stripping her as he looked his fill. She cringed at the thought of his hands touching her.

Before she could take off her cape, he rose to embrace her. She whirled away from him needing to keep her distance yet laughing coquettishly, her hands in front of her to ward him off. “Not now, not yet, we have to talk first. You will have to make a decision. I bring bad news for you. I’m truly sorry.”

“Talk? When you’ve never wanted to talk before? How strange you are acting. Why talk? I want you now, not later. Need to be inside you.”

“There is something important I need to tell you. It’s only fair that you understand the truth since I am very fond of you. I don’t want you to be hurt, to perhaps go mad as many do, I am told. There is no cure that we know of. Perhaps it won’t affect you, perhaps you don’t have it as yet.”

She was rambling, afraid of his reaction. There was nothing she could do about it now. It was, after all, the only way to end this without his posturing and begging. Otherwise, he would not take no for an answer.

Devon Masters downed the last of his hot toddy, weaving slightly as he did.

Perhaps he was drunker than she thought. He was certainly unsteady on his feet.

He spoke, slurring his words slightly. “I’m sure I’m not understanding any of this nonsense you are spouting. Perhaps you should get to the point. Tell me what’s on your mind, sweetheart then take off all your clothes so I can get inside you.” He let out a large burp. “What is it you mean about cures and what not?”

She supposed she should get to the point quickly. The sooner he left, the better she would feel as she recalled Link’s words.

He didn’t share his women.

Well, she didn’t want to be one of his women but her uncle disagreed with her. She knew the consequences of disagreeing with the odious man.

"Sophia?"

A long breath of air and, "I have the pox."

His face lost all color. He could be a ghost. "No!"

"Yes," she told him in a low, very melancholy voice. "The pox. There is no doubt. I went to a doctor. I'm sorry but I did have to share the bad news. I hope I didn't give it to you. That would be horrible."

"You didn't get it from me." His voice was vicious, his hands clasped tightly as if he wished to hit her. "It must have come from one of your other men. Tramp!"

She felt a quick surge of victory. He would go now, leave her. She would have to do nothing more. "Certainly not. I'm sorry you know. I wouldn't be warning you if you gave it to me, now, would I?"

"Oh God," his voice now a whisper then he actually moaned softly, his eyes seeming to cross and bulge at the same time. "What if you've given it to me? I could die."

"There is always that chance."

Devon was always self-absorbed. He didn't care a wit about her, just what was happening to him. He would truly be so relieved to discover he didn't have the horrible disease. She wondered if he would tell his other lovers. Ah, well, it was no longer a concern of hers. She accomplished her mission.

She went on to say. "I don't think it would have been possible for me to give it to you just yet. I'm sure you are safe, clean and will suffer no consequences. You will surely agree with me that it would not be safe for us to continue as lovers. You must leave and not worry about me."

His eyes seemed to bug out of his head even farther as he looked wildly about the small cottage where he'd spent a good dozen nights over the past two months. He looked at her then the bed where they slept together. "Jesus, the pox... I'll go now, Sophia. I'm sorry that you have it. Take care of yourself. Good bye."

"Good bye, Devon. Don't worry overmuch. I'm sure you'll be just fine."

She watched as he grabbed his hat then smashed it on his head.

Truly, she was not surprised when he ran from the cottage. A giggle almost rippled from her mouth. She didn't think she'd ever seen the man run or lift a finger in any form of physical activity. Uncle William had been right.

She also wondered about Devon's reaction when he calmed down enough to think.

Sophia recalled her uncle's words. Devon won't say a word to anyone. We needn't worry about that. No, he'll fear ridicule if he does. When he discovers that he hasn't been the recipient of the fatal disease, he'll look at the other men, just smile and wish the worst. That is the tenor of his character, you realize. He won't even inquire about your well-being.

"He is that type of man," Sophia said letting out a long breath of air. She was more than happy to see him go.

Before she went to bed that night, she sat in a rocking chair looking out over the land surrounding Mayfair Hall. It was chilly. The rain started falling as she left the cottage. She pulled the blanket tight around her shoulders to ward off the cold spring air. Her thoughts flew to Link Stewart as they seemed to do too often, more often than she wished. She wondered how he would have reacted had she told him she had the pox, stifling a bout of laughter at the absurd thought. Undoubtedly, he would search her eyes to see the truth then demand to examine her himself.

He was that kind of man.

~ * ~

Link was sitting in the breakfast room the next morning finishing his second cup of coffee when Edward sauntered into the room beaming, a huge grin on his face. Taking up the pitcher of coffee, he poured himself a cup before looking at Link to see if he wanted a refill. Then, "Did you know that Devon Masters is no longer one of Miss Carter-Brown's lovers?"

News seemed to travel fast in these parts. He didn't think Sophia would have accomplished the task so quickly. Link leaned negligently back in his chair, a feeling of satisfaction sweeping through him. He folded his hands, setting them on the table before addressing Edward. "Bloody eyes, but that didn't take long. Astonishing, but difficult to accept. Who does he say cried off? Didn't you tell me he was at her cottage only a few nights ago?"

He stretched his legs out in front of him thinking and wondering. This was definitely news. Good news, he decided.

Edward grinned then pushing out a chair sat down. "You don't suppose she's cleaning out her stable to make room for you? Must have seen him last night. Told him she couldn't continue with him."

Link was thoughtful for several seconds as he drummed his fingers on the table. He said finally, very firmly, "One could be tempted to think so at first. However, I still can't see her doing something so blatantly noticeable. She is subtle in her attacks. She is not stupid either. No, there is more to this than meets the eye. More to it than the obvious."

"Truly, Link, you might well be underestimating her attraction to you or the gentlemanly charms that seemed to float from you when you are with a woman. You do have a way about you that seems to draw women to you. Perhaps she does want to bed you. Perhaps she admires you and wants you one way or another, anyway she can have you. No ulterior motives. You are not a troll, you know."

"There is no one way or the other about Miss Carter-Brown. As much as I would like to preen myself in front of a mirror and strut around as if I'm God's gift to women. On my magnetism, where Miss Carter-Brown is concerned it would be complete stupidity. No, Edward, if she does want to add me to her long list of conquests, there's a purpose as well as reason for it. She doesn't do anything idly or on a whim. It is my job to discover her reason."

"If what you say is true, then why kick out Devon Masters?" Edward was trying to think of reasons as well. It pleased Link that he had friends here, friends who wanted to help and believed there was more to the goings on here than met the eye.

Sophia played a part but what that part was still eluded him.

"Perhaps," Link said, idly stroking his jaw as he contemplated different scenarios. "Just perhaps he's outlived his usefulness. For whatever reason she doesn't need him."

He was also recalling his words to her, words that if she wanted him for some unknown reason, he didn't share, that he would be the only man in her bed. That would provoke her to get rid of Devon. No, he wouldn't be drawn into that conceit. She didn't even like him.

Things were adding up nicely, he wasn't going to be wearied with an extended stay in Virginia.

He was becoming more and more intrigued and fascinated by the chit. She challenged him. He liked it.

Edward leaned forward, seeming to be interested in his thoughts. "What does that mean? Outlived his usefulness?"

"It's human nature, my friend. People behave in certain manners for various reasons. It's all quite fascinating, don't you think? If she dismissed Devon then there were very good motives for her to do so. Remember, we spoke of incentives as well as motives. We just have to put their intentions for the different men together. Somehow, they are interlocked. Devon is young and handsome, a likely candidate for a woman if she wished a lover. Charles Ewing on the other hand is middle-aged, overweight, stoop shouldered...no, Edward, the selection isn't random. There is a reason as well as purpose for each man. What I want to learn is who pulls the strings, Sophia or her uncle."

"So, what is her reason for selecting you if it isn't for your obvious manly self? What have you got that she wants besides your body?" Edward asked as he laughed.

"I doubt if it's the same as for Devon Masters. She literally despises me. If the reason wasn't imperative, she would avoid me like the plague. Can't possibly understand why she seeks me out at times."

"Devon is telling everyone who will listen that he was tired of her. His interest waned as she took on new lovers. No one believes the tale."

"Of course not, why would they?"

There was silence for a few seconds before Edward began again, "I stopped by the Ewing plantation to say my good byes to the family.

They're leaving at the end of the week. I drank a hot toddy with Charles and learned something of interest but not until his wife left the room. What we heard was true. He did lose money to Devon, a lot of it. He had to sell. They were bankrupt, just enough money to head home to Scotland with his tale between his legs. Didn't my father tell you about Devon's incredible luck at cards? If you get caught up in a game with Devon Masters, take heed."

Link sipped his coffee thoughtfully, wondering if it was luck or cheating. "Yes, yes he did, as did several other men. One implied he cheated, but that may well have been sour grapes. This is interesting, Edward. So, as a result of his losses he must leave Virginia after selling his plantation, which just as a coincidence is situated next to Mayfair Hall. Mr. William Brinkmeyer, because he is such a fine compassionate fellow is buying the plantation. I do wonder what he is paying Ewing for it."

"The price tag should not be too difficult to discover. One only has to ask the right fellows. I should have thought of asking when I was there but didn't. My apologies. Besides his wife returned and she quite terrifies me."

"No matter. There are more pieces of this provocative puzzle falling into place with each passing day. Do you think it will ever get hot here?"

Edward sent him a worldly grin. "Don't tell me you are still cold. You should make use of the fireplace. Go warm your hands. Better yet you should invite Sophia to your cottage and see if she likes the fur rug by the fireplace. Maybe she can warm your hands."

"No, I'd have to ride to Mayfair Hall to invite her. I've no intention of doing that until she comes to heel. I've a feeling that will take a few more encounters before that happens."

"I'm sure it will come about eventually. Until then..." Edward lifted an eyebrow in speculation. "Until then, I suppose you will have to wait for her to come to you. How long do you think that will take?"

"Still," Link shrugged at the sight of Edward's housekeeper peaking around the door.

Edward saw her then frowned at the girl. “What is it?”

She managed to move another inch exposing a tiny bit more of herself, her eyes riveted on the floor in front of her. “I-I must speak with you. I’m sorry. It’s important.”

Edward turned back to Link. “Usually, she doesn’t say boo to anyone, thus it must truly be important. So, I’ll speak to her. Excuse me for a moment. If I can, I’ll return and we can continue this stimulating conversation.”

Link watched them as Edward held her elbow, escorting her from the room. He wondered what was so all-fired important it couldn’t wait a few minutes. He felt a shiver of wind gusting through the closed windows. He thought of all the hot summers he spent in the south of France. He longed for the feel of hot sand between his toes. He wondered if Sophia would enjoy the south of France. He even thought fondly of sweat dripping down the sides of his face while he inspected the grapes at the vineyard.

Sweat would be nice.

He didn’t like it when he couldn’t keep the little tart from his head as he wondered why as well as how she dismissed Devon Masters. It was only a matter of time before he could ask her but still, he couldn’t help thinking on different scenarios. He was pretty sure he knew why she took the man as a lover in the first place then he wondered how the devil he would verify what he believed to be true. Primarily, he wondered why he’d been selected to become her next lover. For the life of him, he couldn’t think of one thing she could gain from having him in her bed.

Chapter Four

Two days passed. Sophia felt a certain air of relief at the thought of not having to verbally battle with Link Stewart. Even though she knew the reprieve wouldn't last, she was thankful nonetheless. It would not be too much longer before her uncle would wonder what was happening and why she hadn't seen him. Why she hadn't lured him to the cottage. She was idly pulling a comb through her damp hair, thinking about taking her sister shopping. It was one of the only pastimes they had any more since William used her love for Clare as a weapon against her.

When the door opened then closed, she tensed understanding the serenity of the past two days was broken. Uncle William finally lost patience. Well, did he expect Link to come to her? He loathed her, despised who she was, hated everything about her. When she finally turned to look at her uncle, he was pale with the anger simmering inside him. She understood what he was like when he wore that particular expression. Shivers of fear swept down her spine.

"Damn your idleness. He hasn't shown himself in two days. You've done nothing to tempt him."

"A saint of a woman couldn't tempt that man unless that was what he wanted. As you well know, I'm not a saint," she murmured turning slowly to face her uncle. "To him this is a game. He's determined to win. His intention is for my complete surrender. For now, I am waiting for him to make a move so I know how to counter it."

"Whatever it is you think the two of you are playing I want it finished. You are to ride over to Leslie Hall today. I want him at the cottage and in your bed, soon, Sophia. Do it anyway you can. Get him to ask you."

He strode to where she was sitting in front of her mirror. Looked over his shoulder then onto the balcony. When he saw there was no one around, he slapped her hard across the face. Her head jerked back from the force of the blow. She fell from the chair. She didn't move. Unwanted moisture welled in her eyes, spiking on her lashes. She learned a long time ago not to cry as she forced the tears back.

His fists were still clenched tight. He looked as if he wanted to hit her again. "Stand up. I'm not certain you understand how important this is to me or the consequences if you fail. In order for this to work, he needs to be your lover. He can't be your lover if you never see him."

"I understand," she spoke softly wondering if he could even hear her tortured words. Her tongue was swollen. She tasted blood.

"Damn you, stand up. If you don't, I'll have your little sister in here and you can witness first-hand how much pain I can inflict on her. She is nothing to me. Just as you are nothing to me except a means to an end. If you don't cooperate, your sister will join you as possibly the youngest whore in Virginia. The talent must run in families."

Sophia complied, seething inwardly, wondering what she could do to thwart him. There was nothing. She learned thirteen months ago he would have his way at her expense. Even though she was prepared, the pain still took her by surprise. The bruises from the last beating were just beginning to fade. The first blow to her ribs sent her to her knees. She shook with rage as well as the pain as another blow found its mark.

He stood over her, watching her, most likely deciding if he wished to hit her again. "So, I believe you understand my meaning. Get yourself dressed and put on your cosmetics. You look pale and sickly. No man would climb into bed with a woman who looked as you do. That tiny tap I gave your face might discolor a bit. Cover it up. Go now and hurry."

She sat back on her knees, staring at him, hating him. "Link Stewart does not like to see my face painted. He will have me wash it off. He will see someone has beaten me. He will ask more question I don't know how to answer."

He turned on her before swiveling back to meet her gaze. "Do as he wants. We don't want to take any chances with him. Don't sit there. Do what you need and don't waste any time."

Sophia understood this to be a dangerous mistake. Her uncle might understand the rules to his game but not to Link's. Now this would not go well for her. She would lose ground in the battle between them. When the door closed behind her uncle, she rose, finished combing out her hair then put on the smallest amount of cosmetics, just to cover the handprint on her face. With that accomplished she selected a riding habit.

For more minutes than she cared to admit, she studied herself in the mirror, dreading the moment she saw Link again and reciting possible explanations for her sudden appearance. Sucking in a long and very deep breath of air, she left the house.

When she walked into Leslie Hall, the three men were just sitting down to luncheon. While she waited in the hallway her arrival was announced to them. She wondered what he would think, what new words he would have for her to bring her down. She wanted to yell at him that she wasn't what he thought but she was and worse.

Edward shot Link a quizzical look. Link was frowning slightly. In a low voice, he said, "I hadn't thought she would come here, to me. I was sure I would seek her out next time we met. This is a surprise. Still, this isn't her style. At least I didn't think it was. Something must have happened to get her here. That, or someone must have put the spurs to her to come."

Standing so she could see the men, she watched Grayson give the servant a fat smile. He actually rubbed his hands together in what seemed like appreciation. "Do show her in."

When she walked into the room, Link's gaze traveled the length of her, taking in her yellow riding outfit. His concern settled on her face where she'd used a minimum of makeup, just enough to attempt to conceal the handprint. In defiance, her chin tilted upward. She wondered if he appreciated her efforts. He would not. He would believe she was still fighting him that she might give up a battle but not the war.

Despite the constant pain in her ribs, she tried to be funny and charming, gay and witty. She knowingly played with striking boldness to

Grayson's besotted look. Purposely, she cast Link sloe-eyed looks, knowingly seductive, knowing also he wasn't the least bit moved by them. As for Edward, she ignored him for the most part.

"Thank you, I would love to join you."

Link appeared content to sit back and watch her perform. All was an act and curse him, he knew it for what it was. He would not give an inch. She understood him even if her uncle did not. He would not enter into this fray until he had her alone. For the moment, he would merely observe and decide on his next course of action. She also knew he would want to be alone with her. As for Edward, he was clearly distracted.

Near the end of the meal, she smiled sweetly while she raised laughing eyes to Link and said, "I'm here actually to ask Mr. Stewart to visit a fascinating place one of our field slaves discovered."

"I don't like caves."

"Oh, I didn't mention it was a cave, but it is much larger than the other one we visited. The ride there is beautiful as well. I'm sure you will quite enjoy our time together. We don't have to go inside if you're afraid."

"You would make a charming guide, my dear," Grayson said in a voice so infatuated that it struck Sophia that he might be the only man left in Virginia who respected her. The other two men certainly held her in the lowest esteem. "Link doesn't like the cold but today could be bearable. The sun is still out and the temperatures are much higher than the way they were the day he arrived. I'm afraid he got the wrong impression of Virginia."

"Perhaps Mr. Stewart could bear up so he might enjoy some of our fascinating landscape," Sophia said trying everything she could think of to get him to comply with her wishes.

She knew he would not. His mind was made up and there was no changing it. No, she quite recalled his words that where women were concerned, he would do the asking.

"I don't know," he finally said, leaning back in his chair. "Perhaps another time when it is not so dastardly cold outside. I would have to wear my warmest coat and gloves just to survive. I'm such a frail weak man where the cold comes into play."

"Truly," she said unable to hide her disdain, "it is not all that cold outside today. We've had real spring weather for the last few days. In fact, it is decidedly warmer than it was the last day we went riding."

"Yes, Sophia. You know I'm not all that strong and my fortitude appears to be at low ebb. The first day weekend me. Yes, I am a weak man, one who must take care of his precarious health."

Precarious health, my foot, she wanted to scream at him. If she couldn't get him to come with her today, she understood what awaited her this evening. She was desperate now and sure that he would see it. "Surely, you can survive a simple ride to the beach."

"Ah, but there is nothing simple about a ride in the cold weather. Do you have a parasol or rain napper I can hold over my head if the weather turns? I wouldn't want to get wet and chance a cold."

"A hat should be sufficient. I'm sure you have one of those." She knew she was losing and did not intend to resort to begging. She still had a tiny bit of pride left inside.

"I'm also worried about my horse," he told her. "He pretends to enjoy galloping around in the rain and snow but I know him better. He wants sunshine and light breezes, none of these gales that are so prevalent around here."

She sucked in her breath. He was a slippery devil, cocky, too, as he played and used her to his own ends.

She didn't like it at all.

What could she do?

She was going to concede defeat. "Very well then, I'm off for a brisk ride along the river. You don't know what you'll be missing. Good bye, Mr. Grayson. Thank you for the delicious luncheon." Her heart in her throat if she didn't have Clare to worry over, she would just keep on riding and let fate take her wherever. If she left, Clare would suffer the same fate she did. She pulled in cold air, air that froze her all the way to her soul.

"You didn't eat anything," Grayson called after her.

Edward began to laugh. She could hear it as she left the room. Grayson hurried after her, catching her by the arm, effectively stopping her close enough to the room she could hear Edward and Link talking about her. She didn't like it.

"You have her going every which way, Link. I fancy this has never happened to her before. It's fascinating to watch. I would like to learn how you do that."

He leaned forward talking softly. She could only make out parts of Link's reply, "Yes, but enough is... She just learned a valuable... now it is time for a..."

She sipped in a quick breath of air trying to fill in the blanks then she heard. He was thinking of teaching her some other lesson. Well, she wasn't about to learn. Her uncle be damned, she wasn't going to be part of this. Let him beat her to death. Realizing she was damning Clare, she sucked in another breath of air holding it for as long as she could. Held it until her lungs burned.

"No attacking the flank? No coming around the back for a surprise?"

"You're becoming impudent, Edward," Link said. She knew him, knew he grinned from ear to ear, and left.

She still wasn't quite sure what Link meant but now she didn't know what to do with herself. She certainly didn't dare go home. William would flay her hide if she showed up too soon. Even when she did make it to the house, she was going to have to lie to him. He would never understand she failed.

She shuddered at the consequences when he discovered she could not seduce Link, could not even get him to go for a ride with her let alone coax him into her bed. This was not going well at all. Unconsciously, she touched her cheek. It was still a bit swollen from the blow. She no longer tasted blood. The powder concealed the bruising but it could do nothing to bury the memory of the pain, the humiliation or the thought of more to come. She wanted to die. Dying wouldn't help Clare.

She wanted to scream to that conceited bastard she didn't wear cosmetics to look like a tart. She wore it to hide bruises. At least she had at first until Uncle William decided she looked more worldly, more seductive, painted like a whore. Of course, he also realized he could hit her more often without chance of discovery if her face was covered with makeup.

Now she had no choices. She could not go home. A small slave gave her a foot up helping her onto her mare's back. Sitting on top of the horse she stared ahead, unsure of anything anymore and cursing the fact Link Stewart came into her life. Her heart thundered in her chest as she remembered all the things he'd done and said to her, recalled how he challenged her.

She decided to go to the cottage and sit outside on the porch swing realizing she was exhausted from all the charades that had been going on since Link arrived. She thought of Clare, worried William would start using her too. When she did go home, she would lie to him. She would tell him Link kissed her, told her he desired her. Was too tired to meet her at the cottage tonight. Those words might placate him for a day or two.

The devil with men.

That wouldn't work and well she knew. William would want to know why she didn't immediately take him to the cottage. He would expect to know every minute thing that happened between them. She didn't have an answer for any of that. In her uncle's mind, a kiss made a man think immediately of sex and bedding the woman. Link wasn't at all like that. No, a kiss would mean little to him. Yet, in her experience her uncle was right. She didn't want to think one more thought about Link Stewart, her nemesis. She would deal with both her uncle and Link when she had to do so and not a moment sooner.

Today she would try her utmost to forget all her problems.

Her decision made, Sophia urged her little mare to a fast pace heading straight toward the cottage. The place didn't always hold fond memories. If she didn't stray inside, she would be fine. She wouldn't be forced to remember all the tasteless things that went on inside the small rooms. From the front porch swing she could see Leslie Hall as well as the river. She would take a few minutes to relax and try to put her thoughts in order. Perhaps she could find a way out of this taxing situation.

Inside, the cottage was neat and orderly. The makings for the hot toddy's sat on a sideboard near the fireplace. The bed was clean, the sheets washed. She shuddered when she looked at the bed, recalling all the things that went on there as well as the part she played.

None of this was her choice. Trying to put all the terrible thoughts aside she rummaged through the closet, finding a warm quilt to wrap around her. The second order of business was to procure a bottle of wine as well as a glass.

Within minutes she was pouring the drink and sipping the sweet red wine. One leg drawn up beneath her and the other one pushing the seat so it would swing, she let her head fill with nothing. The emptiness appealed to her. She didn't want to think of anything or anyone for the time being. By nightfall her life would come crashing down around her again.

Thinking was inevitable though.

Her thoughts turned to happier, better times, a time when she was loved and cherished. She recalled hearing the news of her parents' death and prayed over and over again that it wasn't painful. Her mother had been strong-willed and determined. She accomplished everything she put her mind to. Sophia could remember wanting to be just like her mother. Her father had always been indulgent, giving his wife all the love and support that could be expected of a husband. They both loved their children very much, too much to take them on the journey to America, a journey her mother considered too fraught with danger. She didn't want to go, begged her husband. This was the only time, to Sophia's memory he didn't give her mother what she wanted.

Her father told her, "Nonsense." He didn't have her mother's determination thus Sophia and Clare were fetched from their residence near Glasgow by their uncle William after the drowning of their parents, and brought to Virginia. She recalled clearly her grief as well as her gratitude to her uncle.

She had loved him then.

She also prayed her parents' death had been quick. Even now after four years she still repeated that prayer. Somehow, she knew her mother eased her father in the end. It was who her mother was. Sophia set the empty glass of wine on a small table near the swing. She closed her eyes and felt the warm sun heating the enclosed porch. She slipped out of her riding jacket and unfastened the top buttons of her linen blouse.

Within minutes she was asleep, her head resting on a small pillow.

~ * ~

Link had been riding in the direction where Sophia indicated the cave was located. Heat from the sun warmed him as he thought about his earlier comments to Sophia. He was surprised to see her mare, tethered to a post near the small cottage where she took her lovers, where she meant to take him soon. He grinned. He wasn't meaning to go inside but he would if it meant another encounter with Miss Carter-Brown. He saw her, on the porch swing sound asleep.

Despite all his complaints about the cold weather the day was fairly warm, warmer than usual. During the short ride he generated a goodly amount of heat in his body. He supposed she would have been warm when she sat down. After walking up the steps, he spied the bottle of wine. Using her glass, he poured himself a small amount and drank deeply. This was better than he expected.

He knew exactly what he was going to do.

Now, he stood over her, staring down at her face, still now, and he realized she looked very young despite the horrid stuff painting her face, very young indeed. What had he heard? She was nearly nineteen? Or was it eighteen. Bloody eyes but that did seem young, too young for what she was about. She should still be running around the countryside, chasing boys her own age. She should still be a virgin.

Why had she taken all of those men into her bed?

Why did she now want him?

Quickly, he dropped to his knees beside her. He didn't want to wake her. Very gently, very slowly, he unfastened the remaining buttons on her blouse. The fabric gaped open. She wore a very plain batiste chemise beneath. No fancy frothy lace and such. He scowled as he finished with the buttons.

His intentions were not so honorable but neither were hers. He wanted to see more of her but he couldn't peel the blouse off her because it was tucked tightly into her skirt. He wanted her to stay sleeping for a few more minutes, at least until he accomplished what he intended.

He tugged the blouse back as far as he could, drew a small knife from his pocket and slit the chemise down the front to just below her breasts. Ah, he thought as he eased the light fabric away from her breasts.

Hers were beautiful breasts. She stirred but didn't waken.

He waited a few moments before easing her across his lap. He waited longer, hoping she would remain asleep. She turned nestling her face and hand comfortably onto his chest, moaned just a bit then fell back again. Her dark lashes arced across her soft flesh

Smiling, Link began to work up her skirt, slowly, ever so slowly, until it was bunched at mid-thigh and he could see the plain garters that held her stockings in place. Very nice legs, he thought, long and sleekly muscled.

He was still looking at her legs when he let one hand linger on her upper thigh, the other just below her breast.

How she would react when she did wake up? He wasn't quite certain. In his imagination, he supposed she'd look up at him, a bit aroused already and fling her arms around his neck. Perhaps she would kiss him. Still, he waited, picturing his hand easing up her inner thigh to stroke her soft feminine folds, the crevice between. She'd be eager. She'd beg him to take her here, now, not to wait another second.

He stared at her mouth. It was slightly parted. Her breaths long and slow in her sleep. He found himself mesmerized by this picture for a moment.

His imagination did not do justice to the enfolding scene. She awoke in the next second. Out of that lovely mouth came an actual scream; loud, humiliated and totally appalled. Perhaps horrified might be a better word. The shriek diminished into a yelp then a gulp. Her eyes round with what he could only describe as terror.

He tightened his arms around her, refusing to let her go until he understood what plagued her. She was staring stupidly from him to her naked breasts down to her legs.

"You bastard! Pigswill! What did you do to me? How dare...?"

He showed his perfect white teeth, his grin wide and confidant in what he was about to say. "I kissed your breasts, once, twice perhaps even three times. Don't recall exactly. You moaned, arching your back as you asked for more of what I could give you. You forced your breasts into my face so I was forced to slit your chemise open to help you get what you were asking me for. You're a greedy woman, Sophia. You wanted more and more. So, you crawled onto my lap and lifted your hips to my seeking hands. So, I helped you by pulling up your skirt. I wanted to give you everything you were silently asking for. Are you happy?"

"You're a damn liar. I did no such thing," she gritted out between clenched teeth, her lovely white breasts heaving.

Her face was red with indignation or embarrassment. He wasn't sure which. Her hair was falling down around her shoulders while she was actually stammering with more outrage than he'd ever seen before. He didn't think she was acting. It seemed so real. Link scowled. This reaction was completely unexpected. Where were her teasing looks and flirtatious smiles? What happened to her shameful, coy, very sexual remarks and innuendos?

She was not acting as she was supposed to act.

He stared at her attempting to close his gaping mouth as she slowly recaptured the control he was used to seeing, watched the mortification vanish from her eyes, viewed the stiffness come back into her spine and that damned cool smile set itself into place. She was now a picture of calm serenity.

Sophia returned. What did that mean? Who was the girl-woman he witnessed when she woke? It wasn't the woman he was getting to know and hopefully understand.

He wanted inside her head. Knew he wasn't going to get there anytime soon. What the hell was she thinking?

Slowly, and very efficiently she brought herself into complete control. He watched as she breathed deeply. Her detached persona was back. She gave him a very tempting sideways smile. Slowly, she pulled the sides of her chemise over her breasts then began to work on the buttons he unfastened, all the while keeping her legs exposed to him.

When she finished, she slowly rose from across his lap and stared down at him. She smoothed her skirt then provocatively placed her hands on her hips.

"You damn bastard," she told him, surprised at the mildness of her voice. "Damn you to hell. What are you doing here?"

"Well, if you put it that way," he paused for several seconds, thinking. "I decided my manliness couldn't abide your noticeable disdain. Had to do something about it, you know. Prove I wasn't a mincing fop before you came to that conclusion."

"Most adult men are not different. You are just the same as all of them, with only one thing on your mind."

"No, probably not," he agreed with a grin. "I do, however, have more than one thing on my mind at the moment."

"Oh?" It seemed she doubted him.

"I wanted to take you off guard, surprise you. Needed to see a real unfiltered reaction to what I was doing. I find you extremely unpredictable whenever I manage to startle you. You screamed, just like a spinster who's never seen a man naked." He leaned closer. "We both know that is not true. Most impressive and pleasing. It makes life more interesting all these unexpected and unique sides of you. The twists and turns that are so much a part of Sophia have me fascinated. I wonder how many different faces you will show me if I'm fast enough to catch you in the act of showing me."

"You have had your fun, Mr. Stewart. Forget what you think you've seen here today. There are no different sides to me. What you see is who I am. I do not twist or turn."

"A brazen hussy?"

She turned away from him for a moment only.

When she looked at him again, he continued. "Not nearly as much fun as I intend to have. No, not nearly enough as what the promise of your lovely breasts can give me when I do taste them, suck them deep into my mouth. Ah, they will taste like peaches and cream. I would like you to answer something for me, Sophia. Why did you dismiss Devon Masters from your little heard of stallions?"

"Heard of stallions? That's a bit tawdry even for you."

"I only react to the company I keep, Sophia. Why?"

She caught her breath in the back of her throat trying to think of something to say without telling him the truth. She couldn't think. She turned away from him staring at the quickly flowing water in the river. Her lips remained closed for a very long time.

Finally, she turned her attention back his way, the stoic unfeeling expression firmly in place. Then with a small lift to her shoulders, she said, "He bored me. He was a boy playing at being a man. He was selfish and cared only for himself and his amusements. I grew tired, that's all. A woman can only spend so much time with a little boy when she needs a man. A man has to want to give something in return when a woman allows him use of her body."

"You're lying."

"Why would I bother to lie, especially to you? It's so mundane. You mean nothing to me."

Well, once again she firmly put him in his place. "You wish me to believe that you dismissed him because you wanted me and you remembered my ultimatum to you. When we are lovers, I will be the only man in your body."

"Well, yes, I do remember you saying that. Your words have nothing to do with Masters."

"So, you say. Will you dismiss Charles Ewing also?"

She watched the broad grin on his handsome face. She said nothing.

His even white teeth showed his arrogance and all-consuming confidence that didn't fail to astound her. "I won't become your lover until you do."

She looked as if she wanted to smack him with her parasol. Too bad she didn't have one or he was sure that was what she would do. That damn calm settled on her features as well as her stance. "Surely, you think way too much of yourself as well as your demands. Unquestionably, it isn't up to a lady to make herself more appealing to the gentlemen pursuing her. I have it on good authority that I'm already appealing. You should be salivating over me even as we talk nonsense here on the porch of this cottage. There should be drool coming from your mouth. You should be down on your knees begging me to take you into my bed."

He laughed, a rich deep laugh. "Sophia, you are terribly naïve when it comes to men, real men. You play with little boys. You are pretty, yes, even with the absurd paint on your face, but understand me. I have bedded many women whose beauty reduces yours to mere commonplace, to nothing out of the ordinary. You are not unique in any way. You are conventional in a conventional world. From what I've seen of your body, it is quite pleasant to look at and touch as well. It is nothing special. Understand me, Sophia, I won't play games, yours or anyone else's. I won't wait around while you spread your legs for seemingly every man in the vicinity. I'm not an uncontrollable boy anxious to plow every female belly he can manage. I'm a man, Sophia. I've standards developed over years of dealing with the opposite sex."

"Years? What are you, twenty-five, twenty-six?"

"I had my first sexual encounter when I was thirteen. What about you?" he challenged.

He heard the quickly indrawn breath of air. Saw the anger simmering so close to the surface he could almost reach out and touch it. Watched as uncertainty took over her eyes for a moment he was sure she was thinking of all the ways she could reduce him to a pile of rubble. He was about to speak when the fleeting moment of victory vanished. She smiled at him, that coy, teasing smile that made him hard as a rock. He wanted to shake her. No, he needed to best her, set her in her place.

"Miss Carter-Brown get rid of the others, all the others, or I will never bed you. I find what little interest I have for you is fading quickly."

"Very well," she told him, "I will let Charles Ewing down. He will cry, I am sure but he is leaving anyway. Will you come to the cottage tonight at eight?"

"Are there any others?"

"No."

"Ah, you already dismissed Oliver Sheffield, the poor fellow who lost all his money to Devon Masters."

"He wasn't the only one as you well know. Charles lost all his money as well. They both have to leave."

That was true. They both lost sizable fortunes to Masters. Ewing lost his plantation as well. He wondered what else Oliver lost beside a fortune. He supposed that was enough of a loss.

"That's true."

Link found that he was brooding, ruminating, but understanding at the same time he would never get to the bottom of this unless he shocked her, surprised her to her very core. She would always find a way and the words to elude him. At times she showed him glimpses of herself, but she never dropped her guard maintaining the façade of indifference. Only when he did something outrageous that she didn't expect, like baring her breast or pulling up her skirt did she give a tiny bit of herself away.

He rose to stand beside her. He stared down at her, watching her with finely veiled intensity. He grasped her upper arms in his hands and drew her against him.

"Perhaps I don't wish to fall into the same bed your other lovers have used. Perhaps I wish to sample what you're offering before I make my decision, right here, right now on that rug in front of the fireplace." He thought of the fur in front of his fire, pictured her lying there naked as the day she was born.

He tried to kiss her but she expected that and jerked her head away. His lips feathered across her jaw then down her neck. He felt her stiffen in what he could only assume was distaste. Strange. Never before had a woman acted that way when he kissed and stroked her. He gave women pleasure. They adored him.

Smiling down at her, he schooled his expression as well as his intentions. He clasped his hands beneath her hips and raised her, pressing her belly hard against his groin. He was hard and he knew she could feel him.

"Let go of me, Link."

Her voice was too calm and too controlled. Her pulse beating so rapidly at the base of her neck, betrayed her. He wanted to rip that serenity from her and see the real woman beneath the makeup and the stoic veneer. He wanted to see and feel her passion. “On the other hand,” he whispered close to her ear, “perhaps I don’t wish to sample your charms at this instant. Perhaps what I truly wish to do is pay you back. Give you a taste of reckoning. Yes, that’s precisely what I want to do.”

“Link?” There was a small sample of panic in her voice.

He grinned.

Link carried her toward the river, having noticed a large mud puddle nearby. She began to understand his intent, struggling against his greater strength. He laughed as he stood over the large puddle of water and mud created by the river. It was deep enough if he tossed her, she would not be hurt. It was also dirty enough she would have to seek out a bath before this evening. He stood in the middle, ruining his soft leather boots, uncaring. He waded until the water hit his thighs. It would be cold, damn cold. He couldn’t quite bring himself to toss her into the river.

“Don’t you dare, Link Stewart? Don’t!” She was screaming at him, struggling and pounding on his chest, his arms his shoulders. The blows were inconsequential. He’d been hit harder in tussles with his brother when they were younger. He lifted her high then dropped her. She disappeared beneath the surface for a moment. When she came up, she rushed him, throttling him, knocking him over into the depth of the water and mud.

It was his turn to be surprised.

He grinned when he emerged and saw her. He laughed, thoroughly enjoying Miss Sophia Carter-Brown. This was growing more intriguing by the moment.

The water washed some of the makeup from her face, mud replacing it. Her hair was matted and filthy, hanging down in a horrible mess around her shoulders. She was charming. Enchanting. She was shivering as was he. The river water was very nearly frigid. He wanted to haul her out and oversee a bath. This time he laughed at himself, pleased with this afternoon. He lied to her. She was really one of the most beautiful women he’d ever seen.

He stepped from the puddle, his hands on his hips, feet braced apart. “There, you little hellion,” he said with a calm he reserved for the weaker sex. Ah, but she was not one of those at all. There was nothing weak about Miss Carter-Brown, but he was becoming more convinced by the second she wasn’t a hellion. He needed to clear his head. “Don’t attack me again unless you want to pay more reparations.”

He laughed again while he strode back to his horse. Looking over his shoulder at her. “I mean it, Sophia. I am a gentleman most of the time unless I’m provoked into acting otherwise. Understand me. I will never allow you to do your worst to me again without complete retaliation. When you are around me, tread carefully.”

As she stumbled through the water, her skirts dragged her first to one side then to the other. Her boot went into a hole and she fell down on her face. She managed to regain her balance and rose with her fists clenched at her sides.

He mounted and on his horse riding away he looked back. He could not stop laughing. Then he shouted, “Tonight. Eight o’clock. Don’t be late. Ah, and make certain the place is aired out.”

~ * ~

Sophia looked out the door. Snow started to fall about an hour ago. She wondered if he would come. Wondered if he didn’t show up, if it would just be more punishment. When he looked at her breasts this afternoon all she could think about was if he saw her bruises. She prayed he did not. There would be questions if he did. Questions she couldn’t answer.

If he didn’t come just to torment her, she understood her uncle’s form of discipline would be far harsher than what Link meted out today. She’d rather find herself dumped into a frigid mud puddle than beaten black and blue.

A lump formed in her throat. Moisture welled in her eyes. She pushed the hot tears away, swearing that all of this was worth it just to keep Clare safe. Told herself she was a spineless ninny and should stop feeling sorry for herself. Link would come just to see if she would be here.

If she had a choice, she would be as far away as she could get.

Clare, sweet, sweet Clare. Her empty sigh filled the tiny room as she looked at the bed while swallowing another lump in her throat. She didn't want to do this to anyone let alone Link Stewart. He didn't deserve her uncle's plans. She didn't want to be a part of the evil.

Link would retaliate.

She didn't have a doubt in her mind.

Humiliated to the depth of her soul, Sophia paced the small cottage, aware her uncle was smiling and watching her from a corner of the room. He was starring and probably gloating about the outcome tonight, what he would gain when all was said and done. She needed to talk to him, let him know this just wasn't going to work. Finally, she said, "I'm afraid of him."

Waving a hand in the air, a scowl on his face. "Nonsense, he is just a man, ruled by a certain part of him. Don't be a fool now when you have him exactly where you want him." William Brinkmeyer said with finality. "He's young and inexperienced, merely an untried boy. You don't know what you're talking about. So far, he's just been lucky, that's all. He will fall into our plans quite easily. Just as the others did."

"You've no idea who he is truly. I've the distinct impression he's slept with more women than there are in all of Virginia. He knows what they will say, what they will do. He believes women are all the same. Him and his cursed ethics."

William chuckled then shrugged, his eyes cold, brows drawn together. His mood suddenly changed. "We didn't need the other men as we do Mr. Stewart. Get him drunk. You know how to do it. It's nearly time for him to arrive. Don't worry about anything. I'll be nearby. Remember what to do. After tonight you won't be afraid of him."

"I remember everything. How could I possibly forget? I don't like this," she told him with a huge rush of air, wishing quite simply that she could vanish into the night and never have to look at or speak to him again. Link wasn't going to fall into anyone's plans but his own. What her uncle was attempting was dangerous.

"Just do what you always do," he said staring at her as if he was casually imagining her naked. "You know what will happen if you fail."

That would leave Clare unprotected and alone.

She straightened her spine, once again filling her lungs with much needed air. The fear and terror wouldn't go away, the unease encapsulated all of her. She had to think, to control, to manipulate Link or this would never work. She was good at doing so because she was smart and she had a lot of practice. Link was not like any man she'd ever met. She didn't have one idea how he would react. Patience was not going to be the answer with this man.

At exactly eight o'clock there was a knock at the door.

Sophia opened the door. Snow rushed in along with a cold draft of air. He was leaning negligently against one of the posts on the porch, his arms crossed in front of him with a lazy smile. Seeming to ask what took you so long?

"It's snowing again," he said looking toward the sky. "Does it ever stop?"

As he stepped into the cottage, his gaze raked over her. She knew he disliked the way she looked, the gown she wore, the tiniest amount of cosmetics she wore. He would tell her now. God forbid, he dump her in the river again. She could not deal with any more surprises.

"Your attempt at a seductive gown is more of a success than not, I should say," he said as he eyed her critically. "However, harlot-red really isn't a good color for you. A soft blue would suit your coloring much better. To avoid laughter, you should avoid any shade of white. Also, the whalebone pushing up your breasts is a deception I abhor. A woman either has breasts or she does not. That small article of clothing doesn't dupe a man who knows women. You will learn. Come into the light so I can see your face."

She didn't even think to object. She followed him into the light. She was right to be afraid of him.

He clasped her chin in his long fingers and raised her face into the full candlelight. "Ah, very little makeup, good girl. I didn't wish to wash your face before we could get on with the evening. I'm pleased that you've listened to me and wish to please me. We've taken the first step now to a compatible relationship. Now, how eager are you? Would you like to take all your clothes off for me or should we talk for a while? Have a sip of wine. Who are your favorite philosophers, for example? Ah, I can see by your expression that you have read the great minds throughout all the centuries. Yes, there are so many you are very likely completely conversant about."

"I don't want to speak of philosophers. They have no bearing on this, on what we are about to do. You don't even like me. Why would you want to delve into my mind?"

"You are uninformed then."

"Hardly." This was not something she wished to pursue. She turned away from him and quickly poured him a hot toddy. She handed it to him. "It's cold tonight. You will need something to warm you. I'm glad you decided to visit. I wasn't sure you would come."

"I suppose talking philosophy at a time when I should be thinking about the way you will taste and feel is presumptive of me. You are right. We should continue this visit and see what transpires. We can speak of other things when we are sated and don't have the energy to move a muscle."

Link raised his glass and toasted her. He drank it. It tasted just as he remembered and warmed him to his belly. "I see you aren't drinking your hot toddy."

"I prefer the wine," she spoke softly. "I'm quite warm enough sitting here next to the fire with you hovering so close and tempting me with your strange words. That never fail to leave me witless and at a loss how to reply."

This time Link drank deeply. Now it didn't taste at all like the ones he had previously at the alehouse or at Leslie Manor. He didn't realize he was so thirsty. It must be from the witty conversation he was having with Sophia. It certainly wasn't from any kind of exertion. He looked at the flames burning in the fireplace then drank again. It was really very good.

"If not philosophers, what topic would you pick? Surely not a topic about fashion or...the latest gossip of who is seeing whom."

"Never," she said softly. "Tell me of the news from Scotland. I know it has been several months but what if anything is there to report? I miss the land and the people as well."

"Can't really say. I was only in Glasgow for two days before I set sail for Virginia. The only news I have is that my brother—"

"The duke?"

He nodded, "The duke is happily married. At least he will be as soon as he figures out how to bed his young bride. Ah, if they lived here, she could get advice from you and not my incorrigible little sister. You certainly could give him all the pointers he needs in order to seduce sweet Lacie. I'm sure you must know a lot of helpful hints for new grooms and brides."

She looked at her feet before seeming to examine her fingernails and said nothing. Exhausted, she was tired of the verbal sparring between them, wanted to be done with this entire fiasco. She hoped this evening would be over soon and come to its proper conclusion. He would fall in line for her.

Link drank another hot toddy She watched him drink and drink, just like the other men and wondered just how many it would take to put him under. He seemed a man who could hold his liquor. "This tastes better and better." He finished the glass and handed it back to her. "I'm sure you've been told that more than once."

She smiled then poured him another.

"I'm glad you like it. You have a sister too?"

"I do. She is not a normal woman. I pity the poor man who finally weds her. He will not be able to control her. A man needs control so he won't forget who he is. Forget he is a man. Women control men through sex, just as you attempt to do with your countless lovers. The more skilled a woman the more dangerous she is. A woman who knows what she is doing can bring a man to his knees if he lets her."

"Your sister is a skilled courtesan?"

"Of course not. Let's take you, for instance, Sophia." He paused then, shaking his head as if he needed to get his bearings. "Sophia. I don't like that name. It's too contrived. I'm going to call you Sophie. Sophie, yes, it's much better, a shorter version of your name, makes sense. It's more like you, small, petite. It's not fragile. You are anything but fragile."

She looked at the floor, hiding her amusement from him. "You may call me Sophie."

"Sophie, I wonder what you want from me. I'm not like any of your other lovers. I've no real vices to take advantage of. I'm leaving sooner than later. In other words, I don't plan on making my home here. I repeat, what do you want?"

"You are special, Link." At least her uncle thought he was special enough for her to master him as she'd done all the others. Yes, he spoke of control but she would never master or control this man. She wondered how this would all end. She didn't like wondering.

A shiver of fear swept through her.

~ * ~

"Tell me how and perhaps I'll believe you. I wonder what it is I have that you could possibly lust after, other than my body, of course. It is true that I am a Stewart and thus the plantation belongs to my family, however," Link broke off.

He felt suddenly quite warm. Yes, he felt truly, quite wonderful, relaxed. The need for her was growing hot in his blood. He loosened his cravat opened his shirt at the neck.

She shrugged slightly. She didn't say anything, just watched him with a strange expectant stare.

"You don't know?" he asked.

She looked soft and sweet to him, so willing, so anxious to please him. Now she was holding out her arms to him, speaking to him, but he didn't understand her words, which was odd, but he didn't care. He would soon have her.

"Well, you are very handsome, smart as well," her words were softly spoken but they seemed to come from a great distance away. That wasn't possible because she was sitting next to him. Strangely his mind spun. He swallowed hard. Looked at the hot toddy sitting on the table.

"That's nice of you to say, thank you."

Bloody eyes but he sounded ridiculous. He couldn't recall another time he ever thanked a woman for telling him she liked the way he looked. No, this was bloody different. He had no control of his thoughts or his speech it seemed.

He downed the rest of his hot toddy, rose from his chair, and walked to her. Tried to shake off the effects of the liquor. Thought he succeeded. He drew her into his arms and kissed her. Her breath was warm and sweet. She opened her mouth to him. He reveled in her, the sweet taste. His hands swept down her back to cup her buttocks and pull her closer to his hard arousal. As he had this afternoon, he lifted her against him and groaned at the delightful sensations. He didn't want to talk any longer.

He released her for a moment then stepped back and began to pull her gown from her shoulders.

She laughed softly, so very sweetly as she slapped his hands away. "No, Link, you must be patient. Don't want you to rip the material even though you don't like this gown. I had it made just for you."

"Little liar."

"No, I'm not lying. If you don't like the color, I'll have another one made in the shade of blue you suggested. You would like that I hope. I mean to please you, only you, you know."

"Of course, you are but I'll forgive the lie this time." He reached for her again, stroked her shoulder.

She stepped farther away. "Now, let me remove it. Let me become naked just for you." She took his hand in hers, leading him to the bed. "Now you sit down right here and watch. Tell me what you want me to do. Here's another hot toddy to warm you up."

"Don't think I need any more warming."

He drank deeply though, thinking this was odd. He felt strange. He was hot and he hadn't even touched her yet or kissed her. He liked to kiss, to feel a woman melt in his arms when his mouth covered hers, his tongue delved into her dark sultry mouth.

Hell, she wasn't even naked yet.

Link took another drink. He leaned his head against the backboard on the bed, staring at her. His eyes were slitted as he gazed at her, standing in front of the bed, her hands on the buttons at the front of her harlot-red gown. He sucked in a deep breath of air. She was playing a game with him and hell if he didn't enjoy his part in the dance.

But to what end?

Chapter Five

Snow was still falling when Link opened his eyes. A cold draft of air swirled across his naked flesh. The scent of sex hung on the air. He sat up, searching the room for Sophie. She wasn't there. A black woman was in the room with him, not Sophie. Where the hell was she? Then he remembered Edward told him she was never there in the morning when her lovers woke.

When he tried to cover himself, the woman waved at him as if it didn't matter to her if he was naked or wore clothing. She must have seen a lot of Miss Carter-Brown's lovers. Still, he pulled the quilt on the bed over him as he watched the woman busy herself in the room.

He watched her as she shook a finger at him before saying. "You just never mind. You're all the same to me, massa." She went on with her business of cleaning the room. For the rest of the time, she ignored him. She hummed while she worked. He didn't want to get up and dress until she was gone.

Edward was also right when he told him the room would smell of sex in the morning. The room reeked of it. He remembered very little of what transpired. That was abnormal. He never forgot a woman.

Sophie couldn't even bother to stay here, to wake with him. She was gone. Bloody eyes but he felt tranquil and sated, thoroughly satisfied, replete and strangely relaxed. He also felt used. In all his adult life, he couldn't recall feeling this way after a night of sex. Hell, he should be exhausted if even half of what he did remember occurred.

He still felt drunk. He'd also never been drunk in the morning. Drinking to this type of excess was never something he indulged in. How many hot toddies did he have to drink?

This was all very odd, he thought desperately trying to recall making love to the woman, trying to put a face on the body who he had sex with most of the night. He could not.

He remembered trying to kiss Sophie. He'd wanted to taste her. Taste the wine she drank. She pulled away, putting him off, whirling away from his arms with a school girlish giggle, telling him there would be time enough for whatever he had in mind. Most of the night was a blur in his muddled head. What he could recall was the most explosive sex of his life. He didn't remember satisfying her. He hadn't lied to her. He was good, a very good lover. He always saw to his partner's pleasure.

Within his hands, her breasts were large and full, the nipples taut pink buds that responded to his fingers. He did recall fondling them, stroking and caressing them with his hands. Tasting a woman's breasts just as finding enjoyment inside the deep dark recesses of her mouth was something he enjoyed immensely. He didn't do any of those things. At least he couldn't recall. He seemed to be missing a lot of what happened last night yet other parts were vivid.

There was something very wrong.

Well hell, what the devil happened to him last night?

How would he get to the bottom of it? Sophie certainly wouldn't tell. She would smile and flirt. She would say nothing. She would look at him with her stoic gray eyes and he would have to guess what she was thinking.

The bath waiting for him looked heavenly. Steam rose from the hipbath. He needed to ease his muscles and soak for a while, think as well. Yes, there certainly was a lot to think about if he was to begin to find a grip on reality. Slipping into the hot water, he felt even more relaxed. He closed his eyes and wondered when he would confront the lovely Miss Carter-Brown again. First, he would have to figure out what happened here before she left, while they had sex.

It certainly wasn't a normal night, at least not for him. Instinctively, he knew it. Even though he just couldn't figure out how the time with Sophie was different.

As he thought, he remembered how she took him into her mouth, caressed him with her tongue, sucked on him. She did so until he screamed his climax. There were no memories of his caressing her with his lips, tasting her sweetness. Hearing her cry out his name. In his memories it was as if making love to her didn't happen.

No, this was a damn strange encounter. Nothing was as it should be yet he could not for the life of him figure out what really happened or what happened besides the tiny bit he recalled.

He remembered a man's voice, rough hands disrobing him as he suddenly felt violated. Sophie had not been part of that. Her hands on him were something he would recollect.

He remembered something else, something far more important in the scope of things. It was clear to him now just how he'd been deceived. He'd touched her breasts twice before, held them in his hands. He knew their shape and weight. Recalled the soft silken texture and the tender pink buds that tipped them.

The woman in his bed last night was not Sophie. The woman whose breasts he caressed with his hands had not been Sophie's. With a sudden curse he sat up, water splashing around the tub onto the floor. For a moment his fists tightened.

"Bloody hell," he muttered again.

Sophie drugged and duped him then pawned him off to another woman with pendulous breasts. She had a hell of a lot of explaining to do, prevaricating. Nothing she could say would appease him. He would have his revenge. She would regret what she did.

Hell, she drugged him and raped him. He was sure she would tell him a man could not be raped, violated. She was wrong. He'd had no intention of having sex with another woman other than Sophie. The right to refuse or accept had been taken away from him. How to get back at her without forcing her was his only question.

He would come up with a plan, perhaps a little tit for tat.

She drugged him with the hot toddies. He didn't think he'd ever drink another one the rest of his life. Miss Sophia Carter-Brown would pay for her crime against him.

An eye for an eye.

There would be hell to pay. Now he knew just how he was going to proceed. A smile curled on his lips. Miss Sophie Carter-Brown would rue the day she tried to master him to command him. No woman would control or manage him, let alone a young slip of a girl.

He rubbed his hands together, anticipating the battle that would ensue, looking forward to the expression on her face when she discovered he knew what she'd done. Her breasts had done her in. He laughed, pleased with himself as well as his decision. She probably never considered that he touched her twice, held her in his hands twice.

He would make her believe.

Up to the challenge, oh yes, he certainly was. Indeed, he was looking forward to the moment he would see the recollection in her eyes. The plans for his revenge were beginning to take shape in his head. Quickly, he finished his bath and dressed. When he left the cottage, he rode to Leslie Hall, whistling a jaunty tune as the long drive greeted him.

Edward was just sitting down to eat in the breakfast room. His father was sitting at the table sipping a cup of coffee while reading a two-month-old copy of the London Times.

Link wasn't going to say anything now. It simply wouldn't do to speak of Sophie in front of Grayson who still adored the little harlot. Link didn't think he could listen to a defense of Sophie or hear about her innocence and sweet maidenly charms. It was one thing to defend a woman's honor, but to go about with blinders on was something else altogether.

There was simply nothing sweet or maidenly about Miss Carter-Brown nor was she innocent in any way. She would not pawn him off on another woman again. She would not be able to drug him again now that he was on to her machinations.

"How was your evening, Link?" Edward's bland tone and smirk caught his attention.

"Enlightening."

Link poured himself a cup of the rich dark brew he was beginning to appreciate immensely. It seemed to give him a boost to his step, a lifting of his spirits he didn't get from a cup of tea. It made the mornings more pleasant especially when he had plans to make. He found his mental processes improved as well.

"Try some milk in it," Granger said not even looking up from the article he was perusing.

"Like it black," Link said, tonelessly surveying the placid scene.

Perhaps the other men had not caressed her before they were taken to the cottage for a night of pleasure so had not seen as well as felt the truth. Perhaps she had not duped the other men. This was all a puzzle. He didn't like the fact she didn't want him but had wanted the others. No, he didn't like it at all.

Grayson rose. "I bid the two of you good day. I've errands to run in the village. I take it you can find something to amuse yourselves."

Link didn't want to say anything until the older man left plus, he needed to sift through some thoughts on his own.

He laughed aloud then. Thinking once more that she'd be brought down all because of her breasts.

Later that evening his thoughts went back to the man who had stripped him down, bared him for the sexual encounter. He could actually hear his voice, but he couldn't remember the words he'd said.

Nothing made sense after almost twenty-four hours.

Who the hell had stripped him naked? He certainly couldn't remember taking his clothes off, much less Sophie Carter-Brown's. Of course, she didn't get naked or get into bed with him.

She'd drugged him, seduced him then brought in another woman to have sex with him. It was clear enough. Ah, yes, and there was Uncle William who'd come in to see to his clothing. It must have been Brinkmeyer. There was no one else for her to call on.

Link strode through the room, a very grim smile on his mouth. He dressed carefully. He was coldly and calmly furious. He was going to drop in at Mayfair Hall and pay the lovely Sophie Carter-Brown a visit. He had no doubt he wouldn't be invited to stay for dinner.

~ * ~

Sophie sat in her room, refreshed from a long hot bath, all the kinks gone from her muscles. She was combing out her hair thinking about Link and what he must have felt when he woke this morning. He would be angry, furiously so. She wondered, too, when Uncle William would make her to do it again, loathing those times with a hated passion. She would give anything to be able to return to Scotland. She couldn't do that until she was old enough to become Clare's legal guardian. A harsh laugh followed that thought. No court of law would give her custody of Clare, not with her reputation.

"What are you thinking about," Clare asked as she poked her head into the room, a beautiful smile on her face. "Your eye is healing nicely. You should really pay more attention where you are walking. It seems you always have some bruise on your face."

Sophie winced at her little sister's comment. She didn't like Clare seeing her this way, but there was simply nothing to do about it, praying daily Clare would never see her with her ribs battered and colored from the pounding of Uncle William's fists. In time Clare would know everything. She was wise enough to understand she couldn't keep what was happening to her a secret forever. Sometime Clare would hear the gossip or someone would cast an evil word toward her little sister.

"I'm thinking that it's really nice to see my little sister. What have you been up to? Hope it's something fun." She looked pointedly at the bed inviting Clare to sit.

"Uncle William did take me into town the other day. He bought me three new dresses. Do you like this one?" She whirled around, the fabric spinning around her tiny ankles.

"It's very pretty and goes nicely with the color of your baby-blue eyes," Sophia told her wishing for those carefree days of her younger years with their dear parents.

Clare grimaced, wrinkling up her pert little nose. "You don't have to call me baby or any part of me. I'm getting to be a grown woman now."

God help her but she was getting way too close to an age their uncle might find a use for her. She would be thirteen in a couple of months. What would Uncle William be expecting of her when he thought she was old enough? How would she ever keep her little sister innocent of the knowledge her big sister was a whore? Or even keep Clare from falling into their uncle's plans.

She could not. That was the gist of her uncle's maneuverings. If and when her uncle decided to use Clare, he would. There would be nothing she could do about it.

"I won't, darling. It's just that it's what their color reminds me of. How about sky blue? Would that be better? They are truly pretty," Sophie asked, ruffling her sister's hair, receiving another blistering stare in the process.

Clare nodded, a smile forming. "Sky blue is much more romantic," she said matter of factly.

Romance and romantic, there was no such thing. Sophie didn't want to rob her sister of dreams quite yet by speaking her mind. It wouldn't do for her to meet the world blindsided as had happened to her. Once a very long time ago, she had dreams. Now, she knew none of her dreams and wishes would come true. She would never meet a man who would love and protect her. Never find a man who would treat her with respect. No matter where she went, she would always have this nasty business hanging over her head.

Even if I could find some way to escape this horrible place.

After all she was the harlot of Virginia. As Link called her a 'brazen hussy.' She pushed back the tears threatening.

"He bought me bonnets to go with the dresses and some frilly underthings," Clare said.

Sophie stifled a small groan not wishing her sister to know her thoughts or see the beginnings of her tears. Frilly, frothy underthings could mean only one thing. No, Clare was only thirteen. Uncle William waited until she was nearly eighteen to embroil her in his plans. Still a lump caught in her throat while her stomach knotted in pain.

She had to find a way to get Clare out of Virginia. A long slow sigh escaped her. There was no way. At least not one she could think of. They had no relatives in Scotland who would take her in. No relatives anywhere except Uncle William. That was why they ended up here after her parents' deaths.

"That was very sweet of him," Sophie said as she set her brush on her dressing table.

"You should dress up for dinner. Wear one of your pretty gowns Uncle William had made for you. It will be fun."

One of her harlot gowns, perhaps the red one Link detested. "I don't think so. I'm more comfortable in the old one I'm wearing now."

"They are all worn out and ugly. These make you look like a little girl," Clare said with a slight tilt to her nose. "You should buy some new gowns, ones you like."

If only that was possible, "They are comfortable and they don't show things I don't want others to see," she said softly.

"Your breasts?"

Her sister was far too intuitive. She saw and thought things a thirteen-year-old shouldn't. "Yes, I'd rather never have to wear those gowns. When he entertains, he expects me to put them on. I hate them."

"Why do you?" Clare was now standing with her hands on her hips, glaring at her as if she had a choice as to what she could wear. "If you don't like them. Sophie, I heard some bad talk when I was in the village with Uncle William. He hushed everyone up. Wouldn't let them say the nasty things about you. So, they hid behind their hands and whispered them anyway. What is it they are saying? I'll tell them they are wrong."

Sophie tried to smile. "That was nice of him, to stand up for me. I suppose I've done things that are questionable. Come." She didn't want to say anything more to her inquisitive little sister. "It's time for dinner. We don't want Uncle William to be displeased now do we?"

"No, we don't."

Clare's words were said with far too much wisdom for Sophie. She wondered just what Clare knew about her and the things Uncle William did to gain her compliance.

Hand in hand they walked down the stairs. Sophie froze at the bottom, a tiny gasp rippling from her lips. Her heart thundered in her chest. No, this was too soon. She couldn't face Link Stewart tonight. She closed her eyes as she wavered slightly. She clung to the railing. If he hadn't already seen her, she would have turned then fled to her room.

When he saw her, a broad smile formed on his oh too handsome face, his eyes alight with something she couldn't read. She touched her unpainted lips with a finger.

He stepped forward, "You're fetching tonight. Quite surprising too. I like the new look. Not one speck of paint on your face."

"I…" she swallowed the terrifying fear she felt, the sudden all-encompassing need to flee. She moistened her lips. Her hand rose to cover the bruise. "I didn't know you were coming. I'm suddenly not hungry. Believe I'll go to my room."

"Don't be foolish, at least not on my account. You need to eat," Link said, his feet braced apart, his hands behind his back. "You must be hungry after the fabulous evening we spent together. All night." He stopped speaking when he noticed Clare.

He'd never appeared so foreboding, so male, his eyes narrowed, assessing her. The lines of his face were chiseled, his clear blue eyes smoldering. It seemed he looked into her soul and saw everything. She was terrified. This was not how she thought to spend this evening. She thought tonight she would have peace from all the machinations.

He did always manage to surprise her.

"Come, my dears, it's lovely that Mr. Stewart has agreed to dine with us," Brinkmeyer spoke, his furious gaze directed at her as if she'd known Link was going to visit and purposely dressed in an old gown while she chose to wear no makeup. "Perhaps you would like to change first."

"No need for that," Link said, his smile still broad. "I quite like her the way she is; fresh and untouched...unspoiled."

Sophie looked from one man to the other. Despite what she told William, she knew her uncle was thinking Link was an easy conquest. After all, he was here looking for more of her. He would think Link wanted her again, that he succumbed to her charms as the others had done. Her uncle didn't understand this was all a game to Link.

Holding his arms out, he beckoned to her sister then her. “May I escort two lovely ladies into the dining room?”

Clare clapped her hands together clearly pleased while she held back a moment too long. The challenge directed at her was far too evident in his eyes. She didn’t want to touch him, feel the heat of him as she already felt the searing warmth of his gaze.

With a lady on each arm, a grinning Link escorted them to the dining hall. He stopped to pull a chair out for Clare then for her. He seated himself on the opposite side of the table. He watched her with his clear blue eyes that never seemed to miss anything.

She tried to eat the flaky salmon as well as the mashed potatoes and tender peas. Everything seemed to catch in her throat. She drank long and deep of the fine red Bordeaux Link brought with him. Reaching across the table he poured more for her, his eyes seeming to reach into her mind and know everything. She looked to the stairs. Escape was not possible.

Her hand shook when she set the glass on the table. She started to rise. “Will you all excuse me? I’m not feeling all that well. I would like to retire for the evening.”

“No,” Brinkmeyer boomed. “You must stay here and entertain our guest. I’m sure he would like to speak with you a bit. Alone. The two of you must have a great deal to talk about.”

“We could take a walk in the garden, if you won’t be too cold,” Link smiled at her, tipping his head in that direction. “The snow ceased before I started over here. It’s so lovely. I believe I’m becoming more accustomed to the cold weather. I really am quite enjoying myself. A warm coat and a hot toddy keeps the chill at bay.”

She jerked. To Sophie the suggestion sounded more like a command. “You are sure you won’t be too cold.”

“We could walk to the cottage. I’m certain a hot toddy would keep us warm on our way, along with a warm cape. You do have a warm cape. I borrowed one of Leslie’s before I came here. I find it handier than I thought I would. Of course, I was not expecting snow in March.”

For a fleeting moment when he stared hard at her, mentioning the hot toddies she was sure he knew what happened to him. Then he looked away, his eyes narrowed.

He couldn't. There was just no way he could have discovered what happened last night in the cottage. Everything went as usual. The woman taking her place would never say a word.

"If Sophie doesn't want to walk with you, I will," Clare said eagerly. "She is not all herself today. Something is bothering her."

"No, young lady," Brinkmeyer said is a stern voice. "You are much too young to go for walks in a moonlit garden with a man who is twice your age. Now, don't you agree with me?" He rested his gaze on Clare then shot a mutinous look her way.

Link looked amused, his eyes crinkling with laughter. He smiled at her, tilting his head toward the door as if eager to leave this behind, eager to confront her if she didn't miss her guess. At Brinkmeyer's suggestion one of the servants brought in two hot toddies.

"Shall we?" he asked after the servant set one on the table before handing her the second one.

Sophie smiled, nodding and understanding what the servant was telling. She picked the second one up. She handed it to Link, smiling and wishing she need not pretend. She had no choice. *Never a choice*. If she didn't comply, tonight when she returned, she would feel his wrath.

Another servant was there with their warm coats. He slipped the cloak over her shoulders, tying it for her while she still held the drinks. Link's eyes narrowed. Once more she had the uneasy feeling. He understood what she was about.

As they strode through the door of the dining room, she handed him the drugged hot toddy. When he accepted she felt a breath of relief. She half expected him to toss it in her face. He didn't know or he was damn good at pretending. When she sipped, the heat from the potent drink warmed her as she swallowed. From the corner of her eye, she watched him, ever cautious of what he would do next.

Tension had her holding her shoulders up, her neck beginning to ache. They stepped into the gardens, walking along the lighted pathway to the cottage. He meant to take her there. It was too soon. The servants wouldn't have everything ready. Cocoa wouldn't know to be there in a half hour. Panic swirled into her belly.

Icy terror slithered down her spine. She told herself it was the chill of the night and hugged her cloak closer. Next to her he stopped.

"You cold?" He took the glass from her hand then set it on a bench. His eyes shimmered with desire. His smile widened.

She studied the glasses memorizing which one was hers. She didn't dare get the wrong drink. He turned her gently, his hand beneath her chin. She found herself looking into his simmering eyes, smoldering blue eyes that seemed to read her so easily.

"Yes, no, maybe, well," she was stuttering for words. Didn't know his intentions. Wasn't sure if she wanted to know them. She'd much prefer to be safely in her bedroom, alone or with Clare.

He pulled the cloak tighter, making sure the fastenings in the front were secure. He chuckled softly, "Well, that's a definitive answer if I ever heard one. Perhaps you would like to try again?"

She lowered her lashes staring at the pathway for as long as she could. She said nothing.

She didn't remember him being so nice. What the devil was he about? She didn't dare let down her guard. Where Link was concerned, she was in over her head. She couldn't possibly second-guess the man.

"I don't remember kissing you last night or in the early morning when I shouted out your name," he murmured as he gazed at her, holding her so she couldn't easily look away.

She thought on what her uncle would do if he believed she refused to kiss him. Didn't dare cast her gaze to the master suite window that looked down on this very spot. He would be watching her, them. Judging.

Dear lord, what to do?

Slowly, he lowered his head, his breath lightly brushing across her lips. Her body heated then seemed to melt as she anticipated his mouth possessing hers, his warm tongue sweeping across her lips. She wasn't sure she could stand her knees were so weak. Didn't know if she could breathe, her lungs were so robbed of air. Surely her heart would thunder from her chest. She couldn't remain indifferent.

She heard the soft chuckle then realized he released her, pointing with a quick nod to the window. “When I kiss you, truly kiss you and I will, I don’t want an audience. Is your uncle always so watchful of his niece? Seems he should be more so. But then,” he paused seeming to think, “who am I to know? It is your reputation.”

“Audience?” She followed his gaze to the window but if he had been there, he must have vanished when he realized Link was looking at him. He would have wanted him to kiss her, touch her. He would have wanted to see when the drugs would take effect.

She looked at his drink. She looked at Link. There didn’t seem to be anything gone from his glass. He picked them both up, handing her the drink that was hers. She breathed a quick sigh of relief.

He didn’t know or even guess what happened last night. He was acting perfectly normal. She didn’t have to second-guess anything. All she had to do was act normally.

They walked for a few more minutes. She sipped slowly and thought the hot toddy tasted especially good tonight. It was intoxicating, quenching her ever-growing thirst. The sweet delicious brew seemed to go down as if it were water.

“Where are we going?” she asked, her voice soft as they walked past the trail to her cottage. Even now she was unsure of herself more so with this man than she’d ever been.

“I want to take you to my cottage, Sophie. There is a warm fire in the hearth and a fur rug on the floor in front of it. I want to see you stretched out naked on the fur. Your rich, mahogany hair draped across the white rug as well as my chest will please me. I want to kiss you where no one will be watching. I want you all to myself, Sophie. Just you and me.”

Oh God, oh God, oh God, he did know.

She wasn’t drugged. With all her wits about her, nothing she didn’t want to happen would happen. He would never force her. She understood that much about Link Stewart.

He would coax and sweet-talk. He would use all his masculine charms to convince her she wanted him. In the end it would be her choice.

She chose not to allow him to make love to her tonight. All would be fine. A soft sigh of relief left her lips.

For a moment a wave of confidence swept through her. He stopped again, taking her drink form her hand once more. Again, she memorized the location of her glass. It was perfectly still, unnervingly quiet in the secluded part of the trail.

"No audience now," he murmured as he pulled her close, his hands beneath the cape at her waist, his thumbs rubbing gentle circles there then lower to pull her against him.

His mouth hovered over hers. She inhaled the sweet scent of the liquor. She knew she would taste the whiskey as well as the man. She was afraid. Terrified. The power he held over her...

"We should not."

"We most certainly should," he murmured softly as his mouth closed over hers.

Warmth penetrated, they were soft and moist. His tongue parted her lips, delving inside. He kissed her then kissed her again, moving his lips and his tongue on her mouth, inside as well. She was helpless to resist the ardent attention to her mouth. One hand stroked her back, drawing her closer to him. A tiny sound rippled from somewhere deep inside. She never felt anything like his kisses.

She felt the hard length of him pressed against her, her breasts swelling with need, desperate need. She yearned to tell him no, he shouldn't be doing this. He would laugh at her if she attempted something so ridiculous. The tart of Virginia would never say *nay*.

He ran his hand along her side, while his mouth covered hers, nipped its way across her lips, touched, explored, devoured as if he could not get enough of her. Then he cupped her breast, rubbed his thumb across her nipple. She gasped. He held her breast for just a moment. She heard his soft laughter. His lips slowly moved to her ear.

"Your beautiful breasts are unique. I know their shape and texture. No one else's are like yours."

He withdrew from her then, standing back, looking at her, his brows drawn together in a frown. She needed to know what he was thinking now. It seemed there were unspoken words between them a wealth of information.

"Wh-what are you talking about?"

With a small chuckle, he handed her the hot toddy she'd been drinking. She drank long and deep, feeling the soothing warmth caress the inside of her throat. Her legs were tired as she leaned into him, his arm wrapping around her waist to support her. She felt a bit dizzy, thought that was odd.

"Come, let's get to the cottage before you get cold. You're shivering." His voice was husky, deep and so mesmerizing she thought she would do whatever he wanted.

She didn't say anything.

"I'm just thinking about tonight. Did you, Sophie, enjoy yourself last night? Perhaps tonight will be just as pleasant. What do you think? Hmm..."

His voice was pleasing and so very soft. Tranquil, she thought. She needed the feeling of peace.

Still, she was silent as the night, unnerved by the wave of warmth passing through her.

"I found your love making quite satisfactory. Did you find it pleasing when you took me deep into the dark recesses of your sultry mouth? You took me so deeply I was afraid you might gag, but you didn't. At least I don't think you did."

His voice was so bland, so very emotionless. He acted as if he didn't care a wit about what he was saying. He was so very detached.

She could stand it no longer as she was beside herself with the humiliation of her life, of all the horrible things she'd done and said. He would find her out. And then what? "Those things should be left to the privacy of the cottage, don't you think?"

She was swaying slightly and the words she was trying to put together seemed to stick to the top of her mouth.

Something was wrong with her. She just didn't know what. She'd never felt anything like this before. Didn't understand. They reached his cottage. It was just like he told her. A fire was burning on the hearth, a white fur rug spread out in front. She stood very still, unmoving, staring at that damn rug. He was mixing another drink. She thought that odd. Surely, they both had enough to heat them through the evening.

He handed the warm drink to her. Unthinkingly, she drank again. She sat down in a chair by the fire. Her heart was lodged in her throat. She was thinking about his kisses, the way he looked at her when he pulled away.

"No, I don't think so. You need to lie on the rug. I've had this picture in my mind since the day I first met you. You are on the rug, stark naked, your hair spread around you in charming disarray, your legs spread wide to welcome me inside your core. Come here, Sophie. Let me help you from your clothing." He was sitting on the hearth by the rug beckoning to her.

Mindlessly she walked to him, knelt down in front of him. She didn't know what she was doing or why but he was telling her in such a gentle voice it seemed she couldn't refuse him. Didn't want to in any case.

It didn't take him long to slip all the fasteners on her dress. He sat back then, a smile on his face seeming to admire his handy work.

"This dress becomes you much more than the harlot red dress you wore last night. Raise your arms, Sophie, and I will take this simple gown, one that suits you admirably, off. You won't be so hot anymore. Will feel better soon. You are quite warm, aren't you? I will make you feel better."

She nodded then lifted her arms. Her gown was off. She watched him as he carefully folded it then set it on the wing chair by the fire. He walked back to her, showing his white smile.

"Now the shift. Can you take that off by yourself or do you need help? Hmmm... I'd much rather watch."

She felt her eyes widen at his suggestion. He should remove his shirt. She reached out to touch him, parting her lips as if she wanted to caress him with her mouth.

"No, my dear, not yet. I want to see you perfectly and gloriously in the buff. Then I'll give you your pleasure. Will you like that? I'm really a very good lover. I will stroke your feminine petals with my tongue. You will howl with your pleasure."

Pleasure, she didn't have one notion about what he was speaking of. Mindlessly, she nodded anyway. The shift was on the floor by her feet. He folded it then set it with the rest of her clothing. She still wore her stockings. When she bent to remove them, he stopped her. He smiled and nodded, staring at her. Her fingers fumbling, she finished undressing herself.

She was barely able to keep her eyes open. He sat close to her. She felt him looking at her. Felt his length warm against her, heating her. She closed her eyes, waiting.

~ * ~

Sophie sat up. The sun was shining in the windows. When she crossed her arms in front of her, she was startled. A sheet covered her nakedness and a slow fire still burned in the grate. Her hair spilled around her shoulders and down her back. She inhaled a long deep breath so aware of her sensitive flesh where the fabric of the sheet touched upon her.

She felt as if her mind was unclear other than that she didn't feel any different. Never before had she been drunk. Link touched her and kissed her. Did he take her innocence? How did one tell if they were no longer a virgin? Uncle William told her she would remain a virgin. He didn't count on a man like Link Stewart coming along, a man with a fast wit and an understanding of women. Still, Link didn't know she was a virgin. Thought she was the town harlot, at least until last night. Would he understand now that she didn't have any lovers? She just didn't know. For that matter, she didn't know anything.

What did she remember about last night?

One finger to her lips, she remembered his kisses and the sultry promise in his voice. They were slightly swollen. His words had been softly spoken, endearing yet coaxing. She removed her clothing while he folded and placed each article on the wing chair by the fireplace. She remembered the heat, the warmth and the unrequited longing deep in her belly. She wanted him. Yet she didn't feel as if he did make love to her. Wouldn't she remember?

That was the end of it though. He didn't touch her in any way, at least not that she could recall. She slept. Her dreams were restless, nightmares of sort. She didn't know when he left her. A strange, terrifying unease settled in the pit of her stomach then radiated outward.

What if he did the unthinkable and paid someone to have sex with her. "Oh, God, oh God," she groaned aloud thinking of Cocoa who delighted in the sex with all of her lovers. Who would he have found to do such a heinous act? Would it have been someone she knew?

Furious, confused as well she rose holding the sheet around her body as a protective barrier to the pain radiating from her. The hipbath was filled with steaming water. Bread and honey had been set out for her to eat along with a pot of coffee.

He'd taken every consideration in her seduction, in the defiling of her innocence. Bastard! She wanted to hurry now, needed to confront the arrogant man before...

She should go home and not see Link. A story for Uncle William would have to be made up, the details beginning to form in her head. She would have to tell her uncle it was over, that he knew what they were doing. In the hot water, she closed her eyes, thinking, trying desperately to remember. Nothing came to ease her mind. She had no recollection of what transpired between them.

Frantic she soaped herself, rinsed, soaped again. She wanted to wash away whatever happened to her. Blessed hell, but she didn't know. Someone knew. Her body shook with the knowledge that Link took her innocence, breached her maidenhead.

She wanted to yell.

Finished with the bath, she quickly dressed herself and combed her hair. She tied it with the same ribbon she wore last night. Looking in the mirror, she realized she was pale. Her eyes bore dark circles.

She was not the same person this morning as she'd been the night before, before he had sex with her. How could he have done that?

Sophie strode from the cottage down the long path, striding past Leslie Hall all the way to her home. At the stable she saddled her horse. She rode. The wind whistled through her hair. She rode until she didn't want to ride any longer, until the sun was nearly at its zenith. She turned her horse toward Leslie Hall, unable to stay away a moment longer.

Chapter Six

Link thought of the night before with great satisfaction, a smile forming. Sophie would wake up in a furious rage. He supposed he should get ready for her. It was only a little after seven. He was sure she would make an appearance before he finished with breakfast.

The sun was shining. He should suggest a ride along the river. They could look at the damn cave again. He didn't like caves. They could have a picnic in the field where she assured him it would be covered with wildflowers by summer. He wasn't going to be here in the summer. Right now, it was probably brimming with mud puddles. Ah, he recalled the mud puddle he tossed her in with great relish, wishing for something of a similar nature. Her eyes had sparkled with fury and passion.

The parlor in his house might do well for the conversation he knew she would want to have. He wondered if she knew what happened last night. If he told her nothing happened between them, he wondered if she would believe him. Well, he wasn't going to tell her anything. She could assume they had sex. He wasn't going to disavow her of that assumption. He wanted her to sweat and worry about everything until she howled.

All he wanted was to make a point.

He hoped she understood what he was trying to tell her.

Link walked into the dining room. He poured himself a cup of coffee then wandered to the screened in porch. Waiting for her to appear was hard when all he wanted was to see her face, understand the reaction she would have had to the evening. Perhaps he should have waited in the cottage. It would have been interesting to see her eyes when she woke up and realized she was naked beneath a sheet.

He waited. He expected her to arrive within the hour. She was not here and that set him back a moment. He strolled inside, pouring himself another cup of coffee then bringing the pot with another cup with him. He was becoming impatient, tempted to ride to the cottage and see what was going on. That wouldn't do. She would come here. He just needed to exercise patience.

Only about fifteen minutes later, he watched her riding down the long path to Leslie Hall. Her hair flowed out behind her. If he didn't miss his guess, she was mad. He could tell by the set of her shoulders and the tilt of her chin. All her anger would be directed at him. He wondered how much she guessed or thought she knew about the night, about their lovemaking.

Sophie leapt gracefully from her horse then tied the reins to the hitching post. When she climbed the steps to the veranda, her fists were clenched at her sides and her eyes were blazing, her breasts heaving beneath the same gown she wore last night. She was magnificent in her fury, desperate in her need to discover the truth.

He smiled, knowing she wanted to throttle him, thoroughly enjoying the moment. She wouldn't have one soft spot in her body for him. Perhaps she even hated him. Well, she deserved everything she got and more. He didn't violate her nor did he have anyone else do it. She would thank him for the consideration.

Most likely not.

"Good morning, Miss Sophie. You look well," he spoke softly, his words a gentle purr. "Last evening was nice."

"You bastard!"

"Ah, oh well, what did I do to anger you, Sophie? Our night went marvelously well, at least for me. You were soft and warm in my arms. Your legs parted sweetly for me. I enjoyed you very much."

She didn't say a word. A small bird let out a warble of some sort, nearby a frog croaked.

"Would you like coffee?"

"Yes."

He saw that her body was shaking as he poured, handing her the cup, watching her as she sipped, seeming to be thinking of how she would like to cosh him over the head with something hard.

As she sipped, her body seemed to relax, the lines in her face easing.

At least her anger seemed to be ebbing somewhat. He was disappointed as he loved watching the smoldering of her eyes, the way they changed from a soft gray to molten silver. He liked to watch her breasts heave as she struggled for each breath to keep her passions in check. He wondered if her body would do the same thing when he finally gave her a woman's pleasure. Indeed, she might howl with delight.

Ah, but this was all too much to contemplate right now. He must push away his wayward and very wanton thoughts to another time. He would wait and see what transpired next.

"I would have thought, oh, but did you go home before you rode here? You are wearing the same clothes that I folded neatly and left on the wing chair by the fire. No, you woke and came straight to me, your lover. You were eager to start up where we left off."

"Did you take my clothes off," she asked, setting the cup on the table with a clatter.

He slanted one eyebrow slightly upward, studying her, wondering if she was challenging him or really didn't remember. "I kissed you first. Well, you did kiss me back. You slipped your sweet tongue inside my mouth again and again as if you wanted to play the man's role. You leaned into me, your eyes wide with desire, your full and very soft breasts pushing against my chest. It was well done of you. It pleased me immensely. I'm looking forward to the next time."

She had this vulnerable look about her. He didn't like it. Didn't want to give into this very female ploy of hers. Why he thought for even a second she might be innocent in all this was beyond him. Sophie drugged him, let her uncle undress him then sent another woman to have sex with him.

No, no, he would not soften his heart to her. A continuance of the course he decided on was necessary. Her big soft gray eyes could not, would not sway him. He would not be undone by her. She could flirt and cajole to her hearts content, but his opinion of her would not change.

"Did you take my clothes off?"

His attention was once more riveted to her, to the answer she was seeking. "No, I did unfasten your gown though," he spoke softly, assessing her, the way she carried her shoulders, the slight downward tilt to her chin. Then he reminded himself this was an act. Everything about her was a performance. There was nothing remotely sincere or honest about Miss Sophie Carter-Brown. She took part in this to suit her selfish needs. She was a greedy bitch. Why did he have this all-encompassing urge to pull her into his arms, hold her and protect her?

Blessed hell, he'd never felt that way about a woman, especially not a brazen hussy. Not the best-known strumpet in Virginia. The truth as far as he was willing to go, after that he'd have to reassess this role he was playing.

"You disrobed for me. It was quite the little act of seduction. I suppose you've done it countless times. You played me, seduced me until I was so hard, I truly thought I would explode watching you. The little way you have of running your tiny pink tongue across your lips is so endearing and intoxicating. Puts me in the mood. You lay on the rug in front of the fire and stretched. Your breasts swayed provocatively. I kissed each one, sucked them into my mouth while you moaned your delight. The glimmer in your eyes asked for more."

"You're lying." She stood now, her hands at her sides fisted so tight her nails had to be gouging the tender flesh.

By the look in her eyes, she wanted to hit something. Him. Her restraint pleased him.

"Why would I do that? Lie?" He crossed his legs, stretched out in the most negligent pose he could manage.

She sat down again. For a brief moment he was sure he saw moisture in her eyes, moisture spiking her lashes. She wasn't going to cry, was she? Even if she tried to tell him he took advantage of her, he wouldn't believe her. He only gave her back what she gave to him. She deserved everything that happened.

He did not violate her or take advantage of the situation.

Well, he did drug her but compared to what she did to him, it was nothing in comparison. He didn't even remove her clothing. She did.

Well, he helped, he reminded himself before he dismissed the notion as unimportant.

When she looked at him again, if there had been moisture in her eyes, it was gone now. *The actress in her resurfaced.* He was glad of that. Wanted to see what route she would take next.

"What happened after that? Did you rape me?" Her voice held a slight quiver as she said the words.

He stiffened at the single word. Rape. In any other situation he would explain to her what exactly happened and why. Today, now, with Miss Carter-Brown, he would not.

"Violating a woman is not my way. You were willing, no, eager to come into my arms, to allow me to cover you, spread your legs and come deep inside you. Sophie," he leaned forward, "you wanted me, were in desperate need of my attention. Your core was soft and warm. You begged and pleaded. Very nice."

She stiffened at his words, stood, smoothed her skirts then sat down again. "I would not have let you do that. I didn't know. Was not in full..." she swallowed. "You made it impossible for me to make a decision."

"No?"

"No! I was not willing."

"You screamed your pleasure when you climaxed. I emptied my seed inside your warm sultry body. We might even have a child because I took no precautions. Would you like that, Sophie? A baby to hold? Ah, but it might put a bit of a damper on your nightly visits to the cottage. As you will learn I have other children. You needn't fear. I will always take care of the mothers and well as my children. You have nothing to worry about."

By the look on her face and the sudden pallor, he knew he'd gone too far. What did she expect when she had sex? She wasn't an innocent. She must comprehend the consequences of her profession. He couldn't tell her he left her on the fur, gloriously thick auburn hair spread around her, untouched. He pulled the sheet over her before striding from the room. Early in the morning he made sure a hot bath was left for her as well as food and coffee.

"I did not. I would have remembered something like that." Her voice as well as her hands were shaking, trembling so hard, he thought she might collapse at any second.

He tilted his head, watching her, delving into her mind. "You are calling me a liar again? Would you like to meet me tonight? We can proceed from whence we left off."

"No." Yet the single word was said with little conviction. She looked down then away as if she was looking toward Mayfair Hall.

He wondered about the deeper meaning of that. He had more suspicions just now

that Brinkmeyer was the driving force behind Sophie and her lovers.

Brinkmeyer, he was sure, would have a say if she saw him again. Suddenly, she came at him, her fists flying. She caught him off guard. The chair he was sitting in toppled backward. She was lying on top of him now, beating on his chest and his face. He captured her hands in his, holding them tightly so they would not do him in.

He wrapped his arms around her as she rested her head on his chest. She was breathing hard. It seemed he could hear the rapid, hard beating of her heart. "Let me go, Link."

"You won't do me in?"

"No, it is enough."

He felt the wetness of his shirt where her tears fell. The fear and vulnerability changed to rage then back to tears. She was sobbing now, uncontrollably, gut wrenchingly. He won and he didn't feel any real pleasure from the conquest. No, he felt her shame as well as her fears. Perhaps she would tell him why she had become a harlot, at least in name. At the moment he wasn't at all sure she ever seduced or took any man for a lover. It wouldn't surprise him to learn she duped all her lovers the same as she did him.

His hold loosened as he moved back giving her room. She sat up, pushing her hair from her face, her head tilted regally. The smile on her lips thin, he didn't know what to believe.

"How did you know?"

Link felt a chuckle forming. He held it back. He didn't want to enrage her again although he did enjoy having her in his arms. Tucking a strand of hair behind her ear, he said softly, "It was your breasts. I held them if you recall, twice. The ones I held that night were not yours."

She paled even more, turning her face away from him. When she looked back, "My breasts...?" She sounded thoroughly stupefied as if she thought all woman's breasts were the same.

"Yes, you have quite beautiful ones you know. They are white, perfectly formed, soft but firm. No, perhaps you don't know. In any case they were what did you in."

She heaved a breath of air, searching his face. He thought she was looking for a weakness but there was none. He won. Fair and square. He did her in and it was simply something she deserved.

"I was a vir—" She stopped short of finishing the word, her eyes wide, her hand at her mouth. She would understand he would never take her word in this.

There was only one way he would know the truth of that statement. It amused him, knowing this lady was about to twist the truth again. He truly had enough of her lies. "You are not a virgin. I think it has been a very long time since you were. I don't care. Just be honest with me and we'll deal well together. I've seen your bruises, Sophie. Perhaps you should tell me how you got them."

She grimaced, made a strange face and looked away from him. A few moments later she stared at him hard. "It is as you say. I'm not a virgin. I've had three lovers. You are my fourth. My bruises are none of your business. You can mull that over in your man's mind as long as you want. What do we do now?"

"That is entirely up to you."

He wasn't ready to stop seeing her or discover the source of her bruises, although he had a good idea. He did want to make love to her, watch her delightful face as she climaxed. He didn't want their lovemaking to be something sordid and dirty. He drew in a long breath as he watched her, waited for some sign from her as to how they would proceed.

"I'm going now."

It was only a minute before she was galloping down the path away from Leslie Hall. He supposed what happened next was up to Uncle William. He also supposed she would not have a say in what was going on. She would do her uncle's bidding. While he wanted to believe she might be as innocent as she appeared last night in the old serviceable gown with all her cosmetics washed from her face, he doubted seriously if it could be possible. He wasn't averse to discovering her truth.

His desiring something did not make it so. In any case he knew when they finally made love, he would thoroughly enjoy the act. There was nothing now to stop that from happening. He knew she would have no say.

At least for now he would have to wait. He still needed to discover what Brinkmeyer had in store for him. Most likely he wanted Leslie Hall. Why else would he have started all that ghoulish nonsense? The ghosts as well as blue and gold sulfur would have made more sense if it had been closer to All Hallows Eve.

He didn't understand.

He meant to learn more.

If this all revolved around Sophie acting the slut and she wasn't, what then? What did Brinkmeyer hold over her head to make her do his bidding? Time, he was sure would tell the tale. He didn't have that much time. He wanted to be home by summer, midsummer at the latest.

He really did need to figure out what he was going to do next.

~ * ~

When Sophia entered Mayfair Hall Uncle William was sitting in the parlor waiting for her. She drew in a deep breath as she saw the muscles strain in his jaw. Her heart pounded deep in her chest. Fear for herself surged and swirled then fear for Clare as well. If she closed her eyes, she could feel his wrath, the ever-constant hatred emanating from him. By the look in his eyes even before she regaled him with the truth, she knew he would hit her. One day he was sure to kill her.

In the end to get his way, he would use Clare against her. She didn't have a single doubt.

"Where have you been, Sophia?" His words were curt, demanding answers.

She felt the hate when he said her name. Felt it bone deep. "I want to know now. You weren't at the cottage last night. Damn it, everything was ready. It will only take one or two more times before you will have him in the palm of your hand."

There would be no next time. She wanted to yell at him that this was over now, that Link knew the truth. He figured it all out. "We went for a walk last night. I was at the cottage. It just wasn't ours. I woke up this morning naked and alone, dizzy and terrified just as I left him the night before. It is done, uncle. We are finished. He knows."

"You had sex with him them. You're no longer a virgin." Thoughtfully, he rubbed his chin, gazing at her with disgust clearly written in his eyes. "You liked it, sex with that man, with Link Stewart, didn't you? You were just waiting for a man of his standing. He isn't a duke like his brother but he has more wealth than he knows what to do with. More than he could spend in a lifetime. You're looking for a way out. Well, it's no longer my fault. You're used goods. Now, we have no need of Cocoa. You can service, or seduce all the men. They will all be your lovers."

She inhaled a swift deep breath, fighting the urge to tell him how she felt. Her anger and violence would do her no good with her uncle. All it would do is increase his wrath. "He drugged me. I didn't have sex willingly." She had the need to toss something at him. She wanted to hurt him as he did her. There would be no more lovers, no more men. She was done.

"Of course, you did, Sophie. You're a little harlot. The men adore you and you adore them and the attention they give you. It was just a matter of time before someone had you." His uncle was grinning now.

She was sure he was hatching new plans to use her to get what he wanted.

Her terror grew. "He knows what we did. It's over now. We cannot go back," she whispered frantic for him to believe her.

"Nothing is over until I say it is," he yelled at her, his eyes darkening. "The only difference now is there will be no need for pretense. You will take him to the cottage, have sex with him and continue on in the same way. Eventually, we will have exactly what we want. Blackmailing someone like Link Stewart is so very easy. He will fall into my plans quite nicely."

"You will have what you want."

"True. You will hardly be in a position to ask for anything from me because you will be well and truly used. Perhaps there will be a brothel in town that will give you a room once I'm done with you. What do you think?" He was leaning back in his chair, sipping a glass of brandy as he stared at her over the rim. "Perhaps I'll have you myself. That would be pleasant. You're quite tempting Sophia."

She understood that was exactly what he would expect when he won this game he played. He wouldn't expect to keep her around. She would be a blight on his reputation, his good name. Clare would be his next conquest.

"Link Stewart will best you."

She meant to stand her ground, force his hand. It might be stupid of her. She wasn't going to humiliate herself again. Her reputation was ruined but she could go somewhere else and start over. She didn't know what she would do for money. She was smart though and could figure something out. There was her inheritance. Unfortunately, it would not be hers for another three years. She would have to turn twenty-one.

His features suddenly turned harsher than she'd ever seen them before. He appeared furious. Even now she was trying to back away from him afraid for her life. She'd never before seen his features contorted so harshly or his eyes so evil. For a moment she was afraid she spoke her thoughts out loud.

"You told him, didn't you? You little bitch. He would never figure it out on his own. You've a soft spot for that man. Well, he is rich as

Midas. Can have any woman he wants. He would never pick a whore." Spittle flew from his lips as he advanced toward her.

She backed into the wall as she was shaking her head, denying his words. "No, he figured it out on his own. You see, he told me it was my breasts." She was suddenly afraid she was going to die.

"Liar. You told him."

His fists were balled tightly. He was standing over her, glowering at her. The first blow came before she expected it. He hit her in the face. Stunned, she crumpled to her knees. Before she could stand or protect herself with her arms, his foot connected twice with her stomach and ribs. She gulped for air, her eyes closing as she waited for the next blow. This was nothing like before. It seemed he used all his strength. Held nothing back.

"No." She held up her hands imploring him to stop. "I didn't. I swear I didn't tell him. You have to believe me."

He swung. Her face jerked back as the force sent her head against the wall. He wasn't stopping now. Like a berserker, he was kicking and hitting her as if he was a madman. She pulled herself into a tight ball, trying to keep the blows from doing more harm. Her lip swelled. Her eyes were beginning to shut from the after effects of his punishing fists. Unwanted tears fell from her eyes, rippling down her cheeks. She moaned deep in the back of her throat. The sound was raw and harsh.

The pummeling stopped suddenly. She almost cried with relief as she tried to stand but found she could not. On all fours, she attempted to crawl from the room.

He wasn't finished.

"Felix left me something to use on you beside my fists. It seems fitting today. You deserve this, you little whore." His voice was low and calm. With a brief chuckle she heard the air crack around her.

The whip stung her back, ripped through her gown, shredding the fabric. She cried out as the lash hit her again and again. Her dress was torn then ripped away as the lash cut into her skin. She was on her elbows now, what was left of her gown lay on the floor in front of her. She tried to take her mind off the pain by counting.

"You told him. I ought to kill you." He whipped her again. "But you still have your uses."

More lashes. She lost count then at five. Tears welled into her eyes as she slowly watched the world dim. He hit her again and again until she fell to the floor, the world black around her.

~ * ~

It was later, much later. The room was dark. A soft sheen of moonlight filtered through a window. Her back was on fire. She closed her eyes as she willed herself to inhale deep and evenly, willing herself to ignore the anguish that was her body. Moving was nearly impossible. She gritted her teeth against the agony understanding if she stayed at Mayfair Hall she would die. If she tried to go anywhere, she would not get very far. She had to take Clare with her but the little girl wouldn't understand. She didn't want to frighten her. If she came to Clare now, she would terrify her.

Sophie knew she could not stay at Mayfair Hall with Uncle William.

She didn't have a single option left. She didn't know anyone who would take her in and protect her. Most of the people in the village and nearby plantations tolerated her only because she was the niece of William Brinkmeyer. They wouldn't believe her story. She refused to give up. There had to be some way to survive and keep Clare alive and unused also. She just didn't know what that was.

Until she could stand, she would have to lie here and try to gain strength. She could ask Edward for help, but he thought her just as bad as her reputation. His father would give her aid, but he'd never be able to protect her. Her uncle could ruin the good man. She would die before she would do that.

As she saw it, she had only one option. She would have to throw herself at the mercy of Link Stewart then pray for a miracle. Perhaps he still wanted her. If necessary, she would give herself to him to gain his protection for Clare as well as herself. She could become his mistress for as long as he might want her.

She didn't want to die yet she would not humiliate herself. Could not go to Link, asking him for protection. In any case he would treat her as the harlot he thought she was. A stifled sob tore at her ribs, tears blinding her eyes. She fell back, unable to move. She didn't know what to do even while she understood she had to leave.

Sleep claimed her. Nightmares hovered on the brink of her mind. She saw herself trudging along the road, mud spattered, the good people throwing things at her, crying out that she was a whore. When she moved all of her hurt. So, she tried to do nothing but breathe. Even that small effort caused stabbing pain.

Sometime before dawn booted footsteps passed by her. She heard the sound of her uncle's voice, his laughter as well as the closing of the door. She couldn't move or escape.

Clare stopped by the closed door asking, "Do you know where Sophia is? I haven't seen her since the day before yesterday. It's not like her to leave and not tell me where she is going."

"Sophia? No, she's not been about. She must have gone off to see Mr. Stewart," Uncle William said. "She will be back soon. Don't worry your pretty little head about your sister."

"Why would she do that?" Clare sounded confused for a moment, "She barely knows him."

"She knows him better than you could imagine. Come, I'll tell you a few truths about your sister then you can judge her for yourself."

"Oh, God." He was going to tell her about the cottage and why the women in town whispered about her behind their hands. There was nothing she could do about it. When she finally could move, she would have to leave Clare here. Against the pain she closed her eyes again listening for her uncle to leave the house. She would have little time.

A few hours must have passed. She dozed. She could tell from the chimes of the clock in the hallway. Finally, he left. She would give him a few minutes then she would see if she could walk upstairs to change her clothes. The gown she wore was in tatters. With the whip he ripped it to shreds. She couldn't wear the dress. It would be as if she wore nothing at all.

Sophie found she could climb the steps on her hands and knees with her dress bunched around her waist. She was breathing heavy, her back still on fire when she finally reached her room and managed to close the door. Gritting her teeth against the pain, she found a clean shift and gown.

When she was dressed, she packed a small bag with a few necessities then left. As she walked down the steps one hand griping the railing, she felt old and frail. She had to stop every so often just to drag in a breath of air and remind herself there were no choices for her. Clare was too young for William to use. She would help her when she could.

I cannot stay, one step in front of the other.

She decided she would ride to the cave. There were a few things she could use, an old tattered blanket to keep her warm until she healed enough to move on. She would have to come back for Clare. Clare was only thirteen. Her uncle would wait a few years before he used her. He could not prostitute a girl of her age without repercussions.

The little mare seemed to know where to go. With little effort on her part the horse turned toward the path along the beach and the cave. It seemed to take hours to go the distance. The sun slowly climbed to its zenith. She was glad it wasn't snowing. Every hoof beat seemed to cause her more pain, more agony than she'd ever known before.

The path turned from the river. She was nearly there when she heard hoof beats behind her.

"Sophie!"

No! She recognized the voice. It couldn't be. She didn't have the courage or the strength to speak with the man. At the moment she was bent over her horse barely able to sit, nearly falling off. He would demand answers. She didn't have them for him.

She pushed the mare harder, the jarring agony seeping into her soul. He was beside her, his hand on the reins of her horse, stopping her. She felt his gaze raking over her, questioning. In that moment she realized she both liked and hated him, despised his arrogance as well as the knowledge he controlled her. She was tired of finding herself controlled by men.

"What are you doing? I stopped by the house and no one was home. I thought you might have gone for a ride." His voice was husky but it wasn't desire. "Thought to look for you at the cave."

She heard the concern in his voice. He had no reason to care about her. When he looked at her, there was no way he would miss the bruising on her face, the swollen eyes and lips where she still tasted blood. She couldn't do a damn thing about it except keep her face turned away. He wouldn't allow it though. He would insist she tell him everything.

She could not. Uncle would kill him, get rid of anyone who got in his way.

"Look at me, Sophie," he commanded his words intense, binding her to him in ways she refused.

He was riding beside her. Gave her no quarter. She understood he would never stop questioning.

She knew he wouldn't let this go. Felt the heat of his gaze sear the back of her neck. Unable to help herself the pain so intense, she moaned. He brought her horse to a stop.

"Sophie?" There was a question in his voice, also a demand. The tone of his voice held a wealth of questions.

She didn't say anything, just slowly turned his way. The shock she saw on his face nearly made her laugh. She didn't dare. The ache would be too much to bear.

He was going to talk to her now. Demand answers. She wasn't certain she could talk. All she could do at the moment was to shake her head. Even that slight movement hurt. Tears slid down her battered cheeks.

"Who did this to you? Never mind. I suppose I know." He reached out as if to touch her. It seemed the agony reached from the top of her head to the tips of her toes.

When she flinched, he pulled his hand back. "Where do you think you are going? Why didn't you come to me?"

"Come—to—you?"

A tiny smile flitted across her lips before she winced then nodded toward the cave. She couldn't come to him. He wouldn't believe her if she told him. Well, perhaps he would at least about her uncle. What he wouldn't believe was that she didn't want to come to him because her reputation would be shredded farther if she did so.

He wouldn't believe she feared him, what he could do to her without even trying.

"Enough of this foolishness. You won't make it through the night in that cave. What else did he do to you?"

He was looking at her, really looking at her. Except for her face he wouldn't be able to see the damage. Unless the blood from the lashes seeped through her dress.

He kept asking question she wouldn't answer even as he turned her horse and led her toward Leslie Hall, past Mayfair, down the long drive to his home. She had to get away. Uncle William would make sure Link ended up dead.

"Clare?" she asked, her face turned toward her home, a home she would never return to.

She wanted to know where she was. She needed to know Clare would not be harmed.

"I will see to her after I've got you safe in my home. What the hell did you do to provoke him?" His question sounded angry to her. "No, never mind."

She stiffened then wanted to laugh at him, blaming her for the outrageous beating, which she'd done nothing to deserve. She wanted to yell at him it was his fault. He was too damn smart. He caused this. Tears ran down her cheeks. She couldn't even lift a hand to wipe them away.

When they reached the stable, she slid off her little mare into his arms, wincing at the new onslaught of pain.

"I know it hurts for me to carry you, but I don't think you can walk the distance. Do you want to try?"

To answer, she buried her face in his shoulder. Her hair fell across her swollen and bruised face. As he entered the house, he bellowed orders to his staff, asking for hot water and soap, towels, bindings, laudanum. He would have no idea her back was raw and on fire, that her ribs were bruised and she was sure at least one was broken. Her breath caught in her throat as he juggled her in his arms; agony, hot and burning ripped through her.

"So sorry. Grit your teeth against the pain, Sophie. You will be on a bed soon enough and I'll see what he was done to you. Just keep your words behind your teeth. It will all be better before you can blink."

She didn't think so.

He would undress her now, look at her. She reminded herself he'd already seen her naked. It didn't matter. Nothing seemed to matter any longer. Except the agony.

"I don't..."

"Hush. With that swollen lip you should not be talking. I know you don't want to be here with me, but you are. Don't see that you can be anywhere else. I will take care of you, Sophie. Don't worry about anything." His words were spoken softly, so sweetly she could almost believe he cared about her, that he harbored a few good feelings for her.

Gently he set her on the bed. Knew he tried to be as careful as possible. She looked around the room. It wasn't his room. Thank God.

"No, Sophie, I didn't put you in the master chamber with me. I'm not going to ravish you. What kind of monster do you think I am?" His white teeth showed in the flash of a smile. "Truly, I'm a very nice man. You just need to get to know me."

He stepped back, hands on his narrow hips as he seemed to survey her. She closed her eyes and said not a thing. There was silence for such a long time she finally opened her eyes.

"I'm going to have to take your gown off. I'll be as gentle as possible because I know it hurts. He beat you and left you, did he not? There is yellowing around your eye so he must have done this last night. Nod if I'm right." He turned from soft and sweet to hard and demanding.

She did, her eyes wide as he slowly unfastened the gown then eased if from her shoulders. His breath sucked in at the sight she made. She wanted to tell him it was only her shoulders he was looking at but he shook his head, silently willing her silence.

When he tried to slide the dress from her back, the fabric stuck to her, the blood having dried. He cursed then swore again. She tried to swallow the cry of pain but he heard it, knew something was terribly wrong.

His arms where tense, his hands firm when he saw what else had been done. "There is blood on your back. What the bloody hell did he do? Did he whip you?" He sounded astonished.

She nodded, her lips quivering with the pain.

"I'm going to have to soak the blood away before I can take the gown off your back. Can you lie on your stomach?"

She tipped her head, her lashes fluttering closed. She would lie wherever he put her. Not one position existed that didn't cause agony.

"I'm going to cut the shift off. It will hurt you too much to lift your arms and take it over your head. Hold still now." He quit talking to her, seeming to concentrate on his task.

She felt the back of the knife, felt the sensation as her chemise was slit in half. Now, in front of this man she was once again bared to the waist. He was sucking in his breath. Somehow, she knew he was only looking at the damage inflicted. She swayed slightly, needing to rest now, needing to sleep. Staying upright was becoming increasingly more difficult.

"I'll kill the bastard," he murmured, his voice harshly soft, threateningly so.

He turned his attention back to her. His voice was still soft and soothing even with the hateful words. "No," she murmured. She didn't want him to kill anyone.

It seemed he ignored her plea, "I have to see to your back first. Can you lie on your stomach? Do you need help?"

She tried to turn. Cried out in pain instead. He picked her up before tenderly placing her stomach side down on the bed. The springs creaked as he sat down next to her. She felt the gentle glide of the water and soap across her back. He worked for what seemed like hours, calling for a servant to bring a salve once the fabric of her gown and all the threads were washed from the slashes. The potion was cool and eased the pain.

"I will wait until tomorrow to bind your ribs. You've two broken ones. Blessed hell, but he must have kicked you."

She saw his fists tighten and wondered at that. She was just a whore, a harlot at least in his mind. Why would he care?

He left for a few minutes. When he returned he held a glass of water. "It's some laudanum. Should ease some of the pain. I'll help you." He held her while she drank. "Drink it all."

She wanted to refuse, needed to stay clear-headed.

"I'll—be—fine," she told him slowly and so quietly he had to bend close to hear her words.

He touched a fingertip to her bottom lip. "Aye, you will be fine. Tomorrow I intend to visit Brinkmeyer."

She was shaking her head, frantic in her need to keep him from doing something so foolish. "No..."

"Don't fret. I won't hurt him. I'm just going to explain how he'll never hurt you again or he'll have to answer to me."

A part of her felt the swift current of joy that someone would care for her. Another part felt the fear, the all-encompassing fear that followed defying her uncle.

He was a man.

She wanted to trust him.

"Will—you—bring...?" She tried so hard to talk but it hurt so much. Her teeth scraped her bottom lip. She grimaced.

"She will come visit, I promise. Clare can sit by your side and make sure you are behaving yourself and not running off."

She was shaking her head trying to tell him Clare needed to come here to stay, but she couldn't say that much. She couldn't tell him why because he'd never believe her. Would never believe William might hurt Clare, that he held Clare over her head to make her do the things for him because she cared so very much for her little sister. Uncle William was an outstanding member of the community. He would do whatever he pleased. No one would believe her.

"You must relax now and sleep. I'll send someone to get Clare. When you wake, she will be here, holding your hand. All will be fine."

She was frantic now as she tried to swallow her fear. He helped her with a bit more water then stepped back. She closed her eyes, not thinking she would be able to sleep.

Sophie did sleep. The dreams were horrible. They filled her with terror. When she woke a light was shining on the table near the bed. True to his word, Clare sat beside her on the bed.

"Uncle William did this to you?" she asked in a small voice, an unbelieving voice. "How could he?"

Still, she could barely talk. "He is," she moistened her lips, "not a nice man."

"I believe she would like some water." Link sat on her other side, lifting her head, helping her drink. "Now, before you fall asleep again you will listen to me. You won't be afraid for Clare. Nod if you understand."

Sophie noticed he was grinning at her, his white teeth showing neatly in the semi-darkness of the room. She wanted to curse at him. Tell him she wasn't stupid just in pain. The laudanum must be wearing off because her back was on fire again. Although she had to admit it was not as bad as this morning.

"Nod your head."

She did and he began to talk again.

"Clare will stay here tonight and until you are well. Your uncle has agreed to this but I can't keep her here longer nor can I keep you. He is your guardian. He has the ultimate say in where you live. I've no power here. You will have to go back to him. Simply put, it's the law. I cannot take it into my hands to defy it."

Her body started to tremble. She was shaking her head, "No!" She tried to make him understand she would not go back.

"I agree with you, Sophie. You will not return. Trust me. I promise you I will think of something. Edward as well as Grayson have seen your back. I might be able to gain guardianship for you as well as Clare. We will see how it goes." Gently he touched her cheek, settled a fingertip on her lips. "Hush now, we needed witnesses to what he did to you. He tried to deny it when I confronted him earlier today. It is of my opinion he will not protest much when I insist you stay here but it will not help your reputation."

"I don't care..."

"Hush," he said again. "I've found a nice lady. She is in her fifties and has agreed to come and act as a chaperone. You need not worry about your reputation. It will not be tarnished further."

She laughed. It sounded harsh and disbelieving. It also sent a jolt of pain through her ribs. "My what?"

"Yes, well as we both know your reputation has been trounced on, roughly annihilated, demolished beyond repair. I won't let it be tarnished farther and by me. Now, Sophie, you will go to sleep, rest. You will allow me to worry about you and your sister. Rest assured I will think of something."

For a few more minutes she was going in and out of consciousness. She heard him speaking with Clare. They were talking about her as well as how she would heal then be just as good as new. She didn't think she would ever be as good as new. All she could do now was pray her sister would not end up like her. Pray too that Link Stewart found a way to make himself Clare's guardian.

When she woke again, it was still night. Her back felt a little better, at least no longer in flames. She wondered if she slept the day away. Clare wasn't sitting beside her. Her sister must be back at Mayfair Hall.

It wasn't good. Clare was in danger there.

Link promised Clare would be safe and that he would take care of things. She tried to roll onto her back and push her legs over the side of her bed. She had to relieve herself. The distance seemed too far to walk. A small groan slipped from her mouth. This wouldn't do. Gripping the bedpost, she pulled herself up so she was standing. She was breathing hard. Her heart thundered. Her knees were weak

She could do this. She had to or humiliate herself even more. It took more time than she would have ever imagined. When she finished, she realized the bed was very far from her. It seemed she used up all her strength. So, now what? Her body shook with the idea of walking back to the bed. Perhaps she should crawl. That might be easier.

When Link walked in, she was on all fours in the middle of the room, her hair falling around her shoulders in tangled disarray. She let herself down, her elbows and head on the floor her bottom skyward. She couldn't seem to draw in a breath of air, horrified beyond words.

"What are you doing out of bed?" His voice boomed above her.

Out of the corner of one eye, she saw that his boots were polished to perfection. Strange, the things one notices when they are in abject mortification, humbled beyond measure.

She turned her head to one side, "I'm trying to see what is under the bed. You know, I might have lost something."

"You must be feeling better." He laughed his soft chuckle echoing around in her head. She didn't want to look at him even though she would have to in the next few seconds. "Next time you need to relieve yourself pull the bell cord and I'll come help."

"Don't think so. Something I'd rather do myself."

"Should I remind you that I've seen you with nothing on?"

"Don't need reminding."

His long fingers were under her arms helping her to stand then bracing her against himself. She was on the bed, not lying on her stomach but sitting against the backboard.

"I've brought you some food. After you eat, I'm going to bind your ribs. They will ache less." He nodded his head toward the bedside table. "Are you hungry?"

She didn't know. Every other part of her still ached. With her finger on her lip, she found the swelling to have gone down. "How do I look?"

"As if someone beat you near to death."

That good? "Where is Clare?"

"She is at Mayfair Hall. She will be here soon."

~ * ~

He didn't like the look in her eyes, the fear still too prevalent. Even though her face and her lips were swollen he understood her desperate need to see to her sister, to make sure she was protected. "At the moment that is where she is staying. I've thought a lot about what to do in this situation and threatened Brinkmeyer, the sorry excuse for a man. With a little help from my solicitor, we will get her back. It will take a little time though."

"He won't' give her up."

He lifted his broad shoulders in a manly shrug. "I'll make him a proposition he can't refuse."

He was determined now to see the sisters safely ensconced at Southcliff Hall in Glasgow. They needed to be out of the man's reach. At the moment he was more concerned about Sophie than Clare. If he guessed right, she would sacrifice herself to save Clare. That wouldn't do at all. Sophie should not have that responsibility heaped on her shoulders.

"I need to see him, talk to him." She was pushing away from the wall, trying to swing her legs over the bed.

"Good God, no! You couldn't even walk the short distance to relieve yourself. How the blessed hell do you think you'll get to Mayfair Hall? I'm not going to help you do something so stupid. It will put you in more danger."

He cringed at the thought of Sophie speaking with the man. He decided then the only way any of this was going to work was if he wed her. His smile didn't stretch very far. Marriage when he arrived in Virginia was not something he anticipated. Thought he'd be a bachelor for at least ten more years. Life was good for him. It was his brother's job to produce an heir. Getting her to agree to marriage with him would not be easy. After what he did to her three nights ago, she must detest him. She thought he had sex with her in the cottage. He'd done nothing to disavow that assumption.

"He won't let me go." Her eyes wide, she was shaking her head. "Now it's a matter of principle to him. He doesn't like to lose."

"The man realizes he met his match. He has no choice if he wants to remain a pillar of Virginia society."

Link studied her then handed her the bowl of soup. It had nothing meaty in it, nothing that needed the use of her jaw. He didn't think she could chew yet. When she looked at it, there was a hint of distaste in her eyes.

"Perhaps tomorrow you can handle something a bit more palatable. The cook assured me it will taste just fine and will go down easily to settle in your stomach."

"You eat it then."

He didn't want to argue with her nor did he mean to laugh. An argument would get them nowhere. "The courts will not want to separate sisters. You will wed me, Sophie. I will gain guardianship of Clare. As I see this conundrum, it is the only way."

She appeared beyond herself, speechless as well. Her brows narrowed in mocking disdain. He knew she wanted to vent her spleen. So, he waited, giving her a chance. She didn't remark.

At her look of horror, he said, repeating his earlier statement. "It is the only way."

"No! You detest me."

Ah, but that wasn't true. He quite enjoyed her. Now, he respected her. They would deal well together. He wasn't going to tell her that. Not yet.

At the sound of the door opening, he motioned Clare into the room. "I sent for you. I'm glad you came in a timely manner. You have come to reason with your sister? She needs you to convince her that my marriage proposal is the one true path to embark upon."

"I don't believe you talked to Clare before me," she said.

He saw the anger and the helplessness. He wanted to see the witty tigress he'd come to know. The one he wanted to be married to until he cocked up his toes.

Beneath the simple fabric of the nightgown, her breasts were heaving. He decided it was a fetching sight. They might just do well together. At least she wouldn't bore him. "I'll leave the two of you to talk then I'll make the arrangements. Did you bring a suitable dress?"

"Of course," Clare grinned.

"I will leave the two of you now to discuss the upcoming nuptials in a sisterly manner."

He left whistling. Before the door closed, he heard her.

"I will not marry you. You detest me."

We will see. It would do no earthly good to provoke her further. In any case the arrangements had already been made. The justice of the peace would be here bright and early in the morning. He'd already purchased a special license. All that was left was to figure out how to get Sophie Carter-Brown soon to be Sophie Stewart, to say yes to the justice of the peace.

In the dining room Edward and his father were finishing their dinner. Link sat down after pouring a liberal glass of wine. He drank it down, poured another then thought he should have brought Sophie a glass of wine. It might have made the soup as well as the news more palatable. The alcohol would have relaxed her. A glass of brandy might have been even better.

"You are a fool," Edward told him a curious look casting his features in shadows. "You know what she is, who she is. You won't be able to trust her. She will betray you with other men."

Grayson cleared his throat. "I believe Link has seen her true colors. He knows even if he won't come right out and admit it, Sophia is not a harlot. She's a kind, innocent young woman who has been sorely wronged."

Link stretched his legs out, his wine glass in hand thinking that perhaps Grayson was correct in his assumption. In any case he would discover the truth soon enough. As soon as she healed, he would bed her. "Don't really know who she is. Suppose time will tell. I like her. This is the only way to rescue both young ladies."

Edward made a noise in the back of his throat. "She's had three lovers, four counting you. Well, I suppose you don't count as of yet. You can't really think she won't cuckold you once you're wed."

"She won't. I will make sure of it. As to the other, she says she's a virgin."

Link was having trouble believing her words. Again, he decided he wouldn't spend time thinking on it because it was very simple, time would tell the true story.

Some of Edwards's wine shot from his mouth. He started

coughing and choking, “You mean she truly had the audacity to tell you that?”

“It’s what she said. I didn’t say I believed it though.”

He was curious. He would be surprised at nothing where Sophie was concerned. What he wanted to believe and what he was willing to concede were far apart.

Chapter Seven

Link didn't think he'd ever been so nervous in his entire life. Good God his hands were sweating. The justice of the peace silently sat in the drawing room sipping coffee. Edward was pacing and Grayson looked as if he was the proudest papa in the world. The man was going to give the bride away this morning if Clare and Sophie appeared.

He trusted Clare to convince her older sister this was the right and only course they could take. Clare had been in the bedroom with her sister for well over an hour. She promised to let him know as soon as Sophie agreed. He stared at the clock. He felt his insides churn. Was heartily glad he had not eaten more than a scone this morning.

When he fetched Clare this morning, she had a cream gown with her. He'd instructed her to find something suitable. Something she would not be popping out of or make her look the harlot. Clare nodded her head at the request, telling him she knew the perfect dress.

Footsteps on the stairway caused him to turn. Clare was walking down them a hesitant smile on her face. Link felt pleased suddenly.

"She will say yes?" He felt his heart stop for a tense moment while he watched and waited.

Clare smiled more brightly, her hands clasped prayer fashion beneath her chin. "I believe so. She is dressed. If Mr. Grayson wants to go upstairs and bring her down, I believe she will come with him."

"You didn't have any trouble?"

Link didn't know why he asked something like that. It had taken the better part of two hours before Clare appeared. He knew for a fact it would not have taken that long for her to bathe and dress.

"I wouldn't say that," Clare laughed her eyes twinkling with mischief. "She says she is doing this under protest. That it will be a marriage of convenience only. Perhaps you should have talked to her more thoroughly about that. This convenience thing."

"Brat!" He laughed enjoying Clare almost as much as his own little sister. "What do you know about marriages of convenience?"

He was thinking that it was most likely more than a thirteen-year-old should know. When he thought of Merry, well hell, she knew more than she should have known at that age because she eavesdropped. Clare didn't have two big brothers.

"I would never reveal my source. You might cut it off. Are you really going to be my guardian?" She grinned at him before she led Grayson up the stairs.

"It's my fondest wish."

Sophie would have a quick wedding, something most little girls probably didn't dream of. He wondered if Sophie ever dreamed of such things, weddings and grooms. In the last year she must have given up on any dreams she might have had. He felt disgust with himself as well as his thoughts, knowing he wanted to bed her. She intrigued and fascinated him from the first time he saw her. In that instant he knew he wanted her for his wife. If not, he would have found some other way to thwart her uncle.

Blessed hell he wanted her. His body hardened when he saw her on the white fur, completely naked. No, this was not ever going to be a marriage of convenience. Sophie could hope for such a thing. It wasn't going to happen.

Grayson and Clare walked upstairs to retrieve the bride. He walked with the Justice of the Peace, Mr. Fink, to stand beside the fireplace. It was a nice enough place to say one's vows. He wondered if Merry would have protested this wedding and thought about his brother's wedding, both of them. There had been nothing fancy either time. Leslie's wife Lacie had not cared. Would Sophie care about the simplicity?

He knew then that he would send Sophie and Clare home ahead of him while he finished up business here. The thought of Uncle William finding either one of the girls alone, especially Sophie, sent a cold shiver down his spine. Despite his threat to the evil man, he feared for Sophie. Uncle William must have been very nearly mad to have beaten her within an inch of her life.

Link ran his hands through his hair, discharging a long slow breath of air as he watched the stairs. His future wife was about to descend. She would come to love him.

What the devil was taking them so long?

If she changed her mind, he'd throttle her. He'd take her without the benefit of marriage until she carried his child. No, he wasn't going to humble her that way. She'd been through enough. Until or if she showed her true colors, he meant to respect her as his wife should be respected.

First, he saw the tips of her ivory shoes then the lace around the hem of her gown. Clare stood next to her in an ice blue muslin gown befitting a thirteen-year-old. By the time he could see all of Sophie and Clare, he also saw the bouquet of flowers Clare must have picked for both of them. There were only a few, daffodils he believed.

At the bottom of the steps Edward joined her. They walked the remaining distance together before taking their places opposite each other.

He saw Sophie. Her hair was piled high on top of her head, a few auburn curls framing her face. Clare was correct in her choice. The dress was perfect. While it was cut low, it wasn't too low. The modest corsage trimmed with Belgium lace was perfect. He realized he was staring at her like a besotted fool while trying to memorize everything about this day, his wedding day. He wasn't in love, but he wanted her. Lust was a powerful force.

Sophie wasn't smiling though she was staring at him. Her lips parted slightly. Her eyes slightly dilated. Still in obvious pain, she was walking very slowly in an attempt not to jar her bruised and broken ribs. He wished he had a choice and could have waited a day or two.

It was impossible to predict how Brinkmeyer might handle this deflection of hers. Link understood he couldn't take any chances. While Sophie would be in his bed tonight, he realized he would have to put off the consummation of the marriage until she was feeling better. He was not going to become a rutting stoat just because he would have a wife.

A wife he wanted very much.

When he stepped beside her and took her hands in his, she was trembling while staring at the ground. "Look at me," he prompted.

Her eyes opened wide, long dark lashes framing them. Her teeth clutched her bottom lip. "This will all work out for the best. You'll see. There is nothing left for you here, at least not right now."

She didn't look as if she believed him. He found she was holding her breath. Afraid she might faint before she could say 'I do' he said, "Breathe deeply, sweetheart."

He watched her inhale a long drink of air then wince at the movement it caused. Under his breath he cursed Brinkmeyer. Mr. Fink shortened the ceremony at his order to do just what was absolutely necessary. It was over before it barely started. He was wed now.

A married man.

It would surprise his brother and sister. After all, he swore he would be in his thirties before he would even consider marriage. Bachelor life was just too much fun to give up.

Holding Sophie by the arm to steady her, he led her to the sofa. She sat down, a grateful half-smile on her slightly parted lips. One of the servants brought in a tray laden with champagne.

When everyone held a glass, he raised his. "To Sophie Stewart, mine, my wife now."

He felt a surge of pleasure sweep through him and marveled at that. Everyone drank. It was delicious. Even Clare was allowed one glass.

He wondered what Sophie would be expecting tonight. They had not spoken since the night before when he proposed this event. She appeared nervous as hell. This would be different for her. No one was drugged. He thought of her breasts, the way they felt cupped in his hands. Recalled the feel of her parted lips as well the taste and scent of her. She would come to him smelling of roses. Well, not tonight.

Sitting beside her, he could stare at the sweet curve of her breasts, see the way they rose and fell with each miniscule breath. She was barely breathing. Her pain must still be intense.

Link leaned close to her, inhaling the sweet scent of roses. “Don’t worry about tonight.”

She jumped slightly startled by his voice. “I,” he watched her swallow, “I was not worried about it.”

“Little liar,” he whispered close to her ear, saw the tiny shiver of what he knew to be passion. “As soon as you are well though...”

Her head jerked toward him, a fire simmering in her eyes. “It is to be convenience only.”

“Sorry, but there is where you are wrong. I’m not going to spend the rest of my life celibate. I do think, however, this conversation is better left to the privacy of our room later tonight.”

Turning her head, she drank deep of the champagne, “You are right of course.”

He rose then, bringing her another glass. A tray of breads and meat as well as cheeses was brought in. The food was good and plentiful. She still had trouble chewing though. He heard her stomach rumble.

“Do not drink too much of this bubbly stuff. Seems you have an empty stomach.”

“Already married only a few minutes and you are telling me what I can and cannot do.”

There was no anger in her voice. It seemed she was resigned to a husband along with his manly rights.

“You would not like to wake up to a pounding head, coupled with your bruised ribs and flogged back. Although a little will surely ease some of the pain you must be feeling.” He toasted her with his glass and a wry grin. “To your bedding, my dear wife. I will discover the truth about your numerous trysts.”

“No. I would also not like to wake up with you beside me.”

“You will come to beg for my presence beside you. I will give you so much pleasure you will never want to leave my bed.”

He wanted to chuckle when her back stiffened and her chin tilted regally upward but held it behind his teeth when he watched her grimace. Her look was sour now. Well, what did he expect? She was no blushing bride, understanding everything that went on behind closed doors.

Edward stood in front of him. Link rose, extending his hand. "I just wanted to congratulate the two of you on your nuptials. I hope you get everything you want from this." His words sounded heartfelt and sincere.

"Thank you. I'm sure we both will," Link said watching Edward leave followed by Grayson who also shook his hand but furthermore slanted him a bemused smile.

It seemed as if the man was telling him she was the sweet innocent virgin she claimed to be.

Even if Sophie was still a virgin there was little of her that was sweet or innocent. She could banter with him about sexual things better than any man. Hell, she might be sweet if she wasn't forced to give herself to men. Jaded might be a better term to use to describe his possibly virgin wife. He did laugh then. It was soft laughter, not loud and boisterous. The sound did catch Sophie's attention as well as Clare's.

"Clare is going to stay the night. I did promise, however, to have her home at Mayfair Hall by noon tomorrow. There is no other recourse until I can legally gain her guardianship. That should happen in a few days."

Also, he didn't understand why Brinkmeyer was being so nice. The man didn't have to allow Clare to come here at all. What did William have on his mind?

Well, he couldn't fathom it. He would have to wait and see while trying to stay one step ahead of the man.

"Thank you," she told him, as she looked at him a slight blush on her swollen face.

"She will be staying in your room." He watched for her reaction and what she might say or expect. Her expression remained the same.

"Will you have a daybed brought in?"

"No."

"Oh, well," she paused, her lips pursing slightly, "I suppose we can both sleep in the same bed. It isn't that large but neither are we."

"No," he said again amusement playing at the corners of his mouth while his shoulders were shaking in silent laughter. "I did just tell you this was not a marriage of convenience or did I not? In any case you will sleep with me in our bed tonight and just about every night there after until I stick my spoon in the wall. Clare will take the bed in your old room. She will sleep by herself."

If she could turn scarlet beneath the yellow and blue bruising, it seemed she did just that. She turned away. He understood her desperate need to refute what he told her. In any case he would not change his mind or allow her to dictate. She would obey his wishes.

"But tonight?" she queried, her voice shaking.

It was either a damn good act or she was afraid of him, of the night and what would happen between them. He flashed her a smile, an all-knowing grin, one he hoped would help her understand he would not be controlled or managed. Actually, he thought she already learned that lesson.

Apparently not, this would have to stand as reinforcement.

"This is our wedding night. I'm asking less than any groom. You, my sweet, will share my bed tonight. Nothing more."

"Ha!"

"Ha? What does that mean? You don't believe me. I've never lied to you, Sophie. I won't begin now. You are hurt. I would be a cad, a bastard to claim my husbandly rights this evening."

"You've deceived me. Played word games. I'm no match for you as I don't have any experience, but..."

A raw deep laugh rumbled from his chest, surprising him, "You expect me to believe that? To simper and cower to the fact you've had three lovers before me and you are a virgin. Sophie, heed me in this. I'm not stupid."

"No, no you are not stupid. Perhaps an idiot though."

He was finding all his good intentions were being overridden and slipping away by the anger she was creating by her words. "Well, if you keep this up you might find yourself beneath me tonight despite your injuries. I'm attempting to act the gentleman. Don't try my patience. I only have so much. What I have is quickly slipping away." He let out a long slow and very calculated breath of air, one meant to calm the nerves she so easily provoked. He didn't understand how she did it.

She looked away then back to him. "As you wish, husband."

His grin widened. He was amused at her emphasis on the word husband. She was a fighter. "Husband, that is what I am now to you. I find I like that sound. You will obey me as you promised not very long ago. Do you recall or was your memory damaged by the flogging?"

"I'd like to try some of the cheese and perhaps ham. The bread also looks delicious."

She sounded resigned to her circumstances. She needed to eat.

With Sophie one rarely knew. Her change of subject was nothing short of expedient.

He didn't expect this to continue. "Have some more champagne. It will make me more palatable to you."

"I believe I will. Then I wish to sit on the veranda. It's too soon to retire for the night. What time is it?"

It was only a few minutes past two o'clock in the afternoon. "If you were not so under the weather, this would have been a perfect day for a ride, Sophie. Would you have gone to your cave with me? We could make love there, in the dark. It would be private."

He saw her stiffen.

"You must be remembering the whipping and where you tried to escape. I'm sorry, Sophie. Shall we talk about Clare? She is a lovely girl, sweet and so very innocent. One could hope she does not inherit the habits of her older sister." He saw her mouth start to open. He held up his hands to stop her from speaking. "Keep your words behind your teeth. Clare will not be in danger much longer. I don't believe even Brinkmeyer would dare lay a hand on her. She does have my protection even though I'm not officially her guardian."

"You overestimate the scope of your power here in Virginia. This is not Glasgow or your Bordeaux. You have little influence over William Brinkmeyer, a man who does what he pleases."

"Men are men wherever they live. I know men and I know women as well. In any case my solicitor is drawing up the documents to make

Clare my ward. Both Edward and Grayson have given testimony as to what your uncle has done to you and since Clare is your sister, it will go well for me, for us. She will become my responsibility."

"I should be her guardian." Sophie's back stiffened, her chin tilted in an upward slant.

"You are a woman and thus incapable of being the guardian of a young lady. In addition, you are known as a woman of lose moral scruples. No judge in his right mind would name you the guardian of a young, innocent girl of the tender age of thirteen."

He saw her distress, watched as her shoulders slumped just slightly as if deflated. He could tell she wanted to argue with him. Searched for the words that would change his mind.

There were none.

She appeared defeated.

He didn't like it. No, he didn't like it at all.

"So, you will take her from me. That is not well done of you." She no longer sounded angry just dispirited, resigned as well. "I'd like to sit on the veranda now and have another glass or two or even three of champagne. This other food is too hard to chew. Perhaps if I soaked the bread in this bubbly, it would go down without sticking in my throat."

Gallantly he rose, offered his arm and motioned for the servants awaiting an order to do her bidding. "As much champagne as you can carry and bread lots of bread. Some cheese perhaps, that might be soft enough for your pour jaw."

He touched her there, traced the line then down her neck to her pulse, which leapt at the gentle caress. She was soft and smelled sweet. He wished he could take her to bed tonight.

He walked with her to the veranda then offered the most comfortable chair to her. She didn't smile, but she acknowledged once more appearing accepting to whatever was going to happen.

"When will all this go away? When can I relax and let my guard down?" She drank deeply, setting the glass down as she seemed to search his face for an answer.

"In two to three days. Then, Sophie, I will put the two of you on a ship to Glasgow. Give you a letter to Leslie, the duke, my brother, which you will present to him. He will not believe I have wed. So, no matter what, you cannot lose the letter or no one will believe you to be my wife. Why, if you don't have the message on your person, the duke might kick you out on the street."

"You are such a rake then? Women show up on your brother's doorstep claiming to be your wife. Does it happen often?"

"Bite your tongue, Sophie. No, I've always been up front and forthright about my dalliances. I've never kept a mistress, but I've had numerous lovers. I'm a very good lover. You will enjoy your woman's pleasure when I bed you. I want you to think on that."

~ * ~

That was that she thought.

Clare was to spend the night. She disappeared though. Perhaps Edward took her for a ride. Clare loved to ride. Edward seemed to enjoy being with her in a brotherly sort of way. Perhaps a bit like the way they used to be before her heart had been ripped apart then torn to shreds.

"Do you have horses at your home in Glasgow?" She no longer had any idea what to say to this man who was now her husband, this man who was going to sleep next to her every night until he stuck his spoon in the wall, or so he told her. She was afraid yet she didn't want to tell him. Didn't want to make herself any more vulnerable than she already felt. She wanted to know everything about both his homes.

"I don't have a home in Scotland as yet. It is something I intend to take care of as soon as I join you and your sister. We will have horses. I've two in Bordeaux I'll send for. I will take you there sometime so you can meet mother. A horrific thought if I do say so myself. Do you speak French?" He was watching her over the edge of his champagne glass, judging her she assumed.

"My home then, until you arrive will be with your brother and his wife? I do speak some French. Enough to get by." she said, trying to figure out what was going to happen to her, what exactly he intended. What did a man who didn't want a wife do with one? "I'm having trouble just thinking about tomorrow and the next day. I don't want to leave here. Clare doesn't really remember any other home while I have visions of the cottage we once lived in."

"In this you have no choice. Southcliff, yes, my sister lives there also. You will enjoy her candor. Also of course, Lacie, my brother's wife. The two of you are close to the same age although Lacie is a little older. The duke and duchess will make sure you are comfortable."

"They will not believe you married." Her voice held no emotion. She didn't want to show him the fear encompassing her. "What will happen to me if they don't accept me into their home. I will be penniless and on the street. What would I do?"

"No, they will not believe the fact but they won't turn you away. I'm sure of it. They would wait to find out the truth until I arrived home. Even if Leslie didn't believe the fact, Lacie is a tender heart. She would not approve of turning you out. Leslie would do anything for his wife. You should know I have other children. As soon as we find our new home, I will search out another place close by for the children to live."

"Children?" Sophie downed the rest of her glass, stiffly holding it out for more. She was stunned by the disclosure. He never mentioned children before. If he did, she didn't recall. But then why would he? Until today she was nothing to him. She was more curious than ever about him, realizing she knew very little. "You've had another wife? What happened to her?"

He smiled setting his glass on the table before stretching his long, muscled legs out in front of him. "I've had no wife. You are my first and only one. There will be no more because you will live a very long time. I will make sure of that."

"Then? They are all illegitimate." She felt confused and irritated with him. Meant to ask the pertinent questions. Perhaps anger was the emotion she felt. An urge to toss the champagne at him assailed her. He wasn't forthcoming and by the looks of it, didn't intend to be. "It's alright for you, a man to have children out of wedlock but it is wrong for me, a woman, to have lovers. That is not right."

His eyes were hooded. He didn't answer her for several seconds. Then he said, "Yes and no."

Quickly she stood, immediately regretting it as she moaned before sinking down into the cushioned chair. She let her head hang down for a few seconds, trying to ignore the pain swamping her. She should know better than to move too fast. When she finally felt in control of herself, she looked at him again.

"I'd like to rest now."

"Perhaps that would be a good idea. Go on to the master chamber. I'll be up in five minutes. I want to check your ribs as well as your back."

She sipped in a quick breath of air, holding it while she thought on his intentions. "I'm fine," she told him.

"I need to see for myself." His words were curt. "Your mine now, Sophie. I take care of what is mine."

She understood there were no words that would change his mind. Obey. It was not something she intended with her new husband. She was sorely afraid he would not let her do anything less.

"Very well."

He would have to drag her from her old room if he wanted her in the master chamber, something she was sure he was loathe to do given her condition. She would only go fighting and screaming.

He helped her stand which was a good thing. She didn't think she could have done so on her own. Mayhap it was not such a wise idea to defy him in this endeavor.

In the end she didn't have a choice. It seemed she taxed all her strength for the day. When he discovered she could barely walk, he hefted her into his arms then carried her to the master chamber before setting her on the bed.

"You meant to defy me, didn't you? You had no intention of returning to this room."

She looked at him, not wanting to answer. In any case he knew her thoughts.

He stepped back, his muscular legs braced apart, arms crossed over his chest. "I trust you can take your gown off without help."

She cursed her ribs, wishing she could run past him to her room then bolt the door closed. She couldn't even walk up the stairs. A curious detachment as well as acknowledgment of her fate with this man filled her.

She spoke slowly, understanding where this man was concerned she had no choice. He wouldn't hurt her though. He would just persevere until he got his way. "I believe I can."

"Good. I'll be back in five minutes." Giving her the privacy she wanted but didn't expect, he turned on one of his perfectly shined boot heels and left her alone in the spacious chamber.

For a few seconds she did nothing except inhale and exhale. From the exertions of the day her body was exhausted, strained until she didn't think she could move even her fingers. She had done nothing except drink champagne and eat a few appetizers.

Were there two or three days left before he sent her away so he could finish business? She couldn't remember. What was that business he needed to complete? It must have something to do with Uncle William and her role. She didn't know what her uncle wanted from him. She wished she could tell him so he'd be forewarned.

His pacing outside the door reminded her she had little time to remove the gown. She would be his to inspect. The shiver was unexpected. She had to remind herself he'd seen her with nothing on. So, why was he being solicitous now that he was her husband? He could watch as she removed the layers of fabric hiding her. Despite what he thought, he was the only man who'd seen her naked, except for her father when she was a child.

She tried to unfasten the gown. The task was beyond her. There were at least twenty tiny buttons down the back of her dress. Clare fastened them when she dressed. This frailty, this inability to do for herself was beyond anything she endured before. Hopeless and resigned, she looked at the door, waiting for him to enter.

Clare poked her head into the room. "I'm back. Link told me you would need help and were too stubborn to ask him to unfasten your gown. Sophie, I know I'm only thirteen. He is your husband now. You should not be so determined to have things your way. Link only wants the best for you."

The slow glide of tears traveled down her cheeks. She gulped in air trying to stop the sob. "I know." She plucked at the fabric of her gown, staring at the color, then looking at the Belgian lace around the bottom.

"You had to marry him." Clare sounded so matter of fact Sophie gasped as she looked at her little sister. "You had no choice. If you want to know, I think you did the right thing. He will protect you from Uncle William. There have been marriages made for less."

"There was no other way." Sophie didn't want Clare to be brought into this anymore than necessary. She needed to know the truth though.

"He's a very nice man. You might have been stuck with that arrogant Devon Masters or the old curmudgeon, Charles Ewing. Well, no not him. He has a wife. Perhaps even Oliver Sheffield." She continued unfastening each button. "You are truly lucky, Sophie. You should act better."

Sophie could not keep her mouth from dropping open. Her heart leapt into a tailspin. "How...?"

Clare lifted her slim shoulders, tilting her head slightly. "I don't live my life secluded. I've been to town, heard the whispers behind hands. People talk about me, too, wonder if I'm going to grow up like you, a harlot. I know you're not loose with your favors. If you were, you would undoubtedly have a child on the way by now. Mother and father didn't bring you up with loose morals. I don't remember a lot about them but what I do remember is all the love they gave us along with the knowledge to be good and true."

She pushed the tears from her eyes with the backs of her hands, knowing she needed to be strong for her sister. This was horrible. They had no right. Uncle William had no right. Perhaps that was why he insisted on taking Clare shopping so often. He wanted her to hear all the gossip. He wanted her to know what was in store for her when she was older.

"I'm not a harlot," she said, stifling the pain in her gut. "I know it looks that way, but I'm not what the townspeople think."

"If you were, Link would not have wed you." The girl's voice was so matter of fact, so sure of herself, it startled Sophie. "He's a man who knows what he wants. He knows women too. Don't ask me how I know but I do. I feel it deep in my gut. He is so kind, a sweet man although I believe he can be ruthless when called upon to do so."

Clare's innocent statement made her think, gave her pause to reconsider the man. "You don't think he would have wed me if he truly thought I was a harlot?"

"He's not the kind of man to bind himself to someone he thinks will be unfaithful to him. He has no reason to wed a woman he believes to be a whore. Nobility do not do things like that."

Her sister's statement was beyond what she expected. It gave her hope. "How do you know so much about men? You're only thirteen."

"I like watching people and I listen in when no one is expecting it. Since I'm only thirteen, they speak their mind. Now we need to finish with the buttons. I don't think he means to do anything tonight except check you out."

Check me out? That from a thirteen-year-old.

"I do want to check Sophie out." Link stepped into the room, his amusement clearly written in the lines of his face. "I see you don't have the gown unfastened. Run along, Clare. I will take care of my wife. She will see you in the morning if she wakes soon enough."

Well, he was here. He would do what he wanted. "See you in the morning." Clare was beside her giving her a gentle hug then a kiss to her cheek.

"I love you," Sophie whispered.

She looked at her husband of only a few hours, his expression grim.

"You and Clare are going to be fine," he reminded her again. "Trust me."

She didn't know how many times she needed to hear those words. It seemed he repeated them often enough. Still, she didn't entirely believe him. Uncle William held so much power. She was afraid for Link.

Her hands were folded in her lap, clasped tightly together. She studied them intently, looking at the way she clenched them. "Thank you. I'm afraid."

"I know you are. That is because you haven't as yet learned to believe in me and my instincts. My power far exceeds your uncles. Clare will probably be gone when you wake up in the morning. I'm taking her to the ship then I will come back for you. She will be safe there. Edward will go with us and stay with her until we can arrive. The ship will leave the next day. Sooner than I expected. All that is for the best."

She found herself nodding at him, listening to his words. Still, she had this sick gut feeling something would go wrong. Uncle William would do something to stop all this from happening. She couldn't erase the feeling.

He was sitting on the bed beside her now, his fingers making quick work of the buttons as well as the laces to her corset. The gown, her wedding gown was now pooled around her waist. She wore only her chemise. He touched her ribs, the broken ones first. He seemed to measure the pain by the depth of each gasp.

"They are mending nicely."

Then, his lips touched upon her shoulder, lightly. He placed tiny kisses along her neck then higher to her ear. Her body shuddered, even though she willed it not to respond.

"You like this, Sophie. Be honest. You should not hold back your feelings for me any longer. There is no reason for you to hide from me."

She nodded, thinking it was causing hot sensations deep down inside her as well as an ache between her legs she'd only felt when he kissed her. Her head fell back against his shoulder. She tried to suck in a dutiful amount of air.

"I'm not going to hurt you. It would hurt if I made love to you tonight. You are going to sleep by me while I hold you in my arms. That's all. I want you to feel safe and secure. No more fears, promise me."

He was telling her this, she knew so she wouldn't try to refuse him. Suddenly, he was no longer sitting beside her. He was at the door, looking at her, a brilliant smile etching his handsome features.

"I trust you can put on your nightdress by yourself."

She nodded, wishing he was touching her again. Wishing he would kiss her as he did only a few nights ago. Too stunned to say anything, she watched him back from the door. Her feelings confused and angered her. She didn't want to feel anything for this man. She did.

"I will be up later with some food for you. Perhaps a bit more soup, you really need to fill your belly."

With that he was gone.

Finally, she rose from the bed and walked to her armoire. She found a nightgown, one that covered her from the tips of her toes to just below her chin. She wandered onto the porch outside his room, wrapping a quilt around her. The view from his room was spectacular, looking out on the river. It was nice. Perhaps later, after everything was resolved they could visit the plantation. The sun would set soon as the sky was beginning to darken a bit. She was sure the snow was over for the year. She didn't understand why she thought that.

Perhaps it was because she was leaving.

She was going to Scotland.

It was what she wanted.

At least an hour later, she heard the door open then softly close. Heard the tread of his boots as he walked through the bedroom. He opened the double doors to the porch. She turned to look at him. His white shirt was unbuttoned. She could see his chest, the dark hair running across. He was grinning at her as if he knew a secret.

"As promised, I brought something to eat and drink." He paused for a few seconds. "It's damn cold out here."

"Invigorating," she told him unable to keep a smile from her lips, "There is an extra quilt on the bed," she spoke softly refusing to get into a verbal sparring match with her new husband. Peace was what she needed now and rest. Soon she wouldn't have to do Uncle William's bidding, nor at least for a few weeks or maybe a month would she be Link's to command. She would be free to do as she pleased. There would be an ocean between them.

A tangible weight lifted from her shoulders. She let out a long slow cleansing breath of air.

"Thought you might want to share yours." He set the tray down, fumbling with the glasses and plates.

The food was obviously leftovers from the wedding. She could chew the cheese and the bread. It would certainly be nice when she was more normal.

"No, you should get your own blanket."

He did after handing her a plate of delicacies she could eat. "I would like to share warmth with my wife. Suppose that will have to wait until we retire for the night."

He flashed her a grin that nearly melted her heart. Where Link was concerned, she vacillated with emotions. She wanted to know what it would be like to have him hold her and make love to her then she didn't. She was a seething bundle of different thoughts.

She wanted to be immune to him, to his devilish may care attitude, to the charm that seemed to exude from every pore of his manly body. She didn't know how to reply to him. Didn't know how to keep her woman's body from responding to his smile and soft caresses with his eyes. She tugged in a shaky breath.

He poured her a glass of wine, a fine red Bordeaux she assumed from his vineyard.

"Is there a reason why we are not going to France?" she asked speculatively eyeing the wine and him. "That is your home."

He shrugged then, gazing out at the river. "I want to make my home in Scotland. My brother and sister live there now. Wine country, the vineyards hold no interest to me. They are all managed quite well by families who have lived there hundreds of years. I couldn't possibly do better." He stopped speaking for a few seconds. "My mother lives there and she is truly very independent. She can be very threatening to any female she doesn't know or like. You, my dear, will be much better off with Lacie as a companion."

"I never thought of you having a mother," she laughed softly then smiled at him when he turned to face her a look of wry amusement on his well-chiseled face.

He arched one perfectly shaped, dark eyebrow, "We all have to have one at some time."

"Of course, you're right. I don't suppose you want to tell me about her." She sipped the wine, still feeling more at ease with liquid nourishment rather than real food even though she admitted there was nothing nourishing about the alcohol. The drink slipped down her throat with an ease she might regret come morning.

"No, but I'll tell you about my brother and sister. Leslie is the typical duke, stoic and reserved. It always made me laugh when he and some of his friends dubbed themselves the bad boys. He never did anything that could remotely be considered bad until he met his wife." He paused for a moment appearing thoughtful. "He was a spy, you know."

"Really?" she asked clearly amused at Link's description of the older brother. "Aren't spies bad boys?"

"Don't know about that and yes, really. His now wife was only fifteen at the time. He was so enamored of her he chased her down three flights of stairs into the MacTavish stables so he could steel a kiss. Indeed, the lecherous old man compared to the innocent maid wanted to steal more than just a kiss, but all the ducal training in him kept him from tossing her skirts right there to claim her as his own. Her brother and another bad boy would have had to call him out, demand seconds. He was forced to wait three years for her." Slowly he sipped the wine, watching her as if he was trying to see inside her soul. "As to his spying, he's given that part of his life up. Don't know what exactly he did for the government all those years. Suppose it was to keep boredom from setting in."

"And Merry?" She did want to learn about his siblings as she was to live with them.

He laughed, the sound a soft chuckle as if he thought about his little sister with love. "Merry can be an incorrigible little twit. She's decided on her husband." He leaned forward, placing a piece of cheese between her lips, desire shining in his clear blue eyes. "However, she doesn't know the man's name. She saw him once in Paris and then again in Glasgow. I do wish her luck with the endeavor. Suppose she will need all the luck she can get."

Sophie lowered her eyes, thinking about that turn of events. Once she thought she would wed Edward. When she was thirteen, she fell in love with the man. Thought he was everything a man should be; kind and gentle, handsome as well as debonair. When Uncle William started using her, all those starry-eyed romantic notions left her. Edward turned away from her with scorn in his eyes. He believed every unkind word said about her. He didn't deserve her love.

"Did you ever fancy yourself in love, Sophie?" Again, he assumed his negligent pose. "I would have to call the man out if you still feel that way."

She started at his question not wanting, in any case, to answer. "It's getting cold. Perhaps it's time to go inside."

"Ah, so you were in love with someone." He waited for her to answer. "Care to enlighten me?"

She wasn't going to say anything. Instead, she rose and walked into the room. Perhaps she didn't want to go to bed so soon. When he stayed outside, his gaze remaining on the river, she let her body relax. While she knew he would join her soon, the more time she could gain by herself perhaps she would fall asleep.

He told her this wasn't going to be their wedding night. He wouldn't come inside her and see if she was still a maid. She let the quilt slip to the floor knowing she should fold it neatly. Somehow, she just didn't have the energy.

In the bed she turned away from the empty spot where Link would lie down, clutching the pillow tightly to her chest. She waited. Seconds turned to minutes that changed to hours, at least it seemed that way. The room grew dark. She heard the river in the distance. The balcony doors must still be open. She waited and dozed. Still, he didn't come to bed.

Sophie heard the boot hit the floor. It was her first indication he was going to join her. Her heart fluttered even while she held her breath. The sound of him shrugging out of his shirt then his pants, came to her.

The bed dipped slightly. She wondered if he wore a nightshirt, wondered too if he would hold her. His large hands circled her waist, tugged her against him. His arousal was hard, pulsing against her buttocks. She shouldn't know about such things. She should be innocent.

She wasn't. It would do her no good to pretend.

He kissed the back of her neck. His lips touched softly then again, seemed to caress her neck while one of his hands rested on her belly. She wanted to yell at him. Yell that he told her he wouldn't make love to her tonight.

His hand roamed up her torso, cupped her breast then slid back to her belly. She didn't know what to think or do. Her body seemed to quiver with his onslaught. Nothing like this had ever happened to her before. Of course, not you ninny, all your lovers were drugged and Cocoa came to them.

This was wicked, the strange ache between her legs.

"Link."

"Yes." His long fingers were on the fasteners of her nightdress.

She felt the fabric float away as he tugged the gown down her arms. His chest was pressed against her back.

"Lift your hips."

Mindlessly she did his bidding not understanding why she didn't refuse. A second later she heard the soft thump as the fabric hit the floor beside the bed. There was nothing between them except air. Her breath shuddered through her body, her breasts swelling, the tips growing hard. Her eyes were closed tight as if that gesture would make those wonderful strange sensations disappear.

One hand closed around her breast. She gasped. The ragged breath of air was not nearly enough to fill her lungs. His palm rubbed across her nipple.

"I thought you weren't going to have sex with me tonight." Her thin wail of words was barely discernible.

He laughed softly, his whisper fluttered across her ear, his tongue lightly touched her earlobe. "True, I said I wouldn't hurt you, wouldn't make love tonight."

"Then, then, what are you doing?"

~ * ~

At this point Link wasn't at all sure what he was trying to accomplish. He simply could not resist her siren's call. If he was going to sleep next to her, well, he thought he might as well torture himself. It didn't really matter. He was hard and in need just thinking about her lying next to him. Whatever else he did would make little difference in the scope of things.

"Thought I would give you a woman's pleasure," he murmured, his thumb and forefinger massaging her hard pink nipple. "Feels like velvet and looks like pink. Do you think you will taste that way, velvet and pink?"

He felt the quivering of her body next to him and was pleased. She was responsive. Even though she pretended to be disinterested, her body was anything but.

How far did he mean to take this?

"Would you like a woman's pleasure?" He lowered his hand to her belly, very close to her woman's mound. The need to turn her over and kiss her was powerful.

She pushed at his hand, a feeble attempt to rid her body of him. "There is no such thing." The words were followed by a tiny mewling sound. The noise told him she had no idea.

In the darkness of the night he grinned, knowing she couldn't see his amusement at her false words. He should have left a candle burning. It was going to be weeks before he could actually look at her, thrust into her parted thighs.

"Ah, you will find out differently. Have none of your lovers seen to your pleasure? The ecstasy is quite delightful. After you experience the rapture, you'll beg me every night."

For some reason her gasp surprised him. It shouldn't have. He'd already determined she was most likely a virgin. Problem was that wouldn't account for other experiences.

"I don't want..."

He nipped lightly across her shoulders, one hand covering her mound, caressing her petal soft folds. She twisted, arching and moving with his rhythm. He found she was hot and slick with her wetness. She squirmed, seemingly not all that sure of what he was about. Ah, but he still had work to do before he could hear her scream with pleasure.

"You will like this. Your pleasure. You will also know that I received none. That I was left in need wanting to feel you surrounding me. Perhaps I should find Cocoa. Would that please you if I used Cocoa to ease my manly needs to give me pleasure?"

"Go away, Link."

He couldn't help himself. He turned her, felt her full, ripe breasts flush against his chest and grinned. His mouth covered hers, his tongue slowly sweeping across the lush bottom one. "Open for me, my tigress. I want to taste you. I suppose you taste of sweet red wine and you, velvet and pink."

Only a besotted fool would think someone tasted like pink or velvet. He was shaking his head while his hands and lips explored her more thoroughly.

Her hands pressed against his chest, her fingers digging into his skin. When his lips pressed on hers, she opened for him. He delved into her dark sultry mouth, the warmth and sweetness overwhelming, kissing her again and again. Holding her close his hands swept down her long back before finding the rounded curves of her buttocks. He squeezed then pulled her closer. She was pressed against his arousal. Lord, but he did want to bury himself inside her. Not tonight, he reminded himself with another groan.

No, he was not a besotted fool. He would maximize this pleasure he wanted to give Sophie. He would control his manly parts.

He would give her pleasure then he would leave her to sleep and dream of him. He wanted her to dream of this night until they could have a real wedding night. His groan of rampant desire rumbled up from his chest.

Moving lower, he captured her hard pink bud between his teeth, laving it with his tongue while his hands continued to find soft, satin flesh to stroke and fondle. To bring her closer and closer to that pinnacle where she let go completely. Her fingers wound into his hair pulling him closer, seeming to beg him for more. He sucked on her breast dragging it deeper inside his mouth. She arched her hips, squirming closer, a soft cry reverberating. He felt the ripples of her body as she softened for him.

She was pliant and accepting. He thought of all the different ways he could pleasure her without hurting her back and her ribcage. Still, her ribs were not healed. He needed to finish this not-so-subtle coaxing.

"Part your legs for me, Sophie. You won't regret it. I promise you." He slipped his knee between her legs, making room for his questing fingers.

She was shaking her head in denial even while she was doing as he asked, letting him lift her legs farther apart. He pressed kisses on her soft belly then lower to the insides of her thighs. She was open for him. His eyes focused on the sweet flesh that now wept for him. Just for him. No one else.

"Don't be alarmed. I'm going to give you your pleasure now."

He found the silken knot that would give her the delight she would soon never want to do without. Soon she would beg him to do this. During the trip across the ocean, she would have time to think about what he was doing to her woman's body and what he would do again and again.

Touching her feminine softness, she cried out. "Link!"

Lazily, he smiled knowing he had her just where he wanted her. She would learn about sex today. Later she would learn about making love. He slipped his finger inside, stretching her slightly. God, she was small and so tight he nearly exploded. Her fingers dug into his shoulder. He pressed farther, slowly moved within her. She squirmed and twisted against him, begging for more. She was his.

There was nothing to do about that. Yet he was pleased. She was passionate, her body responding.

With his thumb he massaged the small nub he knew would bring her to her climax. She was moving then, desperate in her need for him to end this. He wanted to push her to the brink, pull back then start it all over again. Make this pleasure build and build until she could stand it no longer.

Suddenly her body convulsed around his finger, her body arching and shuddering, "Link!"

"It's all good, Sophie. Just let it all come." He didn't have to speak the words. She was writhing, moving convulsively to the rhythm he set. He continued until he finally felt the calming of her body.

He rose above her, pushing her hair to the side. A soft sheen of perspiration covered her flushed skin. The grin spreading across his face could not be stopped. He was pleased with himself and her. She was passionate and responsive. Despite everything she'd had no real lovers before him. While she might not be entirely innocent there was no doubt, she had never felt a woman's pleasure. She was his now.

"You are mine, Sophie. Don't ever deny it."

The insistent wrapping on the door woke him.

Chapter Eight

The trip across the Atlantic seemed to take an eternity even though the winds were good. They were plagued by only one storm, which sent them a bit off course according to the captain. Except for the storm, each day seemed to be much the same as the one before, stretching off endlessly just as the horizon seemed to be always the same. At one-point dolphins followed the ship playing alongside. Seagulls were constant companions. Clare was an angel, pleased with her new guardian. One moment, Sophie felt as if they would never arrive in Glasgow, the next, she prayed it would take longer. Each day she checked to make sure the letter to Leslie, Duke of Southcliff was safely tucked away in her reticule.

Now they sailed up the Firth of Clyde, mist clinging to the sails and anyone foolish enough to stand on deck. If she could figure out how to keep from landing in the little port so close to Glasgow she would. Ineptly, she tried to keep the fear at bay. Always cheerful, Clare managed to keep her spirits up. The little girl had nothing to worry about. She was cherished by Link. Sophie assumed the residents at the duke's townhouse would feel the same.

"We are almost there, Sophie," Clare said eagerly, smiling as they both stood by the railing watching the small villages come into sight then disappear behind them.

Excitedly, Clare was stepping from one foot to the other. Clare was looking into her eyes. The hopeful expression tore at Sophie's heart, as she truly had no idea how they would be received at the ducal mansion. "How are we going to get into Glasgow and find Link's home?"

Sophie felt the lump in her throat grow with each passing second.

This thought not once left her mind since they boarded the ship without Link. The tick of the clock sounded the death knell. She lifted her shoulders understanding whatever was yet to come might be distasteful. Link had been adamant that any cab they hired would know where the duke's townhouse was located. That in itself seemed absurd to her. How could one man be so well-known by so many?

"I am to tell the driver to take us to the Duke of Southcliff's townhouse then pray that someone is in residence there. Someone who will let us in, accept our word for who we are." She inhaled deeply, fearing the very real chance they would be tossed out on their ears. Link told her no one would expect him to be wed. The fact would be shocking to those who knew him.

For the first time since they boarded the ship in Virginia, Clare looked hesitant. "What if Link is wrong? What if the cab driver doesn't know where the duke lives? What will we do then?"

Sophie thought about that fact every day. Indeed, the worry never left her mind. She had a little money. Everything happened so fast she was sure Link forgot or assumed she would have funds of her own. Probably just enough to hire the cab, after that... Well, she didn't want to think about the what ifs. If no one was home, she did have several addresses in her reticule to fall back on. It seemed the duke's wife had siblings in the area, a bakery nearby. Perhaps she could work there if need be. She was more than willing to work as she was so happy to be away from William. Her back and ribs healed nicely over the weeks at sea. They would manage.

"We will figure something out," she said on a half-sigh, feeling her knees weakening as the ship drew close to the dock. "Link told me the butler's name is Weston and he rarely leaves the townhouse. Someone should be at the home to let us inside. At least I've been praying for that very circumstance since we left port in Virginia."

"Kick us out," Clare said in a rare bout of defeatism while she tried to reassure. Then she countered, "They wouldn't dare. We will insist that we are who we say we are. You will hand them the message written by Link's hand and all will be fine. We will be fine."

It seemed Sophie's few words dispelled Clare's questions. She wished her words had the same outcome for her. Even now as they waited to leave the ship a fine trembling ran through her body. Her knees quaked. Sweat beaded on her forehead.

It felt nice even though it was wrong that Clare was encouraging her instead of the opposite. She drew in a deep breath of air, filling her nostrils, attempting to gain the confidence that escaped her. The air stung and did nothing to fill her lungs or give assurance. Hauling in its sails the ship was getting ready to dock. The captain was calling out orders as the sailors busily scurried around the deck. Sophie tightened her hold on the railing, staring at the small port town of Clydebank, Scotland.

This was it. A few raw seconds later she let out her breath in a rush of air. This was the first day of her new life, Clare's also. Her husband wasn't even with her. A husband who didn't even like her. What was he doing in Virginia? Perhaps even now he was on a ship headed here. Sophie didn't know what to think or do. She watched the land coming closer. Even with Uncle William out of her life, she still felt a pawn in someone else's game.

She didn't like the feeling.

As they walked down the gangplank searching the area for the cabs waiting to pick up passengers, a slight drizzle began coupled with a stiff breeze. Shivering, she pulled her cloak close around her, wishing she owned a warmer one. The weather was miserable. Her mood wasn't any better. To make matters worse there was only one cab. She tugged in a breath of air, starting forward, grabbing Clare's hand to pull her along. They had to reach it before someone else managed the feat.

"Well, if it isn't the little harlot with the pox? You must be running away from your reputation. Think you could set up shop here?"

Devon Masters stepped in front of her. His feet spread, hands on his hips, he was an imposing figure.

Sophie stopped, her body along with her mind frozen.

He continued an arrogant sneer on his face, the edge of his mouth quirking upward. His dark brown eyes focused on her, holding her in place. "They kick you out of Virginia? Why else would you be all the way across the Atlantic?"

Sophie's back stiffened even more as she decided to address the man, a man she knew, one she wished to perdition. She felt a wave of humiliation so deep and so sever the sensation nearly sent her to her knees. When she finally caught enough air in her lungs to speak, she stiffened her back then tilted her chin, "What are you doing in Glasgow, Mr. Masters? Did you discover you too have the pox?"

"The bigger question is what are you doing in this fine city? You looking for a whorehouse? I can help you find one."

He set his hand on her arm pulling her toward him. She fell against his chest, her hands pushing in hopes of gaining her freedom.

Sophie gasped, tugging away from him. "Let me go." She tried desperately to keep her anger in check. She thought she should be able to end this before the conversation became more public and degrading. She attempted the bland control she was known for, "I want nothing to do with the likes of you."

"Now, why would I do something like let you go, little lady? We had a pleasant relationship, you and me. If we worked together, you could bring me a fortune. I could sell you to the highest bidder. Always been a gambling man, besides in my estimation you owe me," Devon jeered, seeming to watch her for a reaction.

His gaze bored into her.

"How dare you! Keep your hands off me and your dirty mouth shut!" She kicked him, hitting his shin with the point of her shoe, wresting her arm away from his belligerent hold while he hopped on one foot, his eyes blazing with anger.

"Little slut," he gritted out, anger simmering in his eyes as he strode closer to her, grabbing her arm again. "How do you dare? Remaining the whore when you have the pox? Seeing men before you tell them about the disease."

She swung at him with her free hand, struggling to rid herself of his grip. Lashing out. Her reticule flew from her arm. As she reached for it, he grasped it, holding the bag high in the air.

"This what you want?"

"Give that to me!" Demeaning herself even further she jumped trying to reach the bag.

He laughed, enjoying himself immensely. "Come and get it," he taunted, his voice turned soft, deadly soft as he waved it in the air. "If you do, I'll have you. You won't get away from me."

"Come, Clare."

Sophie didn't dare reach out for the bag, didn't dare get close enough for him to gain control. Except for the letter there was nothing of value in the small bag. She would have to take her chances. The duke would have to take her word on the marriage. She took hold of Clare's hand striding once more toward the carriage, which pulled away from them. A groan of despair swirled around her. She looked to Devon who seemed content to stay away from her. He was cocky and sure of himself, his eyes blazing. He probably thought she would give into him.

Their brief encounter drew a small audience. Sophie didn't doubt for a moment the man would bide his time and come for her at a later date if that was what he intended. The letter would give him all the information he needed. He would know where to find her. She tasted her fear, very real. Here, without Link, she had no protection.

What would they do now?

She looked over her shoulder in time to see Devon reaching for her, wrenching her around. When she wasn't looking, he'd come upon them. Sophie supposed this wouldn't be the last time she was wrong about Devon Masters. He wasn't going to let her go. He smelled of sweat and something sweet. Her stomach lurched.

His hands held her tightly against him. Sophie couldn't move, couldn't get away from his brutal hold. He held them together. "Let me go!" Quickly she brought her knee to his groin. She made contact.

Devon doubled over, shrieking in pain. His voice weak while he tried to regain his equilibrium. Husky with emotion, "Bitch! You will regret that."

With Clare in tow, she was backing away, watching him, unwilling to turn her back for a second time. Suddenly, she ran into a solid wall of a man, hands touching on her shoulders. They were gentle hands yet firm. She wondered about that.

His voice was soft with a deadly undertone. “Do you need help, lass? I *ken* that you do.” The words were quietly spoken yet sounded sincere. “My name’s Sandy. I work down here on the docks for Mr. Chamberlin. If this man is causing you any problems...” He looked at the man who was still doubled over in pain. “I’ll be glad to help. Make sure he gets what’s coming to him.”

Sophie straightened hoping this was her chance to find a way into Glasgow. The man was tall and broad of shoulder. His jaw was firm, chiseled, shadowed with a day’s growth. His blue eyes seemed to be dancing, “If you could help me rent a carriage. I need to go into town.” Her body was shaking, her voice a trembling whisper as she prayed for help. “I’ll see that you’re compensated for your time.”

The mist turned into a steady drizzle, rain soaking her through the thin wool of her coat. Sophie pulled the hood around her head, wiping moisture from her face. She knew she was staring at the man with hope-filled eyes as if he was her savior. He wasn’t. He could be. She assumed he would not be able to help; realized her request was far too much for her to ask.

“There are no more cabs. You’ll have to stay the night here in the village. There is a small inn down the road. I’ll walk with you.” He told her, his eyes narrowing as he looked at her, seeming to study her.

“Thank you then. Thank you for caring.” She didn’t move in that direction realizing she didn’t have enough money for a stay in an inn, any inn. Indeed, with her reticule in Devon Master’s possession, she didn’t have money for the cab. Even if she still held her purse, she would not have the funds to stay the night. Moisture formed in her eyes. She tried to push it away without letting the man see her distress. She cursed her stupidity along with her weakness.

“You don’t have any money, do you?” Sandy asked, his hand on her shoulder again as he squeezed gently.

His big hand felt warm, protective as well. The sob she tried to hold back threatened to erupt. This was too much all too much. Everything she’d been afraid would happen was happening. “We did have enough for cab fare but not for a night's lodging. I—well—my husband gave me just enough, you see. He didn't think there would be any problems. I made a mistake by not asking for more coin."

Least of all he didn't expect her to be robbed by Devon Masters. If he'd had the foresight to give her more money, it all would have been lost.

"Really, he couldn't spare a few shillings in case something went wrong," he said gruffly, a silent reprimand to the forgetful husband.

Sophie looked at her toes then back to the man. She had a pretty good idea what he must be thinking, "He's a good man. There was a lot happening when I left Virginia. We were in a hurry. I'm sure he just overlooked it, the money. I'm just as much at fault. I never asked." She was defending Link.

Sandy's eyes narrowed again, seeming to speculate about the hurried circumstances that might leave a lady without sufficient funds. "I'm headed into Glasgow. If you feel comfortable with me, I can take you and..." he hesitated, looking at his boots for a moment.

"My sister." She was quick to say.

Didn't think to answer about the ride. She wasn't at all sure about riding with a strange man now that the request was made. Was having a second and truly third thoughts about it. She didn't have a choice.

When Sophie hesitated, Clare spoke for her without wavering. "We would both appreciate the help. We would have to walk to Glasgow. That wouldn't be wise. I don't suppose. Neither of us knows the way. It's probably too far."

Her eyes were wide with trust, something only a thirteen-year-old could feel for a man, a large man who would have ultimate control of what was going to happen to them. Shivers slid down her spine. She stiffened. Prayed for the best.

Sandy looked to her for confirmation. Sophie wasn't sure at all. She gulped down a ball of air that settled in the pit of her stomach then she nodded. "Th-that would be nice." She paused for a lengthy amount of time, trying to reconcile her fears with her decision. "I think."

Sandy grinned, seeming to notice the insecurities. Sophie noted that his teeth were straight and very white. When he grinned, dimples marked both sides of his mouth. She admonished herself, realizing straight white teeth along with dimples was not a recommendation to a man's character. "I'll not harm either of you. I give you my solemn promise."

It seemed he read her mind. Helplessly nodding her head as if in agreement she followed him to the wagon. After all she truly didn't have a choice. She had to accept his help. She wondered what Link would tell her when he found out. Well, she decided she wasn't about to say anything.

He turned. "Did you want me to try to get your reticule back?"

Sophie waved her hand in the air. "There was little of value in it. I suppose it would not be worth it to try. While I know the man who stole it, I've no idea where to find him. It might take hours to track him down. The rain is falling harder. Clare will get wet. Don't want her to take sick." She gritted her teeth together, praying now more fervently than ever that the Stewarts would believe her tall tale.

"Very well then, where is it you would like me to take you?" He helped her into the wagon then Clare. They were followed by the single trunk and valise.

Her lips thinned as she stared at him, understanding he might not know where the Stewarts were located in Glasgow. A strangled breath of air slipped through her teeth.

"Well?" he asked as he hoped onto the driver's side and urged the two horses forward.

"The Duke of Southcliff's townhouse," she said her quivering voice soft, the thinnest whisper as her courage disappeared right out from under her nose.

"Where?" One eyebrow lifted in speculation or question she ventured to guess.

Sophie wasn't at all sure if the man didn't hear her or didn't believe her. Before she could reply Clare spoke up. In a voice filled with confidence, she said quite matter of factly, "We would like you to take us to the Duke of Southcliff's townhouse. My sister is his brother's wife. She is married to Link Stewart. Mr. Stewart is my guardian. Do you know where the townhouse is?"

Thank God, for little sisters, Sophie thought as she pulled her hood closer to her head. With a vengeance the rain was beginning to soak through her cloak and onto her clothing. She was sure she would appear a drowned rat by the time they reached their destination.

"I do *ken* where the duke resides. Didn't know Link Stewart had a wife." Sandy turned to look at her in a different light than before when she didn't claim to be anybody.

A quick explanation might suffice. "We married in Virginia." She stiffened her back, feeling rain running down it at the same time. She sneezed. Didn't think it had anything to do with the rain and the miserably cold day. "He is finishing his business before he returns here."

They traveled for a good ten minutes before Sandy asked, "Where is Link Stewart? Why did he leave you without enough funds to do more than rent a cab? He should be taking better care of his wife. Doesn't he *ken* anything can happen on the docks to a beautiful lady?"

She wasn't sure but she thought she detected a note of censure. "As I said earlier. It wasn't his fault. Things happened. We were in a hurry to leave."

She wasn't going to tell this man the true story. He already knew everything necessary, probably more because none of this was his business. She wasn't, however, going to tell him that.

"Don't need to get your back up. I've been to this Leslie Hall a time or two. Know that things were happening there and that's why Link went to Virginia. Hope everything got straightened out." He looked at her sideways as if trying to delve more deeply into the truth.

"You know Link?" she asked him a bit in awe of the fact that she happened to hitch a ride with someone who actually knew the Stewarts.

The coincidence didn't go unnoticed. Once again, she found a niggle of fear possessing her.

He pushed his hat back on his head rearranging it in the process. "Not really. Know of, more than know. I work for a friend of his, Donal Chamberlin. My wife is Mr. Chamberlin's cook. Probably better acquainted with the duchess than the duke or your husband."

"Oh, I see." But she didn't see completely.

At least he knew where they were going. Sophie turned to see Clare huddled in the back shivering, her cloak pulled around her. If the two of them didn't catch a cold, they would be lucky.

An hour later they pulled up in front of the huge townhouse. She stared at it as if the structure would just open up and welcome them into its warmth. This was to be her home until Link arrived. Her heart was beating so hard she could barely breathe. She didn't want to knock on the door. She could hardly turn back.

"Would you like me to wait for you?" He asked a bit of a chuckle to his voice. "At the moment you and your sister don't really look as if you could be related to a duke."

"You are right about that. We most likely resembled two women who don't have the sense to come in out of the rain," she said, once more eyeing the home. "The only thing of importance that was inside my reticule was a letter from Link telling his brother that he married me. Link bade me not to lose it, nothing about having it stolen. Told me his brother would never believe he married anyone." *Let alone the harlot from Virginia*. "Suppose you should stick around in case the duke kicks us out. Don't know if it matters though since we've no place to go if he does."

"I'll stay. If anyone kicks you out, and I sincerely doubt if they will, I'll take you to the bakery. There is a spare room above it. I would suspect Daryl, the owner, will let you and your sister stay there until things get straightened out. Link is coming soon. I hope."

"I hope so too."

Sophie thought that to be a fine idea. She didn't say anything as she stared at the townhouse that was not Link's home but his brother's. Sandy leapt from the wagon before helping Clare and her down.

"Thank you."

He followed them up the walkway to the front door then set the baggage on the porch. "I'll just be in the wagon waiting to see if you go inside. If anything happens afterward you can walk down that street, take a left and you'll see the bakery. Justine will be there as I will be for another hour. If you need anything after that, ask for Donal Chamberlin."

Nodding her head, Sophie was trying to remember the names as well as the direction Sandy gave her to walk to the bakery. Everything was a muddle in her brain.

She pulled in a long deep breath, turning toward her sister a falsely bright smile, "Shall we?"

"Everything will be fine, you'll see," Clare told her.

Praying Clare was right and sucking in as much air as possible she knocked on the door with the huge knocker. An older man opened the door, looking down his long narrow nose at them. All Sophie wanted to do was turn and run. Instead, she held out her shaking hand, "Hello, I'm Sophie Stewart, Link's wife. This is my sister, Clare. He told me to come here and wait for him until he returns from Virginia." Then she added hoping the information might help. "I lived at Mayfair Hall until we were wed just before the ship left." She held back, feeling as if she was beginning to babble her life story.

She found she was alternately wringing her hands and holding her breath as she waited. She didn't like it, not one bit. Where was the old Sophia, the one who seduced men with ease? The butler stared at her. What was his name? Given time she might recall the name Link gave her.

"Do come inside out of the rain. You can set your things in the foyer and wait there while I see if the duke will see you," the tall man said. He turned in one refined movement and left them dripping on the marble entryway.

She nodded. Inside it was warm, a fire burning in the drawing room. Still, she found herself shivering. No matter how hard she tried to stop she could not. The sneeze she was trying to hold back came out when a tall very dignified man walked into the foyer from some place down the hallway. He wasn't smiling. His face was grim. His eyes so much like Link's, simmered with questions. He didn't believe her marriage story.

He looked a lot like Link. His eyes were a deep dark brown, questioning. His lips held a hint of distrust as he stared at them assessing them from their sodden toes to their dripping hair. She felt lacking just as she had when she first met Link.

His shoulders were broad and his white lawn shirt and snowy cravat was tied to perfection. His legs were long and powerful looking. She wondered if this was the spy. He looked to be just as confidant and commanding as Link, perhaps more so.

"Weston tells me you are Link's wife." His voice was harsh, threatening with a hint of disbelief molded into the words. He chuckled though, "Link vowed never to marry until he was over thirty. Of course, we all did vow that at one time or another."

Her hopes sunk to an all-time low. Just as Link explained, he didn't believe or trust her. Link told her his brother would not believe her without the letter and might not even then. "He wrote a letter telling you all about our marriage. He understood you wouldn't believe me without seeing written proof."

The Duke of Southcliff held out his hand, not even a hint of a smile on his hard well-chiseled face, his brows drawing together, studying her. "I would read it now."

Out of nowhere a petite lady with raven black hair and the biggest bosom Sophie had ever seen on such a tiny lady, on any lady for that matter stepped into the foyer from another room. "Leslie, you should be ashamed of yourself. Can't you tell just by looking at her she is Link's wife. She is so beautiful it nearly renders me breathless. She is exactly who Link would wed." Her hands on his arm, she leaned forward, questioning.

"Sophie, milady, Sophie Carter-Brown, now Stewart," she said guessing that this woman wanted her name.

"Sophie is of course Link's wife, darling. As I just said, she is exactly who I would have expected your brother to choose. She is exceptionally beautiful. By the way, I'm Lacie. Leslie is my husband, the stupid man standing beside me who can't see the obvious."

He grunted while he stared at his wife adoringly.

"In any case," he rubbed his chin a slight tilt to his head his voice deep, commanding, "I would still like to see this letter."

"Can't you see she is shivering and about to catch her death from the coldness? She is soaking wet. Can your interrogation come after we've warmed her up a bit? Perhaps she'd like a bite to eat too and a steaming hot bath."

Weston appeared out of nowhere, his hands folded behind his back as if reading Lacie's mind. "I've asked the upstairs maid to draw a nice hot bath for the two ladies as well as prepare Link's room as well as the adjoining one."

"Would you like to warm up with a bath then come down to finish with the explanations along with a bite to eat and something warm to drink? You will have to tell us all how this marriage came to pass. I for one am thrilled Link has found such an exceptional wife. He needs someone just like you."

"Bedraggled?" Leslie asked a dark eyebrow arched in mockery.

Sophie felt the relief from her head to the tips of her toes. At least they were not kicking them out as yet. They could warm up, change clothes perhaps get a bite to eat before she would have to explain things to Leslie. Before he would send her out on the streets. Truly, she didn't want to go into the reasons why Link felt obligated to marry her. They might call for an annulment. She couldn't tell them Link had no choice but to marry her if he was to save her life. Could not tell them she was the best-known whore in Virginia.

"Follow me," Weston said as two footmen appeared to carry the single trunk and the valise upstairs.

As they walked, they heard the duke and his wife talking. They were arguing about her, she was sure but she couldn't make out the words. She let a long breath of air slip from her lips. This was enough to deal with.

Quite enough for the moment they would have to take this one second at a time.

Even if they didn't believe her, they might at least keep them safe until Link returned home on the off chance, she told the truth. There would be enough doubt in their minds. One did not set a brother's wife and her sister out on the streets with no funds and nowhere to go to fend for themselves.

They had adjoining rooms. For a few seconds she stood with her hands clasped tightly in front of her watching the steam rise from the water. A bath had not been possible on board the ship. She smiled as she slipped out of her clothing and into the hot water.

Clare called out to her from the other room, “See, Sophie, I told you so, everything will be fine.”

Thirty minutes later she wasn’t at all sure Clare’s words were true as they sat in the drawing room with the duke peering at them. His hands were clasped behind his back as he rocked from toe to heel.

~ * ~

Link watched the ship slowly move into the Firth of Clyde then onto the River Firth. All the business his brother sent him to complete was finished along with some of his own. Brinkmeyer made Clare his heir. Upon his passing Sophie’s sister would receive everything, Mayfair Hall, everything Brinkmeyer possessed including any newly acquired plantations. Sophie would also be taken care of but he would see to that.

There was now no contest about the guardianship of Clare. She was his responsibility until she turned twenty-one or she married. He would make sure she never underwent the same type of treatment and humiliation as Sophie. He believed Clare might like to meet his other children, perhaps even live with them when she wasn’t in school.

The night-time endeavors meant to frighten him into selling Leslie Hall stopped with a well thought out threat to Brinkmeyer.

He drew a long slow breath of the salt air while he prayed Sophie had been accepted into Leslie’s home. His brother would have raised one, if not both of his supercilious, ducal eyebrows. Seagulls called out overhead, dipping then soaring with the wind currents. The look on his brother’s face must have been eye-popping when Sophie explained she was his wife then handed over the letter. He wished he could have been there.

The ship made good time, the weather exceptional. The separation between the departures had been two weeks. Perhaps he made up some of the time. He was eager to see his wife, finally make love to her. After all he had yet to consummate the marriage. He remembered well, the feeling of her body next to his, the smooth round globes of her breast, the slick petals of her womanhood. He gritted his teeth, tamping down the arousal his thoughts created. He wanted a child with her. Ah, the children, she would have to be introduced to his cherished ones. He would have to give more of an explanation.

The sun was shining today as the ship made port. Once the gangplank was lowered, he quickly strode to the walkway. He hired a cab, collected his baggage and was on his way to the townhouse ready to move on with this new life of his. He was eager, he realized, to introduce her as his wife.

He knocked. Weston opened the door, one finely sculpted eyebrow arched toward the heaven above. "Master Link, good to see you again." He stepped back allowing Link to enter.

"Is my wife at home?" He looked down the hall then into the drawing room. The house was amazingly quiet almost as if no one was home. He hoped he wouldn't have to wait a moment longer to see her.

"No," Weston said a hint of amusement in the deep timber of his voice. "No, she isn't."

"You going to elaborate or keep me guessing?" Link strode farther into the hall, gazing up the steps around the corner into the drawing room then up the steps again. Perhaps she was in his bedchamber. Thoughts of her spread out on his bed started more carnal thoughts spinning.

"Keep you guessing might be fun for me but no, Leslie might fire me. Your wife and the duchess are at the dressmakers. Milady said you were abominable for allowing your wife to travel with none of the necessities befitting her station. She also said she has no decent clothing. Everything is outdated and makes her look years younger than she is."

"Abominable, is it? So, she is out spending my money. Married only a short time and she believes my pocketbook is her pocketbook."

He chuckled, realizing how very correct the duchess was in her declaration. Sophie's clothing was horrid. He realized suddenly he liked the idea of Sophie spending his money. He just wished he was there to give his opinion.

"I believe that is what she said. Her ladyship is more than happy to spend your money even while Mrs. Stewart tried to tell her she didn't need anything. I should say nothing more," Weston said.

"I'm given to think I don't stand a chance. In any case, I'm now guessing Leslie read the letter and excepted Sophie into the family fold." The ever-changing expression on the elder man's face fascinated Link. They also told him a wealth of information without a word being said.

"No, sir, he did not." It seemed Weston was not about to issue forth information that wasn't specifically asked for.

"Why?" Link wanted to see his wife now, needed to find out what happened because surely something occurred that kept her from giving the letter to Leslie. His brother would have believed the letter.

What the devil was it?

Weston flicked an imaginary piece of lint from his immaculate coat. "You would have to ask either the duke or your wife. I'm not given to rumors and innuendos. However, I'm sure Merry would tell you if she was home. Unfortunately, she is not."

That comment left him swearing silently. "Neither one is here in case you haven't noticed." He wanted to race to the dressmakers.

"It is not my place to spread gossip." With that said, Weston took himself off, disappearing into the household.

Link let a long breath of air slip from his lungs before he strode up the steps to the chamber he used when he was in residence, pleased to find Sophie inhabiting the room. Peeking his head into the adjoining chamber he surmised from what he saw that Clare was occupying the room next to theirs. He would find her a new room. She could not possibly reside in the room connected to his by a single door. That just would not do.

He grinned well pleased.

"A bath, Sir?" Weston was standing inside the open door, waiting for an answer. "Perhaps a bite to eat before you follow your wife."

Link nodded, realizing he had plenty of time to refresh himself then make it to the dress shop before Sophie and Lacie would be finished. He didn't doubt that Lacie was indeed enjoying spending his money. He also wanted some say in the new clothing Sophie would be purchasing.

An hour later, Link walked into the dressmaker's shop with a grin on his face eager to see his wife. Lacie sat on a wing chair watching as Sophie modeled a sweet yellow muslin confection. The neckline was low, revealing and tempting without showing too much, so unlike her harlot gowns. The color suited her well. He found for a moment air wouldn't spill into his lungs.

With her hair swept on top of her head, a few errant pieces falling around and framing her delicate face, she looked adorable. His breath caught in the back of his throat when she looked over her shoulder to say something to Lacie and found him staring at her.

"Link? You're home."

Her breathy words raised the temperature of his body. She actually sounded pleased to see him.

He didn't know if he should start the conversations with the money she was spending or on the missing letter or even... They must have believed her about his marriage to her or she wouldn't even now be spending his hard-earned groats. Those conversations would have to wait until they were private. Until after he made love to her because he simply didn't want to spoil the one event he'd been looking forward to for months.

"I am." He stepped forward, taking her hand in his before kissing the top when he wanted to pull her into his arms and ravish her. "You're looking splendid."

"How was the voyage?" she asked, as the seamstress urged her back into place.

"Without complications and yours?"

"A big storm. Delayed us and sent us off course. I've only been here in Glasgow a couple of days." She was breathless. Sounded as if she ran all the way here as he heard tiny pants for breathing.

Link sat down on a chair next to Lacie's then looking at her, "I think, if you don't mind too much, I will finish this. I assume your driver is outside waiting for you and Sophie. The carriage was there in any case."

"Don't be..." Lacie began then turned away hesitant.

"She is my wife. Whatever it is you might be thinking, don't. Sophie and I owe no one any explanations if that is what you're thinking behind those beautiful blue eyes of yours."

"I will take my leave. Don't let him badger you. Men, they will try to bend you to your will."

Lacie rose gave Sophie a quick hug before she regally left the room.

Link took over the ordering of gowns, shushing Sophie only twice when she tried to protest. She would no longer wear the harlot gowns or the ones fit only for a young maid. She was his wife now and she would understand what that meant. He did intend to show her off. She would have to look her part. He meant to go all out with her clothing.

When they left the store several hours later, Sophie was wearing a simple walking dress of deep blue muslin. There were several packages of underthings, bonnets and slippers as well to go along with the dresses. A promise to deliver the other purchases as soon as possible was made by the seamstress.

Link helped Sophie into the carriage, following behind her. He sat opposite, stretched out his legs, eyeing her intently. He felt relaxed, totally at ease for the first time in months. He was in control and he would discover the answers to all his questions.

With his arms crossed in front of his chest, a sardonic tilt to his head, he blandly asked, "What happened to the letter?"

The pause seemed lengthy, the silence overpowering as he watched the pulse at the base of her throat pick up speed. He watched her swallow then look out the window. The carriage trundled slowly along the route. He sensed she didn't want to answer. If she lost it, all she had to do was say so. He remembered his promise to himself not to broach that subject until after they made love.

Well damn.

"Where are we going?" Her brows furrowed deeply as she directed her question toward him. "I haven't been here long but I know this is not the way back to the duke's townhouse."

"A place where we might have a moment of semi-privacy. What

happened to the letter?" He wasn't going to back down. She would tell him. Then they would proceed to more pleasurable topics.

"Oh." She looked out the window again still ignoring his question. "Privacy, of course, that would be pleasant. I've questions to ask you about Uncle William."

"Why do I get the feeling alone time with me, your husband, is the last thing you wish for." She was making excuses, putting him off.

"Did you..." She moistened her lips, "Did you get everything sorted out at Leslie Hall?"

"I don't understand this," Link said, reaching across the distance between them to lightly graze her cheek with his knuckles. "I'm waiting for an answer to a simple question, a simple inquiry that should not merit this hesitancy. Yet, you prevaricate then change the subject with a new question. All matters in Virginia are taken care of. What happened to the letter?"

He enjoyed the slight flush rising to her cheeks coupled with the hesitant lift to her shoulders. What the devil was she about and why won't she answer my questions?

"The letter is gone along with my reticule and the cab fare you gave me." She ran her pink tongue across her lips, clearly unsure of herself. "I didn't have it to give to Leslie."

"You're not acting yourself," he blurted before thinking about what he truly wanted to say. "How did you lose the letter along with your reticule? Did you drop them over the side of the ship?" It was the only logical explanation he could conceive.

"Neither are you, Sir, acting yourself. You are different somehow." Her back was clearly up against a wall, her chin pointed upward.

Hers was a position he easily recalled. Crossing his arms against his chest, he ran her words over in his mind then leaning forward, his forearms braced on his thighs, his hands on her legs, "How did you get to the townhouse?"

He didn't want to think of all the possibilities. Now, here in Glasgow, he assumed she would act more like herself. She didn't have to pretend to be someone she was not. She had no one to fear. It seemed she feared him.

She squirmed in her seat as he tightened the pressure on her legs. “Sandy brought us. He...”

The protective rage he suddenly felt was too far out of character for him to understand. Thinking of Sophie with another man for any reason was intolerable, his mind traveling to places he’d rather not contemplate. The sensation boiled up from deep within until he was shouting. “Who the hell is Sandy?”

She was right. He wasn’t like himself. Feeling jealousy and anger was not something he felt before. He was astounded to realize he was jealous and the emotion involved a woman. She was just another woman, nothing more, just a woman.

She was his woman, his wife.

Sophie blinked several times pushing herself back against the seat, her hands tugging at his to release her. “A friend,” she blurted then seemed to realize that was most likely the wrong reply. Her breasts were heaving now and it was all he could do to stop himself from dragging her into his arms and seeing just how they would feel beneath his fingers. He wanted to forget this Sandy fellow and bury his mouth between her breasts.

“You don’t have any friends here.”

He didn’t want to wonder if she was reasserting her old life here in Glasgow. Link grit his teeth against his thoughts, pushing his fears aside not wanting to believe her to truly be the brazen hussy he once assumed her to be.

“N-n-no, that’s not entirely true.”

To his jaded ears she sounded breathless, lying as well. His fingers tightened again, then he let go of her with disgust not wanting to touch her at least not until he found a way to get his seething emotions under control. For Christ sakes, he didn’t want to hurt her.

“Who are all your new found friends?” he gritted out crossing his arms in front of him as he stretched out once more in the carriage, breathing deeply her scent, roses, as he silently undressed her in his mind.

Blessed hell, but he waited months to make love to his wife. Now he didn't know who had been in her bed. "I don't share what is mine, Sophie. You're mine. Don't ever forget that."

For a minute or two she said nothing, then very blandly reminding him of the past, "I've touched a nerve?"

"It seems you've touched more than that." He cleared his throat, "Let's get back to the letter. What happened to it?"

The whereabouts of the letter seemed innocuous at the moment in light of her revelation to him. She had friends. What the hell was Leslie doing allowing his wife to entertain men? That was another conversation that needed to happen sooner than later.

She lifted her shoulders again. "I don't know what happened to it. Just that I don't have it. As I said it is gone. There is no need to continue."

"Then you lost it. Why was that so hard for you to say?"

He wasn't in the mood to play verbal sparring games with her. Answers were what he wanted. He was her husband not some damn beau or possible lover.

"Yes, in a manner of speaking I suppose I did misplace it," she said in an incredibly vague tone.

He wasn't going to let her get the better of his temper. "How did you misplace it?" he asked in a voice so calm he didn't recognize himself.

Still pursuing the question when he was pretty sure she didn't intend to answer. He would have to figure out what she was up to and beat her at her game.

Her fingers pleated into the folds of her skirt for several seconds while she watched with seeming avid interest. "Stolen, it would be more accurate to say it was stolen from me. Rather, I did not lose it. However, I also don't know where it is so in that vein, I lost it."

"Again, why didn't you just tell me and be done with it? Why the secrets and hedging? You make no sense."

There was more to this story than he understood at the moment. It might be prudent to bide his time and wait her out. Eventually, he would discover the missing pieces. Perhaps she told Leslie or Lacie.

With wide shimmering eyes she stared at him, shaking her head.

She was always a puzzle. There were always gaps in any information she might give him. Would the rest of their lives together be like that? Ah, but Mrs. Sophie Stewart would never bore him. That he supposed was that. This tendency of hers was also part of what attracted him to her in the first place.

The carriage rolled to a stop. The door was opened and the stairs put down. He got out then politely helped her from the vehicle. "Are you hungry?" he asked deciding that for at least long enough to eat the meal, he would stow his anger.

She nodded, accepting his arm as he led her into the restaurant. "Thank you, this is nice of you."

He was not feeling the least bit nice. Answers were what he wanted. *Friends?* Blessed hell, how many friends had she acquired in Glasgow in so few days?

Placidly, he ordered wine then baked salmon and small potatoes in a wine sauce. Bread was brought to the table along with the wine. He poured, hoping she would drink enough to loosen her tongue. He thought of the drugged hot toddies with a loose grin. Thought of her beautiful white body on display for him on the fur rug in front of the blazing fire. Thought of the other men she'd been with before him.

His gut tightened.

He watched her eat, stared at her lips then the tops of her breasts. He drank the contents of his glass, poured himself another then topped off hers. Tapping his fingers on the table, he waited.

"What have you been doing these last few days?" he asked searching for a topic that might not cause his anger to flare.

She looked to the door as if she expected someone. "I rode with Lacie, Merry as well. Both your sister and sister-in-law are very nice to me."

"Everyday?"

"Yes."

"What else?"

"The duchess introduced me to her sisters. We ate several times at the bakery. I've met the children." She toyed with her napkin. "They are all very nice. Clare likes Merry very much. As you told me, Clare is only a few years younger. They get along quite well. I'm happy for Clare. She's never truly had a friend before. Except me."

"Do you like Merry?"

"Yes." She looked up from her baked salmon.

What the devil was she hiding from him? Even these answers were simple with nothing to give them substance. Once more he decided a change of topic might serve to improve his mood.

He thought of tonight.

"There will be nothing keeping us apart tonight once we return. Are you as eager to share my bed as I am?"

He watched as her eyes darkened, flashed a deep pewter gray. Her cheeks held the flush of embarrassment. He thought to talk of sexual things to her. Thought to see if she flushed a deeper shade of red. Perhaps he could tell her all he wanted to do to her pure white flesh.

"Link..." She ran her tongue across her lips. Her fingers tightened around the wine glass. "I'm a vir—"

He waved his hand in the air interrupting her before she could spew such nonsense. "We both understand you are no simpering virgin. There is nothing maidenly about your body or your sensibilities. You speak with the aplomb of an experienced whore. It is not your fault. I don't hold it against you. Have some more wine. While I was sure before you left Virginia, no one had actually had sex with you, I'm no longer positive as I listened to you spew words about friends you've met here. Still, what you've seen of men's bodies, and how they pleasure women hardly makes you a virgin even if your maidenhead is intact. We will speak of it no longer."

Well, he thought a change of topic might have been in order. He had not thought she would tackle the subject of her virginity again. It was utter nonsense. They both understood the truth. Over the long weeks of the ocean voyage, he had the necessary time to come to grips with the knowledge she was far from innocent as well as put it to the back of his head.

He didn't care how many lovers she had in her past. It was her future that mattered now. He would make sure she knew only him.

The rest of the meal was spent in relative silence. Tension encircled both of them. She picked at her meal as if it was her last one or she wanted to prolong this evening's entertainment as long as possible. The ride back to the townhouse showed no improvement. She said nothing.

Showed even less expression on her beautiful face.

Back in Virginia he wanted to believe her tall tale about her virginity. Now, he simply didn't care. He wasn't a besotted fool. Didn't care if she was an experienced tart. However, he would make damn sure their children were his.

He took her elbow as he guided her up the porch steps then into the foyer where he divested her of her pelisse, his outer coat as well.

"They're back," Lacie's voice floated to them from the drawing room. "Do join us. A glass of fine Bordeaux? From your own vineyards. Leslie tells me it was an exceptional year."

Link gritted his teeth against the need to be polite and join his brother and his wife. "Of course."

In the drawing room a tray of delicacies was set out. There were all sorts of pastries and tarts to delight the pallet. It seemed the duke along with his wife wanted to keep them out of their marriage bed for a while longer.

"You cannot have spent all that time at the dress shop. Whatever did you two do afterward?" Lacie asked as she sipped her glass of wine. Her eyes were laughing. He remembered the time he walked in on his brother coaxing Lacie into a compromising position. She was very pregnant now, very beautiful. He looked at Sophie, imagining her belly swelled with their child.

He would damn well make sure it would be his child.

Even if he had to lock her in his house. That was another matter. He needed to find a place nearby where there was room for all his children as well his hopefully expanding family. He would begin his quest tomorrow.

He wanted to know who Sandy was, what she was hiding about

the lost letter as well. He could tell by the glint in her eyes she was hiding something. Idly spending time chit chatting with his brother was not going to serve his purpose.

He rocked back on his heels after ushering Sophie to a chair. "So," he began, "you believed I was well and truly married to this beautiful woman. Even without the letter?" The statement was as much a question as anything else. Link watched his brother's eyes and understood quite explicitly that Leslie had not believed a word of Sophie's tale.

"No, but my wife believed her. By the looks of things, I owe my wife. Did wager a tiny bet."

Sophie gasped slightly her gaze resting on Lacie for a moment. "You didn't?"

Lacie gave a slight lift to her shoulders. "It was either that or let Leslie kick you to the curb so to speak. He would have found some place for you to stay, but I wouldn't have anything to do with that. The moment I looked at you, I knew Link would have been hard-pressed to leave you alone. He had to marry you. Or ruin your reputation."

"How did you truly know, brat?" Leslie asked his gaze shifting from Link to Sophie. "I certainly didn't see anything special when I looked at her."

"When she spoke his name, I saw the love in her eyes, the absolute adoration. No one could look that way and lie," Lacie said softly. "It was actually quite simple."

Link tried to keep his jaw from dropping, noticed that Sophie had not succeeded. Her face scorched with color. "I'm rather left with nothing to say at that. My wife and I do love each other. Don't we, Sophie?"

"I suppose the two of you are more than eager to be alone," Leslie's voice held a bland note and one brow was arched in ardent speculation, still seeming to disavow the marriage as legitimate.

Link thought he knew, understood theirs was not a love match. He supposed it was true. What he did know was that he wanted Sophie desperately, had for too many months now that he didn't want to count them.

"Oh, I would love to spend more time here. This is..." Sophie was speaking softly and smiling while she sipped the wine.

"Time for us to discover all that we've been missing since our wedding."

Link held his hand out to his reluctant bride determined at least to make use of her luscious body even if she would tell him nothing about the letter or the man she now called friend.

~ * ~

Leslie shot his wife a tepid grin, one brow arched with ducal precision. "You won. Now, how are you going to collect?"

Even though he lost, he appeared inordinately pleased with himself.

"Hmm..." The duchess tapped her fingers on the armrest. "It might not be too hard to collect. There are certain favors I can withhold if you deem to deny me my rightful winnings."

"Little brat," he mumbled, pouring more wine for both of them. "They are wed but there is something wrong in paradise. She doesn't have that rosy glow of a woman well pleasured or even pleased to see her husband. She looks terrified of him. You did say she loves him though."

"Yes. You're right. They don't act like a happily married couple, do they? You should speak with your brother. Give him some pointers on lovemaking since you are such an expert."

Leslie sat down beside his wife, grinning hugely, pleased thoroughly with his wife's comments. "Do you suppose Sophie is the harlot the documents I received spoke of? That puts an interesting spin on all of this intrigue. My brother fell in love with a well-used woman and is now hesitant to bed the woman, his wife."

"I believe there is a very strong possibility. That woman is not a whore, no matter what the papers said about her. I know things like that just by watching her." Lacie leaned into her husband, his hand now resting possessively on her swollen belly, a pleased smile on his face.

"How many whores have you known?"

Leslie wanted to laugh at the absurd notion his wife was gifting him with. In this case, however, he agreed with Lacie. Sophie did not appear to have the ability to part her legs to any man willing to pay for her.

"None." She looked up, staring at his lips before moving her blatant stare lower, to moisten her lips as she reached his groin.

He groaned softly as he bent lower to caress her lips with his, touch gently at the corners of her mouth. "Then," he paused, to place more tender kisses down her neck to the throbbing pulse at the base, "how do you come by this notion she is not a whore?"

Lacie lifted her bountiful mouth to meet his as her fingers wove into the hair at the base of his neck pulling him closer. "There were several indications."

She ran her sweet warm tongue across his mouth, so warm where she touched, cool where she no longer stroked. He stuffed his rumbling groan behind his teeth.

"And those were..."

One hand caressed her belly, the other he held beneath her chin. Stroking, nipping, tender flesh, he traveled lower to the line of her corsage, daringly, boldly caressing lower with each pass. He teased and taunted. A tiny mew of pleasure rippled up from her throat then another.

A sound he delighted in. A noise that emphasized his expertise in giving pleasure to his wife.

"I can't think any longer. What you do to me? I'm liquid in your hands" Her fingers deftly opened his shirt, her hands running across his chest, lower to his abs as he sucked in a deep breath of air, the sensation exquisite, arousing. This conversation might have to be put off to a later date.

"Perhaps we should take this upstairs since we have guests," Leslie said as he nimbly pushed the sleeves of Lacie's gown down her arms, holding them still while revealing the tender pink buds he sought.

"Oh!"

Quickly, Leslie swept Lacie's gown into place. Turning, "Clare?"

"I'm sorry. I didn't know. Wouldn't have interrupted." She sounded panic-struck. Her eyes wide as she seemed to absorb the scene.

Her blush turned to scarlet.

"Of course, you wouldn't know," Lacie said seemingly able to think more clearly than he could. He didn't possess a coherent thought.

"I'll go up to my room now." Clare backed out.

"I believe your room has probably been changed, dear. Allow me to go with you." Lacie rose, slanting a wistful look at his lips, her eyes promising more when they were alone.

"I'll be up in a minute," Leslie said, his gaze on his wife as she walked not so gracefully from the drawing room then up the stairs. With each day, she grew more endearingly and adorably awkward. She would undoubtedly be waddling around the room soon. He looked forward to each stage except the torture of the birth.

He chuckled to himself while he poured a brandy and drank it down. Lacie turned out to be the perfect duchess. In her pregnancy she was more beautiful and appealing than ever before. Her breasts were even larger, the tips tender and pink. They drove him wild. His arousal pulsed against his britches as he thought about the next few hours. Tonight, he was going to tease and tempt until she begged him for more, until the warmth and tumultuous passion couldn't be controlled.

Grabbing a bottle of wine, he eagerly two-stepped the stairs to their room. Once inside he poured them both a generous glass setting each on an end table. She would refuse the wine. She always refused telling him she didn't see how it could be good for the baby. He didn't disagree or agree. A few minutes later he was naked, stretched out on the bed, waiting for her to enter.

Chapter Nine

"I need to see to Clare," Sophie told Link the moment she walked into their chamber. "Where is she?"

"I moved her," Link said blandly, watching her closely for a reaction. "With Lacie's suggestion."

"Without asking me?" She stopped midstride and stared at him as if he lost all wits.

"Don't want her to inadvertently walk in on us, do you? Don't you think she's a little too young to watch her sister make love with her husband? It wouldn't do now, would it? No, her seeing us would cause you to blush and stutter. You wouldn't be able to think of anything to say to her."

He waited for an answer. Wouldn't be surprised if she remained mute. Watched the ever-changing expressions of her face.

Finally, with a long slow breath she was resigned. It appeared so, "Where did you put her?"

"Actually, Lacie did the honors. Do you truly need to see her or are you stalling?"

He felt wicked, sinful actually. This was, after all, their wedding night. He wanted her all too himself. Wasn't about to share. His wife would be naked in his arms within the hour.

He poured her a glass of wine while he undid his carefully tied cravat. He handed the wine to her, watching for an indication of her decisions.

She said nothing, a serene expression crossing her face. He wanted to know what she was thinking.

He set his wine on a table before striding across the room to return, “This is for you.” Link handed her a small package. Reading the label. “It’s from Lacie. For your wedding night.”

Sophie’s eyes widened. She sat. “What is it?” She held the gift up, turned it over several times with a strange look of awe. “For the wedding night?”

He saw the hitch in her breath. His smile stretched across his face. He could guess. “Open it and see.”

The small gasp held him enthralled as did the sheer soft apricot colored negligée and robe she pulled from the brown wrapping paper. The gown was created from the thinnest of material, so sheer he saw her through the fabric. As she held it up, light caught the material, deliciously. “I can’t wear this. One can see right through it.”

“That’s the idea, my tigress.” His laughter was nearly a whisper in the room. “It is meant to give the female confidence because she is covered while it allows the male to see the woman he wed. It will make everything more exciting. I promise. Go put it on.” He wanted her to wear the negligée so he could slowly take it off. His imagination ran wild.

The gift rested in her lap, her cheeks as well as the tops of her breast a tender shade of pink almost matching the gown. If she wore it now, he wouldn’t know where one stopped and the other began. “You actually want me to wear this?” She held it up, the expression on her face priceless.

He noted her hesitance. Saw the fierce look of denial. She wanted to refuse him, deny their relationship as well as everything it could become.

He wouldn’t have it.

“If you don’t want to put on the negligée and robe, well, then we’ll proceed without them. Nothing will change what is going to happen between us tonight. You do recall your woman’s pleasure, the rapture, the splendor?”

He stepped toward her caressing her cheek, bending to stroke her mouth with his, his fingers now resting on the fastening of her gown.

“I’ll put it on. Give me a minute.” She stepped away, hurrying into the dressing room.

"Do you need help?" he called after her, watching.

He wanted to laugh. This was the woman who traded sexual innuendos with him as if she was a practiced whore. Now, she was shy. The thought turned over several times in his mind before he denounced it.

This woman was never shy where men were concerned.

While she was gone, he stoked the fire then poured more wine into his glass. She hadn't touched hers. He was going to enjoy this night to the fullest, give her time to adjust to a husband as well as her wifely duties. Perhaps she was nervous because she wasn't coming to him a maiden.

Perhaps not.

With Sophie one never knew.

Link contemplated all that happened since he arrived in Virginia. He supposed he knew from the first time he spoke with the elusive miss Sophie Carter-Brown, she'd be his. She fascinated him from the beginning. This maidenly, innocent act of hers had to stop. She was no retiring female without a wit of experience. He wanted to see the willing, passionate woman he anticipated when he decided to marry her.

He looked up.

Sophie stood framed nostalgically in the doorway, the gown and robe covering her but not concealing, exactly as it was meant to do. He inhaled swiftly then let the air out very, very slowly. While she was gone, he'd unbuttoned his shirt and pulled the fine lawn from his trousers, leaving it hanging.

He stepped forward, his hand outstretched. As she backed up, he stopped.

"Come here." Smiling, he held out the glass of wine he poured earlier for her, motioning for her to sit on the couch facing the fire. This beautiful exquisite creature was his. In less than an hour, he'd know her intimately.

With unfaltering steps, her chin high, she did his bidding. Stiffly, she sat down where he patted the seat beside him. He caught the subtle scent of roses. Accepting the glass of wine, she drank. When she finished, he watched her inhale a long breath of air.

"You look as if you're going to your execution," he murmured softly. "I promise you it won't be that bad. You will be deliciously delighted."

"Perhaps this would be easier if you drugged the wine," she said serenely. "I wouldn't have to feel anything."

He tossed his head back laughing. "Then you wouldn't remember what we did or even how it felt as we are doing it. You are going to want to feel this so much you will beg me to make love to you again and again. You will never be sated."

"Not feeling would be preferable."

His eyebrows drew together thoughtfully as he tried not to let anger temper his emotions. She wasn't going to allow an easy coaxing into their lovemaking tonight. He didn't want to fight with her. Willing, she would be willing, he determined.

So be it.

"Would you like something to eat?"

She shook her head as she stared at the tray of cheeses and meats sitting in front of them. "Food doesn't sound appetizing. My stomach is churning as if tiny butterflies are flitting about."

She was nervous.

"Perhaps later." He slipped from his shirt unsure how to start with his unenthusiastic bride of two months. He supposed seducing her as if she were the virgin she pretended to be would be the wisest course of action. He could do that.

Slowly, he traced a line down her neck to the pulse point beating out of control. He let his finger rest on the sensitive spot for a few seconds. Moving upward to her chin, to her ear then back down to the throbbing pulse. She appeared wild and flighty, her eyes darkening, widening as he followed the path of his fingertip with his lips, kissing every inch of exposed skin. He felt an unmistakable shiver pass through her. He wanted to set her naked on the bed and lick every tender, silken part of her.

She squirmed, her breath rasping in and out, her breasts heaving. Her hands lifted from her lap then fell back down unresponsive as of this moment.

"Link."

"Yes."

"What are you doing?" Her whisper thin voice quivered with the desire he created in her.

"Mmm..."

He grinned, toyed with the ties on the gown. Couldn't completely reach them until he removed the robe. This shouldn't be such a delicate matter. If all her lovers were drugged, this would have been a one-sided affair. She would have been the person coaxing, seducing, enticing the man to need more. This might well be uncharted territory for her.

"Link?"

"My love."

He chuckled softly as he slipped the robe over her shoulders his hands grazing her arms as he slid the sheer fabric lower then lower still until the robe pooled on the chair around her hips leaving her nearly naked body revealed behind the sheer fabric.

Her hands on his chest, she pushed at him. He brought her hands upward to his neck. "Wrap them around me."

"No."

"You're my wife, Sophie. No? Whatever do you mean?"

"You don't trust me."

Her voice was a thin wail as one palm touched her nipple, rubbed gently her head falling back inadvertently to give him greater access to her supple flesh, flesh he wanted to taste, savor, relish to the ultimate extent. He inhaled deeply. Her body held the essence of roses.

"What does trust have to do with this? With this moment?" He didn't want to get into a discussion now. Of all the things she needed to be honest with him about this. It would have been nice if she told him about the lovers, if that fact were truly behind them. They could have that conversation after they made love, after he had the proof he was indeed not her first. Why should it matter? She certainly wasn't his first.

His mouth encompassed hers, fully, passionately, fervently as he delved ever deeper inside the dark inviting recesses. The hot sultry warmth he found enticed more pleasures as it flowed into him, surrounded him. Her body provided a paradise for his. He longed to plunge himself deep inside. First, he would give her the woman's pleasure as he did on their wedding night then he would bury himself deep inside her woman's core.

"Everything." The whispered word stopped his onslaught for a moment as he tried to recall the query.

He chose to ignore the question or the statement. Recalling her earlier declaration, he wouldn't trust her until she confided in him. He assumed this was all about her friend as well as the stolen letter. Why the devil should he trust her? She'd naught but deceived him from the first meeting.

As his lips closed over one veiled nipple, she inhaled swift and deep, her body shuddering with raw hunger. He played with the tip, bit gently, licked then sucked the beautiful rounded globe deep into his mouth. Her breast was swollen, aroused and ready for more lovemaking. He turned his attention to the other breast.

Her fingers rose to his head, wound themselves into his hair, tugging him closer. She responded ardently with a heated yearning he didn't expect but longed for. The warmth of the fire he built created a circle of heat around them. The blaze leapt as high as the fire within him, burning to reach and coax her to an inferno she never felt before.

He returned his attention to her lips, kissing, laving, nipping, again and again. He trailed kisses across her chin upward to her ear, biting gently on the tiny pink lobe. She jerked with the contact then moaned softly, her purr of delight filling him. He chuckled. Her flesh was silk and satin, so very soft, velvet to his touch. Her body fragile, delicate yet inviting his attentions, she pleased him. Slowly she was succumbing to his ardent attentions. Soon she would be his. All his.

When he pulled away, her eyes were closed, her slightly swollen lips parted and moist in wickedly sinful invitation. He waited. Her eyes were open, darkened with the desperate desire he created within her sweet woman's body.

"Link? Is something wrong?"

"Keep your eyes open, my love." He kissed her again slowly, deeply until she moved against him, her hips seeking, imploring more, twisting against him. He pulled her onto his lap, his hand on her leg, sliding upward then down. He repeated the caress. She parted her legs for him. He grinned.

This was what he expected. *Her willing and eager compliance.* Not a virgin's passion but a woman's passion, one who understood the outcome of their play. He stroked her inner thigh, felt the constricting of her supple, sleek muscles. She was almost there, so very tense, anticipating, almost ready for him to give her the release she craved. He would bide his time. She would reach her climax when he decided she was ready.

His hand settled on her belly, his fingers resting on the light thatch of curls hiding her most intimate parts from him, from any man. Beneath his hand her body quivered with need. After tonight he would know the delights that waited for him, no other man but him.

No just met friends.

No past lovers.

If need be, he'd guard her from herself and her seemingly obsessive need for the male of the species.

He kissed her again. She met his tongue with hers, parried and danced. Sighs of pleasure flowed from her throat then into his while she arched searching for his caresses for the strokes, he gave her body that aroused and excited, created the enchantment she would not refuse. With his teeth, he untied one bow of the peignoir, letting the fabric fall below her exposed breast. The tip was tight, hard, waiting for his mouth and hands. He sucked the breast deep into his mouth again and again while his hands ran the length of her legs stopping at the apex of her thighs, teasing until more delightful sounds rippled from her throat. He turned his attention to the other perfectly swollen and rounded globe.

Link sucked in a long deep breath of air, willing his over eager sex to calm. His fingers rested on the petals of her sex without parting them. They were swollen and wet, hot to his touch.

"Would you like your pleasure now?"

His voice was bland yet his desire spiraled higher with each moment. He tugged on the other tie until it too fell below her breasts. Lifting her he sent the fabric of the negligée pooling to the floor along with the robe. He remembered that night he interrupted his brother and Lacie. Her peignoir and robe were in a similar position. He looked away but he saw her. She was beautiful but not nearly as beautiful as Sophie. He liked Sophie's breasts. They were perfect for him.

"I..."

He laughed, delighted with her, with her response to him. She was so aroused she couldn't form a coherent word. Parting the sweet feminine folds, he stroked and caressed, discovered the satin knot, massaged and teased until he thought surely she would buck herself off his lap.

"Relax," he whispered while his lips touched and teased her ear then found her mouth one more time, with his tongue he delved deeper, retreated then delved again inside her mouth in a parody of the sex they would soon have. "Let it come."

He felt the tightening of her muscles, felt them clench and heave against his hand. She was mindless now, her head thrown back, caught up in the beautiful climax, her woman's pleasure. "Open your eyes. I want to see them."

She did.

He watched the ever-changing emotions as they crossed her face. She moved now with frantic need, her head back, hair streaming wildly around her face. It was a moment he never wanted to forget. She cried out his name as her body convulsed, tremors wracking her over and over again until she slowed. Limp, now, she let her head fall against his chest, her breaths ragged.

As she calmed, he rubbed her back, whispered words to her that had no meaning. When she was relaxed, sated, he slipped his arm beneath her legs. He carried her to the bed, set her upon the quilts, propping pillows behind her back staring at her beautiful body.

"Wine?"

Flushed with the pleasure he gave her, she nodded, reached out and accepted the glass, her breasts swaying slightly with the small movement. He stepped back to admire her. She was naked, a beautiful shade of pink covering her from her cheeks to the tips of her toes. She looked at the floor in the direction of the robe and negligée, a wistful look on her face. For a moment she tried to cover herself with her hands.

Seemed to give up.

Drank the wine he poured for her.

"I've kissed and stroked every inch of you."

He sat down, yanking his boots off then his pants. Standing before her with nothing on, he was pleased to see she didn't look away, seemed to examine him with appreciation. Her eyes widened when she focused on his sex. He was hard and throbbing with need for her secret depths. He wasn't a randy goat. No, he would make sure to see to her pleasure again, in unison with him this time. While this would be their first joining tonight, it would not be the last.

"I still feel..." She lifted her shoulders in a hesitant shrug, her hair tumbling around her. The long strands provided minimal coverage. The tips of her breasts peeked out from behind the auburn curls.

It seemed she was at a loss for words. He sat beside her after bringing the tray of food to set on the bed. "Eat something."

She picked up a piece of cheese, nibbled a moment before she finished her glass of wine. He poured her another. Watched her.

"Why?" She tried to keep her focus on his eyes.

He wanted to laugh when she couldn't help herself. She looked lower. He laughed again, appreciating her failed efforts. She turned away.

"Why? Why what?"

The pulse at the base of her neck thundered again. He knew she wanted him. "You know."

"Had I known I wouldn't have asked?" He broke off a piece of bread, handed part of it to her along with another piece of cheese. "So, why what?"

Unhurriedly, she ran her tongue across her lips. Looked away. When she returned her gaze to look at him again, "Why didn't you...?" She paused once more, fiddled with her hair.

"Why?" he prompted pleased with the idea she might ask the

question on her mind.

"Go to hell!" She drank down the glass. Drank long and deep from the bottle.

He roared with laughter. She would always surprise him. "Why didn't I come inside you?" He leaned over kissing her lusciously swollen lips, which eagerly parted for him. He'd done that to her. Fashioned the wicked picture in front of him. "I will in time. We need sustenance first. Eat. Drink. Should I open another bottle?" He rose from the bed, slipping quickly into his trousers as he made the decision without an answer from her.

Link headed downstairs for the second bottle, delighted so far with the outcome of this evening. The time with her was going as he planned with a few delightful deviations, side trips one might say. He hadn't expected her to drink straight from the bottle or tell him to go to hell. Amazing.

When he returned, he expected her to be clothed in the negligée and robe, covers drawn to her chin. He would have the fun of removing the clothing again.

He whistled.

~ * ~

Furious with his overbearing audacity, she swore for several minutes after the door closed behind him. His nerve outranked anything she'd known before. She drank from the bottle until she emptied the contents. The room tilted slightly. A warm haze filled her from her tummy to her brain. She was getting intoxicated, something she'd never done before.

She didn't care.

She hummed a tune.

He would discover soon enough there were no other lovers in her life. She would insist on an apology. The only man who knew her intimately, touched her breast, kissed them would be her husband. She shouldn't have hedged. Should have proceeded straight to the bedding.

After all, it was what he wanted. She wanted to prove to him he could trust her. She didn't lie. Sometimes she didn't tell him everything.

But she didn't lie.

Her peignoir lay on the floor a few short feet away from her. Desperately she wanted the sheer fabric's protection. He would expect that. She intended to do the unexpected. Surprising him, the look of utter astonishment on his face pleased her immensely. She must attempt to stay one step ahead of him at all times.

She arranged herself on the bed, artfully draping her hair across her to conceal and entice, telling herself she could do this. She could play the seductress. Tonight's outcome would be more than gratifying. Moistening her lips, she counted to one hundred, wondering how much time it would take him to retrieve another bottle of wine. She closed her eyes to stop the spinning room, vowing then she would not drink more wine even if it would ease the next step in their lovemaking.

She didn't know what that was except that he would thrust inside her. He would hurt her. Having turned away when the men filled Cocoa, she wasn't all that sure. Her mind would not let go of the screams of pleasure she heard those times. Curious, she touched a nipple, feeling a quick and sudden jolt of pleasure. His touch did that to her, more so. Generated the heat and warmth, the hot wet feelings that ignited such strange sensation within her.

Blessed hell, he needed to return before she lost the newfound courage. The tiny bundle of sheer pink fabric lying on the floor became ever more enticing. She turned away from the sight of the fabric. Her stomach growled. A small bubble of laughter ripped through her throat. The sound was harsh, so unforgiving she wanted to stifle the sensation. She yearned to get this over with. The anticipation along with the fears, threatened to make her crazy.

Sophie picked out a piece of cheese. Ate it quickly. Finished chewing, she downed another piece, feeling a little more satisfied. The foggy haze produced by the wine diminished. Perhaps Link was right. To deal with this evening she needed nourishment, a lot of it as well as more liquid courage. The empty bottle of wine sat on the nightstand.

The door creaked open.

Link stood in the doorway, grinning lasciviously at her. His gaze focused on her breasts then rose to her mouth. She moistened her lips. His wicked smile stretched across his face, heating her body. A surge of wetness between her thighs caused her to writhe. She held her ground, determined to seduce him. He held two bottles of wine, enough for the entire night she assumed.

He handed her the open bottle, watched as she brought it to her lips and drank deeply. It tasted delicious. She held it to him. He drank then set it on the nightstand. He stepped out of his trousers.

"Enough for now. You didn't dress. Expected you to do so. Expected your covers to be drawn to your chin. Why am I surprised? You always do the unexpected," he told her sitting beside her his long powerful legs stretched out in front of him.

She saw the surprise in his eyes and was pleased with herself. He did expect to come in here and find her clothed. "No. I did not."

"It would have been entertaining to take your clothing off you again. I did so appreciate tugging at the pink bows with my teeth," he paused, still grinning, "again."

"Ah, it will have to wait. Maybe tomorrow night I will allow you to do that." She reached across him, one nipple sliding provocatively against his chest eliciting a groan from him. Grabbing the bottle, she drank deeply. He took it from her then did the same.

Sophie needed to continue with the surprises as long as she could figure out what to do. Having no idea how to seduce a man, she would have to take the cues from Link then perhaps rely on gut instinct. She straddled him. Her legs caressed his. She felt the rough hair, felt his body touch hers intimately between her thighs. Caught his musky scent coupled with something spicy.

His look of surprise gave her reason to grin. She spread her fingers around his hard arousal. Saw him jerk in response. Heard the male groan rumble from his chest.

"Ah, you never cease to amaze me, my love, shatter my male ego, strip it into tiny shreds. If you want control, I happily hand it over to you.

Do what you will with this man's body."

She couldn't think of one word to say. *Control. Yes.*

"What now?" he asked.

Sophie ran her hands along his chest, stopping to stroke each tiny nipple. She bent to lick each one. He caught her breasts in his hands. Held them. "I want to do to you what you did to me." She felt his body shudder at her words.

"You're the commander. Lead on." His grin of pleasure showed even white teeth as he waited.

She touched the pulse at his neck, ran her finger up the length of his neck, along his chin, felt the stubble there. Hesitantly, she brushed her lips against his, ran her tongue between them felt the sweet sensation as he opened for her.

He groaned again. His body jerked.

Pushing away she looked at him, wary, confused a bit by his reaction.

"That was a sound of a man well-pleased. Carry on."

His hands rested on her waist, moved downward to cup her bottom. They were strong hands, callused. She liked it when he squeezed. She twisted. Her squirms brought a deep chuckle from his lips.

Slowly, she moved against him, felt his rod pulsing against her intimately. "You have to sit still and let me seduce you," she purred softly before realizing that was truly her voice.

"Don't know if I can do that. Sit still."

He ran his hands along the length of her spine then back to their lower resting place.

"You're naughty, not playing by the rules."

"There are no rules. Kiss me, wench."

Sophie bent, sucked one of his nipples into her mouth, bit and laved, mimicked what he did to her. She turned her attention to the other one before she trailed wet kisses lower to touch upon his hard abdomen then lower still. Her hands found his legs, stroked from his ankles to his hard thighs. She followed with kisses. His fingers wound into her hair, tugged until she rose higher, until his lips found her mouth.

He kissed her hard and long, his tongue delving deeper and deeper. She played with his until he sucked hers into his mouth. In the back of her throat, she moaned softly again and again as her need rose ever higher spiraling. Once more she kissed him, lowering herself on his chest. Kissing lower and lower until she felt his sex pulse against her cheek, then trailing light teasing caresses along his shaft.

It was then he lost the control he'd sought. He flipped her over, spread her legs and came between them, capturing one breast in his mouth, sucking deeply on the tender, sensitive flesh.

"Blessed hell but you unman me."

"I don't mean to," she murmured softly, realizing how much she appreciated his hard body flush against the softer curves of her own. She ran her fingers through his dark hair wishing for more of this hot deep pleasure.

His hands under her hips, he lifted her. His mouth touched upon her intimately. He laved kisses, sucked, stroked until she was wild with her pleasure, frantic in her need. She twisted and wiggled, sensations coiling deep inside. Arched her back begging.

"Do you want me, my love?"

Her nods were wild, unrestrained, God how she wanted, craved the wonderful feelings he fashioned within her body. She wanted to feel the undulating intense pleasure again and again. Wanted these feelings to never stop.

"I want to hear the words."

She closed her eyes, knowing this was the moment of truth. There would be pain, perhaps more so since he didn't believe her virgin status. Vindication would be hers. What came after that, she had no idea.

"The words, little one. I'm waiting not all that patiently."

"Yes."

"Yes what?" He grinned, kissed her again and again effectively keeping her from saying what he wanted to hear. He pulled away, gazing down upon her, his fingers lazily rearranging her hair.

"I want you, Link."

"Do you want your woman's pleasure now?" His voice was sultry, seductive no longer coaxing but demanding she give all of herself to him.

"Yes."

"Yes what?"

Deep in the back of her throat she moaned softly, a feminine sound of desire. His hands touched everywhere followed by his lips, teeth and tongue.

"Yes, I want my woman's pleasure now."

Each breath she inhaled was shaky. Her legs were quivering, her body so tight, waiting to reach that pinnacle where she had no control of her body.

"Now, there will be no more discussion of your maiden status. We will both know and accept the truth."

At that moment, he thrust inside. She cried out, tears welling in her eyes as she pushed and shoved trying desperately to remove his body from hers. She had not thought it would hurt this much. Pounding on his back, pushing on his shoulders, she felt the pain sear through her, burn deeply.

"Sophie, lie still. Please." His voice so soft it reached inside her. He sounded hurt yet relieved in some strange way. "I'm sorry."

"You didn't believe me."

He held himself rigid over her. "The pain will vanish then there will be only pleasure for you. I promise."

She tried to buck him off. "Go away. I didn't think it would hurt this much." Tears threatened to fall.

"I'm not going anywhere. Is the pain gone now? We're going to finish what we started. I've never made love to a virgin. You're my first."

It vanished nearly as quickly as it came upon her. He began to move again. His hand caressed and stroked her, bringing her higher once more. It did not take long to bring her back to that coveted pinnacle. Convulsive shocks engulfed her, tremors seized her, mindlessly she moved against him. With her beneath him, she cried out. Heaved against his body. Felt his power.

He yelled at the same time as he pumped furiously. He settled down upon her. She felt his weight atop her. For a moment he remained unmoving. She closed her eyes, content, unable to use any muscle she possessed. He rolled from her, pulling her with him, cradling her head against his chest, stroking her hair.

Finally, she felt the deep rise then fall of his chest as he breathed deeply. "I've no idea what to say to you. I'm stunned, a little bit in awe. Appalled at myself."

"An apology might be in order." Thrilled he finally understood the truth of her life, she ran her fingers down his chest to rest on his belly, noticed him come to life again. "So soon?"

He laughed then spoke softly. "Yes, my love, so soon. You do that to me." The pause was long and silent, so very silent she watched moonlight drift in through the window. Heard the trill of a bird outside. Then, "I do apologize for not taking your word on the status of your untried body. You, however, must also admit I had good reason to believe otherwise."

"You did."

"This is over then. You are mine."

"Yes, as you are mine. Know that I don't share."

Sophie supposed this was a victory of sorts, a small skirmish to be won something she might recall in her old age. He sat up taking her with him, placing her next to his side, a possessive arm draped around her shoulder.

She stiffened, thinking he was going to begin his interrogation all over. She supposed she could tell him about Sandy much easier than she could speak of Devon Masters and her stolen reticule. Devon now had the names and addresses of all the people Link held dear and who lived in Glasgow.

He should know.

She should tell him.

Telling him could wait another day. She didn't want to ruin this evening. He would be angry that Devon was in Glasgow. Once more he would question what she was doing with him, her intentions. He would know for sure though that she was never Devon's, never would be.

Sophie let out a long slow breath of air. He should no longer have reason to question her morality, her innocence or anything else. She was sure he would, even though he now had proof of her true nature.

She wasn't a whore. Not a brazen hussy or a harlot. She didn't giver herself to any man who asked. He had no reason to call her names.

Except wife.

When she looked at him, his eyes were closed. He seemed tired yet...she could not be sure of anything.

"Wine?" he asked her, his eyes now focused on her. He drank deeply before handing the bottle to her and retrieving the tray of food.

She drank again. Listened to a clock somewhere in the house chime twelve times. He pulled from the bottle again, washing down the food he ate.

"What are you thinking?"

She couldn't stop the question. Didn't want to in any case.

"Let's wait." He drank again then set the bottle aside. He bent to brush a swift kiss across her lips. "I want to make love to you."

"You did or have you forgotten already?"

She was blatantly sarcastic. She wanted him again. Didn't want him to know how much.

"I need your warmth, the heat of your body surrounding me. Need my wife beneath me, atop me or in front of me," he murmured softly, nipping light kisses across her mouth from one corner to the next then back again. "Do you want me, Sophie?"

He rose, walking across the room to toss a log on the fire. Naked, he was beautiful, magnificent. His muscles flexed as he moved, his grace fluid, so very masculine. He poured water into a small basin then picked up a cloth.

"Open for me, your virgin's blood is on your thighs. I'll wash it away from your skin but not my mind. Remembering this moment will stay with me through time. I'm your only lover, Sophie. Didn't think I cared. I'm a man well pleased by the notion."

Sophie was suddenly shy, hesitant to reveal herself to this man who coaxed her, teaching her the ways of the flesh so tenderly. She found herself shaking her head, denying him even as he sat down next to her.

With him staring at her, she didn't want to open her legs for him. She would be too vulnerable.

"I've seen and kissed every part of you, Sophie. Open for me and I will take care of you. Is there pain?" His hands rested on her thighs while he waited for her to do his bidding. "I'm your husband. I will do this."

He didn't need to remind her. She did then, parted her legs for him. Felt the blatant rise of heat over her body. While he soaked the cloth in the tepid water before gently washing her, she closed her eyes. He touched her so very lightly. Her breath shivered into her lungs in ragged acceptance of her new life. She realized she always wanted him. The first moment she met him, she wanted him. Wanted him even when she knew he would never give in to her, would never accept the scenario she was playing out with him in the lead role.

When he finished, he stood, stretching his lean hard body. Link was an exceptional man. She knew that, too, from the moment she was first introduced to him. Remembered thinking he would discover all her secrets. The thought was not far from the truth.

He popped the cork from the third bottle of wine before handing the bottle to her. She sipped slowly, still feeling the effects of the first two. "I shouldn't," she murmured.

"Why not? This is our wedding night. You can do whatever pleases you. I plan to please myself and, in the process, delight you."

"Not really," she murmured softly, staring at her fingernails. "Don't you think we should get some sleep?"

"Not until I pleasure my wife again. Not until I hear her scream out my name while in the depths of her woman's pleasure." His grin was wickedly sinful, compelling, seducing. "You enchant me."

He tugged her into his arms, striding to the fur rug beside the fire. He set her down. Stood back to let his wicked gaze travel the length of her before resting on her breasts. The nipples puckered, tightening. It seemed she felt the heat of his gaze everywhere it traveled. She thought to cover herself with her hands. He shook his head.

Link lay beside her on the rug. She felt his sex penetrate inside her, touch her womb. He held still for the longest time while he kissed her, stroked her breasts, toyed with the tight buds that seemed to make her arch and squirm against him. She needed release. Needed to feel him move inside her until she could bear it no longer. Ripples of sounds she didn't recognize came from her.

He didn't move. Instead, he braced himself on his forearms to study her. His eyes were the color of the darkest most vivid blue. They shimmered with unrequited fire. Slowly, he lowered himself to kiss her. She felt a sudden shift as he turned. She sat atop him, his shaft still buried deep inside. His fingers played with her breasts, teasing and taunting. Molten fire raced through her.

Without conscious thought she rose on him then settled back down. His hands on her waist encouraged. His face tensed with the strain of holding back. He stroked her intimately. She arched her back, twisting slightly bringing him deeper into her body.

"Sophie, my love," he murmured her name. "I don't think I will ever get enough of you."

His kisses lingered on her sensitive flesh. When his mouth met hers and their tongues danced once more, she tasted the sweet wine. His male scent filled her senses. She was intoxicated with him, with her husband.

It seemed he wanted to make the mercuric enchantment last forever. The clock chimed once. She cried out his name as her body burst into blinding splendor so sweet and so intense, she thought she might have died and gone to heaven.

She didn't want this to end.

Now she lay replete against him, her weight full upon him. She sighed softly as a breeze swept through the slightly open window near the bed cooling her heated skin. She must have dozed. When she woke, the sun was shining. She was tangled in his arms and legs. His eyes open, he was stroking her hair, running his large hands along her back, lower still.

"You're awake."

~ * ~

"I am."

"We only made love twice last night," he told her softly as he brought her lips to meet his. The light knock on the door stooped him.

"Sophie, can I come in? Leslie told me I had to let you know I was here and that I wanted to talk to you."

"In just a minute. I was going to make that one more time before we rose. Now, I suppose I'll have to wait." Bending over he kissed her, an easy gentle undemanding kiss. "I'll leave you two alone. You should probably put the negligée and robe on, well, perhaps you should dress." He handed her the night clothing anyway. "Would you like me to order you a bath?"

She nodded, moving her head as she stared at him, at his arousal he was unable to conceal. He grinned when he caught the focus of her attention.

"Yes," she murmured softly, "I think I would like that, a bath. I'd like you also."

He laughed, pulled on his trousers. He kissed her again, unlocking and opening the door for Clare. "Don't spend too long. Sophie needs to eat."

Link whistled as he left the room and his wife behind to talk to her sister. Perhaps today he would go to his solicitor to see if there were any homes near Southcliff to purchase. He needed to set the process in motion. He wanted his cherished ones close by. Clare needed playmates. She also needed to go to school. He had a lot to deal with in order for his family to thrive.

Today he would also discover a few truths about this friend of hers as well as the stolen letter. She would not keep secrets from him. He wouldn't allow it. Perhaps he should withhold his lovemaking until she could no longer keep the truth from him. He dismissed that ludicrous idea. It would hurt him more than it would her.

By the look on her face whenever the topic was approached, he sensed fear. She had nothing to be afraid of. Didn't she know that? Didn't she understand he had the strength to protect her? She was still afraid of her uncle. She would have to learn her uncle was powerless now.

He sauntered into the breakfast room, feeling inordinately pleased with his wife as well as the direction of his new life.

"You must have had a good night," Leslie said chuckling as he sipped his tea. "Lacie told me I needed to teach you a few things. Don't believe she understood you were the man who could teach most of us."

Link laughed. "You should try coffee sometime. I found the heady brew much to my liking, much more so than tea. I made sure I've a sufficient supply to last until the next transport from Virginia arrives."

"Well, did you..." Leslie paused. "Never mind. A man stopped by this morning, a few hours ago. Said he knows you and Sophie from your time in Virginia. I didn't like the look of him or the sneer on his face when he mentioned your wife. He told me he knows things."

"You don't say. Did he tell you anything else?"

Link didn't like the look of doubt. Perhaps suspicion was a better description, on his brother's face. An acquaintance, he mused thoughtfully, running over the list of men he met in the states.

"That it would serve your purpose to meet with him. He has certain things to tell you. I don't trust the man. Threads of blackmail are entwined with this message."

"When and where did he want to meet?"

Link's gut clenched. This didn't bode, well he was sure of the fact. Sophie needed to spill the truth.

"Didn't give a location. Said he'd be in touch sometime today. You might want to make use of a certain spy you're acquainted with." Seemingly unconcerned Leslie spread peach jam across his scone.

Link's mind whirled with endless possibilities. Two men he knew of had families here. Two of Sophie's supposed lovers. Devon Masters and Charles Ewing both had ties to Glasgow or Edinburgh.

"What did you think of the man?" Link asked, hoping for his brother's insight, which never seemed to fail him.

"From first look, the man's a gambler. He's wagering something right now. What it is I've no idea except that you most likely won't appreciate whatever he's bringing to the table."

"Devon Maters," Link said softly. "Was he relatively young, my age, give or take a few years.

“Yes, I’d say he’s got something in mind. Something you would take exception to. Do you think his sudden interest has anything to do with your wife coupled with the supposed rumors surrounding her life in Virginia?” Leslie asked seeming to see far more than what Link would have liked.

However, if anyone was to see the situation clearly it would be his brother.

“Yes, he believes he was once her lover. When I told her I didn’t share she had to send him away. To get rid of him, she told him she had the pox. By now he’s determined he doesn’t have the wretched disease. He’s also probably seeking revenge of some sort. He wouldn’t like being tricked.”

One of Leslie’s perfectly formed ducal eyebrows shot upward at Link’s statement. “Was he a lover?”

“No.” Link was curt wishing he didn’t have to explain yet thankful he knew the truth now that he finally made love to his wife. “No, he wasn’t.”

His brow still arched in speculation, “You are sure.”

“Absolutely positive.” There was nothing to explain. Leslie would know he spoke the truth.

“Well, then, there is most likely nothing for this gambling man to wager or hold over her head. She doesn’t need to fear him. Did he speak with Sophie, do you know?”

“I’m assuming he did.” Link ground down hard on his teeth, the muscle in his neck jerking. “I’m beginning to think Mr. Masters was the man who stole the letter I wrote to you. Unfortunately, the letter also contained the names and addresses of all of Lacie’s sibling in the unlikely case you still didn’t believe I wed her. Before this goes any farther, they have to be informed.”

“So,” Leslie began, stroking his jaw, “he is in possession of way too much information about our families. This is very interesting. I’ve been needing a diversion of sorts. This will suit.”

“That he is.”

"What do you intend?"

"I'm going to meet him to see what he wants."

"I'll be going with you. Haven't had excitement of this nature for quite some time. Until now, I didn't believe I missed the intrigue along with the exhilaration. Suppose you and I have a bit of ferreting out to do. I'll see what I can uncover about the man that might be useful."

"For now, all I want is to find a home for Sophie to make her own. After one night residing with my brother, despite he and his wife's incredible hospitality, I'm ready for the privacy I crave."

"I would like that too. Clare caught Lacie and me—well let's just say I was—well it was something a young lady shouldn't see. Not used to having company. Merry stays in the country most of the time. What do you have in mind?"

Sophie waltzed into the room wearing a yellow muslin day dress followed by the heady scent of roses. Clare was behind her.

"Sent a note to my solicitor. Should be hearing back from him in an hour or two. We can take a carriage ride to look at a few homes if you like."

Blessed hell, he needed to have her tell him about the encounter with Devon as well as the identity of her new friend. He didn't like surprises. Perhaps he should bring up what he knew.

"I would go with you," Sophie said. "Clare is going riding with Merry who is coming into town to meet her. If we find a house, will she live with us?"

"I don't think so," Link was leaning back, relaxed in his chair, watching the delicate play of emotions on her face. "Believe she should live with the children. She needs friends of her own age." He emphasized the word friend hoping she would get the hint.

"The children?" Her breath whispered. She turned pale, ashen in fact. "No."

Ah, had he told her anything about his cherished ones? He couldn't recall. She deserved to know all of the truth.

Leslie slanted him a look that bordered on disbelief. "Perhaps you should have had that conversation before the vows were said. She doesn't know you have children, as in many?"

He waved a dismissive hand, grinning. She would come to love all of them too. "There was no time for conversations of any sort."

Sophie's gaze seemed to be darting from one man to the other, a questioning look in her eyes. She seemed willing enough to wait. She exhibited patience.

He was pleased.

He would tell her all about his children while they searched for a home this afternoon. She would tell him what part Devon Masters played in the stolen letter and even if he was lucky what the man's intentions were.

"Children? That does seem a puzzle to me. Have you been married before and neglected to inform your wife?" She was all smiles as she sipped her tea while she toyed with the food on her plate.

They had that conversation once before. She must have forgotten. Either that or she was after something else. No one truly knew about his children. "You need to eat, Sophie. What if you are carrying my child as we speak?"

She gasped in a quick breath of air, choking on the small morsel of food she put in her mouth prior to his words. Her face turned a ghostly shade of white. She didn't say a word.

"You do want children, Sophie. Yes, that conversation should have come up before we married in such haste. There is really no choice in the matter. I intend to make love to my wife every night. The consequences of that action of course are the cherished children. The more the better."

He knew she wanted to toss a glass of water in his face. Ah, he enjoyed the battles and would enjoy even more the making up. He wanted to take her hand and run upstairs to their room. He wanted her beneath him, her lips parted and damp ready for his kiss. Ah, he wanted so much. His cravings would have to wait.

She threw the glass of water in his face.

He roared with laughter.

At least he knew it was fresh water.

Chapter Ten

Five full days passed before Link found the perfect home, situated ten miles from Glasgow toward the River Firth and five miles from Southcliff. It sat atop a hill, looking over the countryside, trees surrounding the home, the view magnificent. Once there had been tenant farmers on the surrounding area. Now there were independent men who worked their land. About a quarter of a mile away there was also a large six-bedroom home, perfect for his children. Tomorrow he would send for them.

He supposed he would also need to purchase a townhouse in the city. That could be put off until these two new homes were furnished and ready for habitation. He was more than pleased to give Sophie a chance to decorate the home where she would live. He intended to also listen to Clare and Sophie about the home for his special children. If she wanted, Clare could play an intricate part in their education, telling them of Virginia, the culture as well as its history.

The time to speak more clearly with Sophie about Devon Masters eluded him. Every time they'd been in the carriage someone accompanied them. First, it was Clare then Lacie decided she needed to see for herself if the home was good enough for her brother-in-law. Merry tagged along the day before when he made his final decision. Sophie hoped Merry and Clare would become good friends. They were only two years apart in age.

Now, they sat at the restaurant where they ate their first meal together on this side of the Atlantic. The one they ate the day he arrived didn't count because she failed to eat. Sophie was toying with the napkin, folding and unfolding the linen cloth while they waited. Her gaze alternated from him to the linen, the intricate folds having vanished.

"We need to talk about Devon Masters." He spoke softly, watching her, studying her reaction. He didn't want to stress or worry her but this knowledge was vital.

At the statement, her face seemed devoid of anything hinting at emotion. She assumed the stoic role she played so very well as she was able to hide all she felt behind a bland mask that told him nothing. Perhaps it told him she was terrified as she must have been when Uncle William pushed her.

She learned that, he supposed, as a necessary survival tactic, a way to keep Brinkmeyer from beating her. Blessed hell but he wished he could have beaten her uncle within an inch of his life. "I don't want to talk about that man. He's a posturing fake. Overly fond with what he sees as his manly self the personification of a man's man. His postures were always absurd and laughable."

The venom in her voice took him off guard, set his mind spinning. He didn't expect the hated and very heated emotion she expressed so vehemently. Supposed he didn't fully understand Sophie's experiences in Virginia. He expected these emotions where her uncle was concerned, not Masters. In some ways Devon Masters was also Brinkmeyer's victim.

Sophie wasn't about to tell him or explain the encounter she must have had with Master's who would still believe he'd been her lover. So, he decided to weave the story for her he believed to be true. "Devon Masters stole your reticule hence the letter also." He leaned forward expecting a yes or no answer but sat back abruptly when the waiter brought the bottle of wine. When the man left, "What did he want in return?"

She paled so swiftly he inhaled a quick drink of air, wondering at the sudden and dramatic change in her demeanor. The fork she was playing with tumbled to the floor. He picked it up, setting it and the remainder of her silverware away from her fidgeting hands. Seeing her reaction, he assumed Master's wanted her in his bed and was willing to blackmail her to force her.

"N-nothing," she stammered, her voice a whisper in the noisy surroundings, her face too pale, her dark lashes forming an arc across her high cheekbones.

"Of course he wanted something. If I have to guess, my thoughts might be far from the truth." By the expression on her face the man wanted her as his lover. "So, tell me. I don't want to guess."

"They won't be far from the truth. I'm sure the truth is exactly what you are thinking." Her voice so quiet he had to lean forward to hear what she said. "If you must know everything, I fought him. That's how he managed to get my reticule. Sandy rescued me, came along and frightened Devon."

A sudden blinding rage encompassed Link. He tried to calm the anger, needed to present a reassuring voice to her. He saw the moisture simmering in her eyes spiking her lashes, immediately regretting his fury. "Tell me and I'll decide. Tell me about Sandy too."

Sophie was shaking her head, leaning on the table as if to rise and walk out of the restaurant. "I..." He watched her swallow. Watched the sudden rise in her pulse. "I can't." She sat down. Stared at her fingernails.

He decided a small lie in this case would do more good than harm. "I'm meeting Devon tomorrow. He will tell me everything I need to know. It would surely help if I understood your side of this tale he's going to try to tell me. I know you were never his lover. It would also be nice to understand why he confronted you." While he did intend to meet with the reprobate, it wasn't going to happen the next day.

"You can't."

"What was that you said?" He leaned forward his hand now resting on top of hers. If possible, her face was paler than before. He needed to proceed with caution.

She stiffened in the way of Sophie Carter-Brown. Her chin tilted up while her eyes blazed. "You will not meet that man. He has no good intended for anyone, including you."

Good, he was getting somewhere. Now that he tapped into her emotions, she would tell him what he needed so desperately to comprehend. The hold Devon Masters had on his wife had to be broken before it was nurtured to a point where she was paralyzed with fear.

"He will not stop until I meet him. If you speak to me, I will go into the meeting with the upper hand. If you don't," he bent closer, "he might well win in the end. I've the feeling you are the sole recipient of his vileness. Didn't you tell the man you had the pox? He might well seek revenge since he now understands the truth. You lied."

Beneath his hand he felt the fine trembling, saw the tiny beads of perspiration dot her forehead, watched as a single tear slipped from one eye. "You will hate me, distrust everything I've told you. I've no wish to be with this man yet you will believe the worst in me. You always have," she blurted unthinking, unaware he could easily refute her words.

Nothing Devon Masters could tell him about his wife would have a ring of truth.

Guilt at his actions jolted him back to Sophie's reality. Perhaps he had always believed the worst. That was no longer true. "Don't forget our wedding night," he told her softly. "Don't forget I was the man who deflowered you. There is nothing he can tell me about you that I'll believe."

She jerked away, her eyes narrowing. "No, I won't forget."

For a moment, he was afraid it was the pain she was remembering not the pleasure. He would have to fix that. Tonight would be his choice. "Obviously, nothing he can tell me will ever convince me he was one of your lovers. I'm the only man you've known."

He didn't know how to convince her the horrible pathetic man had no hold over her or him.

She sat up straighter, her chin higher than before, "You're right. I will strive to remember that."

"Good girl, should we eat?" he asked as the dishes were set in front of them.

He poured the wine. After several minutes passed, he sat back still waiting for answers.

She needed to eat.

His patience was being called on again.

She seemed to focus on his lips over the rim of her glass. The sight was seductive and appealing. He wanted her this instant.

He had more patience now that he understood more fully what the gambling man was most likely expecting. He wouldn't get what he wanted.

Link waited until they finished their meal before he broached the next subject, hoping to learn everything before they left the restaurant. He leaned forward, his forearms resting on the table. "Tell me all about Sandy, the man who was kind to you, the man who drove you from the docks to the Stewart townhouse. The man you trusted with your life as well as Clare's with no reservations." *Dear God.* "He was a stranger."

She pulled in a long drink of air as she pushed her plate away. Drank deeply. "He works for a man whose name is Donal Chamberlin. He told me he knew people who knew the duke."

He leaned back setting his napkin on the table before resting his folded hands on his belly. "That, my love, is a good start. Please continue. Donal Chamberlin is a friend of Leslie's. He is also married to one of Lacie's sisters. Still, what made you believe him?"

For several seconds she stared at him, at his mouth. He wondered where she learned that or if it was something women knew. He felt the restless stirring of his body. Ah, but she meant to intimidate, to change the focus of his thoughts to sex. She could try worse ploys to stall him. Here in the middle of a public domain her game was useless. He wouldn't react until they returned to the townhouse.

"The man rescued me from Devon. When Sandy wanted to go after him, he vanished into the crowds of people."

She swept her tongue across her lips. Nerves or seduction, he couldn't be sure. She tapped one slim finger on her chin.

He chose nerves.

"In hindsight, I should have had him find the man. If he were in jail now for stealing, we would not be hounded by Devon Masters." She finished in an explosion of emotion that surprised Link.

"True." Patiently he waited.

"Sandy offered to give me a ride into town. Clare and I would have had to walk. In the rain."

"You accepted. Why?"

A slow rise of anger started deep in his belly. She trusted a man she didn't know with her life as well as Clare's. He could not halt that fact from tormenting him. Fear rolled within, pooled deep in his belly. He would have to fix that. Her innocent trust could get her violated or worse, killed.

Her shoulders rose a fraction as she looked at him through dark veiled lashes. "He seemed nice enough, harmless. Truly, I could see no other choice. We had no money, nowhere to stay the night. Clare and I were alone. With no funds, I had to trust someone. I trusted him."

"Is he a big man?" Link asked not that size made a lot of difference.

Most men could overpower her. She could have lost her life that night. In part he was responsible. When he rushed her onto the ship, he'd not thought farther than getting her from the Glasgow port into town. He'd not given her the means or the direction that was needed. Didn't expect any problems to arise.

He should be shot.

"Bigger than you."

That wasn't what he wanted to hear. "I suppose he's just a large pussycat."

She grinned at him then. A smile quite capable of melting his heart, "I don't know. He didn't say. Clare seemed to trust him too. Silently, we agreed."

"That's nice to hear."

They were both little fools. Neither had been anywhere, had always in some way been protected from the world. Even what Sophie encountered with her uncle, he protected her. She had not been touched sexually.

No, just beaten when she didn't get the desired results.

"You've no idea what it's like to be a woman alone, with no options." Once more she was staring at her fingernails. He'd rather she focused her beautiful eyes on his lips.

Well, of course, he didn't. Yet he was willing to listen to her story, try to see why she made certain choices. He made a mental note to seek out Donal Chamberlin and discover more about this man, Sandy.

"Acting foolish is not a choice."

By the pursing of her lips and the sudden narrowing of her eyes, he could tell she heard his anger.

She set her hands on the table, standing and leaning toward him. "What would you have me do? Walk to Glasgow? Offer my body in exchange for funds so I could hire a cab? Ah, send a message perhaps by carrier pigeon."

Sophie sat, her arms across her chest, belligerence written clearly on her face while her eyes blazed.

For a second, he found himself at a loss for words. Then, "No."

"What should I have done?"

Now that she put the question on him, he felt a slight rise of heat to his cheeks. "The answer escapes me."

"I bow to your superior knowledge and expertise. Of all the possible scenarios what should I have done?"

"You trusted a man you didn't know."

"Yes."

It appeared she waited for him to come up with a course of action. He gave her the win. "This was my fault. I suppose you did the best you could under the circumstances." Even to his ears, he sounded condescending. "I have no reason to be angry with you. The anger should be directed solely at me."

"Thank you." A small grin formed then grew. Her gaze returned to his mouth.

"Don't gloat. The chances you accepted by your choice are still untenable. Perhaps you should have walked."

"And left Clare's trunk on the dock? I could have carried my valise. I ask again, what should I have done?"

"You make a strong point. So, why did you trust this big man?"

He supposed a woman might have a strong feeling about a man, a gut instinct she trusted, perhaps. Sophie, his wife, did have experience dealing with men. She knew them almost as well as he knew women. She spent more than a year deceiving the male species for her uncle.

Discovering their every desire then countering it with words and quick wit.

She softly cleared her throat, sitting up straighter, her chin high. “He rescued me from Devon who was trying to drag me away on the crowded waterfront. He had no fear. It didn’t seem to me he had a hidden agenda. Devon wanted to make me his whore, pimp me out for his personal gain. I’m sure he would have done the same with Clare given the opportunity.”

“Sandy did, did he? Rescue the two of you?” He would strangle Devon Masters next time he saw him. His audacity went beyond anything he encountered before.

“Yes.”

“So, you trusted Sandy with your life.”

“Are we back to that? We’ve gone full circle. You’re still saying the same thing. Again, I ask what should I have done?”

Her words hinted strongly at sarcasm. There was also an undercurrent of anger. She was furious. It was clear she wanted the conversation to end.

Link knew she was angry. Blessed hell, he was furious with no way to vent his rage. He should have been there with her. Should have never left her and Clare to find their way by themselves. Should not take this out on her. That was exactly what he was doing.

“Sandy took you to the townhouse. A duke’s home?”

“Yes.”

“No questions asked?”

“A few.”

Well, at this point in time, he didn’t deserve more than simple or one-word answers. He put Sophie in a less than a pleasant situation. “Did he wait for you to see if the duke would allow you in the house?”

“Yes.”

“What then?”

Her eyes were dark simmering pools of molten gray. “He was going to take me to Donal’s home if your brother turned me out. He said he would vouch for me. If Donal didn’t accept us, he would take me to the bakery. Said we could stay in the apartment above as long as we needed or until you arrived. He was positive, Daryl wouldn't mind. Justine would also see to our comfort."

"He had it all figured out, did he?"

Link wasn't at all sure why he was being so obtuse and hard-edged, annoyance and irritation a major component of his seething emotions. He wasn't ready to completely admit he might have made the wrong decision in Virginia. Although earlier he acknowledged the possibility. Even when he knew Leslie might not accept Sophie as his wife, he would have never put her on the street.

Or would he?

If he had a single doubt, he would have never put her on that ship alone. Leslie would have thought the scenario amusing, might have seen it as a scam.

Not a very good one.

"Tell me what you want from me," he said, taking her hands in his. "I'm willing to listen."

"Your acknowledgment that my choices were good ones."

He stuffed both hands through his hair. "Can't do that."

"Sandy is a very nice man. I know that because of how he acted toward me. He wasn't ever going to hurt Clare or me. He waited for us on the street outside the townhouse, just in case your brother was not accepting of us. You can talk to Donal and Sandy. He goes with Justine and Daryl when they take bread to the needy. He rescued Lacie one night when she got into a bit of a scrape. Sandy is a good man."

"I believe you," he told her with a long-drawn-out sigh. "So, it's all out and I'm a bastard. Am I right?"

"Yes. You can act like a bastard. In this case there is no question. Acting as one and being one are two different things."

A spinster could not have appeared primmer and more proper than Sophie at this point.

"Should we speak of anything more pleasant?" he grinned at her, waggling his eyebrows at her, hoping to change the mood of the evening. "Would you like to take a long carriage ride home? We could explore each other." He had other things on his mind now. The argument somehow managed to arouse him. What better way to makeup than sex?

"Can we spend the night in our new home?" She avoided his question, supposing the trip to the new house would result in a long carriage ride.

"There's no bed." He thought of the dust and cobwebs that all needed to be cleaned before the home was inhabitable. He thought of seeing her on a rug in front of a fireplace, making love to her with no possible interruptions such as Clare knocking on the door. He thought of burying himself inside her sultry warmth and watching the intense expression of her animated face when she found her woman's pleasure.

"When has that stopped you?"

Once more, she was gazing at his mouth, running her warm pink tongue across her lips. Her gaze dropped lower. The table stopped the view she seemed to be seeking. She looked at his eyes again.

His body hardened. He was sure now. She was thinking along the same lines that he was. Abruptly, he thought her idea had merit. Thought of her naked body with firelight reflecting off it. "Never." His voice husky with the desire he wanted to quench this instant.

"Perhaps you can think on it a bit longer. I don't want to go back to your brother's home. Do you?" She slanted him a quizzical look. Perhaps the new home will be pleasant. We can start a fire in the fireplace."

"Perhaps long enough to gather together necessities for a few days. I don't want to spend the night without food and drink, without blankets and pillows."

"You will keep me warm." Her voice was soft.

He did like the change of subject. He did mean to make love to his wife every night of his life. "Maybe not a long carriage ride home. We'll stop at the townhouse first. Gather together what we'll need for a few days. Would you like that?"

Her smile, warm and welcoming touched his heart.

Their carriage ride to the townhouse was short. Weston helped them put together a trunk of necessities as well as several baskets of food and drink to last them three days with the promise of more to come tomorrow. Weston told him he would oversee everything to keep them satisfied.

When he swept her into his arms, carrying her into their new home, she buried her face against his chest, laughing softly. He felt her happiness bubbling. Felt his relief. They would find a way to deal with the men in her past. The men who believed they were her lovers who were not. He was sure they would resort to blackmail. Devon and Charles wanted her for themselves. To them she was a delicious morsel. Charles would never be able to attract a female of Sophie's caliber. For that matter neither could Devon.

~ * ~

"What did Weston pack for us?" she asked as she rummaged through the trunk.

Sophie's head was down, looking into the trunk her rear pointing skyward. "You look delectable."

Link stood behind her, his hands on her waist, smoothing them across her buttocks. She shuddered with his caress, wondering what exactly he was up to. He tempted her in so many ways. "I'm looking for glasses. Suppose we should clean something first, as we need a place to sit."

"We need somewhere to lie down. A soft fur rug is preferable."

"Is that all you think of?" When she looked up from her rummaging there was a shimmer of desire in his eyes. She knew he wanted her. He might not wait.

The carriage ride to their new home lasted a few hours. Lord, but he tempted and teased her in so many ways she was in dire need of his man's body. She didn't want him to know. Didn't want to tell him she wanted him deep inside her this instant.

"I have other thoughts." His voice seemed to purr from deep in his lungs, a masculine purr, deep and seductive.

Slowly, she felt the fabric of her skirts rising, cool air flowed across her legs and between them as he pushed a booted foot between her feet subtly suggesting she open herself to him. Sophie tried to stand. She wanted to turn in his arms, feel his lips on her mouth. One of his large hands held her still.

"I want you."

"Y-yes."

He stroked her, kissed the naked flesh he uncovered as he held her bent over the trunk, breathless, panting. His teeth grazed her bottom. A small sound bubbled out. Then, "Link?" Her voice quivered. Her legs trembled. She was desperate for him, for what she knew he could make her feel. His hands cupped her breasts.

"Sophie?" There was humor in his voice as he continued to seduce. "You are wet and slick, moving for me."

"Like this? You can't mean..." She squeaked the words unsure of what he was doing.

"What do you think? Should we? Why not?" His fingers found slick, swollen flesh. He pushed inside one then two.

"I-I don't know," her voice didn't sound like herself. His hands upon her generated heat and that same ache he always found ways to create between her legs in the most intimate parts of her.

She swallowed the lump in her throat, moistened her mouth, running her tongue across her lips. She pushed and squirmed against him. Tried to turn. He stopped her.

"We should try everything at least once. Don't you think?"

Link was a practiced lover. She should trust him. But this... "Oh, God."

His hands stroked her, parted and caressed her, found the places that drove her wild. His body pushed against hers in a delightful way. She felt his shaft pulse against her, probe. Unexpectedly, he was inside her. At her gasp, she heard him laugh softly.

"What do you want, Sophie? Tell me. I'll try my manly best to please. As your husband it's my duty." He moved slowly. Deeper.

Handily, expertly, he brought her higher, until she was moaning, moving against him seeking more. "I don't think I can stand. My knees..."

"Hold on."

He thrust deeper, harder and faster, his body meeting hers generating more and more sensations until tremors swept through her, engulfed her. Her muscles clenched, quivered and shuddered. She was mindless. Her scream brought an answering low growl from Link.

Slowly, he withdrew from her, smoothed her skirts. Pulling her into his arms, he held her. Spoke nonsense to her as he calmed her. "That was nice, don't you think? Should we have something to drink then do this a little bit different in a new and unique place?"

"What were we doing? Before?" she asked, her words a soft whisper. "I don't remember."

"Looking for glasses, I believe," he chuckled, nipping at her ear as her body shuddered in response. He spread a blanket on the floor by the fire. "You sit. I want you to conserve your energy so we can have more fun. Try some new ways to make love. Do you think the dining room table would be nice?"

"We don't have one."

"Oh, well, there is that. We should store the idea away for a later date. It does have merit. Don't you think?"

She had no idea what to think.

A little while later, the small area in front of the fire was cleaned, a fur rug set on the floor in front. Link retrieved blankets. They spent the night blissfully tangled in each other's arms. While she had not been sure of the marriage, it seemed he meant to make the best of it. She even thought she was beginning to fall in love with her husband. Link Stewart, she sighed softly. He certainly did know what he was about.

Waking up next to Link the next morning, she pushed a few strands of his dark hair away from his face. She studied him. He was a beautiful man. She would do her best to be obedient. Ha! She grinned. She didn't think he wanted obedient. He disliked boring. Well, she would do what she wanted when she wanted.

She had no regrets even though she always thought to marry for love. Her parents loved each other dearly.

"My love." He held onto her wrist keeping her from her

explorations. "What are you feeling?"

She inhaled sharply fearing he might guess at her newfound feelings for him. Telling him she might be falling in love with him could not possibly be wise or prudent. The words would make her too vulnerable. No, she would hold back confessions.

After all, he didn't love her.

She thought on his question, deciding to tell him certain things that would not compromise her in any way. "Last night was nice."

"Nice? That's a tepid word for what transpired." He tugged her close, his hands exploring, stroking, coaxing. "We will have to try again. Where my wife is concerned, I strive for better than nice."

"If you keep that up, the house will never be ready." She set her hands on his chest in a feeble attempt to push him away. "Link, behave yourself. We cannot—"

"Anybody home?"

"Blessed hell. We don't have privacy in our home."

Leslie was standing in the doorway, gazing down at them, a huge grin on his handsome face. It was quite obvious they were naked beneath the blankets. A slow burn traveled from her cheeks down to her toes.

"Leslie..." Link croaked out, unnerved by his brother's sudden and unexpected appearance. Link felt sure this was done to get revenge for the time he interrupted him and his lovely wife to be, Lacie.

"Seems to me I recall you catching me in a similar situation. Your cleaning entourage will wait outside until the two of you are presentable. It is well past noon, dear boy." He left the room laughing, his strides long.

Sophie buried her head against Link's chest, blankets pulled as high as she could get them. Mortified she didn't ever want to see Leslie Stewart again.

The crew Leslie brought with him was comprised of about twenty people, mostly family along with their servants. By the end of the day the drawing and dining rooms along with the kitchen and master chamber were thoroughly cleaned, minimal but necessary furniture installed. Everything was spotless.

They feasted on baked salmon as well as a variety of vegetables cooked in delicious sauces along with small potatoes. In a large wagon, Leslie brought the bed from Link's room at the townhouse as well as the bedding to go along with it. Included were a few more pieces of furniture for the master suite necessary until more were purchased.

"You did well, little brother. Did you send for the children?" Leslie asked when they finally found a moment alone to talk. "How does Sophie feel about your cherished ones?"

"Yes. Weather permitting, they will arrive in a month. Should give us time to fix up the second house. Both Sophie and Clare are eager to meet them. I haven't told them much though. I'd like to wait until they arrive so they can form their own opinions."

"There are no new arrivals to your brood? I take it you've spoken to Sophie about your ever-expanding list of children. From here on out they all should be yours and your wife's. I trust you will stop acquiring children from other women." Leslie's words were stern as if he expected Link to continue his dalliances.

His brother didn't understand about his cherished ones. Of course, he never took the time to explain the details or the truth about how he acquired his cherished ones. All children were special. All deserved a safe home where they could live without fear. "No, I've not gone into detail with Sophie. There are no new children to add to the list."

"Thank my lucky stars." Leslie wiped his brow. "Don't think your bank account can survive too much more."

"Liar, Link has more groats than he knows what to do with," Merry said laughing as her long-limbed stride ate up the distance between them. "You should tell her the truth. She deserves to know. Or are you going to keep her guessing?"

"Brat," Link shot back sending her a glare that would tell anyone paying attention she was to keep her mouth shut.

Sophie felt heat rise to her face once more. Link's gaze focused on her eyes, now dropped to her lips. She knew what he was thinking. Her pulse throbbed anticipating something that wasn't going to happen until the entourage found their bedrooms this evening. He would continue to torment her of that fact, she was sure.

"Don't you think you should tell her about all your children?" Leslie continued to pursue the question.

"Sophie understands. Don't you, my love?" His gaze touched her breasts. Travelled lower then back to her mouth as he grinned knowingly.

She squirmed and heated. Her breath stopped for a moment along with her heart. Wickedly, he flashed white teeth. She could do nothing but nod. True, he told her he had children. Didn't elaborate save to tell her he'd never been married before her. If sex with his other lovers had been like it was with her, she understood why he had all the children. The consequences were undeniable. What could she expect? Now that they were wed, she did expect faithfulness.

"How long will you stay?" Link asked turning to his brother the duke. He did need to explain the children to his wife. She would understand.

"Tomorrow afternoon is the longest we're going to intrude," Lacie said, looking to Leslie for confirmation. "Leslie cannot behave himself any longer than that. He would end up embarrassing me."

"He's behaved himself so far?" Link asked, a solid look of astonishment slanted in his brother's direction to see a stoic ducal expression. "Nothing untoward in a closet? Or on the dining room table?"

"You don't have a dining room table or I'm sure he would have thought about it and accomplished the deed without anyone except Lacie and me knowing."

"You would not want me here if I was not behaved," Leslie said in his most ducal posturing voice.

"No, you would not," Lacie agreed, "although our definition of good behavior differs."

"So, it does," Daryl laughed as Donal's arm wrapped around her waist, tugging her closer. "He considers himself well behaved if he only embarrasses me a little."

"We did find a closet," Donal said, a sinful grin on his handsome face. "We used it well."

Daryl punched him in the arm.

Flynt stood, dusting his hands together. "Should we retire?" He held out his hand to his wife, Hope, who accepted it. The rest of the siblings and wives followed suit, heading for their newly cleaned and partially furnished bedrooms.

"Alone together at last." Link brushed Sophie's lips with a hard deep kiss, his hand stroking her breasts, tugging on the corsage so he could reach her nipples. "Are you looking forward to our first night in the master chamber? We even have a bed."

"Do you always have one thing on your mind?" Sophie countered, thinking how lucky she was to have a man who cherished her.

She prayed, too, he would not seek out other women. She didn't know if she could bear that.

"Just as you do, my love. Saw you looking at me, and it wasn't my mouth you were always staring at." He brought her hand to his arousal. "See what looking at me does to my most manly parts. You are a little minx. I wouldn't have you any other way. Do you wish to sit on me now or later?"

She stepped away from him, convinced she needed a great deal of distance. Otherwise, he might toss her skirts and make love to her here in the drawing room despite the startling lack of privacy. Even though they retired for the night, anyone of their guests could wander downstairs at any time.

He turned her, nuzzling her neck. Her heart racing with excitement as well as fear of discovery, she said, "Link don't, not here."

It seemed he didn't heed her words, continued to coax a response, continued to kiss and fondle. "Why? It's our home. All have gone to bed and won't be seen again until the morning. I'm sure they are all pursuing the same ends as we are."

"Oh! Needed a glass of water." It was Chelsea, another of Lacie's sisters stepping in through the door. "I'm sorry. Didn't mean to disturb you. I'll get it quick then the two of you will be alone."

"That's why," she whispered softly, burying her head against his chest as she pulled her dress the best she could to cover her exposed breasts.

"Don't let us stop you." Link lifted Sophie into his arms, striding up the steps to their bedroom. "You're right. I would have been very angry if it had been Cam or one of the other husbands who came searching for a drink of water and saw your breasts."

The next morning Sophie read the note left on the kitchen table. It seemed she was the last one downstairs for breakfast. Over a cup of tea and a scone, she reread the missive. Her heart sank. She tucked it away in the corsage of her mint-green day gown.

How the letter found its way to the kitchen table troubled her. The scenario frightening to think Devon or Charles had been in the house. The thought that Link had not seen the missive also terrified her. Her hands shook as she touched her bodice, knowing she needed to take care of this herself. Involving Link was out of the question. He wouldn't understand. Would believe she encouraged this during the brief encounter with Devon Masters on the waterfront.

She breathed in deeply. Courage did not come to her. Didn't want to leave her new home. Didn't want to see Devon or Charles ever again. She had no choice. Something had to be done.

She jumped, startled when two arms suddenly wrapped around her. Her breath caught in the back of her throat.

"My love." Link's mouth found her nape, nuzzled then stroked with his tongue. She shuddered. Heat poured through her. She brought in a staggering breath of air. "You're up. You look fetching in green."

Before she heard his voice, she recognized his scent, a bit of spice mixed with male musk, his masculinity so very apparent. His closeness never failed to give reassurance. Since those first days, months ago, it seemed they'd come so far.

"It's you." Her sigh left in a soft whisper.

"Who did you expect? No one else better wrap their arms around you." He bent over sending a barrage of tiny kisses along her neck.

"You startled me, that's all."

"What's wrong?

He knew her too well. In his arms, she turned, her hand resting lightly against his cheek. "Nothing. I'm tired. You kept me up most the night."

He lifted both eyebrows, his white teeth flashing against the tan. “You were wicked. Scandalously so. Indeed, if I’d your strength...” He left off as she interrupted.

“Sinful man.”

Her fingers wound into his hair tugging his head closer to her mouth. She wanted nothing more than to distract him so he wouldn’t pursue his line of questioning. While his lips brushed hers and he deepened the kiss, she melted into him. She always turned to liquid when he kissed her.

Pulling away, he swatted her on the bottom, laughing, “We’ve work to do, wench. There will be time for more playing later. Insatiable hussy.”

She bristled, “Wench? Hussy? You were the one distracting me.”

“You touched me first. Am I complaining? Certainly not. Where shall we start?” he asked.

“Did not. Oh, never mind, since you’ve been up for hours, you tell me what needs to be done.”

The cleaning continued. Sophie continued to wonder how she would escape Link’s attention to meet Devon and Charles. While she wasn’t afraid of either man, they could force her. Going alone was risky. If she were to meet them this afternoon near the river, she couldn’t contrive of anyway to do so without involving Link. After what happened at the docks, Link simply would not allow her to go off by herself.

The chance came unexpectedly when Merry, growing bored suggested a short ride. To her surprise, Link not only agreed but he encouraged her. It would be a good way, he suggested, to get to know his sister.

When they started out, the sun was shining, the sky a deep summer blue. A soft breeze blew from the river, cooling the air. For a moment she was reminded of the color of Link’s eyes. She smiled.

“Where are we going? You seem to have a destination in mind.”

Merry rode beside her, her hair flowing out behind her. She was an exceptional rider. Quick witted, Merry would be a wonderful mentor for Clare.

Sophie toyed with the idea of telling Merry all the truth. Perhaps in return she could learn more about Link's cherished children. To her it seemed Link was hesitant to explain the situation to her. She was sure there was more to the story, not believing he sired that many children himself. It puzzled her that Leslie seemed to believe the story. No, they were not all Link's children. He was too cautious when it came to sex, remembering how angry he was when he discovered someone besides her had sex with him the night she drugged him.

"To the river. If you can keep a secret from your brother, I'll tell you everything." Sophie grinned at Merry. "He does not need to know. Will get all over protective and demanding if he knew."

"Which one?" Merry slanted her a half-smile.

Sophie sent a glare Merry's way understanding why both Leslie and Link called her brat at times. "Both. Primarily Link. Leslie seems to have taken an interest in my affairs as well as Link's. Don't think the duke trusts me even though Lacie does."

"Secrets? Certainly, if keeping something from either of the male species with the last name of Stewart, count me an accomplice. Those two believe they should know and control every aspect of my life. I'm sure Link feels the same about you. I, however, understand you are a grown woman and are capable of making good decisions."

"Good, then you can tell me what you know about Link's cherished ones. Agreed?" Truly this was something she wanted to know. "I've a right to know. They aren't all his. I'm sure of that fact."

"Agreed," Merry said. "I'd be pleased to tell you what I came to learn through artifice coupled with eavesdropping. But," she paused, "don't you think it should be Link who tells you?"

"Yes, but he seems reluctant. He's had several opportunities and avoided my questions. Let's get on with my secret. It might not be a wise or prudent decision. I've no recourse however. Feel as if I need to take care of my past problems on my own."

"I'll plan on sticking by you."

For a second Sophie had a change of mind about the telling of secrets. "Even if it might be dangerous? Do you still think you would want to know?"

"Better," Merry said with a giggle and a grin. "As the stronger of the species, I'm sure we can handle anything that comes our way. Men are so arrogant. I'm sure Link believes he can solve everything himself."

Sophie smiled crookedly at Merry's words, thinking. "In some ways women are stronger. We can begin with Link's special children?"

This time Merry shot her a full-sized grin. "As you guessed, they aren't really his children. Well, they are but they aren't either. Link has this deep-seated need to help children as well as women who are down on their luck. He is a generous loving man. When he can, he finds husbands for the women who are pregnant with no one to take care of them."

"What if he can't find a husband?" Sophie asked.

"To my knowledge he always has. One child he found abandoned in Paris, left on the ground to die. All of the children were homeless before Link found them. He takes care of them. Loves them with all his heart. He loves women, too, but he doesn't have children of his own. He's very careful not to plant his seed inside a woman. Probably until you," Merry finished with a slight blush to her cheeks. She lowered her dark lashes then looked up. "Has he taken any precautions with you?"

Sophie flushed, heat rising. Merry spoke of sexual things she should have no concept of. Link was not carful with her. She was his wife after all. Didn't need to be careful. "I could be pregnant." She spoke without thinking, her hand resting on her belly. "I could carry his child." The thought pleased her. She always wanted children. Didn't think she would ever have them.

"Indubitably true. Now, tell me what's got you keeping secrets from your brand-new husband. We both know he won't like you doing that. In his mind he should know everything about you and what you are thinking. He will puff out his chest and ask how he can protect you if he doesn't know your problems."

Hurriedly giving Merry the backstory of the events in Virginia, Sophie went on to explain the letter she received a few hours ago.

"Charles and Devon are blackmailing me. What they don't know is that Link knows everything that happened and there is nothing to blackmail me with. Link knows neither man was my lover. They have no hold over my future or me. All I need to do is explain and they should go away."

"They could spread nasty rumors," Merry said softy. "Why meet them?" Merry wore a puzzled expression. "The solution truthfully is quite simple. Ignore the letter as well as the men."

"I wish I could. It is of my opinion they will continue to hound me. They will never go away unless they are dealt with." Sophie knew that to be the truth. "The best way to get rid of belligerent men is to confront them."

"What do you want me to do?"

"Go with me. If something unexpected happens, ride for Link." Sophie found herself breathing hard, terrified she made the wrong decision. No, she had to show confidence. "You can probably out ride Charles Ewing. Devon wouldn't go after you. He's too pretty. Too refined."

"Link wants control," Merry reminded her. "He will be angry if he discovers you've done this without him. You will have to do some fast-talking. What's best in these situations is to coax him to make love to you. Stare at his lips or his crotch. That way they'll forget their anger. At least for a little while."

Sophie gasped at Merry's advice. "You are not old enough to know those things."

Merry laughed merrily, "I know a lot of things I shouldn't. I do believe the knowledge will come in handy in a few years when I meet my future husband."

"Well, he can't have it all," Sophie told her with a long deep sigh. "After I've put an end to Devon's preoccupation with me, Link can have all the control he desires. How do you know the best way to coax them out of their anger?"

She lifted her shoulders nearly to her ears. "I've done a great deal of listening. I'm able to sit in a room quietly while no one seems to know I'm there. No, I don't suppose any man should have that kind of power over their wife. Unquestionably, you understand when he discovers what you've done without his approval my brother will be furious," Merry said again a small chuckle following her words. "There will be hell threatened then he will make love to you. Next, he will grumble and strut telling you to always confide in him. He is your husband after all. You will agree then do exactly what you think best."

"Really listening while no one knows you're around?" She gifted Merry with a half-smile. "Yes. I've considered that fact. Don't see a way around his anger."

Sophie bit down on her lip. She needed to feel something more than the fear encompassing her. Unexpectedly, she had a bad feeling about this endeavor. Her stomach rolled. She rubbed her temples, wishing away the escalating headache.

"If you are positive this is how you mean to proceed, we should ride to that house by the river where they want to meet you. The sooner you confront this man, the sooner you will be home. If all goes well, Link need not know anything of this."

Merry urged her horse forward.

For a few seconds, Sophie watched.

She pulled in a deep breath of air then followed.

~ * ~

Link paced the floor of the drawing room. Leslie was readying his family to leave. Merry was missing. She should have been back but then it was Merry they were looking for. Link told him he encouraged her to go riding with Sophie. She'd return to Southcliff either in the afternoon or in the morning. She would be fine.

Everything was perfect.

"Nothing is perfect by any means," Link murmured, wishing he didn't have this bad feeling in his gut. He wished his stomach wasn't curdling. He usually listened to those sensations. Something was wrong. Dead wrong. He was helpless to do anything to change that fact. "Sophie was acting strange. I didn't notice until I started thinking about the things she said this morning when I surprised her. He was anxious for no other reason he could discern. The sensations were all in his belly, churning and rolling with ferocity that couldn't be explained. He stabbed his fingers through his hair then again, distraught beyond anything he felt before. "Did Merry say where they were going?"

"No, she told me she agreed to ride with Sophie. Also said they had girl things to talk about. That was all," Leslie said beginning to sound a bit more concerned. "Didn't say if she would be back before we left."

"That translates into they wanted to talk about me," Link said feeling a bit paranoid.

"Sounds suspicious."

The hairs on the back of his neck prickled then stood at attention. "Something happened this morning. Sophie wasn't acting at all the way she usually does. At the time I wasn't worried, just a little puzzled. Said she was tired." He strode to the door looking toward the west. "I don't know what to do."

"I suppose you have to wait. Do you want me to stay?" Leslie asked appearing a concerned brother. "I don't mind. You might need help. It is Merry out there with your wife. We both understand the kind of trouble she can get herself into."

"No."

"You sure?"

"What kind of trouble can a woman get into going for a ride?" Link asked still fighting the foreboding feelings assailing him, still staring at the countryside beyond his home. "She found a great deal of trouble in Virginia. Had not instigated it though. Part of that danger followed her here." He groaned and thought of Devon Masters.

"Well," Leslie paused with a small shrug, "one day when Lacie and Merry did that same thing, they were both kidnapped. Held hostage. Luckily, we rescued them before anything could happen. Trouble abounds. Our ladies seem to find it just as easy as breathing."

The breath rushed from Link. His sarcasm was evident in the next statement. "That's reassuring."

He didn't like hearing these things while he was worried about his wife. While his mind shot to Masters and the hold he thought he had on

Sophie.

His impulsive, headstrong wife. She never came to him for help even when she'd been beaten nearly to death. Why would he think she would ask his advice now?

While Brinkmeyer controlled certain elements of her life, he never entirely controlled Sophie. Now, it seemed Sophie was up to something she didn't want to tell her husband.

He didn't like it. Didn't like it at all. She was keeping silent.

"Perhaps Lacie knows where they rode. Merry tells my wife things she doesn't tell me."

"I'm going to the stable. You did bring Kelly with you."

"I did along with a few horses."

Both men headed toward the horse stable. Kelly was taking over the running for the time being even though he was a horse trainer, not a stable hand. He did know horses better than most any man in Scotland.

Link's hands were clenched into tight fists when he finally reached the stables where he could find and question someone who might know where his wife was headed.

When asked, Kelly shook his head, "No, neither lady said where they were going. Weren't in any hurry though. Took their time picking out a horse. Rode out of here as if they didn't have a care in the world."

"Did they act secretive?" Link asked, distraught more than before.

His fear grew more intense the longer he didn't have her in his sight the longer he didn't have a definitive answer about her whereabouts. He'd never thought, especially where Sophie was concerned, he'd be so possessive. There were elements in her life that threatened to destroy her. When he sent her from Virginia, he thought her life there was behind her. She was far too sure of herself and her abilities to handle men. Her confidence might well be her downfall. Devon Masters was in the city. "Blessed hell."

"What do you think will happen?" Leslie asked.

Link never wanted to be put in the position of explaining his wife's past life. What she'd been through at the hands of her uncle. Secrets were supposed to be kept within families. He trusted his brother. With a heavy breath of air escaping coupled with reluctance, "One of her supposed lover's showed up here in Glasgow. He suggested certain things, blackmail the most important. She would take exception. Would try to solve the dilemma on her own. Would believe she could do so. She wouldn't want to see me hurt."

"Why blackmail?"

"The man thinks she was his lover. He is going to threaten her. He has done so already."

"Was he? Her lover?"

"No. Haven't we been through this before? If it needs repeating, I was Sophie's first."

"Look at this." Kelly approached with a folded crumpled piece of paper, which he handed to Link. "Thought you gents might be interested. I read it. You should know that too."

Link's gut clenched. He gritted his teeth before he opened the letter. His hesitancy gave him pause. The lump in his throat grew. The breath he'd drawn remained in his lungs. Without reading the words on the paper, he was sure Devon Masters threatened Sophie. He was also sure Sophie meant to solve the problem without consulting him.

Damn her sweet hide. He was going to thrash her until she couldn't sit down.

She was overconfident. Her abilities were limited.

"She obviously involved Merry," Link said as he stuffed the note in his pocket. "Don't like that. Don't like it at all."

"No, Merry would jump willingly into any conspiracy. Need to be part of it. Secret keeping is her main modus operandi. Her life thrives on controversy." Leslie was stroking his jaw thoughtfully. "I do believe we've intrigue here. I'll send the rest of my household to Southcliff. You and I will see what is transpiring at this home near the River Firth. We will solve this little problem promptly then be home for dinner."

Leslie left while Link had the horses saddled. He thought to do this on his own, but he needed his brother near to keep from throttling his wife when he found her.

What to expect?

He certainly didn't have any idea.

Chapter Eleven

Sophie and Merry stopped on a hill above the home they'd been sent to. Trees surrounded the house with a long drive in front of it. One horse was tethered nearby. A slight breeze ruffled the leaves in the trees. She thought she heard raised voices coming from inside the house, an argument. Devon and Charles would never agree to anything.

"Devon Masters?" Merry asked, leaning on the saddle horn as she stared ahead of her. "What do you think? Does he truly think he can blackmail you or my brother?"

"Probably, Charles Ewing as well. They were both pawns in my uncle's schemes to own all the plantations in the area."

Sophie felt the fear settle bone deep. The fine trembling of her hands threatened to overwhelm her. Her palms were sweaty. She wiped then on her gown. She swallowed the lump rising in her throat as she tried to settle her cramped nerves into something normal. Confronting the men would have to be done sometime. Now would be as good a time as any.

"We can turn around. Understandably, it's up to you," Merry said, seeming to watch the house with diligent eyes. "I'm intrigued though. Would like to hear what these men have to say."

Sophie didn't answer. She was thinking, looking for a clue. She wanted to know who came, if it was just Devon and if Charles was about to show up. Who was the argument with? She turned to look over her shoulder. No one was behind them or in front of them. One man would be easier to handle.

"You were expecting two men?" Merry asked as her horse moved restlessly. "We can't handle two men. Do you have a gun?" Merry reached into her boot then drew out a small derringer. "If Leslie saw this, he'd be furious. Says a child's weapon is worthless. I tend to disagree."

"It wasn't right of me to ask you to ride with me. Should have done this alone." She played with the tiny heart necklace Link gave her two days ago. The action seemed to ease her fears. A gift from the heart he told her. Yet he didn't love her. Perhaps now he tolerated her. She didn't believe he still disliked her. He did enjoy sex with her.

He married you. That has to count for something.

"I would do the same for you," Merry said without hesitation. "You're my brother's wife. He loves and trusts you."

Those words took Sophie by surprise. Blinking rapidly, she drew in a long breath of air. "He's never said so."

Merry lifted her shoulders in a slight shrug not knowing what to make of Sophie's proclamation. "Men never do say the words. Either their feelings are apparent so the words are unnecessary or they're afraid of the words. Don't know which category Link fits into."

Sophie's laugh was brittle, nearly nonexistent. "You know too much for a fifteen-year-old. Link doesn't fit into categories. You're wrong. He doesn't love me. Now that we're married, he tolerates me."

"Been told that before. Lacie said the same thing about Leslie's feelings for her not too long ago. Look," Merry pointed toward the drive. "Who is that?"

"Charles," Sophie said softly her heart pounding louder.

She was terrified. She should have told Link. "Now they are both here." Sophie remembered how easily she handled these men.

You ninny they'd been drugged. They expected sex. You've no idea what they'll do now.

"Should we?" Merry asked.

"Go? I haven't the foggiest notion. Don't know what to expect from either man. Don't know what to do. I'm sure they are angry. They want what they thought they had in Virginia. It was Cocoa they had not me. That will make them even more furious." She drew in a labored breath debating with herself.

"Expect the worst? Leslie always told me where men are

concerned, expect the worst." One perfectly arched brow rose skyward, reminding Sophie of Link.

"If I'm going to do this..." Sophie drug air into her lungs as she stared at the two men. Devon was outside speaking with Charles. "You should leave me here. Don't want you to bring Link. Just go so you won't be in danger."

"Thought you said the men were harmless or practically harmless." It seemed Merry reminded her of things she didn't want to consider. "They don't look harmless to me."

"I did. Just go. I can take care of them. They are nothing. Was always able to before. There is no reason anything has changed. They are only men."

"No."

Sophie turned to stare at her sister-in-law. Pursing her lips, thinking, "No? You're just like your brother, too damn stubborn. Don't listen to a word I say." It wasn't true, though. Link listened. He just usually had a different idea. "You have to leave. I won't put you in danger."

"I've ridden with you this far. I intend to see this through, big sis." Merry grinned at her. "If it's not dangerous, what are you worried about?

Good question.

"If I let you do this, I'll have everyone angry with me Leslie and Link as well as Lacie. I'll never be forgiven."

"Do you care?" Merry laughed then.

"Yes. Not enough to talk you out of whatever you've made up your mind to do. Promise me if things get threatening, you'll leave."

"Promise," Merry said albeit reluctantly. "If I have to leave, I'm going for Link and Leslie. That's final. Not about to leave you alone with two men without reinforcements on the way."

"Alright."

Sophie didn't understand her easy capitulation but she felt a weight fall off her shoulders when she finally did agree. She knew she should have spoken to Link. Having a husband was new to her.

She urged her horse forward, ready for whatever happened. She knew these men. Understood what drove them. Could handle them. Despite the number of times she said the words to herself, doubt niggled at the back of her mind. She was no longer in control. They were. Sweat slipped between her breasts. The palm of her hands slipped on the reigns.

When they noticed the women, the men stopped talking to watch. Sophie straightened her back. Tilted her chin skyward, the effect one she practiced including a smile of disdain for the men. They were weak. She stopped in front of them deciding to stay on the horse. They would listen to her. They would leave.

"What do you want, Devon. I thought I made myself clear when I saw you at the docks. I don't want you or anything to do with you. Still, you sent me a blackmail note requiring my presence. Go back to Virginia."

Devon's grin sent a shiver of revulsion through Sophie. "I want you again. You will be my lover until I grow tired of you, Sophia. Just as you were before, I want you beneath me."

"No. You didn't have me before. You were drugged. You had Cocoa. It was William's idea." By his expression she was afraid she'd said too much.

His eyes narrowed. His voice harsh, "Don't believe you about the drugging or Cocoa. What I remember is seeing your face, holding your breasts in my hands. They are lovely large breasts." He looked to Charles then back to her. "I don't mind sharing. Charles wants you again also. Since neither of us has the pox, there is nothing to stop us from enjoying each other. That was quite the lie. Were you so eager to have Link that you made up the story?"

"Why would I agree to something so preposterous? Just the thought of you touching me makes my skin crawl and my belly churn." She tried for sarcasm, heard the fear in her voice instead. Something about Devon was unusual. The way he looked at her was different.

This was not the man she controlled so easily a few months ago. He changed.

He reached up, touching her hand. A shiver of disgust rushed through her. Her horse sidestepped. He grabbed the reins from her.

"Get down, Sophia. Now." His voice was harsh, abrasive. "I'm not about to play games with you, a woman. Do as I say. If you don't this will go badly for you."

This was not the playboy gambler she knew from across the ocean. He commanded. She didn't like this. She pointed her chin in the air. "No." To no avail, she tried to grab back the reins, reaching forward and down. She wanted nothing more than to run from him. Coming here had been a mistake. She would have to leave.

Charles was beside her, tugging on her arm, pulling her from the horse. She screamed as she fell, landing on the ground.

Her mind spun. Her breath knocked from her lungs. She was on the ground staring up at these men who were bigger and stronger.

What to do now?

Devon stood over her, his feet braced on either side of her. When she tried to push off the ground, her hair was caught beneath his boots. Tears welled in her eyes. The pounding of her heart thundered in her ears.

"You will do as I say, Sophia. You've no control here. We are going into the house and you will entertain me as you used to do. Don't have any hot toddies but wine will serve in its place."

"No," she said quite clearly. Her voice was calm. "No. I won't do that. I don't want you to touch me. Link will kill you if you force me."

"You will or you will regret it. Link cannot touch me. He has no power or authority here. It will be your word against mine." He stepped away, catching her wrist then dragging her to her feet. He pulled her against his chest, his hands holding hers.

She kicked at him. Spit in his face.

Furious, his face spotted red with anger, he pushed her to the ground again. She fell awkwardly, wrenching her shoulder. Hoof beats pounded in her head. Merry was coming. *No.* She wanted to yell at her to stay away, to ride for Link. A black cloud encompassed her brain. Once more she found herself wrenched up. This time she was slung over Devon's shoulder.

"Stop!" Merry's voice rang out loud and clear.

"You little she devil." Devon's words were clear. "I will whip you with that riding crop you're holding. Stop now."

Sophie didn't know what was happening. She was twisted around. Merry was hitting Devon with the riding crop, not the other way around. The spinning stopped. Merry was riding away. Sophie heard the horse leaving, felt relief as well as despair. She had to use her head. Telling the man she had the pox again obviously wouldn't work. No, she would have to be smarter than the man.

Than both men. What to do?

The question remained. The door to the house creaked open. He tossed her on the mattress in the back room.

"Stay put." He spun on his boot heal and left the room, the door banging shut behind him.

He was back, staring at her. For a moment he watched her, his hands on his hips. She clenched her teeth. Inhaled slow deep breaths. Calm nerves would do best.

Ignoring his order, Sophie scrambled to a sitting position, pushing herself against the wall. Beneath her chest her heart pounded. She was aware of every sound, all his movements around the room. He was striding back and forth swearing, beneath his breath.

Devon paced, stopping every few minutes to look at her. "You're a damn harlot, a whore. You've no say in what happens here. You owe me," he finally said. "I've been inside you. Why are you, a woman with no moral character, protesting now? Why would a man like Link Stewart wed a brazen hussy? Makes no sense. I want you to tell me how you did it?"

She started laughing. He didn't listen to anything she said. Either that or he didn't believe her. To her ears she sounded hysterical. She couldn't stop though. Her laughter continued. Tears ran from her eyes. She brushed them away with the backs of her hands. Still, she laughed, mocking him. "I will tell you again. You revile me. You were never inside me. It was Cocoa who had sex with you. Didn't you ever notice any difference? I thought you were an ass when you posed naked in front of me."

She recalled Link told her that her breasts did her in. Devon never touched her breasts. Surely, he could tell the difference between a white woman and one of color. But then none of the others had.

His brows furrowed together, he sat down next to her, drew her close. He kissed her hard. She gagged, hitting the side of his face with her fist. That stopped the hysteria welling up from deep inside her. “I’ll fight you with every breath in my body. You should let me go. Merry went for Link. She’ll bring him here. He will kill you.”

“Whore!” He punched her hard in the stomach.

Sophie cried out, sliding down the wall, losing consciousness for a moment. She tried to swallow. Uncle William hurt her more than this. She would not fall victim to Devon. This was nothing. She could bear whatever he wanted to dole out.

“You never had me,” she told him again as she began to right herself as the pain began to vanish. “Never. Not even one time. I left you and let Cocoa finish the game. It was all a game derived by Uncle William.”

Now, he stood in front of her, his arms crossed in front of him. His face mottled red. “Liar. I fondled your large breasts, stuck my rod inside you, time and again. I heard you moan your pleasure. Don’t deny it now. I won’t believe anything you say.”

She drew herself up, her courage slowly returning, “That was Cocoa. Never me.”

She knew he would hit her again. Knew he wanted to hurt her more now than before. He was not a man who could be lied to by a woman. He believed himself to be invincible. Believed she let him make love to her. That she wanted him.

He kicked her in the stomach. As she doubled over, the pain excruciating, she thought he was just like her uncle. Her eyes closed, she waited for the next blow, wondered, too, where Charles was.

It seemed he read her mind. “Charles is outside. Your little friend is sure to bring help. She will be too late for you.” His hand closed over one of her breasts, squeezing. He ripped her shirt then the chemise she wore beneath. “No, you are much smaller than I recall. A black girl, you say? I would have treated her differently. I know I had you.”

He didn't sound quite as sure of himself. As he fondled her, his eyes seemed to scrunch together.

Her shirt was now a tattered rag hanging around her shoulders. She pulled what she could of the fabric over herself. She was not going to be his victim. When he reached for her again, she battled the pain, ripped at his face with her nails, drawing blood. He slapped her hard, her head jerking back. She fell against the wall before landing on the dirty mattress.

"I won't!" Her words whispered through the waterfall of tears slipping down her cheeks. "I will always fight you. You will never have me, never know pleasure from me. Not like Link. He loves me," she lied hoping to give him a reason to pause.

She needed time to think. Needed time for her circumstance to change.

"There's where you're wrong. If you don't come to me willingly, I'll spread the truth about you around Glasgow. Everyone will feel pity for Link Stewart, the Duke of Southcliff's brother. They will all look at you with scorn. You will lie beneath me, a willing participant or your beloved Link will face the consequences of your promiscuous ways."

"Link doesn't care what people think about him, or rumors or ugly gossip. He loves me. He will defend and protect me. There is nothing you can do. No blackmail. Link as well as his family know what I was forced to do in Virginia. None of that matters to any of them. They are not women hating scum like you. Blackmail is useless against them. The Stewarts will stand united against you as well as any rumors you generate." She hoped what she said was true even though she knew Link didn't lover her.

He was honorable.

He would do right by his wife.

Seemingly surprised by her words, he sat down on the bed beside her. "He cares. Every man cares. A real man doesn't want a woman who spreads her favors from one man to another. He will divorce you. Then I will have you."

From what Merry told her today about the pregnant women, the little helpless children as well, she was sure Link did not put stock in the venom spewed by people. When he loved, he loved unconditionally. When he loved someone, he would defend them to the death if necessary. She laughed softly, understanding if he could find her, he would do just that. If Merry reached him, he would come to her aide. What she also hoped was that he wouldn't care if Devon did manage to rape her.

He didn't love her but he would come for her. Defend her.

She closed her eyes, waiting for the next onslaught of pain. Devon walked into the kitchen, returning with a glass of ale. He drank long and deep. He paced the room, looking at her then out the window. He must have thought along the same lines. Perhaps he didn't want to be vulnerable.

"You don't want to have your pants down when Link comes for me," she taunted, pleased with the sudden paling of his cheeks.

Once again, he drank long and deep. Drank again. His shoulders trembled slightly. She wasn't sure if she'd managed to frighten him or give him second thoughts about the precariousness of this situation.

"He might come for you, only because you're his wife. He will come so he can get rid of you."

"He will come. You should leave now while you're still alive. Although after what you've done to me, he will find you."

"You think he will come for a whore? I will tell him how you begged me to take you. That you were more than willing as well as eager to lie in my arms, eager to feel my manly parts inside you. You spread your legs without being asked. He will understand how much you want me."

Her entire body shuddered with aversion. The thought of him doing the same things Link did to her body, the idea of his touch intimate or otherwise caused her skin to crawl.

"He won't believe you."

"Ah, but I hear the doubt in your voice, read the fear in your eyes as well. Should we let him see us together?" He laughed. "Naked together in this bed? That would change his mind. Would it not?"

This was insane. Devon was not the man she knew from Virginia.

He drank more ale, his eyes growing red with the alcohol he consumed.

She sat up straighter, tilted her chin higher. “I’m not afraid of you.”

“You should be terrified.”

He pulled her from her sitting position. His mouth captured hers. The kiss was hard and demanding. She struggled against him, pushing at him. When he stuck his tongue between her lips, she bit down hard.

He bellowed his rage, hitting her with his fists again and again. She crumpled into a tiny ball on the dirty mattress curling inward, drifting into a world where only she existed. Nothing for her changed. She endured. That was all that could be expected. Long ago she learned to tolerate.

Link would come for her. He would set her aside. No, they were wed. He could have the marriage annulled or seek a divorce. Secured in a tiny protective ball, she didn’t move, only waited for whatever Devon and Charles had in store for her.

Sophie understood now she made a horrible mistake coming here. She should have brought the letter to Link. Asked his advice. She overestimated her abilities. If she trusted her husband, he would have decided how to proceed. At home, Uncle William was always the man in charge, in control. He told her what to do. Told her what to say. He saw to all the details. Here she needed to learn and trust in her husband. Ah, by the time he found her it might be too late.

She didn’t want to admit defeat. Needed to present a strong front. Her ribs hurt. Devon was stronger than her uncle or perhaps William had not used all his strength when he hit her. Except for the last time when he whipped her and broke ribs. Maybe all he sought was to teach her a lesson. Devon meant to hurt her.

What did she know about Link? If presented with Devon’s facts, he might allow her to be used by both Charles and Devon. She closed her eyes fighting a new wave of terror. At least Devon wasn’t in a hurry. She had a few minutes to escape into oblivion.

The hoof beats woke her. She didn’t know if she’d been asleep for a few minutes or a few hours. The time had been nearing noon when she left with Merry. Now the sun seemed to be going down. The tiny room was darker than before. Her stomach growled. When she pushed on the bed to sit up, her body rebelled with the pain he inflicted. She fell to the mattress with a groan, agony spreading around her ribs. She counted her blessings. These injuries would heal quickly. Nothing was broken.

The damage to her marriage, she had no idea if they would ever heal? She had so much to lose. The thought of Link's rejection shook her to the core. In Virginia, well, she lied to him endlessly. If she told him neither Devon nor Charles violated her, would he still believe her word?

No.

Yes. He broke through my maidenhead.

Now, she had no proof of her innocence. No proof she wasn't a willing participant. From past experience he wouldn't believe her. When it came to her, he always thought the worst.

She felt the tears well up inside her, felt the fears as well as the sadness. After the last weeks, she thought her life changed. There was nothing to do now save start over.

Devon was no longer walking back and forth. She heard voices outside the house. Couldn't understand what was being said even though she strained. She tried to stand, to walk outside. Pain washed through her so vivid and intense she fell back.

Panting, she waited. Trying again she made it to her feet. The breath she sucked in didn't help. One hand braced on the wall she walked to the doorway of the bedroom where she closed her eyes. Seconds ticked by. The voices were louder now.

"Where is Sophie?"

She heard Link. Felt gratitude simmer up from deep in her belly. Merry found him. Told him where to go and he came for her. Perhaps he cared for her a little. She wanted his love. Would settle for her rescue.

The door in the front of the house opened. He stood just inside, his body highlighted by the setting sun. It was the most beautiful sight she'd ever seen.

"I should throttle you. Turn you over my knee and give you a child's punishment so that perhaps you would learn to come to me, your husband with any problems."

She smiled before she slumped to the floor, darkness surrounding her.

~ * ~

"Bloody hell!" Link's heart seemed to fall to the pit of his stomach.

He raced forward, kneeling beside Sophie, his hands touching everywhere. A hand mark on her cheek left him swearing again. He should not have let Devon and Charles leave.

They told him she was unhurt. Nothing had been done to her, nothing she didn't ask for. He drew in air. The top of her gown was shredded, her breasts spilling out when she moved. He lifted her, wrapping his frockcoat around her, covering her. A bruise was forming near one eye.

"Is she unharmed?" Leslie stepped toward him, offering help.

"No." Link's voice wavered.

He remembered when he found her after William beat and whipped her nearly to her death. His gut coiled into hard knots. His arms shook.

What he needed was a carriage. When he ran his hands over her ribs, she flinched. Keeping her in this hovel one second longer than necessary was not a passable notion. It would take an hour each way to bring a carriage here.

"Shouldn't have let those two men leave," Link muttered beneath his breath.

He felt helpless. Wanted to beat Masters as he did Sophie. His wife in pain, he'd not made it here in time to help her.

"You had no choice," Leslie said.

"Got to get her home. Devon hurt her just as her uncle did. He beat a defenseless woman. What kind of man does that?"

It was a blessing that Sophie was unconscious. Link was sure the pain would have been horrendous.

Link swept her into his arms, carrying her tenderly to where the horses were tethered. It seemed he and Sophie had been through this once before. At least Devon had not whipped her. He drew in a deep ragged breath of air. Thank God for Merry's timely arrival.

Sophie would heal. Then he would throttle her.

Leslie helped him. In a matter of minutes, they were riding home, Sophie cradled in his arms. Tears slid from his eyes and down his cheeks. He didn't know how he would survive if he lost her. He loved her, he realized. Loved her more than life.

Sophie was everything to him. He'd never before felt anything so intense, so very life changing. The ride home took an eternity. Once, she opened her eyes, smiled at him then gratefully, fell asleep again.

Over the top of the hill, they met Merry who had more questions. Had thankfully obeyed. Leslie answered them the best he could. Devon gave us an abbreviated account of Sophie's arrival. Elaborated on how she begged him to take her on the dirty mattress. Told him how she missed him and his lovemaking."

As Leslie told the story, Link gritted his teeth. Devon lied. So, Leslie threatened him as only a spy for the British government and a duke could do. Apparently, Leslie still had connections. That fact didn't come as a surprise to Link.

By the time Link got her home, she was drifting in and out of consciousness. The soft moans infuriated him. As he was torn between venting his anger on his wife's stupidity and wishing he could beat Devon Masters to a bloody pulp.

"I'll see to her. No need for a doctor. Nothing is broken. She just needs time to recuperate. We can do that here."

Link set Sophie gently on the bed. He stepped back to stare at this woman he loved. A myriad of memories flashed through him. Her defiance, her lack of emotion that first time he kissed her. The way her breasts filled his hands when he shoved them inside her gown the night of the ball when she smiled blandly at him. Grinned as if what he did meant nothing to her.

He poured water into a basin. With the water and a soft cloth, he bathed her face as well as the cut near the corner of her eye. He washed her breasts.

"Justine stayed here. Evidently told the others we might need her. She is a wonderful chef. I'll tell her we need food. Merry is staying the night also. For now, I'll leave you two alone."

"Justine? Sandy's Justine?"

Leslie laughed, "Yes."

He was left alone with his wife. He bathed her face, spread her bodice aside, bathed her again looking for the bruises that would soon blossom, felt her ribs to confirm his earlier diagnosis.

"Link?" Sophie opened her eyes. Tried to reach for him. Her hand fell back as another moan rippled through her.

"You will be fine, Sophie. When there is no more pain, we'll discuss what you did today. It was very stupid of you."

"Angry?"

"More so than I could ever hope to explain." He covered her with a quilt from the foot of the bed. "You will sleep now."

"I don't think I can." Her voice wavered. "I want to know if you still want me to be your wife?"

He heard the unspoken agony in her voice. "That is a ridiculous question. I will get you some willow bark tea. It will ease the discomfort. He hit you?"

She sucked her bottom lip into her mouth. He saw the even white teeth as she stared at her hands in her lap. Understood her reluctance to speak of what happened. They could talk later.

"No. Don't answer me. The truth is evident."

It was too much, all too much. Would she always court danger?

She ignored his command. "He hit me, nothing else."

"Don't think about it." She wouldn't tell him if he forced her. He understood that better than anything. How would he ever learn the truth?

"When you are well, you will be honest with me. There will be no lies between us."

His voice was harsh, unrelenting. He didn't like that fact. Didn't like the doubt he harbored.

"Devon," he watched her swallow, saw the pain in her silver-gray eyes. "He, he told you..."

"Yes, he did. We will not speak of it now."

Her smile didn't reach her eyes. "He told me you would believe him if he told you I begged him to take me. You believe the lie, don't you? Despite all we've shared, you believe the liar and not me. Will you ever trust me?"

Link turned away, unwilling to answer, unwilling to hurt her further. He didn't understand himself or his willingness to think the worst. While he knew she didn't submit willingly, he did believe Devon forced her. She was too small and helpless to fight a man, keep him from forcing her. She was fragile.

When he didn't answer, her voice was stiff, "I've always told you the truth. You know that. Why would I change now?"

He heard the despair in her tone, "If he did force you, would you tell me?"

Her expression changed. Then in a whisper, "I don't know. Does it make a difference? We both know it doesn't."

"What am I supposed to think?" Gently he touched her swollen cheek with his knuckles. "In any case it doesn't matter. If for some reason you carry his child, I will still love the baby as if it was mine."

She turned away from him despite the pain the small change of position must have caused her. His unwillingness to believe her caused her a deeper agony than the physical ones. More than anything he wanted to believe her.

What to do?

He couldn't change his position. Could give her his trust. She would see through the ploy. "I'm going for the tea. You will drink it all. Then you will sleep." His voice was harsh, holding a wealth of emotions he didn't want to share with Sophie.

She didn't say a word. She stared at him instead. He was disappointed she wasn't staring at his mouth. The pain was too great.

He left then, seeing Leslie in the drawing room. In the kitchen he rummaged through the items that arrived today. He found the willow bark. Justine already had the tea brewing. He added milk and honey.

When he stepped inside the room again, she turned away. "Here it is." He sat behind her. Helped her with the warm liquid until she finished. "Go to sleep now."

Sophie didn't speak. Tears streamed down her cheeks.

When he strode into the drawing room. Leslie handed him a glass filled with brandy.

"How is she?"

"Well enough, considering. Much better than when her uncle beat and whipped her." He sat down staring at the fire. "She is angry with me."

"Because you believe that odious man?" Leslie lifted and eyebrow derision rampant.

"Don't you?"

"Where Sophie is concerned what I believe doesn't make a bit of difference. What you believe does," Leslie murmured softly.

That tidbit of advice did him no good. Link watched the flames in the fireplace. He couldn't help what his gut reaction told him. Couldn't understand why Sophie's simple denial didn't take precedence over Devon's harsh unfiltered words. Devon had every reason to hurt him. Devon was a well-known liar and cheat.

Sophie had every reason to deny the intimacy.

"Before she wakes again, you need to figure out what is more important to you, to your life with your wife."

"If I tell her now that I believe her, she'll think I'm lying."

"Be convincing. The words should come from the heart. If that's what she hears, there will be no doubt in her mind."

Silent minutes swept by. He tried to think of all the reasons he might change his mind. There were none.

"You're right. It matters not what you think. I still want to know." With deep feelings of despair, Link waited for an answer from his brother.

Thoughtfully, Leslie sipped his brandy. "Perhaps we should put this entire situation in perspective. What do you know about Devon Masters?"

"Mostly hearsay."

"Gossip is often the foundation for truth of a man's character."

Leslie was always the voice of reason. "So, tell me what you know."

Link listened to him now, thinking of his life so far with Sophie. "This must be why you were such a successful spy." Link plowed both hands through his hair. "He's a gambler. Devious. From what I heard in the tavern he wasn't beyond cheating to win. He ended up owing enough money to William that he had to sell. He was distraught, left town right after Sophie told him she had the pox."

Leslie leaned against the mantle of the fireplace. "Well," he sipped, "his character is far from sterling. A known cheater and gambler, a womanizer, a man who would force a woman..."

"What can you tell me about Sophie?" Leslie tried to hide the grin on his face from Link.

"She has never lied to me. She has, however, glossed over the truth. Has denied me important knowledge." He stopped for a few seconds thinking about his wife. "She was a virgin when she came to me. Told me as much from the beginning. She did tell me she didn't know what she would say if Devon did force her."

"Indeed..."

"I just don't know." He wanted to know his children were his. Not that he wouldn't love and care for any child of hers. He groaned deep in his belly. He told her that. She must think him the worst cad ever. He would have to do something to change that.

"What would it hurt to believe what she says over Devon Masters? By your own words a devious liar and cheat?"

"I've a lot to think about before tomorrow morning."

"I suppose you do."

Later that evening, Link sat on the bed beside his wife. Her face appeared peaceful. The strain and lines of stress from earlier vanished. Why was it so hard to believe her? He didn't know. Compared to him she was a paragon of virtue. He spent his life doing just as he pleased.

She spent her life the pawn of an evil man.

Was it just the fact he might not know if a child she might

conceivably carry was his?

He just didn't know.

From the facts Leslie pointed out, he had every reason to take Sophie's word over Devon's. He didn't want this to dirty their lives together. Never before in his adult life had he trusted a woman.

Maybe it was time to start with his wife.

Gently, he ran a finger down her cheek. She was so soft, tiny, fragile. He wasn't a jaded man. He loved women, all their quirks and weaknesses. Before he married Sophie, he had many women friends as well as lovers. Until him, she knew no other man. Her virginity was not something he expected. When he discovered the small barrier, he was pleased.

No, I was more than pleased.

He took off his clothes. Stretched out beside her, pulling the quilt over them both. Even if he did an about face with his feelings, how could he explain the change of heart?

Tell her what you know about Devon Masters, what they both knew about his character. Tell her you realized the only person he trusted with the truth was her.

She woke in the middle of the night, thrashing about, tears flowing down her cheeks when she finally pushed herself from the dreams. He gave her more tea. She slept again. His eyes remained open, watching the coming dawn. Wishing he could make her feel better. In her short life she'd been through far too much.

Sophie woke. Light shown through the open window. A soft summer breeze drifted inside, redolent with the scent of roses. Link still didn't know what to say to her. Nothing Devon told him held the ring of truth. Sophie fought the man. Devon was a man who could easily overpower her. Why didn't he take her?

Link didn't blame her for anything that happened. No, that wasn't entirely true. He blamed her for meeting Devon alone and unprotected. Blamed her for failing to tell him about the rendezvous so he could shield her. That was the crux of the matter. Nothing would have happened to her if she told him.

"Sophie?"

For a moment she smiled at him then the small sign of affection vanished. As if she suddenly recalled the events of the day before, she turned away. He understood she would continue in that vein.

She didn't say a word.

"Are your ribs hurting?" He ran his finger down her arm, wishing she would turn over and yell at him, anything but the strangled silence.

"My love," he spoke softly. "More tea? Food?"

"I want to go downstairs."

"We can try that." He would do anything for her. "Do you want to get dressed?

"No."

"Alright then, I'll fetch your robe." He rose, slipping on a pair of doeskin breeches and a white shirt. He brought her the robe, helped her put her arms through the sleeves.

With ease he swept her into his arms, carrying her down the steps then into the drawing room. Leslie was sipping a cup of tea. He smiled.

"How are you feeling, Sophie?" Leslie asked, his gaze shifting from Link to Sophie as if asking the silent question.

"Much better, thank you. I shall be healed in no time. This beating is not nearly so bad as the one my uncle gave me when I failed to seduce your brother." She didn't look at him. Essentially, she was using this opportunity to ignore him.

Leslie nodded, saying, "I certainly hope so. Link should be grateful that is all that happened to you."

So, his brother was going to hang him right here and now by making it perfectly clear he believed Sophie's story.

"It's nice to know someone believes me." She accepted the tea Link poured her. Smiled pleasantly at his brother.

"Are you and Merry going back to town today?"

"I am. Merry is going to ride to Southcliff. She much prefers the country life. I'm afraid to say she is a bit of a recluse."

"You don't worry about her?" Sophie sipped her tea, placing the cup on her saucer.

"Nothing to worry about. I maintain a full staff at the manor. In fact, she can get into less trouble there than she can in the city."

She seemed to hesitate for the longest time. "You believe me. Nothing happened except the beating."

"I should remain neutral," Leslie murmured as his gaze settled on his brother.

Link felt the condemnation of that gaze. His brother's sarcasm blatant. "Please don't hold back. Why not tell Sophie exactly how you feel?"

"If that's what you want. Yes, simply because I know men who would do anything to make a woman's life difficult. Devon Masters is a man such as that. Since you spurned him, he intentionally spread seeds of doubt in my brother's head and heart. He's a jealous man and doesn't want anyone to have what he covets. Appears it was not difficult to do. Link is usually wiser than this," he sighed softly. "Sometimes a man in love cannot think straight."

"Thank you, perhaps you could contrive to convince Link of my honesty." There was a wealth of hurt in her voice.

"My brother is a stubborn man. We discussed the matter last night with no changes."

"I see. Since Link already took my virginity there is no proof of the truth I'm saying. Devon Masters told me Link would never believe my claims of innocence. What would it matter in any case? If Link arrived much later, he would have forced me. I was lucky. It, you see, was a matter of timing. Nothing more. I suppose I shouldn't care. Unfortunately for me, I do."

"You can still tell me the truth," Link blurted, sickened by his careless and hurtful statement. He regretted the words as soon as they left his mouth.

Sophie would recover sooner from the beating than she would from his verbal abuse. Not a word. Her chin tilted into the air. It was a pose he'd seen often.

"I believe you should stick a sock in your mouth, Link." Leslie rose then turning to Sophie, "I hope you have a pleasant day. Don't think too harshly of your husband, my brother, whom I would love to disown at the moment. He has many faults. Obviously, the ability to trust the word of a woman over that of a devious, well-known liar and a cheat, is one of them. In time I hope you can forgive the poor man. At the moment his wits have abandoned him. For your sake, I pray he finds them soon."

Openmouthed, Link watched his brother walk from the room, Leslie's diatribe grating on his already stretched thin nerves. He supposed Leslie was right about the loss of his wits. He should swallow his pride and tell her, tell her what? It was too late to recant his statement.

Or was it?

Better after the fact then never?

"Sophie."

He placed her hand in his. Quickly, she withdrew it, her eyes narrowing.

"I'm sorry. I'm a fool."

By the look in her eyes this was going to be more difficult than even he suspected. She was just as stubborn. Right now, she was also a woman scorned. He'd never been in this position before.

"If I could do it, I would walk right out of here. I'd go with Leslie. Don't want to be here with you. You have taken all my pride. Beaten it to death. I've nothing left to hold on to, not even your trust. A husband should trust his wife."

Blessed hell, but he loved her. Loved to watch her eyes turn to molten silver either with desire or rage. She was amazing. Would it hurt him so much to bury his pride?

"You are right to be angry with me."

"If you pretend to tell me you believe me now, I..." She picked at the fabric of her robe. Refused to look at him. "I don't see how I can believe you."

Her anger was fading. He was sure she would find it in her heart to forgive him. "What can I do, idiot that I am? I'm only a man."

He noticed a faint and very brief smile. She caught her lower lip between her teeth. Suddenly, she was no longer looking anywhere but at him. Her gaze settled on his lips then drifted lower. He hardened instantly.

"Is this our first argument?"

"Am I forgiven?"

"If you tell me the truth about your children. Didn't realize I would be an instant mother." She rested her hand on his chest. "I couldn't stay angry with you forever. I'm trying to understand why you would take that man's words over mine. I can't. Decided I would have to live with it."

"I understand. My first child is ten years old now. His name is Jeffrey. I found him in Paris huddled between two buildings. His clothing was ragged. He was dirty and needed food. When he looked at me with his huge brown eyes, my heart melted. I took him home with me, gave him a bath, bought him new clothes and fed him. The problem I realized all too soon is that if I left him to his own devices, he would end up back on the street. A woman I knew and loved..." he held up his hands. "Not in that way. She was a friend, an older friend. She lost her husband as well as her child in a freak accident. Janey, is her name. She agreed to take care of the boy. I gave her money to keep him fed and clothed. Brought him gifts. Saw to his education. We decided the day I found Jeffrey would be his birthday. Janey is a saint. She has taken in all my children and loved them with all her heart."

"Merry told me a little, not how it got started. How many?

"I believe the count is somewhere around seven. I have to list them all in my head to know for sure. Clare will have a room at the new house. She will thrive around children."

"I believe she will."

"Am I forgiven?"

"Yes."

~ * ~

Janey arrived on a drizzly day about three weeks later. It took three wagons to bring her and the children to the home Link bought for them. Besides the wagon Link drove, Leslie and Sandy drove the other two.

Link met the children with gifts and hugs. Inside he beamed, adoring the cherished children each and every one of them. Sophie waited with Clare at the new home. He couldn't wait to introduce them all.

When they arrived, Sophie and Clare stood on the porch. The children swarmed the new house, exploring all the rooms, claiming the empty ones. Watching them Link swelled with pride.

He wanted more children. Longed for ones of his very own and Sophie's. Over the past weeks he watched her carefully. So far, she showed no signs of pregnancy. He would have to be patient. The good news for him though was now he would be sure the child when it came along would be his. She had her woman's time two weeks ago. He hated himself for the thought. Couldn't help it though. Sophie sensed his feelings.

Tension still existed between the two of them. When he looked at her, he saw doubt in her silver eyes. Didn't know what to do to change that. Leslie told him time would eventually heal the wound. He prayed his brother was right.

On the porch, he wrapped an arm around Sophie, introducing Janey to her. The dinner table was moved indoors because of the weather. They spent several hours with the children before riding home.

They sat together on the porch, sipping drinks; he a brandy, she a glass of lemonade. Unexpectedly, she stopped drinking wine. Told him it upset her stomach. He wondered about that but didn't ask questions.

She leaned into him when he wrapped an arm around her shoulder. He felt her relax, a soft sigh ensuing. He needed to tell her how he felt. Needed to tell her he'd fallen in love with her. When they wed, he knew he was infatuated with her. He felt lust. Pure lust. Believed that was all the sensation would be. Didn't realize the feelings would deepen over time.

"Link?" She ran a small fingertip along his shirtfront.

"What is it?" He picked up her hand, sucked the exploring finger into his mouth. Her shudder brought an answering one to him.

"Even though you still don't believe me..." she paused.

"You don't forgive me?"

"I do." She placed a kiss on his lips. "You are only a man with a lot of weaknesses. Lacie told me men sometimes can't think clearly when it comes to their women. So..."

He felt her breasts push against him. "What is it?"

"I love you, Link Stewart. Call me a fool for falling in love with a man who doesn't believe in my honesty over a lying cheating man. I love you with all my heart. Think I could forgive you most anything." She stopped then with a tiny shudder, "If you bedded another woman..."

"Never?"

She didn't answer. Closed her eyes instead, sighing softly.

He continued to suck her fingers into his mouth. Then, stopping for a moment, "I love you too. I've wanted you from the very beginning. My feelings have changed. I do believe you."

She pushed away from his staring into his eyes. "You do."

"Yes."

She said nothing

"Will you spend the rest of your life loving me?" he asked. "All I want is you."

"All I want is you. Hmm... I like the sound of that."

He drew her into his arms for a long slow kiss that spoke of their future and the goodness that would follow. They had so much to look forward to. They had the cherished children then hopefully more. Yes, *All I want is Sophie*. Forever and ever.

"All I want is Link," Sophie murmured softly.

Epilogue

Link was surprised as well as pleased at the warm day. May, oh, he wished the first time he came to Virginia it had been in May. The weather was remarkable as he watched the children along with Sophie play on the grass in front of Leslie Hall. He would join them soon. First, he needed to find out as much as he could about Michael Flannigan. He was the manager at Mayfair Hall. Had been for close to five years now. That was when William Brinkmeyer passed on, killed in a duel.

The man managed the plantation the last five years. He did it well. What Link needed to discover was the type of man he was. Clare convinced him she wanted to live her life now. She wanted to spend her time in Virginia. In less than one year when she turned twenty-one, this would all be hers. For the time being he drug a promise from her that she would live at Leslie Hall until her birthday. He would not allow her to move into Mayfair. After all, he was still her guardian.

A pain curled in his stomach. He would not be here to protect her, Sophie's sister. She grew up. A fine young lady if he ever saw one. He was proud of her. He would have to return to Glasgow.

So immersed in his thoughts, he didn't hear or see Sophie come up the steps to the porch. She sat down beside him, taking his hands in hers. She grinned, staring at his mouth. Her silver blue eyes sparkled.

"She will be fine, you know. She's a good head on her shoulders. Edward along with Grayson have promised to watch out for her. Nothing untoward will happen."

"Doesn't mean I'm happy about any of that. What if something does happen? We'll be on the other side of the Atlantic. Won't be able to help."

"Nothing is going to happen." Sophie stared at his crotch now.

Instantly, he was aroused, hard as a rock. "I'm losing all my children." He turned his attention to her bosom. He needed her now. Could hardly toss her skirts while their children played below them on the grass.

"Are you telling me you want another child? I would not want to cross the ocean in a few months while I'm increasing with the babe and losing everything I eat. Perhaps we should wait until we return." She grinned at him before looking at his crotch.

He was instantly ready. "You want another child?" Link was instantly pleased. He thought Sophie would not want more than three. While she came to him with no idea how to be a mother, she learned quickly. At times he was sure she loved all his children more than he did.

"If you do, we need another girl. I would put in a request." She laughed as she watched the oldest boy tackle his sibling. The little girl giggled before she caught him in a fierce hold that Link taught her. Her efforts brought her brother to his knees then his back. She was on top of him now, laughing while pounding on his chest.

The littlest one, another boy, not wanting to be left out threw himself on top of Callum. All three, Callum, Mia and Dallas rolled down the small hill. The movement stopped by flat ground.

"You should join them. I for one am worn out and ready for a nap." She ran her sweet pink tongue across her lips before smiling at him. Slowly, she lowered her lashes.

"Witch."

His attention found another spot to concentrate on. He pushed the thought of hefting Sophie over his shoulder aside as he watched Clare, Michael and Edward ride down the lane to Leslie Hall.

"She is infatuated with the man. He is too old for her." Link stood, his hands clenched at his sides thinking he needed to do something. He just didn't know what that should be. He realized anything he decided on would be met with resistance. "I don't like leaving her here with no chaperone. He will do whatever."

"Clare will not let the young man take advantage of her." It seemed Sophie tried to calm him. The ploy wasn't working.

Clare kicked the mare she was riding. The horse took off leaving the two men behind. He heard her laugh, devoid of pins her hair flying out behind her.

"Young man my foot. He must be twenty-six or older." When he said the words, he knew Sophie would call him on the fact. He'd been that age when he seduced his wife, when he touched her intimately before they wed. She was barely eighteen then. The thought made his gut curl even more.

"Clare knows her mind. You've got to trust her. Yes, if she fancies herself in love with him, she might do something you obviously won't approve of, but you will have no say because you will be in another country. She wants to spread her wings and fly. Give her the chance. Trust her." Sophie stood behind him now. Her slim fingers on his shoulders, she massaged the tense muscles. Tense because he worried about Clare.

"As long as she doesn't fly too high and, in the process, get her wings seared," he growled, decidedly hating the idea they were leaving in two months. The trip was planned only to accompany Clare to her new home.

"She won't. Clare understands men and what they want. We've both made sure of that fact," Sophie spoke softly from the heart. The tender words did not assuage the fear rolling in his stomach.

"Trust her. Trust in the way we brought her up. We've got our own little devils to worry about. I'm sure they will be growing up way too fast."

The trio was suddenly in front of him. She was grinning as she stared at Michael. Edward dismounted. For a moment, Link thought he saw her tongue sweep across her bottom lip. He groaned.

The devil.

She was breathless and beautiful, her hair curled around her shoulders falling down her back. "Michael and I are going riding to the caves. He insisted I tell you even though I told him it wasn't necessary. I am twenty. I'm a woman grown."

Links fists clenched and unclenched. "Be home before dinner." *Or there will hell to pay.*

"We are going to watch the sunset on the river. So, we won't be home until after dark. I've packed a basket of food along with a bottle of wine," Clare spoke softy all the while watching Michael.

"I'll have her home by dinner," he said.

Clare shot him a furious glare. "You might be but I'm staying for the sunset. Dinner and wine while I watch the sun disappear in the west."

With that said she whirled her horse then spurred the mare to a gallop.

"Don't worry, Sir. She's willful as well as stubborn. I'll try but I do promise you I won't leave her by herself even if we are not home until dark. Clare will be safe."

Link watched resigned as Michael caught up to Clare. *Will she be safe from you?*

"Short of following them and in the process ruining their day as well as our own, there is nothing you can do." Sophie leaned to kiss him on the forehead. We should proceed as planned a few seconds ago.

"I'm not going to ruin our afternoon seeing the nanny has taken the children in for their nap." He lifted her into his arms, starting for the steps.

"Good, because all I want is you, Link," her voice purred tenderly in his ear.

Eager and desperate to bed his wife, he took the steps two at a time. He set her gently on the big bed then came down beside her. "I love you, Sophie. You are mine. You are the only woman I want. All I want in my life is you, Sophie."

Coming Soon by the Author
at
Rogue Phoenix Press

Devlin's Angel
Bad Boy Book Eight

Late spring 1828
Southcliff Hall Glasgow, Scotland

Merry Stewart walked from the kitchen in Daryl's bakery with a tray of her newest accomplishment, cream puffs. Justine, Donal's cook and Daryl's helper in the bakery, had been teaching her to bake with great success. Merry could list the string of conquests and it seemed she had an aptitude for baking.

She set the tray on the huge round table where her sister-in-law's sisters sat chatting and letting their children run around the empty tables. It was after closing time and they all made it a habit of meeting in the bakery once a week,.mostly on Saturdays. Their men would join them in a few hours to walk them home.

Five boys ages a few months to four were gathered around the table. The newest addition to the family was Lacie's and Leslie's little boy who would grow up to be the next duke of Southcliff. Except for the littlest one, each was given a cream puff and each managed to get the powdered sugar and whip cream everywhere but in their mouths.

Before too many minutes they would be sticky from head to toe and need to be dumped into a bath before dinner. Merry knew from experience growing up with her brothers, little boys just found ways to get dirtier than little girls.

"Auntie Merry, can I have two," Grant asked, tugging on her apron.

"If he can have two so can I," Garret's little voice followed. "Wouldn't be fair otherwise."

Bliss cleared her throat ruffling both boys' heads, "Neither of you can have two so do stop asking."

Merry laughed at the boys, wishing she could have one of her own, but that opportunity was taken away from her nearly three years ago when her brother, the Duke of Southcliff, ended her elopement with Douglas simply by informing the man she was fifteen-years-old. Well, she understood her lie would be uncovered but she had just hoped that Douglas wouldn't find out before they were married and had consummated the vows.

He did end the hasty engagement and immediately cried off. In less than a year he was wed to another heiress and now he had two sons. Well, he wasn't worth her time anyway. All he wanted was her money and she'd been brought low by his beautiful body coupled with the twinkle in his sky-blue eyes. In any case she intended to wed the Duke of Weston.

She set her sights back to the man who stole her heart when she first saw him in a coach in Paris then on a horse in the streets of Glasgow. It had to be love at first sight. At the time, she didn't know who he was. She often wondered if she would ever find out the man's name who stole her heart.

Two months ago at a masquerade ball in Glasgow given by some earl, she couldn't remember his name, she discovered he was there. At a distance, she'd seen him, standing so tall and broad shouldered, his dark black hair falling rakishly over his forehead. She couldn't quite make out his features but she knew it was him. His introduction cemented her opinion. By the time she pushed her way through the throngs of people to ask for a dance or at least to introduce herself, he was gone.

Vanished. Her despair caught at her heart, moisture filling her eyes but she didn't intend to lose this man of her dreams.

Despite the fact she searched every room in the mansion, disrupting several liaisons, she failed to find him. For a minute or two she slumped to the floor, sitting with her dress splayed out all around her and fought the tears. At the time she was two weeks from turning eighteen. While she didn't have any illusions he would fall in love with her the very moment he saw her, she still needed to find a way to meet him. She couldn't do that unless she learned his name. Despondent once more, she slowly made her way back to the ball and asked permission to leave. She couldn't bear to be there one more second, knowing he left.

It was just her luck as her carriage began to draw away from the mansion that he stepped from another carriage, striding up the steps to return to the festivities. She would have turned the carriage around but Lacie had pleaded exhaustion and the ever present need to feed her baby was accompanying her home.

Now, back at the bakery, "Your mind is in the clouds." Lacie sat down beside her holding the young heir on her lap. "Are you thinking of the Duke of Weston again? Glad you finally discovered his name. I've met him before and he's very handsome, but boring if you ask me."

"Just stoic like my brother. Believe it goes along with the title as well as the responsibilities. You changed my brother though."

"Perhaps he's really a bad boy at heart. He could be just like our husbands," Chelsea said with a smirk as she wiped her son's fingers after smearing the sweet mess over his chubby little cheeks.

"I am and just how I'm going to go about meeting him, I haven't the vaguest idea." She sipped the tea in front of her as she placed a cream puff on her plate. "How do you think I can do that?"

"Well." Lacie paused to hand the young heir a ginger cookie, "I did hear he might be in Glasgow for the summer. Seems there was some scandal he was involved in and he's escaped London to a quieter place."

"Probably to avoid a duel. I heard that too," Daryl said. "Your duke got himself in a fine fix. He must have a temper. If you do meet him, you need to be careful."

"I heard he's gone to ground it was so bad," Merry muttered. "Nobody is going to see him, least of all me." She swiped her finger across the powdered sugar on the cream puff top then licked the sweet stuff. Think I'll spend the summer at Southcliff. At least I've free reign of the countryside, with no one there to tell me what I can and cannot do. You and Leslie will be stuck in town most of the summer, so I won't have to explain to anyone what I'm doing or where I'm going."

"No nightly rides," Bliss pointed out. "You know it's not safe. Promise us."

Merry avoided Bliss' eyes, staring at her hands resting in her lap. She would do as she pleased. There was no danger in the nightly rides that she could see.

"Yes, you will have the house pretty much to yourself but if we hear of any exploits, Leslie will be the first to drag you back to the city so he can keep a brotherly eye on you," Lacie said, apparently recognizing the simmering need to do her own thing in her eyes.

She lifted her shoulders in a deceptive shrug, "What would I do? There is absolutely nothing for me to get into trouble with. Besides I'm eighteen now and very capable of making my own decisions. I don't need a guardian or a chaperone, thank you."

"While I don't doubt that for one instant we both understand certain things." Lacie winked at her. "A girl doesn't have to do much to get into trouble, especially with their men folk."

"I've no men folk," Merry pointed out with a wistful smile.

"There is the river and the pond," Chelsea said as she wiped the mess from the mouth of her boy. "All of us know you have some kind of attraction to the water and swimming."

"Well, if I do go swimming, it won't be naked," she muttered as she looked from one lady to the other, heat creeping up her face. Last time she swam that was exactly what she did.

Garret and Grant took that moment to run yelling around the table, their younger cousins chasing after them. Bliss grabbed one of the twins around the waist then stalked after the other. Her intentions clear.

"Believe it's time to take these little hellions to the park so they can run off some of this extra energy before they see their doting papas," Bliss said with a determined air. "Of course if I took them home, I would tell Broc it was time for him to do his duty with the boys and play with them."

All the little boys except Daryl's and Lacie's were herded out of the bakery to run off steam. Daryl and Lacie were left with Merry who was still moping, mostly for effect. Yet there was a certain depression that had settled around her, weighing down her shoulders. She needed a diversion.

"You're set on marrying this Duke of Weston then," Daryl said watching Merry closely. "Perhaps you should go to a few more balls and with an open mind. It might lead to something. You don't know who you might meet. There could be another man for you."

"Just as there was another Donal for you," Merry shot back clearly angry and unwilling to compromise in this. She did know her heart better than anyone.

"Promise me you won't wed him if you don't love him. He could be awful, you know, a real bounder. With the scandal there is a hint of that," Lacie told her.

She let out a long dramatic breath of air as she tilted her head thinking about the man she wanted so desperately to meet that she could just barely inhale air. "I'll promise. Just because he's devilishly handsome and owns a magnificent stable doesn't mean he's a nice person."

Lacie laughed, obviously amused by the stable part. "There is more to a man than his stables."

"It's all true. I could meet someone and fall madly in love at some ball, but…" She drew in a deep breath of air feeling as if her eyes were crossing. "I've been to five balls in the last three months. All the men I've seen are boring and simpering fops. I want a real man. One whose body is like Leslie's and Donal's, all muscle and hard. And I want him to challenge me, give as good as he gets. I don't want a man who will cow tow to my every whim."

"Be careful what you wish for," Daryl murmured slanting Lacie an all-knowing glance before she laughed softly. "You might get more than you've bargained for, especially if you like your freedom."

"That is hardly giving the men a chance if you've already made up your mind," Daryl pointed out

"Why was it so easy for you? I'm certainly not going to settle for a simpering dandy. None of you did." She had thought so long on this she was sure mazes of confusion were forming in her head, labyrinths she would never decipher. "I would rather never marry than settle." She sighed then, envisioning the Duke of Weston, his long well muscled legs to his broad shoulders and strong chin. She wondered what color his eyes were. Merry just knew she would melt when he looked at her with desire in his eyes. She knew what that looked like. She'd seen the passion in Leslie's eyes often enough when he stared at Lacie.

"Of course, you won't have to settle. When you're least expecting it, you will look up and the man of your dreams will be standing in front of you," Daryl said thoughtfully. "That's what happened to all of us."

"I will not hold my breath," Merry murmured and I plan on having fun until then. If pining away would get me what I wanted, that's what would happen." She was thinking of riding her little mare everyday and perhaps even at night since Leslie would not be there to chastise her for her behavior. Come hell or high water she was going to make the most of this summer. Even if she didn't meet the duke there would always be another day, another ball, another chance.

"Perhaps Cam can find some nice man at the university to court you. There are nice men their, perhaps a student and not a professor," Lacie said thoughtfully.

"Immature." Was the one word that came to Merry's mind when she thought on the students at the University of Glasgow. She promised herself she would not settle even while she closed her eyes and saw the Duke of Weston's masked image standing in front of her, holding his hand out to her, asking for this dance.

She would never settle.

Daryl left the table to finish closing the kitchen for the weekend. Tomorrow was Sunday and it was the only day the bakery was not open. Justine poked her head out the door to say goodnight and Emilia, the other lady who helped Daryl, was right behind her.

Lacie set the heir apparent in the stroller before giving him a quick kiss to his forehead. "I'm going to the townhouse. Do you care to come with me or do you want to stay here for a while?"

Merry let out a long breath of air, pushing her hair from her face. "I'll walk with you then I think I'll get a carriage ready to send to Southcliff with my maid. I'm so restless and out of sorts I can barely stand myself. Fresh air and freedom is what I need. Then and only then will I feel better."

Once inside the townhouse, Merry called for her maid, Lucy appeared so quickly it seemed to her she must have been waiting for the summons. "Get my trunk packed yours as well. We're going to Southcliff for the summer. We're just getting started a little early. I'm riding Sir Alistair. You can take the carriage as soon as everything is ready."

With the directions given Merry quickly changed into her riding habit. Less than fifteen minutes later she was astride her mare and headed out of town. While the sun peeked its way from behind clouds, the day was relatively cool. A soft breeze blew from the west and even though it was not a hot day, within the hour Merry's forehead was covered in a fine sheen of perspiration. She longed for the cooling waters of her pond and to laze the rest of the day away.

As she drew closer to Southcliff, more intense thoughts of veering off the road and heading to the small pond near their home captured her thoughts. Mayhap she would give in to her inhibitions later this evening. The water would be nearly frigid but would also be invigorating.

No, she decided, now would be the best time. She would rid herself of the dust and sweat accumulated from the ride, rendering herself refreshed and ready for whatever would come next. Turning her horse off the road, she headed for the pond, sweet relief from the scattered workings of her mind.

When she arrived at the pond, the water rippled a soft silver hue capturing its beauty. She slipped from her mare leaving her where she could graze. As she walked toward the water, she noticed a huge black stallion tethered nearby. Perhaps she should leave but curiosity drove her, needing to see who dared invade private property, her very own pond. Well, the pond was Leslie's, but what difference did that make?

The stallion, the horse was amazing; tall, sleek and well muscled, his hindquarters strong, made for running. He nickered when she stepped close, stroking his nose, murmuring sweet nonsense words to him. She couldn't help but stare at its sleek clean lines the beauty of its coat.

"Now, who has left you here. I've a mind to ride you, you sweet guy. I bet you're the gentlest male in all of Scotland." She continued caressing the horse, her mind lost in images of her on top the horse, racing the wind.

For minutes her gaze was focused on one animal. Then, as if sensing something, she turned to see a man rising from her pond, his shoulders broad, his body lean and muscular, his dark wet hair fell rakishly long around his head before dipping to nearly his bronzed shoulders. His chest was broad, his abs hard. A tiny gasp parted her lips as she could not stop her unruly eyes from lingering on him. She liked everything about the man.

She drew in a quick ragged breath of air even while she walked to the edge of the pond. Her gaze having switched from the stallion to the man, she could not force herself to look away. Her stomach somersaulted. Heat flushed her cheeks

Merry's parched throat made it difficult to swallow.

The man stopped, wiping droplets of water from his face as he stared at her, his gaze almost as intent as hers. With a bit of laughter to his voice, he spoke, "You might want to turn around."

"And why would I want to do that? You are trespassing, Sir. This is Stewart land and that is my pond you're swimming in. Did you ask anyone's permission? I should send for the magistrate." She knew she was all bluster. No way in hell would she have this man tossed off her land.

His brows drew together, eyes narrowing. His hands were placed on his slender hips. "You could join me. That might prove interesting, lass."

A gasp of air filled the silence then she stepped back, thinking it might be prudent to walk away while she still could, having noticed a pile of clothing near his horse.

"You're naked." Her words were a bit strangled and she wasn't sure he heard, wasn't sure she wanted him to hear. Didn't think her statement warranted a reply since it was blatantly obvious.

"Would not be swimming in my clothes, sweetheart. At the moment though I'd like to leave the water behind me. It's a bit cold. Unfortunately right now, not cold enough."

"I'm not you're sweetheart," she grit out suddenly angry yet she didn't know if she was angry with herself and her wayward thoughts or with the man who dared swim in her pond.

Now you know good manners should have you turning away and riding on home.

If I did that, I wouldn't see him naked. As you well know, except my brothers when they were young boys I've never seen a man with no clothes. I'm sure he's a fine specimen of a man.

You would regret it. He doesn't look like a man who would let you see him, without their being repercussions.

Do be quiet. I'm going to go in just a minute.

"Ah, but you could be my sweetheart."

More curious than she had any right to be and ignoring the voice of reason in her head, she crossed her arms in front of her, thinking perhaps if she could soak up the beauty of the man for a few more minutes she would leave. She really did want to see what he was hiding beneath the water. This man was no simpering dandy. She could tell by the arrogant tilt of his head and the way the lighthearted note of his first words had changed tone when she confronted him.

"Turn around now or leave. I care not but I'm coming out." His voice rang out, loud and clear. Threatening.

She was far too curious.

Merry gasped as he started walking again, the water covering less and less of him. Her gaze followed the water line as it dipped downward. She saw the dark hair on his chest narrow. "How dare you?" Not as curious as she thought she was she turned tail, mounting her horse and racing home.

From behind her she heard his laughter and, "For some reason I thought you had more courage."

She almost turned the mare around, the need to confront the arrogant man foremost in her mind. Prudently, she thought better of it.

Merry felt the heat of the encounter on her cheeks. Even the light wind caressing her face did little to cool her flaming face. An eternity seemed to pass before she was in the safety of the stables. For at least a minute, she leaned against her mare's neck and tried to calm her racing heart.

The man was an arrogant cad of the worst sort, playing with her emotions with his nakedness. Finally, feeling more in control of her shaking body, she slipped from her horse. She saw to the mare, taking the saddle off, feeding and watering the horse. After that she brushed her, stroking her, thinking of the man and the way he stared at her, remembering his rudeness as he threatened to show himself to her.

A noise from the front of the stables caught her attention. She stepped from the stall only to find the man of her thoughts standing at the large door, the reins of his stallion in hand, a dark wicked smile gracing his arrogant features.

Her breath caught in her throat as she fearlessly strode toward the man. "What are you doing here?" She was pointing a finger at him and had every intention of poking him in the chest before she thought better of it, dropping her hand.

"Nice to meet you again." His gaze raked over her just as hers had done when he stood naked in her pond. He settled on her bosom then lifted his eyes upward to her mouth. She couldn't help herself. She ran her tongue along her lips.

"I will thank you to answer my question." She endeavored for all the authority in her voice she could gather. Stiffening her spine her chin tilted high she waited.

He quirked a dark eyebrow upward before turning her question back on her, "Then don't thank me. What are you doing here?"

"Of all the..." Merry was at an obvious loss for words, something that never happened. Her verbal aptitude was well known. She could spar and hold her own with anyone. After all, she practiced with her brothers. She wasn't sure if she liked him staring at her or not. Heat throbbed in strange places, and butterflies danced in her stomach. His gaze was appreciative and that gave her a bit of a thrill, thinking he might like what he was looking at. Not even Douglas had looked at her that way.

"Nerve?" He supplied the single word for her, a half smile tilting the corner of his mouth.

Thoughts of him kissing her came to mind, his lips touching hers. He had the most beautiful mouth, full lips that beckoned. "I would appreciate an answer," she told him as her anger with this man simmered deep in her belly and her confusion about how she felt about that, raged. "Why are you standing here?"

He strode closer, his stallion following behind. "I'm your new horse breeder." Insolently his gaze locked with hers, challenging her in a way no one had ever done before.

"Kelly O'Brian is our horse breeder." She spoke with a confidence she didn't feel. Surely Leslie would have told her if he hired someone to work at the stables. Surely...but Leslie was out of town for a while, ensconced in London with Drake Montgomery. If Lacie had known of this, she would tell her.

"Horse trainer," he corrected, "and he's away on his honeymoon. The duke told me he had mares coming and he wanted to breed them. I'm in charge of that. Breeding. You do *ken* what that is?"

With his gaze focused on her mouth then dropping to her bosom more heat flooded her, warmed her as well as her face once again, felt the fire as if he stroked her. She placed her hands on her cheeks in a feeble attempt to cool herself off.

It seemed he realized the effect the direction of his attentions had on her, his grin widening for a moment before he sobered.

He crossed his arms on his chest still staring and frowning, his dark blue eyes simmering with heated emotions.

"How do I know you speak true?"

"Why should I not toss you from the stables. You've yet to explain your presence here," the man said, his voice filled with confidence.

She clamped her hand over her mouth, stopping herself from giving him a few choice words. "You've no right to speak to me that way and in that impudent tone of voice. You're hired help and a commoner and that."

"Ah, now we have part of the truth. A commoner who dares to return a noble's rude gaze or should I say stare? You were more than gazing at me now and also when I was naked. I know you found me quite to your liking. Didn't you? Tit for tat, why not?" He stepped even closer, his presence overpowering, stripping her of what sanity might remain.

She moved back, her heart in her throat and tried to look anywhere but at him. She found she could not stop looking at him, all of him, and remembering the Adonis rising from the water, his muscles, the sleekness of his flesh as water sluiced from his form.

"I trust you should apologize. I'll go to my brother and he will fire you for your impertinence." She stepped back again, bumping into her mare, groping for words. With nowhere to go she tried to step around him, but he blocked her way from the stall.

His arms crossed over his well-muscled chest, "You can try." This time he smiled, an all-knowing smile, an arrogant smile as if he knew she would get nowhere if she went to Leslie with any type of complaint. "Didn't you say he's in London? Was that my imagination?"

He set the challenge and she meant to win. "If he won't dismiss you, I'll have his wife fire you."

"Ah, so you do agree I work here." He extended a hand. "I'm Devlin Mathews. Would you mind telling me exactly who you are and what you are doing here? Perhaps even why you believe you can have me fired with the snap of your fingers." He bent closer, his breath whispering so close she could scent mint on his breath.

She sipped air, unable to get a real breath into her lungs. Heat flooded her body, an inferno, slicked from her toes to her head, "I'm Merry Stewart, the duke's sister."

"Ah, the youngest of the tribe, Angelica. I've heard much about you."

"How?" She had her hands placed on her hips in defiance. Now his words were a set back for her. She couldn't think of a single reason why her brother would talk about her to a man such as this, a commoner. "Leslie would not have spoken about me to the likes of you."

"Here we are again, this commoner noble thing you have going. Doesn't your older brother have several very good friends who are minus a title?"

He implied so many things by his comments least of all was that she was the baby of the family. She had this incessant urge to prove to him she was no child, least of all a baby. Yet she could think of no way to do such a thing.

"I'll show you to your room." This time he didn't block her way when she marched past him. He didn't follow either but continued to watch, making her feel self-conscious without saying a word.

"Should take care of Windwalker first." He set to work on his horse, ignoring her as well as the firestorm building inside which he was singlehandedly responsible for.

She stood nearby unable to leave, unwilling to stop looking at him while beneath his fine white lawn shirt his muscles moved and bulged with his work. After his dip in her pond, he had failed to fasten his shirt.

When he finished and with that same rakish, devilishly handsome smirk on his face, he said, "Now you can show me where I'm to bed down." The way he said the words seemed to take on a different meaning, almost as if he was asking her to join him. That couldn't be. He couldn't be. No, it wasn't possible for a commoner to imply that.

Or was it?

Her breath caught in her throat as she was sure he meant more than what he said. There were subtle innuendos in his words and tone. She wasn't sure she understood, but she'd been around the bad boys long enough to make significant guesses. Curiously, she wanted to ask him what he meant but prudence, something she rarely had, stopped her.

~ * ~

Devlin Mathews enjoyed the brisk cold water as he swam beneath, surfacing then diving deeper. It had been his intention to wash the dust and sweat from the road before he walked into the Stewart stables. Leslie Stewart told him many things, but the foremost was that even though Angelica was expected to summer in Glasgow, she could always be a surprise. She changed her mind often and could invariably turn up unexpected. Leslie also told him she could be a very real thorn in his side.

Doing the unanticipated had long been her agenda. As Leslie told him, she improved with age but still, if he was to live in the stables and breed the new mares that would be sent within the week, he would have to learn to deal gently with his unpredictable but lovely sister. Merry would be under his step and in his way most nearly all of the time.

Because she could not be trusted to stay in the city despite her promise. Because she would do as she wished. Leslie had not entrusted him with the need to make sure she did nothing to risk herself, but he implied that if he needed to do just that, he had free reign to handle her in a way he deemed appropriate. In short, she was his to discipline if necessary.

The week traveling here, he enjoyed the Scottish countryside, enjoyed the playing of the pipes and everything Scottish. Half way he stopped at his great aunt's home letting her pamper him with an amazing meal and soft bed, understanding that until he was able to purchase a bed and have it delivered, the pallet in the stable boy's room was not worth sleeping on. So, he remained in Glasgow longer than he intended and despite everyone's wishes until the bed was delivered.

Well, it had been delivered this morning. He would be there in less than an hour, as soon as he was fatigued enough and was able to drink enough brandy to fall asleep. Nights were an impossibility, drifting into the depth of Morpheus eluding him. His best friend called him out over the most ludicrous of stories. He didn't even like Teddy's sister. There was know way in hell he would get her pregnant so he would have to marry her.

His lungs near to bursting, he surfaced. Wiping water and hair from his face, he looked up. What was left of his breath caught in his throat. While she wasn't the most beautiful woman he'd ever seen, she was intriguing. He very much liked what he was looking at. When he looked again, he found she was staring at his horse, stroking him, murmuring soft words that only Windwalker and she could hear. More intrigued than ever he strode to shore only to stop short recalling he was buck-naked and his clothing was piled near his stallion.

When she focused her attention on him, her smile was devastating. Now she was staring at him, at his mouth to be exact, her gaze drifting lower to remain at the waterline as if she wanted to see him intimately. When he told her to leave, she stayed there for the longest time, challenging him with her blatant perusal of his body. By the time she finally left he was aroused beyond anything he'd felt in his life and he was ready to ride after her and throttle her.

She told him this was her pond. That led him to believe the girl must be Angelica Stewart, the unpredictable lass Leslie warned him about. If she was going to be a handful, she would be his handful, at least for the duration of his stay here at Southcliff. He began to whistle, thinking he might come to enjoy the summer here in the country outside Glasgow. Leslie also told him she would use the argument that she'd come of age to justify any ridiculous and dangerous behavior she was inclined to perpetrate.

He would see her again soon. Just how he would handle this delicate situation without getting into hot water with the Duke of Southcliff eluded him, but he would figure something out. During the ride from the pond to the stables, he went over various possible scenarios in his mind, all of which ended up with him in bed with her.

Well, hell, that just wouldn't do. Angelica Stewart was not just a skirt to be tossed and enjoyed for the summer. She deserved better and better was not something he could do. So, he would have to find a very real way to leave her alone, which might be a nearly impossible task given the fact he was still aroused.

When he strode into the stables on the Stewart property, he wasn't surprised to see the woman of his tangled thoughts in the stable once again staring at him. She was stroking a horse, her horse this time while murmuring sweet nothings to the beast. What he wouldn't give to be on the end of her whispers. Wrestling with his thoughts of her murmuring in his ear and caressing him, he cleared his throat, pushing everything from his mind except the present and how he would deal with this willful and thoroughly spoiled woman-child who burned him with a smile.

He stared at her waiting for her to notice him. Several seconds ticked by. She did notice. The coming confrontation was heated, simmering with passion between them, passion he could not, would not touch. The heat would flame.

When he was finished grooming the big stallion, he followed her through the stables to the back room. She told him she would show him where he would sleep. With her so nearby and untouchable, his nights would most likely be restless.

"Your room," she said, bending over to peek inside. "There's a new bed. I didn't know Leslie ordered one."

"Thank god," he said laughing before offering, "Care to try it out with me?" He leaned over her, his hand splayed across her back as she was bent slightly peering into the room. Playing with fire would be the death of him, pure torture, but he didn't think he could stop.

She stood up so quickly she nearly knocked him over, her head hitting his chin. "What? What did you say?" Her deep blue eyes flashed, seemed to touch upon his soul as she turned to confront him.

His grin deepened even as he regretted his next words. He looked to the bed then back to her, "Care to try it out?" He repeated, needing a way to get her to leave. The blatant invitation might do the trick.

If she didn't go soon, by the way she aroused him, he would have her skirts tossed and he'd be deep inside her before she could tell him what she thought of him. He would tease and flirt, but he drew the line at blatant seduction. Her brother was a friend after all and if anything did happen between them, he would be honor bound to wed. He wasn't ready for marriage. Not to Angelica, not to anyone and especially not to Teddy's little sister.

She was standing now, in the middle of the doorway, stepping backwards again but it was to move further inside his bedroom. He grinned as he watched the play of emotions across her lovely face. Her eyes shimmered and darkened with what he knew to be desire, a passion he longed to test and explore. Even though he understood the consequences, he couldn't help himself. He stepped forward watching her once again move in the opposite direction, ever closer to the big bed occupying most of the room.

"You didn't answer my question," he told her, his voice softening, tempting her to run he hoped. If she didn't, he wasn't sure he could be responsible for himself.

Suddenly her arms whirled and it seemed she was losing her balance. "I..."

He moved quickly, holding on to her then falling with her he turned them so he caught the brunt of the fall as they landed on his bed. He grinned at her, "Guess I've your answer, brat." He laughed as she fell on top of him, her slight weight settling down on him. This was not the outcome he wanted from his teasing, but he meant to enjoy the few seconds he would have her in this position.

Her hands on his chest, she pushed, "Let me go," she said, but there was neither command in her voice nor any realization of the situation she was in now. She was sprawled on top of him, her breasts pushing against his chest. Until he rolled with her, presenting his body atop hers, she could have gone anywhere she pleased. Now she was tucked nicely in his arms. She was beneath him.

"Not yet," he said, resting on his forearms, staring at her lips then the valley between her breasts, wondering about the size and texture of the twin morsels on either side. "Not until you answer me. Well, I guess you decided it would be a good idea to try out the bed. What do you think? Should we crawl under the covers and see what happens next?" The invitation was blatant and another attempt to frighten her to remain far from him.

She glared at him as if he was a mad man and perhaps he was a bit crazy challenging her in this way. He meant to provoke her to get her to leave when in truth he was enjoying her company far too much. She would leave soon enough, and he'd be left to tamp down his lust. A powerful lust that if she cared to look was quite obvious.

"I didn't answer and you know it. Did you push me?" She hit him on the shoulder. He grunted simply because he thought it was most likely what she wanted.

"I would never push a lady." He fiddled with flyaway strands of hair moving them away from her face, wishing he dared kiss her. A commoner kissing the daughter of a duke just wasn't done.

Well, hell.

This wasn't at all what he thought would be happening tonight. At this point in time he was liking the feeling of her breasts pressed against him. Turning her again, he ran his hands down her back until he reached her nicely rounded bottom.

"Sir." The single word sounded breathy and filled with passion.

"Devlin," he reminded her.

He was amusing himself with ungrounded hope. Moving away from her he held out his hand.

She blinked a few times before she accepted the offered hand, her cheeks flaming with color. Quickly he pulled her to a sitting position then off the bed and into his arms again. Pressed close to him he held her for a few more seconds.

"I should go." She smoothed her skirts, looking to the floor.

"You should." He agreed with her even though he would have liked her to stay. Damn the consequences.

Merry wiped her hands on her dress, plucking at the fabric as she looked around him. "You might step aside." Her voice was breathy as she finally lifted her chin high enough so she could see him. High enough he had no doubt she was the sister of a duke.

"Perhaps I should require a token from you," he said, sliding a finger along her chin before letting it travel down her neck to the rapidly beating pulse. "A small token before I let you pass."

"And what would that be?" she asked, her voice gaining strength as he allowed her more distance between them.

"A kiss and I'll let you pass." Where did that come from? He just spent a considerable amount of time convincing himself a kiss was not possible and here he asked for one. Damn, but everything he was doing with the girl was out of character.

"You are no gentleman." Anger tingeing her words, she pushed past him as he let her go by.

"True. I never said or implied I was." He laughed, watching the provocative swing of her hips as she marched from the small bedroom he was going to call home until the end of the summer. At least he managed to get her out of the stables for now, yet he was anxiously awaiting his next encounter with Angelica Stewart.

His angel.

Now that he was alone, he managed to look around the room. His valet had been here ahead of him with a trunk where he would find the clothing he would wear and his secretary had also been here. A small desk sat in the corner with papers on top he assumed would be the correspondence he needed to examine before the end of the day.

While his grandmother thought he needed to rusticate for awhile, he still had work that could not be left undone. Finding a bottle of brandy on the desk he made a quick note to ask for a case. If the following days were going to proceed anything like this one, he would need to drink himself into oblivion just to fall asleep at night as well as keep Angelica a virgin.

Sitting against the headboard and stretching his legs out in front of him, he sifted through the papers he held in his hand. Really, there was nothing that needed his immediate attention. He sipped the strong drink, finishing the glass then pouring another. With his eyes closed, he let his imagination take over his thoughts and they all sped directly to the little brat who had felt so comfortable and appealing in his arms.

The second glass finished, he decided to take a look at the stables. The mares would arrive tomorrow or the next day. While he was sure Leslie had seen to the accommodations for the mares he had a pressing need to make sure they were kept safely away from his stallion. Even though it was a distraction for him, the breeding of these horses was important.

As he wandered the stable, he realized Leslie was most competent. The wandering changed to pacing until his restlessness took over his body. It wouldn't do to finish off the bottle of brandy so he decided a midnight ride might be in order. Perhaps it was now closer to dawn, he couldn't be sure. His pocket watch was in his jacket and he couldn't be bothered to discover the time. Somehow, in the country with so little to occupy his days and nights the hour of the day just no longer seemed to matter.

He wondered then when Angelica would make her next appearance. The sooner the better he decided. Her very demeanor challenged him, kept him on his toes and he realized he couldn't wait to see her. He decided that perhaps sleep would do him well in this circumstance. A midnight ride could be had any time and perhaps he could convince her to go with him.

You're playing with fire, and if you don't watch yourself you're going to get burned. Aye, he might but the pleasure would well be worth the ensuing inferno.

Or would it?

He would have to leave that question unanswered for the moment.

He disrobed eyeing the bed and remembering her splayed on top of him then his body over hers. The groan leaving his lungs surprised him for a moment. She would never agree to bedding him, a commoner and a noble. No, but it was worth it to see just how far she would go. Perhaps he would push her a bit farther today. The sun might shine upon them. He fell asleep with thoughts of Angelica filling his dreams.

The scent of strong coffee wafted in through the slightly open door to his room. The hinge didn't work; was one of the things on his list to improve before he left. He was surprised to smell coffee. Unlike most in the British Isles, he preferred coffee to the tea that was most often served.

With one eye open, he saw that light filtered in through the one window, the day giving a promise of warmth.

"Devlin? Devlin are you up?"

So, she was back and bringing coffee as an offering of sorts. Was it a peace offering or did she want something from him? Perhaps she thought the strong brew would replace the kiss he asked for last night and didn't receive. If it was strong enough, it would at least for the time being replace thoughts of the kiss. Perhaps not.

He pulled on his soft doeskins before striding shirtless into the main area of the stables. She'd set up a table and two chairs, the coffee and something else on the table.

“Would you like a sticky bun? I just learned how to make them a few days ago.” She held out a cup of coffee.

“A sticky bun.” He grinned accepting the coffee, his mind taking a different route than what she would expect. As he sat down, her stare travelled along his chest, lower then lower until it stopped at his unfastened pants. Heat flamed inside him at her blatant perusal. What had he expected? He chose not to wear a shirt for his own purposes, wanting to see if the heat from the night before still existed between them.

It did. Now if flamed brighter and hotter.

“Daryl taught me. I made some for the bakery and was told they are really quite good.” She sat down on one of the chairs, sipping the hot liquid she held in front of her, watching him expectantly a hesitant smile.

“I bet your buns are very tasty.” He bit into one, chewing thoughtfully, studying her, realizing she had no idea what he meant.

Her brows drew together, chewing over his words. “They are,” she agreed with him. “As is the coffee.”

“How did you know, brat?” he asked.

“Know what?”

“That I preferred coffee over tea.”

“Do you? I always thought coffee tasted better with my buns,” she said straight faced. “Link brought a lot back from Virginia.”

The liquid in his mouth spewed out with a cough. “What did you say?”

“You heard me. Coffee tastes better with my buns,” she told him so much indignation in her voice.

Keeping his laughter behind his teeth, “That’s what I thought you said.” He’d like to try that particular combination as he wondered how much of what she said was feigned innocence or if she knew exactly what he was talking about. He’d like to discover that too. Did she have any clue what he referred to?

“So, what do you think?” She leaned forward, her eyes sparkling with anticipation of his response.

His heart twisted, lightened, changed from his usual jaded thoughts. With his mouth full of sticky buns, his eyes catching her gaze, he said. “They are really very good with your coffee. Or is it your buns with the coffee? Maybe it's the cinnamon and sugar with the melted butter that makes your buns so delicious."

She smiled, her twin dimples, changing her face, so much he gasped, "Thank you. I can make them for you every morning if you like. You can taste my buns every morning along with all the cinnamon, sugar and butter you want."

He inhaled then very slowly he said, "I would like to taste your sticky buns every morning, thank you."

She beamed even more. "Ask and you will receive," Her eyes were alight, her smile beautiful, overpowering.

Inwardly he groaned. *Ask and you will receive*. There were a lot of things he could think of that he might want to ask of her. Trying to stick his wayward thoughts to the farthest recesses of his brain, he finished eating.

"Are you wanting to ride this morning? I'd be happy to go with you since the mares aren't here yet."

Her face fell, her lips turning downward in a small pout. "Of course, if that is what you'd like."

After such a good beginning he didn't understand her reticence. Didn't understand why she appeared disappointed by his invitation. "Why don't you want me to go with you?"

She pursed her lips together, stiffening. "Yesterday you were in my pond and I couldn't swim. I was..."

"Wanting to swim today. Do you think that is wise? Swimming all by yourself?" He would go with her, but he would never be able to keep his eyes from her. To save his soul, he couldn't help uttering the next question. "Do you swim in the buff?"

Her lips quirked, her eyes smoldering with defiance, "Yes."

If she kept this up, he wasn't going to be responsible for himself. Trying to keep his body in check was increasingly impossible as every word from her moist pink lips aroused and inflamed his senses. "You don't want me to go with you then." He wasn't sure if he should allow her to go by herself. Leslie implied he might want to keep her from doing something stupid. In his mind, what she planned was indeed stupid. "Perhaps you could swim in your shift."

"And what good would that do?" she asked him with more

defiance. “As soon as it got wet it would be like swimming in nothing at all. My shift would be soaked through.”

She was right of course. “Can’t let you go by yourself.” His voice was harsh when he spoke, but the thought of anyone coming along and finding her as good as naked sent his gut rolling as anger built within. His imagination sped to what might happen.

“It’s really quite safe but that’s why I usually go at night. Even if someone would ride by, it would be too dark to see anything. They wouldn’t even know I was in the water.”

His gut tightened even more. He stood so quickly his chair fell over hitting the floor with a loud bang. “No. You are not to go riding at night, brat.” While Leslie had mentioned keeping an eye on her, he didn’t think she would ever do anything quite this reckless or stupid.

“I’ll thank you to keep your orders to yourself.” She stood also, striding, back stiff to the stall where her little mare was housed.

“Don’t thank me then.” He raced after her, grabbing her arm, swinging her around. “I’m coming with you, brat. You’ve obviously no idea just how dangerous this endeavor could be.”

“Then I can’t swim. You would keep me from one of my few pleasures?” Her voice was incredulous as if her intentions were not something other than absurd and dangerous as hell.

“You can swim as long as I am there to guard your buns.” He grimaced as her face flamed, regretting his words and undermining the few minutes of peace they shared this morning.

Well, hell.

“It’s the only way you are going to get wet as well as get what you’re thinking. Choose what you want. Don’t leave without me.” He strode to the stallion deciding he should saddle Windwalker before he saddled her horse. If he didn’t, she would most assuredly take off without him. In truth he thought he was being very diplomatic. In his way of thinking, this was the only solution. He would simply not look at her.

When he finished saddling his stallion, he heard the hooves of her horse pounding behind him. His heart caught in his throat. By the time he turned, she was out the doors. Bloody hell. The frustration and anger simmering deep in his belly, caught him by surprise. If anyone was going to see her wearing what would be nothing, it was him.

He swung onto his horse, racing out behind her. She was incorrigible, didn't take to reasonable commands at all. What he asked of her, he believed was extremely sensible. He didn't understand how Leslie assumed he could ever keep track of her. By the time he was out the door, she was disappearing behind a hill.

When he caught up with her, he'd tan her backside.

He'd rather kiss her senseless until neither could breathe.

~ * ~

Lacie looked up, startled from her musings about her husband when Leslie walked into the drawing room. "You're home sooner than I thought you would be. I missed you."

"Montgomery finally took no for an answer. The man surprised me," he said, placing a kiss on his son's forehead then Lacie's. "I missed you also and couldn't wait to get back. Did the horse breeder show up, Devlin Mathews?"

"I believe he did, a few days ago. He stopped by to say he was going out to Southcliff after he spent a few days here in town. Mumbled something about needing a new bed, among other things." She laughed, remembering the lumpy pallet that was in the room. Leslie had made love to her there. "He didn't seem too worried about the sparse accommodations. Said he would take care of whatever he might need."

"Thought as much. The man is resourceful."

"Why, is there something you're not telling me?" she asked, cocking her head a bit sideways to study him, sure there was more to Devlin Mathews than he was willing to share with her. That didn't sit well with her. Since Merry was at Southcliff, she felt it only right that both understood exactly who the man was. Horse breeder, that wasn't all Devlin Mathews was. She was sure of that fact.

"So you haven't heard anything from Merry." It seemed he didn't want to talk about the horse breeder.

"It's been strangely and eerily quiet around here. Not real sure what to think about it and wonder from time to time if she is sick or if I should be alarmed and send someone out to check on her. Didn't think she'd stay in isolation for more than a day or two." Lacie still watched him closely even though she knew he would never give his thoughts away. His time as a spy trained him well.

Leslie held out his hands for his child before swinging him into the air. "Missed the little tyke." Then changed the subject back to his sister and the horse breeder. "We should wait a while before we send out the troops. I'm trying to keep in mind that Merry is an adult and I've the utmost faith in Mathews' integrity. Nothing will happen between them simply because of who I am."

"He's still a man," Lacie logically pointed out while she watched the play of emotions over her husband's face. She remembered the times when he kissed and coaxed her to his way. He was always successful in his seductions. If Mathews had it in his mind to kiss Merry or do more than just kiss, the deed would be done.

After a lengthy pause, he said, "Perhaps I should pay a visit to see if the mares have arrived. Wouldn't hurt to give them a surprise visit and see what they're up too. It would be interesting to hear Devlin's version of my sister and her antics, because there would be antics."

"Merry won't be suspicious if you show up unannounced?" Lacie was now more concerned than ever if Leslie thought his sister and the horse breeder might be up to something that would only serve to get Merry into trouble. Even with all her considerable knowledge garnered from listening to her two brothers, she was an innocent. If she guessed correctly, except for a few shared kisses three years ago with her bodyguard, Douglas, she was totally untried.

"If I have my way, Merry won't even know I'm there."

"You know that would be impossible. The black stallion you ride is unmistakable and Merry spends several hours every day in the stables." Lacie wondered now if Merry might not spend more time. Devlin was a handsome young man, arrogant to boot, although Leslie would most likely call it confidence.

When Lacie first saw the man, she wondered if possibly Merry could lose her heart to him, suspecting he was more than just a horse breeder. He had a way about him that spoke of complete confidence—of nobility. She stared at her husband, playing with the young lad in his arms who would eventually have so much responsibility. It might be nice for Merry to find someone who could be carefree and take a moment to play rather than spend most hours working.

Leslie seemed to read her mind. Defending himself he began, “I’m much better than I used to be. I’ve made snow angels with you every time it has snowed. Playing with my son has become an essential part of my life. I’ve emitted a few choo, choos when we brought out the toy train.”

“Yes, but you had to be coerced each and every snowfall. It’s time for his nap.” She took the boy from Leslie, heading up the stairs.

“When you put him down, we can play. More than willing.” He was behind her on the stairs. “Need to play with my wife. Been away too long without her in my bed.”

“It’s almost dinner time. You will have to wait.” She set the boy in his bed, covering him with a blanket.

“I’ve waited weeks.” His lips caressed her neck then slid across her shoulders. He moved up her neck, playing with her delicate earlobe with his teeth and tongue then travelling to her lips where he could nibble his way across her mouth.

She shivered with the desire she always felt with his touch. “I suppose I’ll let you have whatever you want. I’ve missed you too much to deny either of us.”

Other Books by Christine Young
Available at Rogue Phoenix Press

Connal's Eternal Love
Sweet McKenna Book One

A few days shy of All Hallows' Eve Connal McKenna, Laird of Clan Chattan stands on the parapets of his castle. Bonfires line the hillsides while his clan prepares for the upcoming festivities. Drawn by the whispering of the wind, Connal McKenna feels a strange restlessness in his soul. Setting out to discover the wickedness that is calling to him, he discovers his mate. With gentle words and sensuous kisses, the auburn-eyed highlander conquers his mate, the beautiful, defiant Wynnie Adair who he comes upon during an evening ride. She must ultimately put her trust in the only man who can save her from the ruthless plans of her father and succumb to his gentle coaxing.

In Brady's Arms
Sweet McKenna Book Two

Forced to run from the only home she knows, beautiful, headstrong Lillian Townsends seeks shelter in the wild highlands where the McKenna clan live. Trying to avoid a betrothal contract signed by her stepfather to an aging lord, she is desperate to find a means to sidestep the inevitable, including a marriage to the oldest son of the laird. Lilly is enamored of the young lord who pursues her with unrelenting determination flashing his devilishly handsome charms. She is hard pressed to resist.

Besotted from the first moment Brady McKenna sees Lilly, he is determined to find a means to coax her into his arms and bed. With only the promise of carnal pleasure as his mistress, Brady relentlessly pursues the woman who has unwittingly forged a place in his heart. She is like no other woman, proud, defiant and enchanting. Despite his father's advice to stay away from her, he cannot. He boldly seeks her out and makes her his own.

Nobody but Walker

Sweet McKenna Book Three

The Highland Lass...

She was brought up, adored and loved by a doting mother and father ardently protected by her brothers. She was everything sweet and innocent until she was faced with betrayal and an unexpected and out of wedlock pregnancy. When she gave her love to a man who couldn't return her passion and commitment, she was left devastated and furious. Faced with the loss of her child if she didn't comply to his demands, Crissie McKenna followed him to Belfast then on to his country home to discover he was already married.

...The Irishman

Stunned to find out his one and only encounter with the woman he wanted to love forever created a child, Walker Endicott, Earl of Briarwood, claimed his child as his only heir. Walker threatened all her previously held values even while he thrilled her senses. From the moment he first saw her to the second she ran after him begging him to make love to her, his captivating masculinity held her fascinated. In his arms she would know tempestuous passion, bitter despair, and a soaring joy that would humble them both before the power of love.

My Sweet Broc

Bad Boys Book One

He's a bad bad boy...

Broc Wallace is a fun-loving rake who never thought any beautiful woman could melt his heart. He lives life in the present enjoying the camaraderie of his friends and the pleasures of his mistress. When Bliss races into his life, he is ill prepared to deal with her secrets or give up the tenor of his life. When the truth is revealed, he finds himself unable to forgive and forget the betrayal.

...but she's sweet for him

Bliss MacTavish knows she's playing with fire when she refuses to tell this bad boy her name. He tempts her with sweet whispers of seduction knowing her innocent nature will be unable to refuse all he yearns to give her. Deciding to follow her heart, she finds the repercussions more than she bargains for when she gives herself to this bad boy.

Crazy for Cam

Bad Boys Book Two

He's a bad bad boy...

Lord Cam MacEwen, Viscount of Rosehill, tries his best to be proper and court the lady of his dreams in the acceptable way. The feat proves impossible when the lady in question uses every means at her disposal to tempt him. He fights his jealousy for another man as well as the need to make her his own, finally giving in to her irresistible passion.

...but she's crazy for him.

Chelsea MacTavish wants the bad boy she fell in love with and kissed just before her eighteenth birthday. With feminine wiles and irresistible allure, the sensuous lady plans to best Cam at his game of hearts and make him forget his need to court her properly.

Falling for Flynt

Bad Boys Book Three

He's a bad, bad boy...

Fascinated by Hope's loss of memory yet haunted by her sultry beauty, Flynt is irresistibly drawn to the stoic miss—and into her troubles with the sultan who wants her for himself. When he discovers she is the sister of his best friend, his pride keeps him from pursuing her and making her his.

...but she's falling for him.

Raised in a harem but now penniless, alone and without her memory, Hope must discover a way to remember all that she has lost. She finds a way to continue with her life as a servant in Flynt's home. The first sight of Flynt steals Hope's breath as well as her heart. Can she overcome her fears and give herself to the man she fell in love with.

Dancing With Donal

Bad Boys Book Four

He's a bad bad boy...

Once a bad boy always a bad boy, Donal Chamberlin's carefree ways come crashing down around him when he meets the ravishingly beautiful Daryl MacTavish, the innocent little sister of one of his best friends. He is determined to win her heart as he sets his sights on marriage and an heir. His past gets in the way of his quest when a woman he once loved threatens Daryl's life.

...but she's dancing with him.

Daryl has seen the control her sister's husbands hold over them. She yearns for a life where she makes decisions for herself. No man will have power over her. But no man kisses her the way Donal does. No man can make her forget all her goals leaving her helpless to give up her dreams. Yet Donal is determined to dance through all the barriers she thrust in front of him, pursuing her until she says yes.

Loving Leslie

Bad Boys Book Five

He's a bad bad boy...

Leslie Stewart, Duke of Southcliff is stoic, set in his ways, a spy who is used to having his life well ordered. He expects life to continue on in this perfectly conventional fashion. He assumes his bad boy status while keeping mamas and debutantes at arm's length. An heir is needed but Leslie has every intention of finding a woman who doesn't covet his wealth and tittle. He is irresistibly drawn to the headstrong young lady who becomes more beautiful as she develops into a woman.

...but she is loving him.

When Leslie kisses Lacie MacTavish, she knows even at the tender age of fifteen this is the man of her dreams. Forced to wait until she comes of age, Lacie withdraws into herself. Now she is eighteen and Leslie has returned from a mission for the British Government ready to claim her as his bride. She refuses him and he must find a way to seduce her and in the process create a burning passion within her, which she cannot deny.

Pleasing Arie
Bad Boys Book Six

He's a bad bad boy...

Arie Demir has never been denied anything in his life. He takes what he wants. What he undeniably yearns for is the beautiful redheaded spitfire he sees in a restaurant in Glasgow. At every turn, she confuses him by disputing his power over her. Alison refuses to accept the fact he owns her. While Arie tries desperately with patience and tenderness to drive her wild with new sensations, his scorching kisses ignite the fires of her very soul to make her understand he is all she will ever want.

...but is she pleasing him?

Alison Fletcher never expected to find herself kidnapped and sold to a whorehouse then bought by a Turkish sultan to become his slave. She vows to never surrender to the arrogant man who believes he owns her. She is stunned by the magnificently handsome man who awaits her compliance. Unexpectedly, she finds Arie the lesser of all the evils. The hidden depths of his mesmerizing dark brown eyes hold her into their power; his muscular embrace makes her weak with desire. She is his to do with as he wishes.

Graham's Wicked Kiss
Bad Boys Book Seven

He's a bad bad boy...

Graham Chamberlin is stunned to find three young boys dangling from the trees lining the drive to Runningmead Manner. On further inspection, he is astonished at their obsession to protect a young woman who has been brutalized by her pimp. The woman he discovers hiding in a third-floor attic room is gravely injured. He takes the silver haired stowaway under his wing. Clearly, Graham's new guest is a lady with many secrets. He is determined to unlock all the mysteries surrounding her.

...But she can't resist his wicked kiss.

The years since Ria left the convent where she was raised have been a nightmare. Her secrets are dangerous—as is the powerful man determined to find her. Handsome Graham Chamberlin is clearly a gentleman with secrets of his own, but staying with him could mean the difference between life and death for Ria. With each passing day, her handsome host turns Ria's convalescence into an increasingly sensual escape. Now her greatest challenge may be imagining anything less than a future in his arms.

Feeling Etienne's Love
Bad Boys Book Eight

He's a bad bad boy...

Etienne Dubois is the son of a wealthy vineyard owner who craves the excitement of putting his life on the line. Working with the French government and as a confidant of King Charles X give him reasons for living. An encounter with a beautiful young woman in a plush bordello in Paris has him rethinking his roguish ways. Etienne never expects to become a father especially from one encounter with an innocent prostitute who whispers his name and has him rethinking his well-ordered life.

...But she can't help feeling his love.

Elisa Moreau, the only daughter of Angelique Moreau, the owner of an exclusive bordello in Bordeaux, France, has loved Etienne Dubois since she was six. Unfortunately, until an unexpected encounter at a brothel in Paris puts the two of them in the same room, Etienne doesn't even know she exists. Confused but wanting Etienne and this chance meeting to never end, Elisa gives herself to the man who has held her heart in hands for what seems like her entire life.

Foolish for Piper

The pickpocket...

Piper has spent her life surviving the streets of St. Giles Parish in London, a den of iniquity and crime. Masquerading as a boy she escapes the whorehouses the young girls are sent to as they come of age. The day she encounters Brett MacLachlan begins the same as every other one. When she picks his pocket, she has no idea her life is going to change irreversibly.

...and the mark

Handsome aristocrat Brett MacLachlan has come to London for his amusement only to find his world turned upside down by a thief and her dog. From the moment he spots her, Brett knows there is something intrinsically wrong. In his arms, Piper discovers passion and joy. Yet secrets of her past haunt her, and a scar will tell the true tale as well as her identity.

Taylor's Destiny

She traveled to another time and place to change destiny...

Enjoying a day of sailing, Taylor Maxwell never expected after a suffering a concussion she would wake up in another century. A resilient independent woman in the twenty-first century, the blond beauty is ill prepared for life in the 1800s. Her first sight of the naval captain who rescues her makes her heart stop, giving her hope for her future.

His life is transformed by a woman who appears from nowhere...

Born to a life of ease, Reid Stewart defies the dictates of those born to aristocracy and chooses a life of adventure in the navy and as a spy for the crown. When he discovers a nearly naked woman on the bow of small sailing ship, his heart warms. His love for Taylor and his need to protect her from a man who pursues her might cost him his life as well as hers.

Caitlin's Duke

She played a fiddle in an Irish pub...

Caitlin O'Shea Is the most beautiful woman Roc Leighton has ever seen. With her blue violet eyes and long black hair she captivates him. In turn he mesmerizes Caitlin. Caught in the power of his gaze as he watches her, she is wise enough to know he desires her but will never give his heart to her. Caitlin has vowed to never be any man's mistress.

And fell in love with an English Lord...

Roc knows the first time he watches her play the fiddle and dance around the pub, she will be his next mistress. Despite her protest, he will find a way to convince her that her place is with him. While Caitlin's determination to keep her vows, fate takes a cruel turn and she is forced to seek refuge with Roc.

Catching Meara

Book One in the McKenna Clan Series

Meara Thorton was a feisty, world-class computer hacker—cornered by the FBI and shockingly given the chance to be their newly acquired technical analyst. Brilliant and intuitive, yet aching with the loss of everyone she has cared about, her restless heart led her to discover a love she fought and a world she didn't know could possibly exist.

Sweet Sexy Sadie

Book Two in the McKenna Clan Series

From the first time Sadie's eyes met those of Brody McKenna in the hot Sierra Madre Mountains, theirs was a potent attraction—not gentle, slow, and easy, but hot, hard, and all-consuming. The daughter of a dysfunctional family, Sadie had dreams no man could wrench from her with hot sex and an all-consuming passion. She'd challenge this alpha male with all the strength she possessed. But her red hair, fiery temperament, and indomitable spirit obsessed Brody...and he knew he had to find a way to show her he was more than he appeared and convince her to make a life with him.

Sweet Misbehavin'

Book Three in the McKenna Clan Series

Cast adrift after fleeing the home of Jokul, the ice demon, Atantsi, a firestarter, grew to womanhood as she moved through time to keep the demon from finding her. Though stubborn and courageous, she was ill prepared to use powers she had not been taught. Her first sight of the intoxicating Carr McKenna left her breathless, and her second encounter gave her hope for a future she never thought she had.

A playboy, a second son and a shifter, a man who thought his life would be carefree, Carr McKenna was shocked to discover the woman he'd paid as an escort is a firestarter who is running for her life. He is the leader of all the McKennas around the world and that he has multiple powers. His passion for Margo and the need to defend her might cost him his life as well as hers.

Sweet Talkin' Sugar

Book Four in the McKenna Clan Series

Lyonesse McKenna, was dreaming, or was she? From the instant Lyn saw Deacon McClain across a black jack table in a crowed Las Vegas casino the unmistakable attraction sent Lyn's senses flying into overdrive. Her family of shapeshifters believed in soul mates. She'd always been skeptical yet she couldn't help but question the way her heart sped when he looked at her.

When Deacon appeared in Las Vegas he knew his first job was to save Lyn from a Sea Demon, but the next order of business was to convince her he would someday mean more to her than she'd ever expected. But her stubborn nature and unbendable spirit consumed Deacon...and he had to chase away all the demons real and imagined in order to win her heart.

Sweet Surrender

Book Five in the McKenna Clan Series

Ripped from her family at the top of Infinity Cliff, Kimi McKenna finds herself thrust somewhere into the future. Dark elements threaten to destroy the earth unless Kimi can work together with the white witch to stop the destruction. Confused by her mate's role in the conspiracy, she refuses to acknowledge the connection. But amidst raging fire and attacks on the people she is coming to hold dear, she allows Maska O'keefe into her heart.

Maska O'keefe has loved the beautiful shapeshifter for years. Unable to save her life years ago, he vows to watch over her as he is given a second chance to convince her that even though he is a witch and not a shifter, they are indeed soul mates. Kimi's divided loyalties between her family and the cause she is now a part of will determine their relationship. Only the part she plays as the messiah can bring this to a conclusion in the final battle.

Dakota's Bride

The first book in the Lakota/Pinkerton Series

When Emma St. John received her brother's letter imploring her to escape her stepfather's vengeful scheme and to trust Dakota Barringer with her life, she was willing to chance it. But the handsome, brooding riverboat owner Emma found in Natchez a danger of another kind. For Emma soon found herself surrendering to an unrelenting desire.

Raised by the Sioux when his parents were killed, Dakota had been betrayed once before by a white woman. He wasn't about to trust another, especially one claiming that her stepfather, a powerful U.S. senator, had framed her as a murderess. But he couldn't let Emma's intoxicating effect on him. Now Dakota would risk his very life to protect the innocent beauty who had seduced him with her tender love.

My Angel

The second book in the Lakota/Pinkerton Series

A BEAUTY IN BUCKSKINS

When her father decided to send her to a finishing school back East, Angela Chamberlain refused to be confined to stuffy drawing rooms. Instead, the daring spitfire who could shoot like a man and ride like the wind longed for a life of adventure and romance—and she knew exactly who could give it to her. Devil Blackmoor was a hired gun with a dangerous reputation. But Angela was willing to go to the ends of the earth to capture the handsome devil's heart.

A DEVIL IN DISGUISE

He'd come to America looking for excitement, but Devil Blackmoor got more than he bargained for when he encountered a beautiful rebel who answered his kisses with a wild innocence that touched his very soul. Yet standing between them were more obstacles than either ever dreamed. For Devil had strapped on a gun for the wrong man. And that made Angela his enemy. Now he'll have to choose between his duty and the woman he loves more than life.

The Locket

The third book in the Lakota/Pinkerton Series

The year is 1894. Seeking revenge for crimes against his family, Misha Petrovich follows a path that leads straight to Ariel Cameron's boarding house in Mist Harbor, Oregon. A family heirloom in Ariel's possession leads Misha to believe she is guilty. The locket has been handed down to the oldest girl in the Petrovich family for generations. Ariel is innocent of wrong doing, but her father is not. Misha is torn by his feelings for Ariel and his need for restitution against her father. Knowing that the relationship between them is fragile, Misha does everything in his power to protect Ariel's father. His efforts are to no avail when her father is shot. Ariel comes to realize Misha's steadfast courage and determination to protect her and her father despite what has happened to his family. Ariel's love and devotion heals Misha's heart.

The Talisman

The fourth book in the Lakota/Pinkerton Series

Running from a marriage that lasted one night, Dr. Moriah McKeown discovers the land she has settled on is coveted by determined and lawless men. Yet the proud young woman who once vowed never to abandon her home has second thoughts when her adopted children are threatened. Her only recourse is to enlist the aid of a dark, dangerous gun for hire.

Haunted by the past and a betrayal he will never forgive, Ian Civanovich uses his fast gun and his reckless courage to forget the faithlessness of a woman in his past. He will trust no female—nor will he rest until the threat hovering over Moriah McKeown is put to rest.

Forever His

The fifth book in the Lakota/Pinkerton Series

Struggling to come to terms with the part she played in Jacob St. John's death, Etta Barringer resigns from Pinkerton Agency and seeks peace and solace in a Rocky Mountain Cabin.

Jacob has vowed to discover the reason Etta has betrayed him, sold him out to his enemy and left him for dead.

Isolated in their cabin, they discover their love for each other and learn to trust. But the trust is shattered when Jacob learns she is married to his sworn enemy; the man who left him in the desert to die.

Allura's Secret

Twelve Dancing Princesses Book One

Allura McClellan is horrified by her father's decision to take out an ad in the Times awarding her to the man strong enough and smart enough to win her hand and uncover her secrets. She's an intelligent young woman who takes great delight in the freedom allotted to her by her father. She's well aware that marriage would effectively curtail the adventures she's shared with her sisters and cousins.

Hunter Gray is nothing like the other men who've arrived to vie for Allura's hand in marriage and everything that goes along with it. However, he is the first to refuse to concede defeat and pursue her despite her attempts to disguise her true appearance. It's her temperament that is of more concern to him than her looks. Hunter has worked all his life with the hope of someday owning his own land. Now that it looks like there's a very real possibility that everything he's ever wanted is within reach nothing is going to deter him – including Miss Allura's disagreeable disposition.

Amorica's Wager

Twelve Dancing Princesses Book Two

Amorica Hepburn was sent to London to find a husband. Finding a man was the last item on her agenda. With her two cousins, Amorica wagers she can dissuade her suitor before the others. Despite her efforts she discovers a chemistry that cannot be denied. Suddenly she is the arrogant man's wife, pledged to a marriage neither desire. But swept off to his ancestral home above the Dover cliffs and into his strong embrace, Amorica is soon possessed by a raging passion for the husband she had vowed to despise...

Damian Andrews couldn't afford to trust the emerald-eyed spitfire who happened upon his secret. Amorica's hatred of all men of his kind only inflames the war that rages between them. Still, he can not control the intense desire his stubborn bride inspires, or make her surrender to his will until he has conquered the headstrong beauty on the battlefield of love...

Ravyn's Marriage of Inconvenience

Twelve Dancing Princesses Book Three

A REGAL BEAUTY

When the duchess decides to wed her to a wastrel and a fop, Ravyn Grahm takes matters into her own hands and declares her engagement to another man. Instead of fessing up and telling her great aunt what she has done, she goes through with the pretense. Ariec Lakeland is the bastard son of an earl and has a dangerous reputation. But Ravyn is willing to do most anything to keep the duchess from discovering the lie.

A DEVIL-MAY-CARE SMUGGLER

He'd bought land in America, looking to put down roots and end his life of adventure, but Ariec Lakeland got more than he bargained for when he encountered a beautiful heiress who made a promise she didn't want to keep. But the promise could not be undone and standing between them were more obstacles than either ever dreamed. Ariec had made plans to spend the rest of his life in America and that was at odds with Ravyn's plan of living in England and running her father's estate. Now, he'll have to choose between his dreams and the woman he loves more than life.

Christel's Sunrise

Twelve Dancing Princesses Book Four

He Made Her An Offer...

Life has thrown Christel McClellan some experiences that could have devastated a less determined woman. Beautiful, self-assured and fiercely independent, she is trying to forget the loss of her stillborn child. But is the child alive?

She Couldn't Deny...

Life is carefree for Ryder MacLaren who loves to see what is on the other side of the sunrise. Laird of Clan MacLaren, he is wealthy, handsome and happily unencumbered...until stunning Christel McClellan enters his life. When he hears her story, he believes the child she thought dead has been sold to a wealthy buyer.

Storm's Passion

Twelve Dancing Princesses Book Five

SHE MADE A PROPOSAL...

Life strikes Storm Graham a shattering blow when she learns her father has bartered her to a man she detests. Storm is beautiful, self-assured and fiercely independent, and refuses to be a pawn in her father's schemes, yet she can find no way out of this bargain made in hell. Going on the offensive she asks the wealthiest man on the eastern coast of England to marry her, never believing she might fall in love.

HE TRIED TO REFUSE...

For Hadden Johnston life has provided everything he ever wanted, including a sanctuary for homeless children. He is wealthy, handsome and happily unencumbered...until stunning Storm Graham marches into his life and proposes a marriage of convenience. Yet this type of marriage to a woman who inflames his senses is far from acceptable. If he's going to be tied down, he will move heaven and earth to have this woman warming his bed.

Gotta Have Fayth

Twelve Dancing Princesses Book Six

A regal beauty with raven hair and piercing blue eyes, Fayth Graham is unwilling to parade herself in front of the wealthy Lords of England during the season. Seeking a means to dissuade any man wishing to wed her, she seeks a way to ruin herself for marriage. When she unexpectedly meets a man with sparkling gray eyes and an infectious grin, she decides this is the man who will keep her from agreeing to obey.

He returned from six months at sea, looking for a few nights of pleasure with a willing lass, but Jarret Kinsley got more than he bargained for when he met a beautiful debutant who responded to his kisses with a wild innocence that touched his heart. Yet the obstacles looming between them might rip them apart. Both had vowed never to marry, so when consequences of their dalliances got in the way, Jarret would have to choose between the life he's always desired and the woman he loves more than life.

Ella's Pleasure

Twelve Dancing Princesses Book Seven

A WHISPER OF PLEASURE

Ella Hepburn was an auburn haired debutant from the harsh Scottish coastline—a wild innocent to be seduced and tamed. A spirited beauty, she captivated Drake Montgomerie's jaded heart—while succumbing to the smoldering desire she felt for her unyielding suitor.

A WHISPER OF DANGER

In Drake Montgomerie's glittering world of money and privilege, young Ella discovered passion and desire could overcome everything she'd been taught to resist—entangling Drake, the heir apparent, in a lethal coil of aristocratic family intrigue. But grave peril would only nurse the sparks of a love that knew no limits and a magnificent ecstasy that would not be denied.

Eveleen's Seduction

Twelve Dancing Princesses Book Eight

A WHISPER OF SEDUCTION

A brutal attack on Eveleen Hepburn's cherished island off the Scottish coastline leaves her shattered and bewildered. Learning a man she once trusted can kill as easily as he can breathe even though the deed saves her life, creates questions that need answers. An innocent beauty, she enchants Logan Maxwell's cynical heart—giving in to the raging passion she feels for her mysterious suitor.

A WHISPER OF INTRIGUE

In Logan's Maxwell's world of espionage and privilege, young Eveleen discovers truths about herself she never expected, and a need for passion and love can overcome all her fears if she learns to accept certain truths. She finds herself entangled in a lethal battle for land that was once owned by French nobility, taken from them during the revolution and sold to Maxwell. But grave peril would unleash the flames of love that simmers, creating a magical union that cannot be refuted.

Tavia's Deception

Twelve Dancing Princesses Book Nine

WHISPERS OF DECEPTION

When her father decides to send her to London for her season,

Tavia Hepburn resolves to see the world instead. The raven haired beauty decides to disguise herself as a lad and find employment on a ship bound for Barcelona as a cabin boy. But she never bargains on finding passion and love to a red haired sea captain who rescues her from certain death.

WHISPERS OF MURDER

For James Macmurra, the world is black and white until he meets a young debutante, who turns his world upside down. He's unable to deny Tavia's intoxicating effect on him. In a match tense with obstacles, unwillingness to divulge secrets, and unforeseen peril, irresistible desire and passion grows into undeniable love. James would risk his life to shelter and protect the innocent debutante who seduces him with her sweet love.

Larena's Fascination

Twelve Dancing Princesses Book Ten

WHISPERS OF FASCINATION

Fiery, free spirited Larena Graham never wanted to marry a duke. She is thrilled to be in love with the fourth son of an aristocrat, Gavin Broon. But when it seems Gavin ignores her, she set her sights on politics and bettering human life. Unsuspecting intrigue and a plot against her, she continues her dangerous plans despite Gavin's wishes.

WHISPERS OF TRUST

Gavin has every intention of properly courting the beautiful Larena until he must leave the city in order to put his affairs in order. Returning to London, he finds the woman he means to make his own is embroiled in political protests that could lead to a prison ship. Larena must learn to trust the handsome Scotsman whose most pressing mission is to protect her and keep her from harm.

Tira's Education

Twelve Dancing Princesses Book Eleven

WHISPERS OF EDUCATION

Learning how to build ships is Tira Hepburn's only dream until she meets Jamie Lundin and her world is turned upside down. With her raven black hair and vivid green eyes, she tempts Jamie and pushes him to defy his vows. She never bargains on finding an irrevocable love and a passion to a man who cannot fulfill her dreams despite his burning desire for her.

WHISPERS OF A BARGAIN

Arrogant and self-assured Jamie is brought up short when Tira captures his heart. All his carefully made plans are put to the test when he decides to teach her the art of ship building if she will spend a week with him alone on his ship. He is unable to deny Tira's intoxicating effect on him. When Tira leaves him behind unwilling to live with him without the benefit of marriage, he races after her. Jamie will risk everything to shelter and protect the innocent debutante who seduces him with her sweet love.

Aidan's Love

Twelve Dancing Princesses Book Twelve

Whispers of Love

Aidan McLellan has loved since she first set eyes on him as a young girl. Spontaneous, wild and eager to grow up, Aidan haunts his waking thoughts day and night, insinuating herself into his life. With her fiery red hair and sparkling sapphire eyes, she seizes Blade's heart even while he tries to resist the innocent child until she becomes a woman.

Whispers of Courage

Blade has waited what seems a lifetime to claim the woman who captures his heart as a little girl. Claiming his inheritance before his younger brother takes what is rightfully his, Blade must convince Aidan of his sincerity after years of avoidance and wed her before his father dies so he can return home, securing his rightful place. Everything is put to the test when his life as well as Aidan's is threatened by the man who once called him brother.

Twelve Days to Love

When Archer Steele shows up at Calanthe Durand's failing plantation with an alligator over his shoulder, Cali thinks she's never seen a more handsome man. During the war she had to defend herself and her servants from both union and confederate soldiers. Independent and self-sufficient, she vows to never marry.

But Archer Steele has different ideas. The first time Archer sees Cali in town, he feels an instant attraction. He decides he will do everything and anything to convince the beautiful Miss Durand he is worthy of her love. During the weeks leading up to Christmas, he gives her twelve gifts in hopes she will fall in love with him. Yet they are faced with challenges they must overcome before Cali can commit to a marriage.

Door to Heaven

Jessica Lawrence is the stepdaughter of a woman born in the twentieth century transported back in time to the year 1868. An acclaimed suffragette, she raises Jessica to believe in the equality of women. Jess Law believes everything she was taught, and when the time is right she becomes a private investigator. Courageous and impetuous, Jess finds danger in her quest to save all women from white slavery. Her passionate mission results in a wedding to Roc Newman, a man she knows can steal her heart...

Roc can't trust the sapphire-eyed spitfire who invades his home in search of secret papers and knocks him flat with her karate moves. Jessica's refusal to obey his wishes serves to inflame the war between them. Still, he cannot control the intense desire his reluctant bride inspires, or make her surrender her independence, until he has conquered the headstrong beauty on the battlefield of love...

Rebel Heart

HER REBEL SPIRIT DEFIED HIS OUTSIDERS SOUL...She was velvet and silk, eyes the color of a summer storm and amber hair. Victoria DeMontville, because of a promise and a codicil to her father's will, was forced to marry one man to protect her from another. She hated Cameron Savage with a fierce passion. But to hold on to her genetic research and find a cure for the deadly Signe virus, she must pretend to love the enemy at her door, come with weapons of fire to melt her icy heart...

HIS OUTSIDERS TOUCH IGNITED RAGING PASSIONS... He wore a mask, disguised as the Phantom, a true legend come to life. Even as war and debate over new genetic research engulfed them all, he would find his greatest adversary in the beauty who'd branded him an outsider and barbarian, the woman he was born to possess, his soul mate.

Safari Moon

Solo St. John, a wildlife photographer, is preparing for a trip to Alaska. Suddenly, Solo finds women of all sorts invading his privacy, his home and his office, all cooing nonsense words and blatantly throwing themselves at him. Solo doesn't know why, and he has no idea how to rid himself of the persistent women. He finally decides to beg a favor of his best buddy Nyssa Harrington.

In love with Solo for the past ten years and knowing he doesn't return her feelings Nyssa doesn't want to talk to Solo. She knows if she accepts his phone call, she will not be able to resist the temptation to hope again.

Straight to Heaven

Running from demons, Alexandra McMurdie stumbles into Forbidden Ground where up is down and elements of nature are contested.

Though a strong independent woman in the twenty-first century' she is unprepared for life in the 1800s. Her first site of the formidable James Lawrence makes her heart skip a beat, giving her cause to reconsider her desperate need to find a way home.

Born with a silver spoon, James' life was torn apart during the War Between the States. Moving west he vows to put the life he once knew in the past. When he discovers a half-frozen woman near Gold Hill, his heart begins to thaw. His love for Alexandra and his need to keep her from a man who has pursued her through time might cost him his life as well as hers.

A Valentine's Anthology

The Lending Library-a fantasy by Christie L. Kraemer

Faeries try to fit into the human world when the forest where they make their home is destroyed by a mysterious enemy.

Chasing Rainbows-a contemporary romance by Genene Valleau

An eccentric aunt, an inventive uncle, a mother who wears poodle skirts, and a brother who wears pearls provide a hilarious backdrop for the courtship of a young woman who yearns for a "normal" family.

The Gift-an historical romance by Christine Young

A man and a woman on opposite sides of the Civil War get a second chance at love after one final battle returns soldiers to their war-torn homes to rebuild their lives.

A St. Patrick's Day Tale

Christine Young, C. L. Kraemer, Genene Valleau

Tumble through time...

...to Ireland in 1817, when tensions are high between Protestants and Catholics and fae people guide the fate of villagers. A lovely Catholic lass stumbles upon the weakly ritual fisticuffing between Irish lads. She falls into the lap of a handsome young Protestant. Family ties, grudges, and two conniving faeries threaten their budding love. But the faeries outsmart themselves when they hijack a time machine that has mysteriously appeared in their forest and are whisked to...

...Eugene, Oregon in the 20th century, amid a property feud between the local faeries and night elves. The conniving faeries from Olde Ireland try to stir up more mischief. However, a warrior gnome convinces the magic folk to control their own destiny, and forces the intruding faeries to take refuge in the time machine again, spinning their way toward...

...A modern day castle in western Oregon. An eccentric inventor is determined to reclaim his wayward time machine and save his beloved wife from her latest misadventure. If only they can travel safely past the black hole...

a May Day Anthology

Christine Young, C. L. Kraemer, Rosemary Indra, Genene Valleau

Highland Miracle — Christine Young

HURTLED THROUGH TIME, Sean Michael Sterling, landed in the midst of a May Day celebration he didn't understand, assuming the role of Laird Sterling.

ILLIGITAMATE CHILD OF NOBILITY, Reagan Douglas searches for a way out of her half brother's house.

Defying the Odds — C.L. Kraemer

The night elves on the hill aren't happy without their magic. They concoct a plan to punish those who were involved in the act that rendered them almost human. Meanwhile, Uther, the rogue night elf, has returned to woo the Librarian to be his eternal mate.

Love in Bloom — Rosemary Indra

When childhood friends reunite it takes two fairies and a matchmaking daughter to help them admit their true love for each other.

No More Poodle Skirts — Genie Gabriel

After drifting for years in the innocent age of the 1950s, a woman struggles to join today's world by finding a career and a new love, with some help from her zany family.

Once Upon a Christmas Moon

Christine Young, C. L. Kraemer, Genene Valleau

TWELVE DAYS TO LOVE

When Archer Steele shows up at Calanthe Durand's failing plantation with an alligator over his shoulder, Cali thinks she's never seen a more handsome man. During the war she had to defend herself and her servants from both union and confederate soldiers. Independent and self-sufficient, she vows to never marry. But Archer Steele has different ideas. The first time Archer sees Cali in town, he feels an instant attraction. He decides he will do everything and anything to convince the beautiful Miss Durand he is worthy of her love. During the weeks leading up to Christmas, he gives her twelve gifts in hopes she will fall in love with him.

BOOTS AND BLADES

An ancient evil from the old country has arrived in the high desert of Oregon. Gnome children are vanishing then re-appearing, showing various stages of traumatization. Tiamoon, warrior gnome, will put her skills to use alongside Killian, a handsome warrior, also in need of a cause.

CHRISTMAS PAWSIBILITIES

With their world destroyed and their space ship malfunctioning, the dogizens of Planet Canid have little choice but to crash land on Earth. They face tortuous experiments at the hands of the Geeks in Green...or they can trust an eccentric inventor and his zany family to deliver the Canine Queen's puppies and help them celebrate new lives.

VISIT OUR WEBSITE
FOR THE FULL INVENTORY
OF QUALITY BOOKS:
http://www.roguephoenixpress.com

Rogue Phoenix Press
Representing Excellence in Publishing

Quality trade paperbacks and downloads
in multiple formats,
in genres ranging from historical to contemporary romance,
mystery and science fiction.
Visit the website then bookmark it.
We add new titles each month.

www.ingramcontent.com/pod-product-compliance
Lightning Source LLC
Chambersburg PA
CBHW061935170626
46813CB00006B/2405

* 9 7 8 1 6 2 4 2 0 6 5 2 8 *